First Comes Love

NEW CASTLE

LYDIA MICHAELS

BAILEY BROWN

Content Warning

The New Castle series features situations that could upset sensitive readers. To learn more about possible triggers in Lydia Michaels' books, please visit her website where you can view content warnings by trope and title.
View Content Warnings at LydiaMichaelsBook-s.com/content-warnings

Dedication

To Blamkins...
There is nothing in this world more precious than you.

Prologue

NEW YEAR'S EVE, 11:58 pm

"Push!"

The pain was heavy. The epidural was in full effect, removing even the slightest sensation from Kat's pelvis down to her swollen and neglected toes. But the pressure was still ungodly. Three hours in, and she was at her limit. Modesty gone, she grit her teeth and pushed.

She'd been poked and prodded more than a pig at a county fair, with no one there to guide her aside from the nurses she'd met that evening and the doctor now staring at her second greatest source of pain. As much as child labor hurt, she'd mentally prepared over the last nine months. But the agony of having no one by her side, *that* was the source of her *greatest* pain.

She was frightened, anxious, and alone. Utterly alone.

Tears seeped from her locked eyelids as her sweat-slicked palms gripped the metal rails of the hospital bed until her back bowed off the damp sheet. She was pushing what could only be an elephant out of her ass. Her strength was waning as every second passed.

"...five, six, seven," the nurse counted as she bore down, "eight, nine, ten."

Like a rapidly deflating balloon, her breath came out in a rush as her body collapsed back on the sweat-drenched linens.

"Almost there, honey."

Peeking through heavy lids, her vision blurred. Telling herself she was crying from the pain and not the fear, she focused on the elderly nurse soothing her wrinkled brow with a cool, damp cloth. Her expression fell into place, completely unguarded, wiped of all bravado.

She apparently was giving birth to the world's largest baby, and she'd take all the sympathy and support she could get. It wasn't like people were overwhelming her with kindness these days.

The next contraction whipped across her spine, and her breath sawed through her burning lungs like fire. She focused on the happy kitten playing with a ball of yarn on the poster tacked to the ceiling. The corner was torn and fluttering oh so slightly from the vent to the left.

In an attempt to distract herself from the pressure, her gaze focused on the coffee-colored stain on the ceiling tile next to the fluorescent light. Grinding her teeth as the next contraction crashed through her like a tidal wave set to destroy the coast, she hissed out a breath.

Screaming through clenched teeth, her muscles locked, and then the wave subsided. Damp hair clung to the back of her neck, as her hands throbbed, the blood slowly returning to her fingertips. Releasing a shaky breath, she eased her white-knuckled grip off the bed rails. How did women do this without drugs?

"Okay, time to push again."

Then there was this motherfucker. Okay, maybe that was a little harsh. He was actually a very nice man and a good doctor—and she was at the mercy of his care.

Dear God, please don't punish me or the baby for calling Doctor Carol a motherfucker. He's really a very nice old man, whom you will surely welcome into heaven one day. Amen.

"Young lady, you're going to have to push if you ever want to be a mom," Doctor Carol reminded from his position between her stocking-clad knees.

Kat bore down as the nurse next to her supported her damp back and started counting again.

"One, two, three—"

"Here we go!" Dr. Carol enthusiastically called.

"—four, five, six—"

"Keep pushing," he coached.

A slick release and a tug had her gasping.

"seven, eight, nine—"

"It's a girl!"

The next few minutes were a whirlwind. Shivers quaked through her body as her heartbeat echoed in her ears and throbbed at the tips of her fingers. The squawks of a newborn vaguely registered in her tired brain as she was told to push again for the after birth. With the biggest hurdle conquered, she obediently applied her remaining strength to finish what she'd started.

When a nurse pressed a soft cloth to her brow, cleaning away the sweat and tears, her eyes slowly opened. Raspy squawks, like that of a fledgling, broke through the blending of adult voices. Searching for the sound, she focused on the squawks, louder now, more like that of a baby calf.

Baby. That was her baby. Her daughter.

Blocking out the nurses' voices, Kat carefully listened to the first sounds of her little baby girl. She strained her neck, trying to catch a glimpse of her, but the ocean of blue medical smocks blocked her view. It didn't matter. She was beautiful. Her daughter's beauty would challenge the most radiant sunset.

The doctor and nurses' heads were bent as their arms moved over the table, cleaning and fussing over her baby as she chirruped and cooed.

"Is she all right?" Kat asked the nurse in an abused voice she didn't recognize. Her throat had gone chalk-dry from emotion and labor.

"She's fine, honey. They're cleaning her up to meet her mommy."

Mommy. Her heart tightened at the title. So significant, so meaningful. She would bring honor to the name, despite what others believed.

The ocean of blue parted as the doctor turned, holding a pink-capped bundle of perfection. All Kat could see was her tiny swaddled form, but she was sure she was magnificent.

"Here you go, Miss D'Angelo, a beautiful baby girl."

Gently cradling her daughter in her arms, shocked at the insubstantial weight, Kat stared breathlessly at her miniature pink face. So small. Surely this wasn't the linebacker who'd been wreaking havoc in her womb for the past nine months? Her head was tinier than a softball, and her body as weightless as a bouquet of wildflowers.

"She's so little. Is she okay?" she whispered to no one in particular.

"Not too little, eight-one. She's a perfectly healthy size," Dr. Carol reassured. "Now, she's probably hungry. Are you planning on nursing, Miss D'Angelo?"

"What? Um, you mean breastfeeding? Yes," she said, mesmerized by the most delicate, teeny hand she'd ever held. It was too small to fully wrap around her thumb, so she placed her pinky in her daughter's palm. The most magical squeeze, as if she were pulling a thread tied right to her heart, tightened around her finger. Breathing in a shuddered breath, tears of happiness and relief welled in the corners of her eyes.

"Do you have a name for her?"

Unwilling to take her eyes off of her perfect face, all crinkled and rosy, she whispered, "Yes, Mia Rose D'Angelo."

"That's very pretty. Well, Mom, would you like to give feeding little Mia a try?"

Her gaze released Mia and focused on the nurse.

A thousand thoughts of inadequacy skittered through her mind. What if her breasts weren't developed enough to produce milk? Would they criticize her if she did it wrong?

A yearning for the bonding she'd read about bloomed in her chest. She was determined to be the best mother in the world yet had no point of reference. Moistening her dry lips, she pleadingly gazed at the nurse. "Can you show me how?"

The nurse tenderly smiled and adjusted Kat's gown. Shifting Mia toward her body, she guided her pursed mouth toward her breast. Mia cried, revealing a mouth full of soft, pink gums. But the nurse massaged Kat's breast to stimulate the flow of her colostrum, something she'd learned comes out of women before the actual milk arrives, and Mia quickly nuzzled into her and latched on.

It was unlike anything she'd ever experienced. Her mind jerked at the pinching sensation, but the discomfort was soon replaced by a stir of emotion she could only describe as a mother providing life for her child. She blushed at the emotional intimacy of their connection.

This must be love.

The room slowly cleared as hospital employees wheeled machines away to serve the next patient. Undisturbed by the movement, Kat watched Mia and fell more and more in love. As the room fell silent, she decided that every hardship, every tear, every fight was worth the gift she'd been given. Her Mia. Her baby girl.

Time passed at an immeasurable pace as she familiarized herself with this new person who would forever be a part of her life. A nurse eventually returned to take Mia to the nursery so Kat could get some rest. Wanting to object but too unsure of her right to speak up, she protectively watched Mia get wheeled out of her room in a clinical bassinette decorated with a pink teddy bear card that said her name. A sharp and sudden sting of separation washed over her, and she tried to rein in her panic.

It's okay. It's okay. She'll be back. It's okay. They can't take her from you.

How could she miss someone so much after meeting her only hours ago? She needed to take advantage of her rest when she was able to get it. Lying on the bed, she tried to relax. Rest, she needed to rest.

Closing her eyes, she smiled, finding comfort in imagining Mia's face, her hands, her wrinkled feet, her fuzzy tuft of brown hair, and her round, curious glistening eyes. She pictured every bit of her perfect little body for over an hour and still couldn't fall asleep. Finally, she sat up and reached for the phone. After several deep breaths, she dialed.

"Hello. You have reached the voicemail of Vivian D'Angelo..."

Kat listened to her mother's voice and waited for the beep, unsure of what to say.

"Um, Mom, it's me, Katherine. I'm at Upper Park Memorial Hospital. I, uh, had the baby. A girl! Mia Rose. She was born at twelve-thirteen am, a New Year's Baby. She's so beautiful, Mom. Perfect. Eight-one, eighteen inches long. We're in room three-seventeen if you want to—"

Beep.

"Shit."

Kat placed the hospital phone back on the receiver next to her bed.

At least she knows where we are.

She tried not to get her hopes up that either of her parents would visit while she was still at the hospital. Chances were Vivian wouldn't be visiting her first grandchild as long as Edward, Kat's father, didn't approve.

The entire situation was a "scandalous disgrace", according to her father—the Mayor of Parkside—who was aspiring to a position in the Senate. There was no room for scandal in their family. Everything must appear neat and tidy, and her pregnancy had been anything but.

In the past year, she'd pushed her parents to their limit, and their solution to her "predicament" was to act as though Kat, and the child that grew in her belly, didn't exist.

She'd hoped to at least finish high school, but her parents refused to assist her with the paperwork for homeschool tutors. Instead, their solution was to have her bags packed on her eighteenth birthday when she was starting to show and escort her to her new apartment. Her father offered her the perk of paying the rent for one year and providing her with an allowance of one thousand dollars a month until the baby was two months old, at which time, she was expected to find a job to support herself and her child.

Aside from purchasing a few supplies for Mia and paying for the essential utilities, she saved most of the money her father provided. To a naïve teenager like herself, a thousand dollars a month was a fortune. But as she noticed the prices on upcoming necessities such as diapers and bottles, she realized her nest egg was terrifyingly meager.

She found a crib and baby swing at a secondhand store near her apartment and learned to crochet. She was set as far as blankets were concerned. She also—after days of researching on a library computer—found out how to apply for government aid for unwed mothers and was now stocked with coupons and vouchers for formula, diapers, cheese, milk, bread, and any other things they'd need.

She dropped out of school when she'd stopped fitting in the classroom desks. Her parents hadn't done much to stop her, their mortification at her circumstances taking precedence over her education. That was at the end of November. On Thanksgiving, she ate a microwave turkey dinner, a pint of Ben & Jerry's Chocolate Chunk ice cream, and watched *Look Who's Talking* by herself.

She'd spent a lot of her time alone in her apartment, reflecting. It wasn't easy deciding to have a baby at seventeen when everyone simply wanted her predicament to go away. It became clear that if she were to have a child, her days of being one were over.

She sometimes missed being silly and hanging out with friends doing absolutely nothing. Jade, her best friend, marveled at how grown-up she'd become in such a short span of time. Kat didn't feel grown-up. She felt like a terrified kid expected to raise a kid of her own.

On Christmas, she shut off her phone and answering machine, so she wouldn't know who did or *didn't* call and hung pictures of ducklings she found at a yard sale in the baby's corner of the room, knowing her baby would arrive any day.

She was right, of course. Five days later, and here she was, ringing in the New Year with a great new beginning. Jade, of course, was completely unprepared for the inevitable, but that was Jade—always flying by the seat of her pants, never worrying about a thing until it was go time.

Kat had called her the moment it was time, but her friend, being a typical teenager, doing what teenagers predictably did on New Year's Eve, was drunk.

"Hello?"

"Jade? Can you hear me?" Kat had shouted into the phone.

"Hey, Kat! I'm so pissed you aren't here. I just destroyed Kenneth Langley in beer pong. He's being a total crybaby, telling everyone I cheated. I'm thinking about TP'ing his car." She laughed as the bass of loud music pounded through the phone.

"Uh, that's great. Jade. It's time."

"What?" The phone crackled as Jade shifted closer to the music. "No, it's not. There's still an hour until midnight."

Kat patiently breathed through her contraction and looked at her watch. "Not time for the ball to drop. Time for the baby. I'm in labor."

Utter silence aside from the thumping of bass in the background.

"Jade?"

Her best friend shouted, "You can't have the baby now! I'm drunk! Can't you tell it to wait?"

"No, I can't tell the baby to wait!" Kat's laugh muffled into a garbled moan as another contraction hit.

"Shit. I need to find someone sober, so I can get a ride."

Knowing how many maniacs were on the road, Kat patiently said, "It'll probably be a while. Just sober up and come in the morning."

"But I'm supposed to be there with you. It's my duty as a best friend."

"I'll be—" Her words cut off as another contraction hit. "—fine."

Jade's voice sobered. "Are the contractions bad?"

"No, not at all." There was no point in freaking out her friend. She hoped she'd eventually have a child so their kids could be friends.

"Really?"

"So far, they're just uncomfortable." But each one was getting worse. "Jade, I really gotta go."

"I wish I could be there."

Kat carried her bag to the car. "I know you do."

"I'll be there first thing in the morning. I love you."

"I love you too, Jade."

A light tap on the door interrupted her thoughts. The sight of Mia's bassinet filled her heart with unparalleled warmth, and she quickly adjusted her position in the bed.

"Someone wanted their mommy," the nurse said, an affectionate lilt to her voice.

Kat smiled. "I missed her."

Taking her in her arms, she breathed in the familiar soft scent and sighed, knowing her days of being alone were over. Now that she had Mia, she'd always have someone to love.

~

Kat was laying Mia down after feeding her breakfast. Her body still wasn't back to normal, but at least she was moving around. She carefully bent over the bassinet and adjusted Mia's cap when a barely audible tap sounded from the door.

"Come in," she whispered as she tucked Mia's sleeping body snugly in her receiving blanket.

The quiet, uncertain shuffle of feet entering the room didn't match the sure pace of a nurse. Glancing down to make sure her gown was tied and that she was properly covered before straightening to face her visitor.

Her already sore legs almost gave out on her. "Jeremy," she breathed.

"Hey, Kat," he said, looking anywhere but at her face.

"What—What're you doing here?"

"I heard you had the baby."

He barely stood inside the room. Head bent and hands in his pockets, his posture was that of a hesitant boy—one who appeared to have gotten caught with his hand in the cookie jar or some such undeniable crime. The way he fidgeted showed he was prepared for judgment, yet he hid any signs of regret, or worse, pity.

"How?"

"Jade called me."

"Oh." *Damn meddling best friend!*

Jade had come to visit her first thing on New Year's Day and, of course, did exactly what Kat asked her not to do.

"What did you have?"

"A girl. *We* had a girl. I named her Mia Rose D'Angelo."

His mouth twitched, possibly disappointed their child wouldn't carry his name, but she doubted that.

"Yeah," he nodded. "I guess that's for the best. How are you doing?"

"I'm sore, but I'll be all right. Do you want to see her? She has your coloring and your eyes."

"Uh, I really can't stay long. I gotta get to school—"

"She's right here," she interrupted, stepping back so he could see the bassinette.

Jeremy froze, eyes huge, as Kat patiently waited for him to move toward their daughter. After several breaths, he finally took a sluggish step toward the bassinette.

"She has your nose," he whispered, his hands still deeply rooted in his pockets as if afraid to touch Mia, afraid to leave a fingerprint.

"You think?" Her voice rattled the quiet moment like thunder on a still morning.

Once she broke the silence, her words fell like wishes tossed into an empty well. "Do you want to hold her? It's awkward at first, but you'll get the hang of it. She's so petite and light. Eight pounds. The doctor says that's normal, but she feels more like two pounds. And you should see her..." Her babbling faded as Jeremy's slack-jawed, panic-stricken face looked at her.

Since the day those two blue lines appeared on a stick, Kat considered herself a mother. But Jeremy had made no attempt to familiarize himself with the foreign idea of parenthood—at least not that she knew of.

Finally, Kat looked at the floor and mumbled, "Right, you don't want to get attached."

"Kat—"

"No, no, it's fine. She's fine. She has all the love she needs."

She tried to disguise the hurt tightening around her heart and constricting her vocal cords. Unwanted emotions choked her. She was stupid to allow herself to get sucked into the fantasy of a normal family. His rejection of their baby had nothing to do with her character, but it was still rejection—still personal.

I have to stop hoping for things that will never happen.

Schooling her expression, she met his apologetic gaze.

"It's just better this way, Kat. With me going to boot camp in June, I just think—"

"I understand."

Her eyes stung as she fought to hide her tears. *Stupid hormones!* "Well, you better go if you don't want to be late for school. Besides, I have to feed Mia soon," she lied.

"Well, I'm glad you're okay. I guess I'll see you around."

He shifted toward the door, and she fussed with Mia's blankets, unable to watch him leave, afraid he'd see the tears in her eyes. His guilt and reluctance to leave were evident as he scuffed his foot over the blue linoleum, but to her, he was already gone. He hadn't been *with* her since the moment he suggested their 'other options'.

An obligatory visit to the hospital was not enough to distort the reality of their situation. He would go, and she would stay behind to raise their child. He didn't want the responsibility, said he wasn't prepared to be a father. Well, they were on Mia's schedule, not his, so perhaps this was best.

"Kat?"

Knowing she'd never see him again made it nearly impossible to look at him one last time. Taking a steadying breath, she glanced at him. "Yes, Jeremy?"

"She really is beautiful."

Smiling, a tear slipped past her lashes. "I know."

His gaze lowered, and he grimaced. Looking back, he smiled sadly, his mouth pulling to one side. "I'm sorry I can't stay."

Nodding tightly, her fingers gripped the bassinet as Mia's father walked out of their lives forever. She was sorry too.

∼

"Katherine, you know I can't do that. Your father needs time to adjust to all of this," Vivian's voice lectured over the phone as Kat dressed Mia in her going home outfit.

"He's had nine months, Mother. It's your first grandchild. You haven't even seen her yet."

She tried not to let her emotions get the best of her, but it was really difficult with all the hormones taking over her body in some postpartum invasion. "Can't you come? He doesn't have to know where you were."

"You know I'll not lie to your father. How could you even ask that of me?"

Accepting defeat, Kat simply cooed at the bundle of perfection before her and ignored the other broken parts of her family. Her mother sighed as she noisily adjusted the phone.

"Katherine," she said in a lower voice as if conspiring to rob a bank. "Why don't you let me call you a cab? I'll even pay for it with my credit card."

"I don't need a cab, Mother. The nurses have a service patients can use. I just figured you'd want to help bring your granddaughter home. I wanted to include you in this special day."

"Please don't make me feel guilty, Katherine. It's difficult enough dealing with all your father's demands. Why don't you get yourself settled? Call me next week, and we'll make arrangements for a visit? How does that sound, dear?"

"I guess."

"Good. And trust me. Everything will be fine.

Your father just needs a little more time. Now, I have to get ready for my charity meeting, but I'll talk to you soon."

"Okay, Mom." Her mother hung up before ever hearing her reply. She looked down at Mia and smiled. "We don't need them anyway." Fighting back her ever-present tears, she released a cleansing breath. "Nope. It's you and me, babe, and that's all we'll ever need."

Chapter 1

APRIL - 3 YEARS later

"Can we get a dog?"

"A dog?" Kat echoed as she and Mia walked home from Mrs. Bradshaw's.

"Yeah. We need a dog. All happy families have dogs, and we're a happy family, right, Momma?"

"The happiest, but I don't think we're ready for a dog. They're a lot of responsibility, and who would take care of the dog while I'm at work and you're at Mrs. Bradshaw's?"

"He could come to Mrs. Bradshaw's with me."

"I don't think Mrs. Bradshaw would like that too much, babe."

"Yes, she would. Mrs. Bradshaw's my friend," Mia replied as if her friendship with her sixty-eight-year-old babysitter was validation enough.

"I know she's your friend, but I think Mrs. Bradshaw's allergic." The fib rolled off her tongue with zero hesitation. They could *not* have a dog. Her plate was full.

"What's 'lergic?"

"Allergic is when something makes you sneeze and makes your eyes itchy."

"Oh." Mia pouted.

She'd perfected the pout by the time she was a year old. Kat hated to disappoint her, but their situation didn't allow for a dog.

"Besides, I'm not sure Dr. Stevens allows pets."

Mia's face scrunched up as she stared off into the distance. She was never silent for long, so Kat quickly tried to come up with a better argument.

The Dr. Stevens excuse was solid. He was the owner of their house as well as Kat's boss, and as the landlord, he'd have the final say in issues such as dogs and other pets. But in reality, Kat couldn't imagine him saying no. The man spoiled Mia rotten. Hopefully, Mia never got around to asking him herself. She could ask for a giraffe, and Dr. Stevens wouldn't deny her.

"A stick!" Mia yelled with excitement as she snatched up the twig.

Crisis averted. Thank God for broken branches and three-year-old attention spans.

As they turned onto their street, Mia chattered about the spring flowers starting to bloom and pretended her stick was a magic wand. During the day, someone had switched the *For Sale* sign on the old vacant farmhouse to *Sold*.

"Oh, look, Mia. Someone bought that house. Maybe they'll have kids your age."

They scrutinized the neglected home from the ramshackle roof and dilapidated shutters.

"Maybe they'll have a dog," Mia cheered.

Shit. Crisis reinstated. Stay calm. "Or maybe they'll have a little three-year-old like you."

"I'm three! They can be my friends!" she exclaimed, finally comprehending.

"I know. Wouldn't that be nice to have some new friends on our street?"

"Yeah! And they're gonna wanna play tag with me!"

"I'm sure they will. I wonder when they're moving in."

"Let's say hi!"

Mia scampered toward the house's driveway, and Kat quickly took her hand, slowing her determined steps. "No, babe. They didn't move in yet. They may not be here for a while. See how there isn't a car in the driveway?"

"Oh. Maybe they'll be back in five minutes."

Kat's shoulders sagged. She pinched the bridge of her nose and reminded herself that her daughter's tenaciousness was a blessing no matter how tedious it became at times. "Maybe."

Nudging her along, they continued home. At the old oak tree that marked the edge of their property, Mia bolted up the porch steps of their cottage.

Two rockers sat on either side of the paned window, adorned with a cedar flower box. The garden needed tending but was lovely nonetheless. Kat loved their home, from the white clapboard siding with black shutters to the brass knocker on the shiny, red front door. The backyard, outlined by a white picket fence, only added to its charm.

Kat unlocked the front door, and Mia dashed through the small, antiquated kitchen and into the living room. The afternoon sun highlighted the wood floors in a deep, honey gold glow as it filtered through the many windows. The TV clicked as the ever-present sound of cartoons filled their home.

Kat hung Mia's backpack on the coat tree with her purse and headed into her bedroom to change. Off came her stockings, skirt, bra, and blouse. And on went her cotton tank top and yoga pants. Grabbing a hair tie from her dresser, she pulled her hair into a sloppy knot on top of her head as she headed back to the kitchen.

"You want apple juice or milk?" she called.

"Apple juice."

Kat poured the juice into a cup and grabbed two cookies from the jar on the counter along with a paper towel. Placing the snack on the coffee table in front of Mia, she sat next to her on the couch and pulled her into her arms for a bear hug. "I missed you, babe."

The familiar scent of baby shampoo and sweet spring air greeted her.

Mia wrapped her arms around her neck. "I missed you too, Momma." Mia then cuddled into her side and sipped her juice as she stared at the television. Quiet.

Running her fingers through the fine, strawberry blonde curls, Kat smiled. This was the best part of her day. Work was over, obligations were met, and all she needed to focus on was her daughter.

"What's today?"

"Tuesday."

"Macaroni and cheese night!"

Her income only covered the basics. They rented the house from her boss, who could probably get twice as much from another tenant, but insisted they take it. Owning a home on her salary never crossed her mind, but renting a house—well, that was the next best thing.

It wasn't fancy. The cottage was the smallest house on the street, one-story with a small eat-in kitchen, simple bathroom, living room, and two tiny bedrooms. It wasn't big, but it was their happy little home, and they loved it.

Kat was meticulous about keeping it clean and organized. She definitely had some strong Virgo tendencies. Her cupboards were labeled, her clothes coordinated by color and season, and her menus were always the same. It was structured, but she savored the predictability of their life.

Every weekday Mrs. Bradshaw watched Mia while Kat worked for Dr. Stevens as a secretary in New Castle. Dr. Stevens was a psychologist. The office was usually quiet and empty except for her, the doctor, and the client of the hour. She spent her days filing, making coffee, answering phones, and sorting mail. Her boss was a very sweet, tolerant man she was grateful to know—grateful Mia had the chance to know such kindness as well.

Her entire world was Mia. Their life was structured at a level she could control, and that was the way she liked it. Aside from Jade, they rarely had company. Kat's parents were forever making excuses why they couldn't visit, and after three years, she learned to take what she could get. Sometimes it was healthier to accept the reality of situations rather than hope for change. They loved Mia, but the reality was Kat's relationship with her parents never recovered from the blow of disappointment they felt the spring of junior year when Kat announced she was pregnant.

Her father only spoke in terms of minimum courtesies, and her mother chose to ignore her opinions altogether, replacing them with her more pretentious beliefs. Her self-important, superficial mother spewed never-ending socialite crap and made an art of harping on the displeasures of life. Kat often agreed with her just to shut her up, because there was no use arguing.

Her parents were both politically active, public figures. They lived in the nicer residential section of Parkside, where Kat's father had been the Mayor for twelve years, and her mother campaigned for many different charities—because it was expected.

All Vivian really ever wanted was someone to validate her feelings. Kat didn't have siblings, so her mother relied on her for such validation. The only thing worse than her mother's phone calls were Sunday dinners, obligatory meetings where Vivian held court to air a week's worth of grievances in one very tedious sitting.

There were plenty of differences between the way Kat was raised and the way she was raising Mia. But at the end of the day, she always knew she was doing right. Their small, cozy house was a home built of love and laughter. Something Kat had grown up without.

"What do you say I start dinner, kiddo?"

Mia nestled into her side and nibbled her cookie, eyes focused on the television. "Let's snuggle a little longer, Momma."

She sighed. "Okay."

Chapter 2

THE NEXT DAY, a truck was parked in the driveway of the corner house. "My friend's home!" Mia squealed.

Reeling in her daughter's exuberance, Kat held tight to her little hand. "Hold on, babe. I don't think that's your friend." The side of the work truck read *Adams Construction*. "I think that truck belongs to workers, people who are fixing up the house to get it ready for your friends."

There weren't any lights or coverings showing in the windows. The house appeared vacant. Perhaps their new neighbors were planning some renovations. It was already an impressive house. Being on the corner, it had the largest lot on the street. The house itself was big too.

It was two stories with a third floor attic accented by peaked dormer windows. Kat wasn't sure if it had a basement, but it was four times the size of their cottage and had a two-car, barn-style garage. It was nice but in need of repair.

Like a mouth full of sporadically missing teeth, the fence was the first of many blemishes surrounding the overgrown yard hiding the rickety, stained siding and shutters hanging from broken hinges. Kat supposed the construction truck was a good sign. The new neighbors would most likely be decent homeowners if they were taking the initiative to fix up the home before they moved. It would be lovely if a family with children close to Mia's age moved into the home.

Mia hopped cracks in the sidewalk as Kat followed, contemplating the difference between managing a house of that size and one the size of her cottage. She couldn't imagine one person signing on for such an undertaking, which added to her presumption that the new residents would be a family.

Sharp longing poked her heart. She couldn't deny her envy for those who did things traditionally, the ones who got the house, family, and white picket fence. Getting pregnant in in a guy's dad's tobacco-scented Bronco wasn't anyone's ideal fairytale. Anxious insecurities and nervous fumbling dulled most of the pleasure, at least from what she could recall. It had been exciting, but the repercussions were permanent. She wouldn't change a thing, but she also would never be that reckless again.

Mia bolted inside their home. Standing in the doorway, sorting through the mail, Kat took one last look back at the house on the corner.

A man paced on the front lawn, speaking on a phone, his boots and jeans coated in dust. Probably a laborer doing some interior modifications for the new owners. Kat chastised herself for being a nosey body and quickly entered the cottage.

~

Tyson slid his phone into his pocket and stared up at the mammoth colonial that would now consume all of his free time. Signing on to such a huge undertaking wasn't the sanest decision of his life. The blueprints would be ready for pick up in the morning, and he could only hope he correctly forecasted the budget. With old homes, one never knew what kind of nightmares lay beneath. And wasn't that the perfect analogy for his life?

Despite his fit physique, his joints ached from too much manual labor, and tension throbbed in his lower back. At thirty-six, he felt more like a hundred, and never did he imagine he'd be starting over again this late in life.

Since he was a boy, he loved building things. Deciding what he wanted to do with his life was simple. Financing his dreams had been the opposite.

He hustled, and he saved. Then one day, he bought his first truck and started contracting out his own jobs. He'd spent so many years focused on making his way in the world, rarely thinking of anything else, he'd somehow misplaced over a decade of time. It wasn't until his sister passed away that he realized how much time he'd lost focusing on what should have been a means to an end.

In the quiet that came after his baby sister passed away, he'd realized he rarely laughed anymore. In the hours after work, he barely spoke unless his other sister, Gloria, or his mother called. While everyone else clocked out and returned home, he simply passed the hours separating him from the next shift—alone. He couldn't even recall the last time he'd gotten laid.

It was never his intention to let life pass him by. He wanted to come home to children shouting and chasing each other through the house, a wife that greeted him with a smile and a kiss at the door. Ty wasn't sure where he would find those things, but he figured finding a house big enough to create such a home was a good place to start.

Exhaling, he ran his hand over his head. For nearly twenty years, he'd worked his ass off to get to this moment. He should be celebrating, but for some reason, he couldn't shake the sense of emptiness, emptiness he'd hoped the house would relieve. It seemed even significant days passed with ordinary calmness when there was no one there to share in his happiness.

Sophia would have liked the house. His baby sister always found beauty in discarded things. She was notorious for bringing home ugly old strays when she was a kid. And as an adult, she frequently dragged him to flea markets where she'd sort through other people's unwanted crap, moving items this way and that, finding some speck of value and beauty beneath the tarnish and dust.

This house had beauty beneath the dust, which was why he chose it after making a promise to Sophia just before she passed—a promise he wasn't so sure he could keep.

His brain raced with a million and one items he

needed to add to his checklist. Upper New Castle was a quiet, small town set far enough away from all the noise of the city, yet near enough to have all the conveniences of suburban living. The lawns were manicured, and the drives were filled with family-sized vehicles. Tricycles littered the patios, and flowerbeds edged the walks.

The stillness of the place brought him a level of peacefulness he wasn't accustomed to. He'd always been a solitary guy, goal-oriented and determined, never needing much fuss or frills. He didn't need much to keep him happy. Food in his belly, beer in the fridge, and sports on the TV, was all it really took to satisfy him. A bit of female attention didn't hurt now and then either. Treating himself to something as monumental as a house didn't quite sit right. He'd likely bitten off more than he could chew, and it was going to take a while to digest. But if he wanted a family to someday fill this house and make it a home, he needed to start laying that foundation.

When a man in a pair of short shorts jogged by pushing a toddler in a stroller, he had a moment of *Toto, we're not in Kansas anymore*. Obscure pride mixed with trepidation at the thought of actually living in such a neighborhood. There weren't a whole lot of people that looked like him in these parts.

Exhaustion seeped in, and he wished he had a couch to rest on before he got back to the never-ending demolition inside. With a fortifying breath, he reached into the cab of his work truck and grabbed a six-pack. The sheetrock wasn't going to remove itself, and he had a home to build.

31

Chapter 3

DISTRACTED by what was taking place on her street, Kat stubbed her toe on an uneven lip of pavement. *Holy hell and hotness, Batman!* A man parade was happening at the old colonial on the corner.

The property was a hive of activity and looked completely different than it had one week ago. Construction workers marked the home like ants on a dropped popsicle. Kat wasn't typically the drooling type, but she had the urge to check if her tongue was still in her mouth.

The front siding had been removed, and a young, burly, blond man was installing blue and silver insulation. He wore reflective sunglasses, and his hair was long, bluntly cut to the collar of his shirt. Her eyes focused on the damp ends of his hair, darkened with perspiration, finding it oddly intriguing.

Loose-fitting carpenter jeans and work boots covered a good deal of tanned flesh. Muscled arms bunched as he dragged the back of his hand over his brow, wiping away beads of sweat. She especially enjoyed the way his muscles tugged the cotton of his shirt as he worked the insulation into place.

Her gaze briefly passed over an older, heavy-set man with a plumber's crack. There was too much goodness on display elsewhere to focus on him.

Her gaze traveled past the dormer window to the steep peak of the roof. The man she had seen a few days before was tearing shingles off the roof. Her throat went dry as he stood, and oh my, once the shirt came off, he revealed more burnished skin and a perfectly sculpted chest.

A yellow bandana covered his head, tied at the back of his skull. The worn fabric was damp at the edges, darkening the material. Her hand crept to the back of her neck as she tried to imagine what such glistening heat felt like, smelled like.

Her heart raced, and she frowned. Shaking away her thoughts, she shifted Mia's bag in her arm and guided her daughter around a pile of debris littering the curb. Focused on reaching home, her gaze kept pulling back to the man on the roof.

Snug jeans, fit at the waist, hugged his ass. Curious flutters filled her chest when his toned arms, corded with muscle, swung another shingle to the ground. His abdomen was tight and rigid as an old-fashioned washboard, with too many dips and hard angles to count. There wasn't a flaw on him. People shouldn't look that good, at least not in real life.

As her gaze roamed over his loosely slung tool belt, snagging on the bulge forming a shadow at his fly. Her mouth went dry. *Maybe she needed a date more than I realized.*

"What are they doing, Momma?" Her daughter's voice was like a bucket of ice water, squelching all her dirty thoughts and bringing her back to reality.

Kat cleared her throat. "They're fixing the house up for when our new neighbors come to live here."

"Maybe they'll build a doghouse. I think my new friends have a dog."

"Maybe," she said, distracted as the sexy man tossed a stack of old shingles into a debris pile by a dumpster.

A radio played Motown over the scraping and hammering. He disappeared over the other side of the peaked roof, and she sighed. Skin hot under her clothing, she had the urge to fan herself. She didn't usually get like this around men. She didn't usually get like this *ever*.

"Are they going to paint the house, Momma?"

"Probably," Kat absentmindedly answered, waiting for the shirtless man to reappear. When he didn't return, a slight wave of disappointment washed over her.

"I think they're going to paint it pink," Mia declared.

Kat loved the way her daughter's three-year-old mind made such absolute predictions. She could imagine what Mia was envisioning—a bright, frosty, pink house that resembled a whimsical cake more than a home. She wished her imagination were that fanciful.

"Hi."

Kat sucked in her breath too fast and choked as she realized the deep voice belonged to the muscular, still shirtless man from the roof. Covering her mouth, she gasped and coughed, offering a futile wave as her mortification grew.

Her fingers fluttered much like the way her daughter waved and her eyes burned and watered. When his dark eyes creased with concern, she wanted to crawl in the dumpster to die.

"Hi," Mia said. "Are you fixing up the house for my friend?"

Kat blotted her eyes and cleared her throat.

The man smiled full lips pulling into a breathtaking grin as a dimple formed in his left cheek.

His eyes were fringed with long, thick lashes. They were the eyes of a pirate, keen and seductive as if brushed in soot, sharp and observant. Kat fidgeted under the weight of his gaze, certain he was noticing all her imperfect parts.

She cleared her throat again, drawing his wandering gaze back to her face. "Hello."

He offered a quick nod, looked down at Mia, and replied, "I'm fixing up the house, but I'm afraid the guy who bought it doesn't have any children."

"Oh." Mia pouted. "Does he have a dog?"

He dropped to his haunches, so he was at Mia's eye level. "Well, he doesn't have a dog yet, but he may get one once he moves in. Do you like dogs?"

"Yes, but Momma said we can't have one cause it's Dr. Stevens' house and Mrs. Bradshaw's 'lergic."

She should probably readdress the talking to strangers topic. Mia, no matter how much she reminded her to be cautious, would tell anyone anything. Kat could only be grateful Mia didn't know their bank account pin or social security number.

The man grinned up at her and back at Mia. "Well, if you could have a dog, what type of dog would you want?"

Mia took the question very seriously. Head tilted and lips twisted, her small finger thoughtfully tapped her chin. To a three-year-old, decisions like what breed of dog the neighbors should own were as paramount as nuclear warfare to adults.

"He should be smaller than me and have to have floppy ears and a long tail. He'd have to like to run, 'cause running's fun. And he has to know not to poo in the house."

The man laughed, gravelly and deep. It seemed to touch places inside of Kat that were normally dormant and unaffected. She looked away, afraid her reaction might somehow be noticeable.

"Well, those sound like good specifications."

He stood and extended his hand. "Hi, I'm Tyson Adams."

"Kat D'Angelo," she responded, shaking his hand. His fingers were rough and calloused but warm and twice the size of hers. "This is my daughter, Mia."

"A pleasure to meet you, Mia," he said, looking back down at her daughter before returning his gaze to her. "You guys live on this street?"

"Yes, that's our cottage, Mia said before Kat could stop her.

That's all she needed, some strange construction worker—twice her size and ripped with muscles—knowing her address and that they lived alone.

Tyson glanced at the cottage, then back to Kat. "Pretty."

He was complimenting their home, but his gaze lingered on her face, the unwanted scrutiny making it difficult not to fidget. She shuffled her feet and glanced away. "Well, it's home. We like it. It has all the amenities we need. Electric, running water, an alarm system."

What the hell was wrong with her? *An alarm system?* Good God! For once in her life, she'd like to be able to meet someone and not start babbling like the village idiot.

Tyson laughed under his breath as if sensing her embarrassment. He squatted back down to Mia and said, "Well, it was nice meeting you, Mia. I'll see what I can do about that dog."

Mia smiled, completely charmed. "You should probably build them a doghouse. Dogs like people houses, but they also like to have their own house too."

"Duly noted," he said and stood again.

"Kat, it was nice meeting you."

"Nice meeting you, too."

She took Mia's hand, completely focused on making her escape.

"I'll see you around," he said.

"Okay. Come on, Mia, we have stuff to do."

As they reached the door, Kat looked back over her shoulder. Tyson still stood at the curb, his gaze connecting with hers and sending a shiver down her spine. She quickly pulled out her keys and rushed inside, where she bolted the door.

～

That afternoon when she got home from work, Kat parked her car in their driveway and walked toward Mrs. Bradshaw's to pick up Mia. The corner house was, again, a beehive of activity. The radio played over the sound of a nail gun attaching shingles to the roof and the hum of an air compressor. Some other kind of machine made a racket in the backyard.

Her eyes immediately searched for Tyson. The burly blond was there, but he didn't seem as interesting as he had the day before. The irrational longing to see Tyson again was an aggravated inconvenience as it altered her typically content state of mind.

The door—now off the hinges—leaned against a tree in the front yard and wore a fresh coat of glossy, black paint. Blue insulation covered the rest of the exterior. The older man was working on the shutters on the front lawn, still indecently exposed.

Regret swamped her when she saw no sign of Tyson. But more than regret was the deep disappointment in her foolish desire.

After she picked up Mia and wished Mrs. Bradshaw a happy weekend, they started back toward the cottage. As they rounded the corner, she heard Mia's intake of breath.

"Hi, Tyson!" Mia yelled.

Tyson unfolded his posture from over a long table made of plywood and two sawhorses, and beamed at Mia. Wedging a pencil into his yellow bandana, he started toward them.

"Hi, Mia. Kat. How are you today?"

"Good. It's Friday!" Mia informed him.

"Is it?" Tyson replied, again dropping down to Mia's eye level. "And what's so special about Friday, may I ask?"

"It's pizza night, and Momma doesn't have work tomorrow!"

"Oh, well, that would make it special."

"Are you drawing pictures?"

Tyson's dark brow creased at the sudden change of topic, and then his gaze followed Mia's line of vision toward his worktable. "Ah, that. No, I'm not drawing. I'm looking at blueprints. They're kind of like drawings, though. They show me what we have to do to the house. Want to see?"

"Yeah!" Mia bounced.

"Okay, come on."

As he gently took Mia's hand, possessiveness gripped Kat. His assumed familiarity with Mia was a bit too forward. He was a stranger working on their neighbor's house. Kat quickly followed them across the yard, intending to force some space between this man and her child, but once they were in front of the worktable, he released Mia, and Kat relaxed slightly.

He showed Mia a sketch of the entire property. "You see I'm trying to find the best place for that doghouse we talked about."

Mia frowned, trying to make sense of the geometric images in front of her. "Maybe there?" She pointed to a room labeled *Master Bath*.

"Ah, well, that's the bathroom. See, this here's the backyard. This is the fence, and these are the trees."

His long, tapered, work-roughened finger traced

the images. A white scar nicked the flesh above his middle knuckle.

"Oh," Mia said. "Maybe under this tree?"

"That looks like a good place." Tyson grinned and winked at Kat, flustering her all the more.

"I can draw it for you. I'm a good colorer. Momma says I'm an artist."

"Is that so?" Tyson plucked his pencil from his bandana. "Well, here you go. Draw me a little doghouse right under that tree—"

"Uh—" Kat interrupted, placing a staying hand on Mia's shoulder as her daughter reached out and fisted Tyson's pencil in her three-year-old grip. "I don't think that's such a good idea, babe. Maybe you could draw Mr. Adams a picture of a doghouse on your own paper and give it to him. Blueprints are very expensive, and I'm sure his boss would be upset if he let someone color on them."

Tyson slowly rocked back, amusement dancing in his dark eyes as he studied her. The side of his mouth curved and a hint of his dimple showed. "I'm sure my boss wouldn't mind—"

"Tyson—"

"Kat," he countered. "It's fine. Really. The blueprints belong to Adams Construction. I'm Tyson Adams. They're mine."

When she shook her head, he continued to explain, "I'm the boss."

Her cheeks heated. Saws buzzed around them, the scent of cut wood lacing the spring air. "Well, you don't want to let a three-year-old doodle on your blueprints."

"Not just a three-year-old—an *artist*. Go ahead, Mia, give it your best shot."

He observed Mia, and Kat frowned at the back of his head, speechless. He arrogantly assumed his permission was enough. Who did he think he was?

Kat wasn't used to people maneuvering her. Well, except for her mother, of course. Vivian was a master of manipulation. But this guy was nobody to her, and Mia was *her* child who should listen to her mother, not strangers.

"Very nice, Mia!" He seemed genuinely pleased with her work. His large hand engulfed her daughter's shoulder and Kat's stomach tightened another degree with unease. Inwardly, she fought the sense of being shuffled aside. She wanted to bulldoze up to him and smack his hand away.

"This is the door, and this is a bowl for his food." Mia beamed.

Kat looked over her daughter's shoulder at what could only be described as a three-year-old's masterpiece. It was a circle with four parallel lines going through it and one patch of scribbles.

"And what color would you paint this doghouse?" Tyson asked.

"Pink!" It was only her daughter's enthusiasm that had Kat restraining herself.

"Hmm..." He dramatically considered her suggestion, tapping his finger on his chin. "But what if it's a boy dog?"

"Boys like pink, but I guess you could paint it yellow."

"I like yellow."

"I'm a good painter. I could help you paint it."

"That would be great."

A Lexus SUV pulled into Kat's driveway. Mia squealed, a wide grin breaking across her rosy cheeks. "Kiki!"

The driver's door opened, and Jade stepped onto the pavement. Kiki was the nickname Mia assigned Jade when she first started to talk. There was no rhyme or reason behind the name, and eventually, it stuck.

When she spotted them, she waved and headed in their direction. Kat breathed in a sigh of relief. Jade had always bolstered her confidence. She was the perfect interruption to distract Mia so they could make their escape.

A bite of inadequacy pinched as Jade approached in her fitted jeans, tight tank top, and cute mini-cardigan. Kat glanced at Tyson and grimaced to see he was studying Jade. An uncomfortable gumminess filled her chest, cold and hot all at the same time.

"Kiki!" Mia screeched again. Jade held out her arms as Mia ran toward her, launching herself at the last moment.

"A friend of yours?"

She glanced at Tyson. "Yes." Jade approached, holding Mia, and Kat did a quick introduction. "Tyson Adams, this is Jade Shultz."

"A pleasure," Tyson said as he shook her hand.

"Likewise," Jade replied. Her gaze moved from his large booted feet to the yellow bandana covering his head, openly appraising him.

"Tyson's running the construction here for the new owners of the house," Kat informed her friend.

"Oh, cool. Did you meet them yet?"

She shook her head. "Not yet."

Jade returned her attention to Tyson. "So what are the new people like? I assume you've met them? I can't have Mia and Kat living down the street from a serial killer."

He laughed. "I assure you the new owner is not a serial killer."

"So if you know they aren't murderers, what else do you know about them?" Jade had zero social graces, but her cuteness seemed to give her license to be blunt.

"He's an independent businessman. Single, no kids, and apparently a future dog owner."

"Ah, single. There you go, Kat." Jade nudged her in the arm with no subtlety whatsoever.

Kat choked, glared at Jade, then laughed nervously.

Tyson cleared his throat. "What about the doctor?"

Kat frowned as Jade asked, "What doctor?"

"Uh, the doctor who owns the house?" he replied, his dark stare moving from Kat to Jade and back to Kat again.

"*Doctor Stevens?*" Jade blurted and snorted in a fit of laughter. "My God, Kat! If you have something going on with that old man, you definitely need to get out more!"

Heat spread all the way from Kat's collar to her ears. "Dr. Stevens is my elderly boss. He rents the property to us, but he doesn't live there." To be completely clear, she added, "He's my landlord."

"Ah." Tyson smirked, the uncertainty fading from his face.

"Yeah, so perhaps this new neighbor of yours will be the man you've been waiting for," Jade continued.

Kat shot her a look that told her to shut up when Mia added, "He's gonna be my friend."

"I have *not* been waiting for a man," Kat growled under her breath, wishing the subject of her non-existent sex life would drop. This was not a conversation Tyson, nor Mia needed to witness.

Perhaps sensing her discomfort, Tyson said, "Well, ladies, I have to get back to work. Thanks for drawing me a doghouse, Mia. I'll see you all later."

As Tyson walked away, Jade whispered, "Well, at least you have a nice view for the next few weeks."

Chapter 4

MIA PLAYED with a bottle of bubbles in the backyard while Kat hung the laundry on the line. The breeze was laced with the sharp scent of fresh-cut grass, tinged with the slight hint of gasoline from the lawnmowers running. Mia's voice carried over the buzzing.

As she shook out the damp bed linens and clipped them to the line, she caught sight of Tyson in his backyard. Jade was right. The view was *fine*.

Tyson's muscles tightened and bunched under the exposed skin of his back as he used a shovel to dig a hole. Sweat coating his shoulders and sides glistened in the sun.

An ache formed low in her belly. What would he smell like? Her palms itched as she rolled a clothespin in her fingers. Would his skin be smooth or rough like his hands?

She shifted her shoulders, her bra irritating her flesh. He pierced the shovel into the ground and reached down to retrieve a bottle of water. She concentrated on his forearm as he rested it on the handle of the shovel to guzzle down several gulps before recapping the bottle.

She wasn't sure if it was his size or the way that he carried himself that had her so mesmerized. Every move he made seemed confident and sure. She craved the sort of resoluteness he displayed, but it went against her indecisive nature. Maybe such confidence came with age.

She gasped as he unknotted his bandanna, revealing a beautifully smooth, bald head. Her pulse thrummed. His lack of hair only made him more appealing. He unfolded the yellow fabric and used it to wipe the sweat from his brow.

Oh, yes...

~

Tyson laughed as he fitted a fence post into the ground, aware his neighbor, Kat, was spying on him. She was a peculiar thing, high strung, but in a charming sort of way—with a natural beauty. She was small but had curves in all the right places, no matter how she tried to hide them.

She didn't have the best social skills. She was skittish, yet assertive with her daughter. He suspected she was in her early twenties, but the fact that she had a three-year-old made him unsure. No matter, he was most likely ten plus years her senior, and that meant he had to keep his thoughts in the PG zone. A task that became more difficult each time he saw her.

However, he couldn't deny that he liked

catching her spying on him. He found her most intriguing when she didn't know she had an audience. When it was just Kat and her daughter, she became animated and lost in her own world, chasing bubbles and twirling with little Mia. The kid was adorable—all wild strawberry blonde curls and pink, pudgy cheeks.

Her friend Jade had said Kat was single. He wondered what kind of man let a sweet woman like Kat walk out of his life.

There was something shy about her, something uptight and guarded that disappeared when she didn't realize others were watching. Maybe he made her uneasy. No unwritten rule said she had to like him. Or maybe her uneasiness had to do with her baby's daddy? Maybe Mia's father had been the kind of guy that made women uncomfortable around men.

She hung another white sheet on the line. Tyson enjoyed the way her loose-fitting linen skirt whispered over the backs of her knees and swelled over her plump bottom.

Her hair was down, the brown waves delicately curling at her shoulders. When she'd been in his yard the other day, he found the way the sunlight played over her hair incredibly distracting.

She bent over—*nice*—picking another item from her basket. He admired the way her white t-shirt molded to her chest. He caught echoes of her humming as she hung the laundry across the line. White sheets blowing with the bubbles in the breeze...the view was prettier than a Norman Rockwell painting.

As the freshly laundered sheets worked their way across the line, he got a whiff of fabric softener. Would her clothes carry the same sweet freshness? His body stiffened at the thought of pressing his face into the curve of her neck and breathing in the mixed scent of her clothes, skin, and hair. He bet her skin would be as soft and as warm as the sun-kissed cotton fluffing in the breeze.

Back to work. She's too young for you.

He thrust the shovel into the ground in an attempt to dispel his arousal. It had been too long since he'd last had a woman.

After digging a few more patches out of the earth, he stopped to get a sip of water. It was damn hot for early spring.

Using his bandana to wipe his brow, he pulled the damp cloth away to see if she was still there. She squeaked and jumped behind the veil of the sheets as his gaze collided with hers. A rush of satisfaction punched through his veins. So much for losing his hard-on. Did she like what she saw?

Dainty feet in plain flip-flops showed under the sheet. Little did she know that the angle of the sun left her silhouette in full view. The side of his mouth kicked up as the shadow of her curvy body fidgeted, and her feet shifted. She sure was skittish.

He had the suspicion she didn't get complimented as much as she probably should, and that was a damn shame. He waited for her to peek around the sheet and wave, but as her slow-moving shadow worked closer to the edge, again and again, she chickened out every time. He had to laugh. She certainly was skittish as a kitten.

~

He'd caught her watching him!

Taking a few minutes to find her composure, Kat took a few slow breaths. Peeking back around the sheet, she exhaled, tension leaving her shoulders. He'd retied his bandana around his head and was shoveling again.

Kat stayed behind the sheet—tilting only her head past the protective barricade—when Tyson looked in her direction again. He grinned and shook his head as if laughing to himself, and continued on with his work.

Frowning, she wondered if he was laughing at her. She ducked behind the sheet and chewed on her nail.

The phone rang. Kat picked up her basket, called Mia to follow. Inside, she dropped the basket in the hall, and ran to the kitchen to pick up the phone.

"Hello?"

"Katherine, what were you doing? You sound out of breath."

"Hi, Mom. I was out back with Mia."

"Oh. How's my granddaughter?" Her tone always reeked of skepticism whenever she asked about Mia's wellbeing as if Kat's parenting skills would forever be in question.

She should talk.

"She's fine. How's Dad?"

"He's well. That's actually why I'm calling. Your father has a colleague he'd like you to meet."

She cringed. Her parents' taste in men was nothing like her own, and while it seemed the entire world was hoping she'd meet a man and marry, she had no desire to do so. The mere thought of dating —the effort of physically and mentally preparing for such fabricated social meetings—exhausted her.

"He's in his late twenties and works on the township's board of trustees. He's never been married and is quite handsome, from what I understand."

"Mom, I'd really rather not be one of your charity cases."

"Don't be foolish, Katherine. You're my daughter. You're a lovely young woman, and some men might be kind enough to overlook your past."

This was her mother's idea of support.

"I'm really not in the market to date right now. I tell you this all the time. My life's as full as I want it. Mia doesn't need to suffer through the complications of me dating."

"Mia needs a father," her mother said as Kat considered how much better her self-esteem would've been if *her* father were absent from her life. "She'd benefit from having a strong male figure in her life. You know your father can only compensate so much for your shortcomings. And you'd benefit from having a husband, someone to take care of you. Then you could quit that job and stay home with Mia instead of shipping her out to your neighbors."

"Mia likes going to Mrs. Bradshaw's, and I like my job." God forbid Vivian D'Angelo acted as a babysitter. No, that would be too much.

"That's not the point. The point is that your father sees this man as a suitable match for you. It

would please him if you at least—*once*—did the du-
tiful thing and followed his request without our
coercion.

"Now, he's asked Dawson to attend Easter
dinner with us next Sunday. I'll expect you to wear
something appropriate and Mia will need a new
dress. I'm taking her shopping tomorrow on our
outing, and I'd like you to join us."

Son of a bitch! The only thing worse than
talking to her mother was shopping with her. "I
have clothes, Mom."

"Your clothes are outdated and Dawson's a successful young man. He's used to moving in high-
class circles with sophisticated young ladies. You'll
need something classy that hides your curves. How
are you doing with your weight, anyway?"

Kat dropped her head into her palm. No one
needed to tell her she wasn't perfect. She was quite
aware. She didn't have Jade's perky boobs, her
mom's trim waistline, or Mia's vibrant hair, and no
amount of envy would change that. What she did
have was an unremarkable chest, love handles, and
hair that resembled a bird's nest without the help of
a flat iron and a good amount of conditioner.

It took years to convince herself that stretch
marks were a mother's badge of honor and that
freckles built character, but her mom could still cut
to her core with one quick question. Vivian assumed it was Kat's life's ambition to be a size two,
which she'd never been. Even at her best, she was a
size twelve. And since Mia, she'd maintained a comfortable size fourteen-sixteen.

Regardless, she made a point to hide how much

her mother's words still hurt. "Um, I look the same as I did last week, Mom."

"Well, if you eat extra healthy this week and drink plenty of water, you could lose a couple of pounds by next Sunday."

Kat said nothing as she picked at a hangnail. *Ignore her. She's superficial. There are more important things than a person's weight.* Vivian always seemed to attack her pride as an attempt to make her more agreeable, weaker, something Kat had spent years trying to build a tolerance against.

"I'll be picking up Mia tomorrow morning at nine. Be ready. We'll start at Nordstrom's and take it from there."

"Fine, but Mom, I do have things to do tomorrow. I won't be able to shop all day. Why don't we meet you at Nordstrom's, and when we're finished, you and Mia can go about the rest of your day, and I can do my running around?"

Vivian was quiet for a minute and Kat, knowing her mother, interpreted her silence as irritation. "I don't understand why you can't do your running around on another day. Is it so much to ask that you spend a day with your mother?"

And here comes the guilt.

"I rarely see you and only get to see Mia on Sundays."

Kat gaped. "That's completely your choice, Mom. You're welcome to visit whenever you want. We're home every night, and I'm sure Mia would love to have you over more."

"You know your house is too small for company."

"My house is fine. It may be too small for a dinner party, but it's certainly large enough to have you and Daddy over once in a while."

"That's my point, dear. You're getting older and eventually will want to entertain in your own home. If you married a successful man, you could afford a bigger house and do these things. Anyway, I have to run. I was simply calling to make arrangements for tomorrow. I'll meet you at Nordstrom's at nine if that's the most you can offer. Give Mia my love."

As Kat hung up the phone, she rubbed her temples in an attempt to prevent the oncoming headache that always followed a conversation with her mother. "Why couldn't I have normal parents?"

~

Kat was cleaning up after dinner when she hit the switch for her garbage disposal, and it made a god-awful noise. Sharp metal scraped and suddenly silenced.

Bracing her palms on the lip of the sink, she stared into the dark hole. "Shit."

"Momma, that's a bad word. You gotta give me a quarter," Mia said.

"Sorry, baby. I'll get you one as soon as I fix this."

She adjusted the spray faucet to dislodge whatever was jamming the disposal and hit the switch, but nothing happened. Reaching under the sink, she pressed the reset button, but that didn't work either. "Mia, can you get me the flashlight out of the hall closet?"

"Okay."

Mia left her coloring to rush off to her aid. She was always such a good little helper. A broken garbage disposal wasn't the end of the world, but it also wasn't something she could afford to replace at the moment. Hopefully, it was a simple fix.

Mia returned with the flashlight, and Kat shined it down the drain. Something dark was lodged in the grinder.

"What's wrong, Momma?"

"Something's stuck in the sink."

Reaching into the drain as far as her fingers fit, she ignored the slimy potato peels clinging to her wrist and grazed the object, but couldn't grasp it. An aggravated breath huffed past her lips as she removed her arm and flicked off the slimy bits of food.

Retrieving her toolbox from the closet, she searched for pliers or something that could grip the object, but there was nothing. Letting out a frustrated groan, she bit at her thumbnail. "Tongs!" Jumping off the floor, she slid the toolbox back on the shelf.

Mia stood in the kitchen as Kat sifted through the utensil drawers. When she found them, she fed them into the hole, but they still didn't reach the obstruction. She tried rotating her hands, but the handles simply wouldn't fit. "Damn it!"

When Mia didn't correct her language, something she always did when Kat let a curse word slip, she looked at her daughter. She stood, head bent, gaze on the floor, as she wrung her hands in unnatural silence.

"Mia, do you know what's wrong with the sink?"

She rubbed her toe on the floor, still not looking at her.

"Mia, did you put something in the sink that shouldn't have been in there?"

She nodded.

"Can you tell Mommy what it was?"

She mumbled something that sounded like, "My wiswa tree."

"What?"

Lifting her teary gaze, she took a deep breath. "My wizard was dirty, so I tried to wash him. But he fell in the hole."

Kat sighed. "Mia, you know you're not allowed to play at the kitchen sink."

"I'm sorry I broke your sink, Momma." A tear rolled down her cheek, and the sincere sadness in her voice nearly shattered Kat's heart.

"It's okay, but don't do it again. This sink is very dangerous. I need to figure out how to fix it, so Dr. Stevens doesn't have to call a plumber. We need to think of something long enough to grab the wizard. I need a tool that pinches."

"I know! You can borrow one from Tyson. He has lots of tools. He'll give you some."

"Good idea." He would definitely have a tool she could use. "Okay, why don't you go watch cartoons? I'm going to run over to see if Tyson's still working. You stay here and don't get off the couch."

"Okay, Momma." Mia dashed into the living room and flicked on the television.

Relieved the Adams Construction truck was

still parked in the driveway, she quickly walked down the sidewalk. *Does this guy ever go home?*

No music played, and the yard was empty. "Tyson?" No one answered, so she knocked on the door. Nothing. She knocked again, anxiously glancing back at the house.

Did she shut off the stove? Shut the broom closet? Visions of Mia waiting on the couch mixed with fears of her climbing up the shelves of the closet filled her with anxiety. She didn't like leaving Mia alone for more than two minutes. Her hand rose to knock one last time when the door opened.

"Kat?"

Words. She needed words.

Tyson stood—shirtless—in the doorway wearing only jeans. Her gaze fixated on his bare feet. Breathing in his clean scent, she noted traces of soap, the green, expensive kind. Her mouth went dry as she looked up and found herself at eye level with his dark nipples.

"Is everything okay?"

He was standing so close her mouth opened, but nothing came out. "Uh..." She shook her head. *Pull it together, Kat!* "Yeah, I wanted to see if you had a long pair of pliers I could borrow."

"Sure, they're in my truck. Let me throw on shoes and get them for you."

He disappeared for two seconds and reappeared wearing a pair of slip-on canvas boat shoes. Was he staying there while renovating?

He stepped close, and she froze. What was he doing?

He chuckled softly, his large hands pressing into

her shoulders. "Pardon. I need to get by." Her eyes widened as he briefly squeezed before letting go.

She took a jolting step back as the smooth flesh of his abdomen brushed her arm. The light scent of beer was faint on his warm breath.

God, what is wrong with me?

At the truck, he sifted through a canvas-lined bucket. Kat waited on the lawn, careful not to get too close. He probably thought she was such an idiot.

"Here ya go." He handed her the pliers.

"Thanks, I gotta run. Mia's in the house by herself. I'll bring these back soon as I'm finished."

"Take your time."

She jogged back to the house. Mia was still sitting on the couch. "You okay, kiddo?"

"Yes."

"Okay, good. Why don't you pick out a movie while Mommy fixes the sink? We'll have to take a tubby in the morning."

"*Cinderella?*"

"Sure."

She changed Mia into her pajamas, situated her on the couch with her blanket, and started *Cinderella*. Kat tried the pliers but couldn't un-jam the wizard. She was sitting on the floor, her head stuck under the sink with a flashlight, tools scattered around when there was a knock at the door. Twisting, she whacked her head on the disposal bin.

"Mother Fudrucker!" She rubbed her head and crawled out from under the sink.

Mia's footsteps pattered to the window, and she shouted, "Tyson!"

Kat froze. She quickly smoothed her hair back and brushed her fingers over her face. Very aware he was in *her* territory, she took her time standing and getting to the door, fussing with her shirt and frowning at the smudge of something on her shoulder.

Taking a steadying breath, she unlatched the deadbolt and gently nudged Mia away from the door.

"Hi, Tyson!" Mia greeted from beside her hip.

"Hi, Mia."

He raised a brow and held out a leather belt full of tools. "I figured you might need some help."

"Oh. Uh…"

Did she really want to impose on the new neighbor's construction guy? Would he expect to be paid for his time? Should she even involve him in their personal affairs?

Oh, for Christ's sake, get a grip, Kat! It's a garbage disposal, for crying out loud, not a therapy session.

"Thank you. Please come in."

He stepped over the threshold. "You okay?"

"Yeah, I was weighing my options, thinking I could fix it. I mean, you work in construction, so I'm sure you've installed, like, a thousand of them, but I'm so worried that the wizard broke the damn thing. I tried my hands, tongs, pliers, but I can't get the wizard out of the hole and—"

"Whoa, whoa, you lost me at wizard. Why don't you tell me what the problem is?"

"I dropped my wizard down the hole," Mia said.

"The garbage disposal," Kat amended. "Mia

dropped a plastic toy wizard down the drain, and I can't get it out. The mechanism froze up, and I hit the reset button, but it's jammed."

"I see."

He walked to the sink, and the air seemed to siphon out of her small cottage. Tyson was too big for her home. She'd never had a man there before aside from Dr. Stevens or her father. His presence totally threw her off-kilter.

"Well, that should be easy enough to fix, but first things first. You *never* reach into a jammed garbage disposal."

"I made sure it was off—"

"Never." He tilted his head, attempting to look stern, but his dimple gave him away. "Who's to say the piece won't spin after you un-jam it? You could lose a finger that way."

Kat raised a brow at the dramatic reprimand, and Mia gasped at the mention of losing fingers. Keeping her tone level for her daughter's sake, she agreed. "You're right. I won't do it again. That's exactly why little girls aren't supposed to play at the sink."

"Good. Now, let's see this wizard."

"Mia, take your milk and go sit down and finish your movie before bed."

Mia headed into the living room, and Kat cleared away her tools to show Tyson the issue. "It's on this side," she said, leaning over the right basin of the sink.

She shined the flashlight over the hole as Tyson looked in the drain. With their heads so close together, she breathed him in. Slowly, she turned. His shaved head was completely smooth, not even a shadow of stubble. She took an uneven step back and cleared her throat.

"Well, your hands are smaller than mine. So if you couldn't maneuver the tools through the hole, I definitely won't be able to. Looks like the base is going to have to come off."

"Is that difficult?" The idea of him going through so much trouble didn't sit well with her or her wallet. Maybe she should just tell Dr. Stevens in the morning.

"No, I'll have it working again in no time."

He dropped to his knees and dug through his tool belt. Ripples of muscle formed under his t-shirt as he pulled out various tools, not an ounce of fat on him. Every nook and cranny was so defined even his clothing couldn't camouflage how fit he was.

Her shoulders subtly rotated as if that could relieve some of the tension low in her belly or soften the tightening skin beneath her bra. Maybe she should get a job in construction. Then her mom wouldn't think she was such a fat cow.

He pulled out his own flashlight and paused before ducking under the sink. Those dark almond-shaped eyes stared up at her, and all breathing stopped. "You don't have to sit here. Go spend time with Mia. I'll get you when I'm finished."

He probably realized she was gawking at him again. Good God, she was becoming a deviant. "Um, okay." She awkwardly hitched her thumb toward the next room. "I'll be in the living room if you need anything."

"Sounds good." He ducked under the sink and

gave her a phenomenal view of his ass. *Holy mother of sweetness!*

About a half-hour later, Kat sat watching *Cinderella* with Mia on her lap when Tyson stepped into the living room

"I have good news and bad news."

Kat put her finger to her lips and motioned toward Mia's sleeping face. She gently slid her daughter onto the couch and motioned him back toward the kitchen. Taking a deep breath, she leaned her hip against the counter and braced for the worst. Hopefully, it would only be a minor setback. Her financial situation did not allow for overly expensive emergencies.

"What do you want first, the good or the bad?" he asked.

Kat rubbed her forehead. "The good, I guess."

"The garbage disposal is fixed."

She exhaled in relief.

"The bad news is I don't think Merlin will be doing spells again anytime soon." He held up a mutilated piece of plastic, and she laughed, his smirk shifting to a full on smile—dimples and all.

"Well, I can deal with that. Here, let me throw that away." She took the toy from him and dropped it in the trashcan.

"This is a nice place you have here. You're a little bit of a control freak, aren't you?"

She faltered as her neck stiffened in offense. He looked around her kitchen as he stretched, gripping his hands behind his head. His shirt slightly rose at his midriff, exposing his trim waist. He seemed utterly unaware that he'd just insulted her.

"What did you say?"

"I, uh, noticed you have little labels under the sink for where things belong, sponges, dish soap, disinfectant." Likely noticing that he offended her, he held up his palms. "Hey, I'm not judging. Really. It's cute."

"Cute?" Since when was compulsiveness cute?

"Yeah, cute. Really, Kat, I didn't mean to insult you."

Her face heated. "I'm a little weird. Jade calls me OCD, so I'm a little sensitive about it. It is a disorder I have. I mean, it's not like a doctor's diagnosed me or anything like that. I just figure, having Mia and all, it's easier to keep things controlled and organized."

"That makes sense."

She nibbled her lip and looked down. Should she pay him? Offer him something to drink? Her toes twitched as an awkward silence fell between them. She sensed him watching her.

"And Mia's father..."

Her gaze jerked to his. That was the last thing she expected him to mention.

He shook his head. "Never mind, that really isn't any of my—"

"Mia's father is out of our lives. She's never met him, and he only saw her when she was two days old. Last I heard, he was in Japan."

"Japan?"

"Yeah. He's in the military."

"So you're okay with him not taking responsibility for his actions?"

She shifted. "Mia was the result of both our actions, but she's my child. She doesn't need a father for me to be a good mother."

"Very true." He studied her, and she fought the urge to fidget. "How old were you when you had Mia?"

"Eighteen." She braced for his reaction.

His dark brows arched. "That's pretty amazing." Nodding, he crossed his arms over his chest, appearing open and at ease.

Unused to flattery, his praise made her self-conscious. Falling back on old defense mechanisms, she brushed off his compliment by minimizing herself. "Hardly, I do what hundreds of moms do every day. I don't have the luxury or patience to wait for some rich man to sweep me off my feet and make everything easy. Although, that's what my mother's hoping for," she joked.

"Do your parents help you out?"

"Uh, no. Not exactly. Other than taking Mia on Sundays, they aren't really involved in my life. They never really got over the disgrace of me getting pregnant in high school."

His expression changed to shocked disbelief. "Seriously?"

"Yup. Pretty shitty."

"And you still talk to them?"

"I tolerate them for Mia's sake. They take Mia every Sunday like I said. I don't usually tag along. I think they have a better relationship when I'm not involved."

"That's pretty tolerant of you."

Her feigned casualness faltered as her stomach flipped and heated at his words. It wasn't safe to let him affect her so much. Back to indifference. "No, I'm just a kid trying to make it as an adult. I can use all the help I can get."

"You're pretty accountable. That's more than most adults can claim."

Mia was her responsibility, and feeling sorry for herself or complaining through difficult times only made things worse. "Well, it's easy to make sacrifices for someone you love more than yourself."

"See? You sum up your hardships with some optimistic poetic line. That's amazing."

She didn't know when it happened, but somehow the conversation shifted to squarely focus on her. The urge to flee hit hard. Her chest rose and fell with shallow breaths. She'd gotten pregnant when she was seventeen. Amazing women didn't do stuff like that.

"It's a compliment, Kat, take it."

Lips trembling into a smile, she looked at the floor. She never found time to pat herself on the back. Back pats didn't pay the bills, so why bother? But still, to have someone other than Jade recognize her accomplishments was really nice.

Nervously blinking, she slowly lifted her gaze. Confidence was hard when you didn't always have faith in yourself. "Thank you."

She didn't know how to get past the awkward emotional exchange. It was good to actually talk like this with another adult, but it was also unfamiliar and painfully personal.

Clearing her throat, she turned the tables on him. "Okay, your turn. Does your boss know you're staying at his house?"

"I told you, I'm the boss."

"Yes, but you work for someone. In this case, the owner of the house."

"Kat, I bought the house. It's mine. I own it. I'm fixing it up to live there."

Her smile faltered. "What? But you said..." she trailed off. He'd said the owner of the house was an independent, single businessman with no children. "Why didn't you tell me?"

"We all hide our cards until we're comfortable with our hand, Kat. Sometimes we even lie."

"*Did* you lie to me?"

"No, but you lied to me when you felt threatened. You told me you had an alarm system in case I was planning on robbing you or something. But I don't see one installed anywhere."

Unease washed through her—cold and unsettling. He was grinning, but there was no dimple, and his eyes seemed flat and untouched. If she'd known he was their actual neighbor, she might have acted differently.

"I didn't say it because I thought you were going to rob—"

"Sure you did. You saw a large, unfamiliar, black man hanging around your house, and you lied to protect your cub."

She gasped. "It wasn't because you're black."

"Maybe not. I'm sure there were a lot of reasons. I'm a man. I'm bigger than you by a long shot, and you didn't know me from Adam. But I'm also not blind. I'm probably the only black resident within a five-mile radius."

She knew better than to judge others, especially

after too many people had unfairly judged her. "I'm sorry I lied. You seem like a nice man." But he was a man, and perhaps that was all she needed to fear.

He nodded as if accepting her apology. "You seem like a nice woman."

It would only take a small movement of her fingers to touch his hand resting on her counter. He was beautiful.

His voice interrupted her thoughts. "You did the right thing with a strange man so close to your home. But I need to know if the color of my skin is an issue since we're going to be neighbors."

"It's not."

"Good, because I like you, Kat. I'd like to get to know you." Soft and gravelly, he asked, "Can we be friends?"

Friends. Tyson wanted to be her neighbor and her friend, yet the way he was looking at her, dark smoldering eyes staring right through her as if she were naked behind only sheer whispers of secrets, told her he wanted more.

She didn't do *more*. Ever.

Her lashes lowered, and she stole a glance at his hand, his arm, and his chest. Heat bloomed somewhere dark and deep within her. Her thoughts fragmented, and a little demon inside prodded her to touch him. What would he feel like? She actually considered accidentally bumping him.

Swirls of breathless suspense rushed through her, awakening her blood like heated honey.

Her gaze softened, and her neck extended as the

tension in her shoulders eased. Her voice was low and raspy, nothing like the way she usually sounded. "We can be friends, Tyson."

A sort of lightheadedness took hold of her as those full, fringed lashes lowered and his eyes darkened. Smoldering. Deep pools of onyx, flecked with swirls of amber watched her. Focusing on the delicate V beneath his lip, she swallowed.

He touched her face, using the soft edge of his knuckle to graze the line of her jaw from her ear to chin. It was enough to ground her, making her aware of the physical space she occupied.

Her skin prickled as though she was falling. Her arms itched to cover herself, but her blood was too sluggish for her to move. She could barely get oxygen to her lungs, let alone her brain.

A strangled whimper tickled her throat as he leaned in. His scent intensified, slipping inside of her as she sucked in a deep breath at the first brush of his lips. Like a laden balloon flies on its last breeze, kissing the air between sky and earth, his mouth hovered over hers, a caress somewhere in the space between.

His fingers pinched the edge of her chin, pulling her lips slightly apart. And then the space between them was gone. His plush, firm lips pressed into hers, and she was drowning. The first slow lick of his tongue had her breasts tightening.

Oh my God, oh my God, oh my God!

He barely touched her, yet she felt him everywhere. This was nothing like the kisses she'd shared with boys in high school, with Jeremy.

He pressed closer. The thin layer of clothing

separating them was insubstantial as his front molded to hers. His weighty palm pressed over the center of her stiff spine, trapping her against him. No one had ever touched her so intimately.

How did she get here? Tongue to tongue, he kissed her, slow and soft. His slanted mouth gently opened and closed. She could no longer deny the effect he was having on her as her body softened as her lashes lowered.

Amplified by her blindness, her senses caught fire. His lips sealed to hers as his large hand slid beneath her hair and a moan of satisfaction slipped from his mouth to hers.

She hadn't been kissed in years, and never had she experienced anything like this. If this was kissing, what the hell had she been doing before?

He slowly slid his tongue over her bottom lip. Palms gently skidding over her clothing to her skin, he caressed her from shoulder to wrist and eased away.

A soft squeeze of her hands was the last warning she had that the kiss was over. Her spine extended as her mouth followed his. His soft chuckle had her opening her eyes. Dazed and intensely aroused, she blinked at him. Holy crap! What had she done?

He was still close, but with the hold he had on her wrists, he had complete control over their contact. He measured her through thick lashes and breathed deeply through his nose as if memorizing her scent, sending shivers up her spine.

"You smell like sunshine," he whispered.

His fingers released her wrists, leaving an impression of heat, making the chill that replaced his touch all the more unsettling. He took a step away, and she stood frozen in place. Was he leaving? Was that it? *Shouldn't* that be it? What was she thinking?

He picked up his tools and took another step toward the door. "Goodnight, Kat. I'll see you around."

His words registered, and she finally blinked. They were neighbors. There would be no avoiding him. Fingers trembling to her lips, she cursed under her breath, knowing she'd just made a terrible mistake.

Chapter 5

HE WAS SUCH AN IDIOT.

Ambling home, Tyson cursed himself for being twenty kinds of a fool. She was no more than twenty-one or twenty-two. She was a baby, for crying out loud. Her youth was evident in everything from her shy, questioning eyes to the way she kissed. Christ, she even smelled young. And he, well, he was a letch.

"You're an old pervert," he mumbled as he crossed onto his property.

But there was something irresistible about her.

Tyson walked through his front door and tossed his tools on the floor. Dim, dreamlike images of Kat played through his mind. His hand closed around the cool neck of a beer, and he shut the fridge. Her face, soft with that wistful look of inexperience, filled his mind.

Fuck. He was strung tighter than a guitar string after a simple taste of those sweet, kiss-provoking lips. Chucking the beer cap across the room, he groaned. His back hit the wall of his sparse living room as his weight dragged to the floor.

This was bad. How had he gone from a little flirting to mauling her in her kitchen in only a couple of days?

He stopped by to make sure everything was all right, but also because he'd been waiting for an excuse to get close to her. There was something so exquisitely simple about Kat. A delicious shyness, so unlike the other women he knew.

Kat was a woman who hadn't been kissed much. Her lack of experience was evident by the way he had to coax her soft mouth open and how timidly she kissed him back. Seizing the moment, he possessively took her sweet mouth when she eased forward.

Ty sipped his beer and let his head hit the wall, hoping to knock some sense into his thick skull. He shifted his legs in an attempt to make room in his pants as his mind replayed her sweet little moans. She probably made all sorts of delicious keening sounds during sex, a mixture of raw, unguarded headiness and untried wonderment. He wanted to see if he was right. But that would never happen.

Two houses and fifteen years—that's what separated them. The chances of him fucking a woman like Kat were so low he was pathetic for even entertaining the fantasy. A pretty young mom like herself probably had high hopes for a nice young husband.

Pushing out a slow breath, he tried to let go of all thoughts of getting Kat naked. For all he knew, she was furious with him. As much as he used the excuse of fixing her sink to get into her house, he didn't want her to think she owed him anything.

His empty beer hung from his fingers, and he massaged his temples as he sighed. The depraved fantasies running through his mind needed to stop. Those sultry lips parted. His name on her tongue. Her smoky gaze crawling over him like little kisses. The last thing she needed was her middle-aged neighbor making her uncomfortable.

Groaning, he acknowledged what he needed to do, but snuffing out his attraction to her wouldn't be easy. There was no telling his cock that she was out of the question when it perked up like a fucking weathervane every time she was around.

Her family sounded like a bunch of assholes. Clearly, they didn't understand one thing about their daughter. Life was messy, and accidents happened. There were plenty of girls who got pregnant when he was in high school. What kind of parents discarded their child at such a vulnerable moment in life?

Who's looking out for Kat?

Retrieving another beer, he popped the cap and then returned to his spot on the floor. He let out a frustrated breath and roughly rubbed his palm over his face.

"Not your concern, man."

He was supposed to be looking for a wife, concentrating on starting a family of his own, not intruding on someone else's. Once the house was done, he'd be back to his normal schedule, and Kat would be someone he passed maybe once a week on the occasion that she was unloading groceries while he mowed the lawn.

Cruising the marriage aisle was something he'd never done. His life had revolved around the simple focus of starting his business and watching it grow. It wasn't until his sister Sophia got sick that he started worrying about shit like mortality. And it wasn't until she died that he realized how goddamn lonely his life had become.

Not wanting to sink into that swelling tide of memories, he finished his beer and hauled himself off the floor. Working a screwdriver under the rim of the paint can, he uncapped the lid. It was time to put pointless fantasies away and get something done.

He should have put on music, but he was already involved and didn't want to stop. The slow spongy swish of the paint roller and his even breathing were the only sound in the empty house. His mind switched to autopilot as he dragged the roller up and down the wall, and his thoughts wandered anyway.

Death was a naked fact of life. Everyone died. Some old, some young, the point of it all was to make use of time while time remained. Since Sophia's passing, he'd suffered a nagging guilt that he wasn't utilizing his time wisely—missing all the opportunities his sister wished she could have had. He didn't want to leave this world without a trace.

He'd spent years building a legacy, but what the hell did a construction company mean in the grand scheme of things? Family was what mattered. He wanted to see his hard work passed onto a son or daughter, not some employee. And he wanted to leave behind more than an investment. He wanted to invest himself in the ongoing life of his children so they could do the same.

Thirty came in the blink of an eye. Thirty-five rung in quick like the bell of a boxing match. By then, it had all seemed redundant and meaningless. His days passed routinely with little blips of interest along the way, but there was never anything significant happening, never anything exciting.

Sure, his friends had gotten married and had children, and that was exciting, but those events were theirs. He had nothing going on in his own life deserving of such celebration. Time was running out.

Moving the lamp and bucket he was using for a table to the other side of the room, he dragged his tarp over the cement floor and replenished the pan of paint. Rotating his shoulders, he fell back into the repetitive motions of rolling the walls.

A familiar empty weight filled him when he thought of his sister. He missed her. Gloria at least had Darrel and the kids to distract her from the grief.

"Ty," Sophia had whispered, her feeble hand reaching for his. She'd become too delicate, barely anything separating her flesh from her little bones. Her curls were too fine to braid anymore, and dark shadows surrounded her eyes.

He wished he could erase those memories of the way she looked in the end. No matter how many flashbacks he held of her looking young and vibrant, his mind always saw her the way she was in the end.

When he gave her a tender squeeze to let her know he was listening, she smiled and shut her eyes.

"I worry about you." Her brow tensed as she released a deep breath, never admitting when the pain was gaining on her.

"You don't need to worry for me, Phia."

It was a terrible impression of bravery. His emotions were simply too strong at that point to hide.

"Hush." She smirked. "You might have everyone else fooled, but not me, Ty. Not me."

He didn't have the energy for deep, so he tried to keep the moment light. "What're you talking about, Phia? You're high from the morphine."

She breathed a raspy chuckle. No matter what, she always had a smile at the ready. "My senses are just fine." Taking a deep breath, she held his hand a little tighter.

"So strong," she mumbled while keeping her eyes closed. "You've done everything you set out to do. Got everything you wanted, but Ty, you're a fool." She peeked at him under sparse eyelashes. "You got them all fooled. But not me, Ty. Not me."

He didn't want to have this conversation. He didn't want to have some final moment, wasn't ready to see his baby sister wither away to nothingness. Her mind had always been so sharp. Her ramblings were only more proof of the cancer's progression.

"Phia," he soothed, fighting back the lump in his chest. "Rest, baby girl, rest."

"There'll be plenty of time for me to rest when I'm dead."

"Phia," he hissed.

"And that'll be soon enough."

Choked by a sense of foreboding, he allowed her to go on.

"I'll never know what true love feels like. I'll never experience a child growing inside of me. Never know what it's like to be called mother or wife."

His jaw locked as his vision blurred. "Jesus."

"Now, Ty, don't you go cussin' God for this. The good Lord's all I got, and the only solace I find is that eventually He'll stop the pain and welcome me into His kingdom."

Losing the battle against his tears, he wept like a child, resting his forehead on their entwined hands. "I wish I could take this from you."

"No. This isn't your destiny. It's mine. But you'll do me this one favor before I go."

"Anything."

"I love you, but you're a dumb ass."

He scoffed and laughed, the weight in his chest slightly dissipating, but there was no room for humor. Only hollow sadness.

"What?" She chuckled and coughed. "You think no one around here can tell you how it is? Well, I ain't got nothin' to lose."

He waited through another crackling cough.

"I want you to do all the things I can't, Ty. I want you to find love. I want you to know what it is to hold a child of your own in your arms. I want you to get out of this area and finally be the man I know you're meant to be."

She wheezed in a short breath. "Dying does weird things to a person. Sometimes talkin' gets too hard, *and all you do is stumble through your mind. You see things, you know? I see you. Not here, but somewhere that the air smells of fresh-cut grass, somewhere that the breeze carries the chatter of children, and a tire swing hangs from an old oak tree or some such quaint shit like that. I see you coaching little league and packin' brown bag lunches with cute smiley faces drawn on the napkins.*

"When I go, Momma'll be there for Daddy, and Darrel'll be there for Gloria. But who'll be there for you, Ty? You know how to build a house, but I want you to build yourself a home. And once you do, I want you to find your soul mate and fill that home with babies and be the best daddy you can be."

Just like that night, his vision blurred with tears. The paint hit the walls in wavering strokes as the memory play like a reoccurring nightmare. Sophia had died that evening. The funeral was on a Tuesday. After everyone left the cemetery to return to his parents' house, Tyson stoically watched the burial of his baby sister.

The hours that followed passed like years. Days were lost in the shuffle of life and grief. Gloria was the first to put on a brave front and get on with her life. His mother and father would probably never completely recover, but they had eventually cleared out Phia's things and figured out how to laugh again.

Ty seemed the only one who still suffered the weight of this unbearable loneliness, most likely because he had no one to fill the void. The tension of tears striving for an outlet drove his mind away from such sad memories. He couldn't keep going back to that time. She was gone, and she wasn't coming back.

He tried to think of some happy thoughts, and there she was—Kat. Soft, brown wavy hair with a dusting of pale freckles across her nose. He gave in and let his mind wrap itself in everything Kat. The relief was swift and powerful. How did the thought of a person he barely knew affect him so strongly?

He wasn't sure why he was so obsessed with this woman, but after so many hollow nights of grief, she seemed the only distraction great enough to pull him away from the sadness. As much as he promised to keep his distance, another part of him was inexplicably drawn to her.

As he finished painting the last coat, his mind decided on three things. One, it was time to let his grief go. Two, it was time to be happy again. And three, getting Kat naked would make him a very happy man. He just wasn't sure if that made him a wise man.

Chapter 6

THE HEAVY, bloated clouds hung low on the gray horizon. Kat stared out the window listening to the pitter-patter of rain, waiting for any sign of Tyson. The air was musty, and she'd settled into a pathetic, misty gloominess suitable for such weather.

You're being ridiculous.

Mia, with her exhaustless energy, had finally settled in with a movie. Without the option of walks to the park or playing in their yard, the cottage seemed to shrink with every waterlogged minute.

She hadn't seen or heard from Tyson since the night he kissed her. This was exactly the reason why she didn't date. She was obsessing over what was probably nothing. She'd replayed the memory so many times she had to wonder if her hazy recollections were even remotely close to what really happened.

Gnawing thoughts that she'd done something wrong, or embarrassed herself in some way, haunted her. Perhaps he was avoiding her, and it had nothing to do with the dreary weather they had been having.

There wasn't much that could be done while the spring showers lasted, yet Kat never stopped listening for the echoes of power tools. It was ridiculous to think of him so much. Almost as ridiculous as lying in her bed the night they kissed, cupping her hands over her face and breathing in his scent that lingered on her skin. And how sad was it that their kiss had been the best kiss of her life?

"You are such a loser," she mumbled, her breath forming a soft sheen of mist on the drizzly glass. She pressed her finger into the steamy patch and drew a big *L*.

"Loser."

The dignified way he carried himself made her self-conscious of all the ways she was still a child trying to play a very real game of house. Other than their street name, they had nothing in common.

She had no right getting upset that he hadn't stopped by again. There was no sense in leading him on. If Kat let Tyson kiss her again, he'd eventually want more—and that was something she couldn't provide. There were too many hidden pitfalls involved with dating. The risk that Mia could somehow be hurt was too great.

She tried to distract herself with everyday reality, methodically going about her normal routine, but nothing took away the inner restlessness. Even Mia seemed to detect something was wrong with her. And, of course, there was something wrong with her—she had a crush on a guy who was the last person she should be fantasizing about.

He was too mature for her. He owned his home. She rented a cottage. He even owned his own company, for crying out loud! Kat didn't even own her crappy, used car. She'd be making payments on that pile of junk until Mia was in first grade. The car probably wouldn't even last that long.

Common sense told her she was being an idiot. Not only that, but she had no desire to date. So what the hell was she doing?

Let it go. Drop it. He clearly isn't interested. And the last thing you need is a boyfriend.

Her head dropped like a broken flower. She had to get a grip and stop acting like a lovesick sixth grader. Starting right this minute—right now— there would be no more thinking about Tyson Adams.

The phone rang from in her lap, and she jumped back from the window. "Hello?"

"Hey, girl, whatchya up to on this beautiful day?"

"Hey, Jade. Nothin'. Just sitting around." She cradled the phone closer to her ear, glancing up at the blackening, stormy sky

"What's wrong? Why do you sound upset?"

She sighed. So much for promises. "Tyson kissed me."

"What? Wait? The hottie next door?"

Kat quickly held the phone away from her ear, wincing at Jade's squeal of excitement. She probably should have kept this to herself.

"Yeah." She turned away from the window and let her head fall against the wall with a thump.

"Oh my God, when?"

"A few nights ago. Mia dropped a toy down the drain and my garbage disposal broke. I was just gonna fix it myself, but I didn't have the right tools so I ran to Tyson's to get a pair of pliers—"

"Nice. Nice."

"—but then he showed up to see if I needed help."

"Oooh, was he all dressed up for the job—work boots, sexy tool belt, big ol' burly muscles flexing out of his tight, sweaty shirt?" Jade made a gargling purr.

"Uh, sort of."

"Okay, so then what happened? Details! I need details!"

"Well, Mia and I watched a movie while he fixed the sink."

"Then what?"

For a girl who had a pretty active social life, Jade acted like she hadn't seen any action in years. "You are getting way too excited about this. I'm telling you it was nothing."

"I'll be the judge of that. Keep going."

"Well, Mia fell asleep, and we were in the kitchen talking."

"About...?"

Kat rolled her eyes. "He asked about Jeremy."

"Because he's into you! I knew it!"

"Settle yourself. He did say I was amazing."

"Awww."

"Oh my God, I forgot the biggest part—"

"—Yeah, I bet it's big."

"Will you get ahold of yourself?" Kat laughed.

"Jade, he's moving into that house. It's his. He's gonna live there."

"No shit? That's awesome. Permanent eye candy. Okay, go on and get to the kiss."

She shrugged. "It's nothing. He just...kissed me."

"You're such a liar. I can tell by your voice it was more than a kiss. Where were his hands?"

"Um, first on my face, then in my hair, and then sort of on my wrists."

"Nice. Dominant. Go on."

"That's it. He kissed me and left."

"Has he called you or anything?"

"He doesn't know my number. You're making this way more than it is. It was a spur-of-the-moment thing. Besides, I don't want it to be anything. He probably regrets ever coming over here." In a smaller voice, she added, "Men like that don't like girls like me."

Jade was silent for a minute. "You don't know that. And what does that even mean, girls like you? You're a woman with a child and not the first one. Oh my God, you should totally fuck him!"

"Jade!"

"What? Come on, Kat, you haven't been with anyone since Jeremy and Tyson's *gorgeous* and seems totally into you."

"He's going to be my neighbor. Technically, he already is. What happens after the fact, Jade? I'll have to see him every day, and my God, what if I got pregnant again? I'm already struggling to support myself and Mia."

"Katherine Marie D'Angelo! First of all, you

aren't a stupid teenager anymore. You're old enough and smart enough to buy condoms and use birth control. And even if it's a fling, so what? People have casual sex all the time. Do you think I've never run into ex-lovers?"

Kat moved at much slower speeds—turtle speeds—speeds of turtles walking backward. Casual sex didn't exist in her situation because there was nothing casual about raising a child.

"Yeah, but condoms aren't always safe."

"My God, Kat. So what, are you going to live the rest of your life as a nun?"

"No, but—"

"But nothing. You have to bang this guy. You owe it to women everywhere!"

While a big part of her wanted to rub her body all over him like a kitten in catnip, another side was scared to death and clung to her controlled, boring life.

"That's not going to happen, Jade."

Her friend scoffed. "You suck."

"I know."

"You should be sucking him."

"Damn it, Jade!" She laughed. In the end, she was grateful for the rain.

~

Sunday morning, after Mia found all of her Easter eggs, they rushed to get ready for church. They didn't attend church on a regular basis—not like it wasn't a nagging thought in her mind every weekend—but there never seemed to be enough time.

The air held the scent of dampness from the rain, but the skies were blue with soft, fleecy clouds. The ground was soggy, which was a challenge in their Vivian-approved shoes, but they managed.

The Christian church in their neighborhood was an old, colonial-style chapel that seated no more than fifty. The picturesque little chapel sat between clusters of sycamores with a loose stone path that led to a forgotten graveyard. She liked that the reverend wore jeans. Mia liked the choir and the fact that Mrs. Bradshaw attended service there.

Mia spotted her babysitter in the front row, wearing a flamboyant Easter bonnet. Mrs. Bradshaw was a no-nonsense woman in her early seventies who somehow pulled off gaudy as stylish.

The service was a little longer than usual because of the holiday, and enforced silence was never easy for Mia. The heavy oak pew creaked as Mia fidgeted. "Momma," she said in a loud, jellybean-scented whisper. "When's this over?"

Kat patted her knee. "Shh."

Mia sat for a few minutes. Her tiny Mary Jane shoes swung as she sighed with impatience. "Momma," her hissing whisper came again, drawing the attention of nearby parishioners. "This guy talks too much."

Hot embarrassment burned Kat's cheeks. Mrs. Bradshaw's raspy chuckle only drew more unwanted attention.

"Mia." She placed a stilling hand on her leg. "Just a little longer. Try to sit still."

Her daughter squirmed, her curious gaze darting from the shelf of bibles on the back of the pews to the windows, to a transparent study of everyone sitting in the church.

Hoping to occupy her, Kat passed her the paper pamphlet they had been given for the Easter service when they arrived. Mia's pudgy fingers lifted the page, and she began to make up a story as if she were reading it. "Once upon a time..."

A wave of creaks and whispered snickers surrounded them as people turned.

"Mia, no talking," Kat hissed, taking the pamphlet.

"Momma," she whined. "This is boring." Her words dragged out so long, not a single person missed them—including the reverend.

Mrs. Bradshaw tipped her chin and pressed her knuckles into her lips as she chuckled. Kat's mortification was complete as her stomach filled with giggles, and she fought the infectious laughter. If she let one snicker escape her lips, she was done for.

Pulling in a deep breath, she forced herself to be serious. *This guy does talk too much.* Her stare followed a filtered ray of sunshine highlighting dust motes, and her heart lodged itself somewhere in the pit of her stomach. Tyson was staring at her from the pew beside the window.

A small curve tipped up the side of his mouth. Kat wondered if he saw Mia carrying on. He was taller than all the other parishioners. The monotone rumble of the reverend's sermon echoed to her right as they stared at one another as if connected by an invisible string that made it impossible to face the front.

Half of his profile shined under the ray of sun streaming from the window. He looked like an angel. He winked, and her belly swooped like a trap door swung open.

She licked her dry lips, tasting the artificial flavor of strawberries in her gloss. She could swear he watched her do it. His gaze, unblinking and incredibly heavy, weighed on her like a physical touch.

The choir started to sing, and she did her best impression of indifference, but there was no ignoring the storm of emotion swelling inside of her. No one had ever had such a potent effect on her.

As the service ended, she headed to the back of the church. The mixed scent of old lady perfume and clinical old man cologne tickled her nose and made their escape all the more urgent. She held Mia's hand and wedged her way through the clogged double doors.

When the fresh spring air hit her face, she took a long deep breath. The lawn was littered with people dressed in their Sunday best. Mia ran off toward where three small children played in the shade.

"Who's that gentleman talking to Mia?" Mrs. Bradshaw asked in a gin and tonic rasp.

Kat knew before she seeing. There, speaking to Mia—all charm and tall, sexy goodness—was none other than Tyson Adams. The same rolling feeling took over her stomach when he smiled at her. She swallowed. Her mouth went from dry to too wet to dry again, and her skin heated yet covered with goose bumps at the same time. She pulled in a deep breath and slowly released it. "That's our new neighbor."

He was wearing a black suit that cut along his muscles like it was custom-made for his body. She couldn't decide which was sexier, Tyson in work boots and jeans or Tyson in a suit. Either way, he was incredibly devastating.

A mixture of trepidation and irrepressible excitement filled her. She casually pressed her clammy palms into her stomach to slow the fluttering of nerves. "Would you like me to introduce you?"

"Honey, the day I stop wanting to meet men of that caliber is the day I'm dead. Yes, introduce me."

She led Mrs. Bradshaw toward Mia, each step causing her heart to beat a little faster.

The smell of his rich cologne over the sweet scent of nearby Easter flowers made her dizzy. The moment they approached he sprung that devastating smile on her.

"Hello, Kat."

His deep voice sunk into the depths of her belly, stealing the last of her breath. "Hi."

He glanced at Mrs. Bradshaw, and Kat introduced them. "This is Mrs. Bradshaw, a dear friend of Mia's and mine. Mrs. Bradshaw, this is Tyson Adams."

"A pleasure, Mrs. Bradshaw." He nodded, and that oh so yummy dimple appeared.

"The pleasure is mine, Mr. Adams. Mia speaks well of you. She tells me you're doing wonderful things to the old Thornton house."

"Thank you. We've been busy. Hopefully, the rain's finished for a while so we can begin the landscaping. And, I believe Mia and I have a doghouse to build."

"How charming. Mia's a magnificent helper and lovely, too, just like her mother."

"You have no argument from me there."

He sent her a pointed look, and her whole body felt awkward. A fluttering laugh, unlike anything she'd ever done before, slipped past her lips. She didn't know what to say.

"Thanks for fixing my sink." The impulsive gratitude spewed from her before she could stop it. *You are such an idiot.*

A soft smirk curved his lips. He seemed to watch her with covert curiosity that had a way of unnerving her.

Looking back to Mrs. Bradshaw, she informed, "Tyson fixed our sink." *Thank you, Captain Obvious. Stop talking now.*

But the meaningless chatter continued to flow. Her faltering tongue clumsily folded over words before she gave them much thought. "Good thing it stopped raining. April showers bring May flowers." *Oh my God! Stop!*

She bit her lip, forcing herself not to say another idiotic word. Tyson grinned at her with the same elusive charm that accompanied every expression he made. Luckily, Mrs. Bradshaw stepped in to save her from making more of a disgrace.

"Tell me, Mr. Adams, do you have any family? A wife? Or perhaps some children?"

"No, ma'am. I've never been married, nor do I have children. But if I'm lucky one day, I might."

"Indeed." Mrs. Bradshaw coyly smirked. "Well,

Mr. Adams, I must be going, but it was lovely meeting you. Perhaps I'll see you again soon."

"I look forward to it, Mrs. Bradshaw." He faced Kat. "I'll see you later?"

She nodded but didn't chance a word, and he walked away.

As they walked back to the car, Kat wondered if he meant I'll see you later as in "of course I'll be seeing you around because we're neighbors" or if he meant he intended to make a point to see her again.

When they approached the car, Mrs. Bradshaw rolled down her window and smiled. "Well, Kat, it seems your life just got a little more interesting. Do keep me posted."

With the enthusiasm of a funeral procession, Kat backed out and headed to her parents' house. A familiar, watermelon-sized, knot of tension slid into the pit of her stomach as they approached their destination.

She wasn't surprised when a man in an understated tuxedo answered the door. Her parents were in the habit of hiring temporary staff for all of their affairs and family holidays were no different. She nodded her thanks to the butler for holding the door while they stepped inside the foyer.

The doorman took her wrap and Mia's backpack, filled with things to keep her occupied. This would not be an abbreviated visit. No, this would be long and about as fun as a root canal. For Mia, it would be worse.

Affluent, lilting voices echoed down the hall as they walked in silence, their dress shoes clicking like an ominous bell tolls. The scent of dinner slipped from the kitchen doors as they passed. At least the food would be good.

They were escorted into the parlor, where other guests mingled. A grand piano dominated the formal room, and eight-foot windows accented the ten-foot ceilings. From the Parisian carpet to the crown molding, the space was as luxurious and antiquated as a museum.

Her parents had money, but their events were always a gross exaggeration of their wealth. She couldn't stand it. Pasting on a plastic smile of serene blandness, she looked for her mother.

Trails of Shalimar perfume and lemon polish tinged the air. She didn't know what wore more lacquer, the women with their pungent perfume and red lips, or the heavily polished woodwork.

Small settees and glossy tables dotted the room, and an ornate bar graced the corner, neatly set with champagne flutes, snifters, and various decanters. Her mother immediately noticed their entrance and zeroed in on her with the focus of a hawk.

Kat grinned with borrowed grace as she approached. Vivian's eyes glistened with cloying sweetness. "My darlings!" she cooed as she kissed Mia on the cheek.

Her mother—always the performer—complimented their appearance with calculated admiration. "You look beautiful as always, Katherine. And Mia! Such a charming little angel you are."

This was the insecure—nauseating—truce she and Vivian shared when in the presence of others.

"The Easter Bunny came to my house, Grandma!" Mia said.

"Hello, Mother," Kat greeted, kissing her mother's cheek as expected.

As Mia chattered about her morning, Vivian covertly eyed Kat, obviously making sure that she'd followed orders and worn the right, pre-chosen outfit.

It wasn't that the outfit was unattractive— it just wasn't her style. The tanned pencil skirt was conservatively cut an inch below her knee with a matching silk camisole and a dusty sage cashmere sweater with pearl buttons. The sweater, Vivian had informed her, was necessary to hide her 'undesirable soft spots'. She'd been given strict instructions that it should stay on her shoulders at all times.

The most unfortunate thing about the whole ensemble was that she had to shop with her mother in order to get it. Five hours of trying on dresses while her mother frowned and critiqued her flaws was enough to drive even the sanest person to drink.

Per her mother's request, she wore her hair in a sophisticated French twist with nothing more than two pearl stud earrings and a pearl tennis bracelet. Nude stockings were a requirement, of course, because bare legs were simply scandalous. The outfit was completed with two-inch bland, brown satin pumps.

The only thing her mother didn't choose was her underwear, so—for the simple pleasure of rebellion—Kat went with none at all.

As Mia finished telling her mother about everything the Easter Bunny delivered, her mother took her performance to an Academy level. "That's wonderful, dear. Your grandfather and I have a little something special for you as well."

Kat was sure their *little something* would be three times the size and price of her gifts for Mia, outshining even the Easter Bunny's efforts.

Rolling her eyes, she scanned the mingling guests. There were a lot of people she didn't recognize.

Just another close-knit D'Angelo holiday.

"Now, you be a good girl and sit down here while I introduce your mother to some of our guests."

She hated that Mia had to endure this. Crouching next to her with a reassuring squeeze on her arm, Kat whispered, "Just for a little bit, Mia, then Mommy will get your coloring books. Okay, babe? And I promise, tomorrow we'll do something fun."

"Like make a cake?"

"Sure, if that's what you want."

Mia eagerly nodded. Kat kissed her cheek with a small smile and followed her mother toward the other guests by the bar. Her father smiled in greeting. "Katherine. How's my granddaughter?"

"Hello, Daddy. She's great."

"Good." He nodded. "Katherine, you remember Dr. and Mrs. Malone and their daughter Jennifer and her husband Christian?"

Kat greeted the two couples. Jennifer was around her age. On her left hand, she wore a platinum wedding band and a three-carat canary-yellow solitaire diamond. Her belly swelled under her robin's egg blue, tailored dress, and she looked to be nearing the end of her pregnancy.

Jennifer smiled with demure composure. Her husband watched her with obvious devotion and adoration that filled Kat with an oppressive sense of emptiness. "Congratulations on your pregnancy, Jennifer," she said as Jennifer preened and gracefully laid her bejeweled hand over her belly.

"That's right, D'Angelo," Jennifer's father chimed in. "Twins! Can you believe that? Two boys!"

It still stung whenever she witnessed pride in her parents' friend's expressions as they spoke of their grandchildren. She never saw that kind of pride in either of her parents' eyes. The lukewarm sentiment in which they accepted her as a mother was nothing compared to the way Jennifer's father raved.

Words of praise paraded about, each syllable trampling Kat's heart and cutting her self-esteem into shreds. She mentally wrapped herself in cotton, safe from the jealousy burning inside of her. This was about the point when she let herself go numb.

Her mother directed her attention to another nearby group of men.

"Pardon me, gentlemen," Vivian politely interrupted. "I'd like to present my daughter. Nathan Lithe, Dawson Price, this is my daughter, Katherine."

Nathan was a short, stocky man in his late twenties with beady eyes, a receding hairline, and one of those beards that was more of a line around his jaw than actual facial hair. Guys who spent that much time on their personal grooming always freaked her out.

Dawson, on the other hand, was generically handsome. Not runway hot, but good-looking enough to be a model in a department store catalog. He was tall, about six feet, with short, blond, wavy hair, sun-kissed skin, and soft blue eyes.

This was the man her mother wanted her to meet. He definitely was better looking than her, but something was missing. He didn't bring about any sense of excitement or jitters, feelings she never would've noticed before meeting her new neighbor.

It was difficult to detect a man's style at functions like this. They all wore the same formal jackets, dress shirts, and pressed slacks. The only variations came in khaki or black. Even the ties knotted at each man's neck stayed in the safe family of political blues and reds.

She shook both men's hands as she curved her lips enough to project a passable smile, hating these staged situations her parents insisted on putting her in every few months.

Dawson grinned. "Can I get you a mimosa, Katherine?"

Prepared cocktails were lined up like pretty, decorated debutants all in a row. It would be nice if she could ask for something a little stronger than orange juice and champagne. "Thank you."

She took the glass while Nathan stared at her breasts from the corner of his beady eyes. As she sipped around the slice of strawberry garnishing the rim, she casually posed her arms, blocking his view.

"We were discussing the verdict of the Triton case," Nathan said with an egocentric sentiment.

The Triton case was a local trial that wound up getting more than local attention in the media. Apparently, the woman was a victim of chronic domestic abuse. She eventually snapped and backed over her husband with their minivan. The trial had been going on for a year, and last week the jury sided in favor of the husband. Mrs. Triton was convicted of manslaughter.

"You'll have to excuse Nathan, Katherine. He's a cutthroat attorney, and cases such as the Triton trial are pure catnip to him."

In other words, he's an unethical sleaze with money. "Oh?" she commented with feigned interest.

"That saucy bitch deserves every hour she spends in that jail if you ask me." No one had. "She drove her husband to the brink of insanity as much as she drove that minivan the night she killed him."

"How so, Mr. Lithe?" she asked, ignoring his inappropriate language and the sense that she shouldn't bait this man.

"He never laid a hand on her until he caught her in bed with the neighbor. She was a harlot, and the entire town knew it."

"And you believe infidelity's deserving of such brutality?"

Mr. Triton had been rumored to do every despicable thing, from slapping his wife to throwing her down a flight of stairs and kicking her until she lost consciousness.

"I believe," Dawson interrupted before the conversation became too heated, "that a husband should know how to keep his wife adequately satisfied in the first place. If Mr. Triton had done that, then his wife never would've strayed."

Kat looked at him and caught a devilish gleam in his eyes. His suggestive comment gave her chills, but not in the way he intended. Who flirted while discussing manslaughter? This was the man her parents wanted her to date?

Kat hid her unimpressed expression behind her champagne flute and raised her eyebrows. Dawson was sure to be another trial in pacifying her mother. She hoped she wouldn't have to take this one too far. There really wasn't anything wrong with Dawson. He just didn't do anything for her.

A servant announced that dinner was about to be served in the formal dining room. Kat excused herself to check on Mia.

All the guests seated themselves at the large table while she found herself sitting with Dawson to her right and Jennifer to her left. Her father was at the head of the table and her mother at the foot. Mia was seated next to Vivian to ensure she was on her best behavior. Heaven forbid she do anything to wreck her parents' special night.

The dinner was a seven-course meal with all the trimmings of a traditional Easter feast. The rack of lamb formed a cradle for the ham. Mint jelly and pineapple soufflé sat in fragile glass dishes to the left of each guest. There were candied yams and smoked salmon crudités, and many other useless tasty treats created for show more than sustenance. The white-gloved service was sure to impress her parents' colleagues. Kat couldn't wait to leave.

"Your father tells me you work in a psychologist's office," Dawson said between bites.

"Yes." She placed the linen napkin in her lap. "In New Castle."

"And do you enjoy working?"

"I started there out of necessity, not interest, but yes, I enjoy my job. I have a great boss. Do you like what you do?"

She was trying to be polite for her parents' sake. Dawson could have very well been a man she found interesting, but having him foisted on her triggered an instinctual aversion. Her mom was a control freak, and she hated being manipulated. Who she dated—*if* she dated—was up to her.

"It's interesting. Being on the board can be tedious at times, but it has its moments. I like the political aspects."

She didn't reply, so Dawson continued.

"Do you miss living in Parkside?"

"Not really. I rent a small cottage in Upper New Castle. Mia loves it there, and that's what's important."

"Mia?" he asked, tilting his head in question but keeping his expression friendly.

"Yes, my daughter." She motioned to Mia sitting next to her mother.

"Oh, yes, and how old's Mia now?"

"She turned three in January. Do you like children, Mr. Price?"

"I hope to have many of my own someday, and please, call me Dawson."

Their conversation lulled as the next course was served. Throughout the meal, she caught Nathan Lithe watching her. Whenever their stares met, he offered a leering smile that made her skin crawl. Dawson continued to make small talk, and her mother appeared pleased, giving her sidelong, approving glances from the end of the table.

After supper, the guests retired to the sitting room for coffee, tea, and cordials. Mia was getting tired, so Kat set her up in her father's study with some paper, books, and toys. The rest of the evening dragged, but sooner than she expected, the guests began to make their goodbyes.

"It was a pleasure meeting you, Katherine," Dawson said as he took her hand.

He moved his thumb back and forth over the top of her wrist. His fingertips were smooth on her skin—fingers of a man with a desk job—not calloused like someone else's. There was no way to withdraw from the caress without seeming rude, so she tolerated it. She gritted her teeth, smiled tightly, and waited for him to let go. When he released her, she tucked her hand safely behind her back.

"I look forward to seeing you again," he said, leaning in to brush his lips over her cheek and lingered a moment too. He smelled nice, but that wasn't enough to relax her in his presence.

With a straight spine, she muttered, "Nice meeting you too."

After the rest of the guests left, Kat went to change Mia into her pajamas. Chances were she'd pass out as soon as they got on the road. It'd been a long day for both of them.

"Dawson seemed to take an interest in you," her mother said from the doorway of the study.

"Mia, why don't you go say goodnight to Grandpa?" Kat suggested as Mia left the room.

Her mother wore a triumphant grin.

"Mom, I wish you wouldn't discuss men in front of Mia. It could confuse her."

"She should understand that you have an adult life as well as your life as a mother."

"She's three." Mia was innocent, and she wanted to keep her that way. Somewhere inside of this woman, there had to be a grandmother who understood that logic.

"Well, either way, he seemed to take notice of you. What did you think of him?"

"He seemed nice enough, but I told you, I'm not interested in dating."

She rolled her eyes. "Really, Katherine, sometimes you're as stubborn as a mule. I swear you enjoy living like a pauper."

"I do not live like a pauper, Mother."

"Well, I hope that you didn't say anything to embarrass yourself. Dawson's used to being surrounded by very respectable, attractive women."

"And how humble of him to humor someone of my ilk for the evening."

"Don't be derisive. It's unflattering. I just meant—"

"Momma, I said goodnight to Grandpa," Mia interrupted.

Vivian dropped the conversation, and no doubt stored away her comments for another time. They said a final goodbye to her parents, and as Kat expected, her baby was sound asleep by the time they pulled off her parents' street.

Kat's stomach was starting to burn from all the

tension of the past few days. The stuff with Tyson, the pressure from her mother, Nathan the nipple watcher, and Dawson was more stress than she was used to handling.

Why did Dawson have to show interest in her? That would only provoke her mother. Vivian was relentless when it came to finding a son-in-law. Kat wasn't interested in finding a husband. She just wanted her normal life back.

Chapter 7

AFTER CARRYING A SLEEPING Mia to her bed, Kat headed into the living room. It looked like the Easter Bunny exploded. There were dyed eggs, candy wrappers, tissue paper, and the dreaded green Easter grass all over the carpet.

After kicking off her shoes, she got on her knees and gathered Mia's things in a basket while raking the Easter grass into a pile with her fingers. Just as the room was beginning to look somewhat tidy again, there was a light knock at the door.

She glanced at the clock. It was only nine-thirty, not as late as she suspected, but a day with her mother would make anyone weary.

Doggedly, she stood and hit the switch for the front porch light. The sight of Tyson had her heart immediately skipping a beat. Smiling, she opened the door.

"Happy Easter." He was holding a plush, brown bunny with a green satin bow around its neck in one hand and a bottle of wine in his other.

Her lips twitched. The idea of a man visiting with gifts was so novel she was afraid to acknowledge the tempting bubbles of excitement popping inside of her. Maybe she had the wrong idea. "Happy Easter. Would you like to come in?"

"Sure. Is Mia still awake?"

She shook her head. "No, she conked out on the way home from my parents."

He didn't appear too disappointed. Was he here for her then?

"I saw this when I was picking up something for my nephew, and I thought she'd like it." He set the bunny on the counter.

"That's sweet. You'll have to give it to her tomorrow, though. She's out cold."

"Oh, well, I can leave it here for her to find when she wakes up. How was your day?"

How was her day? When was the last time someone other than Mia or Jade asked her that? *Act casual. Don't overthink it.*

"Long. How was yours?"

"Nice. I visited my sister." He rubbed the back of his neck. As if catching the nervous gesture, he stopped himself and stuffed his hand back in his pocket. No way was this man uneasy around her.

"That's nice. Do you just have the one sister?"

"Yes. I had a younger sister, but she passed away almost two years ago from breast cancer."

"Oh, I'm sorry,"

"It's okay. She was in remission for a year, and when the cancer returned, she didn't want to go through chemo again. It took her fast. She wasn't in much pain at the end." A flash of grief passed over his eyes.

She motioned toward the wine he held. "Would you like a glass?"

"Only if you have one, too. I wasn't sure if you drank."

"Oh, I have a three-year-old. I drink." She laughed. "But I'm no connoisseur. My wine etiquette is atrocious. I usually drink boxed wine, and I put ice in everything."

He laughed. "Ice is fine. This is Pinot Grigio. It's white, so it's usually served cold."

She retrieved a corkscrew, two wine glasses, and an ice tray from the freezer. He expertly twisted the wrapper and popped the cork as she distracted herself by cracking the ice and sliding out a couple of cubes for each glass.

As she handed him a glass, his hand closed around hers, as the amber liquid poured. She took a wobbly breath. Her belly tightened as he held her hand again.

He clinked his glass with hers before taking a sip, his dark eyes studying her over the rim.

"So, where did you spend your Easter, Kat?"

"My parents'."

The cool flavor slid over her tongue and soothed her tired body but did nothing to calm the fiery anticipation burning inside of her. She knew what it was, but she didn't want to admit it. Admitting that this man could arouse her more than any man ever had was a very bad thing.

Bad Kat. Bad.

Her gaze stroked over his broad shoulders, and a puddle of heated honey pooled low in her tummy.

Mentally she did that gargling purr thing Jade did whenever she was near a hot guy.

"And how did that go?" He sidled next to her with ease she couldn't mimic.

Kat had to get her head out of his pants—*Gutter!*—Head out of the gutter! "As good as could be expected."

"That good?" He smirked. "Did Mia enjoy herself?"

"Probably not, but she made the best of it. My mother doesn't seem to understand the concept of being three. I think she was born middle-aged."

He laughed, genuine amusement playing in his eyes. "Mia's a good girl."

"She is." A contemplative smile curled her lips, remembering how cute she'd been about the Easter Bunny that morning.

He tilted his head. "What are you thinking about? You have the sweetest expression on your face."

Stay calm. "I was thinking about Mia this morning. She's getting so big. She loved that the Easter Bunny hid her eggs, and she went nuts when she saw the basket."

"I can see that."

Her breath hitched as he reached for her face and removed a string of green grass from her hair. Her heart spun into a rapid flutter. She wanted to press her cheek into his palm but forced herself to remain still.

Self-consciously, her hand inspected her hair for any other foreign objects. What a way to make an impression. She was killing it tonight.

"I was cleaning up when you knocked," she explained. Her face and neck were getting warm. She thought of removing her sweater but didn't want Tyson to see her 'undesirable soft spots'. Damn her mother for adding to her list of complexes.

The soft curve of his lips drew her gaze as she self-consciously licked her own. His dark gaze dropped to her mouth. The air crackled. Where the hell should she put her hands? Her weight shifted as she fisted her wine glass like a bouquet of flowers between them.

His fingers gently lifted a strand of hair that escaped from her French twist, and a shiver chased up her spine. He stared at it as if he'd never seen hair before. Fast, shallow breaths lifted her breasts as her senses jumped to full throttle.

"May I?" he whispered as his hand brushed her hairclip in the gentlest caress.

Kat gave a slight nod. She avoided his eyes as her hand clasping the wine stem shook like a leaf.

Impulses, moments of daring followed by cowardice, came and went like the flash of a short-circuiting firefly. The wine must've gone to her head. His closeness was an aphrodisiac, easing her tension, making her thoughts single-minded, fuzzy, and irrefutably sexual.

Her hair tumbled to her shoulders, barely grazing the nape of her neck.

"Beautiful," he whispered as he placed the clip and his wine glass on the counter. His simple comment sent tingles from her head to her toes.

With a deliberateness that made her throat tight, his fingers ran through her hair, raking a ripple of shivers down her spine, leaving her quivering with barely contained arousal.

She shouldn't let him touch her so intimately, but nothing had ever felt so decadent. Her lashes lowered, and the slightest moan vibrated in her throat.

"It's as soft as silk. I knew it would be." He took a slight step forward, and her lower back pressed into the counter. When he leaned his head down to her neck, she arched and stilled as he breathed in her scent. "I've missed you, Kat."

Holy Hannah!

Chills danced under her clothes over every inch of her flesh. Her breasts swelled, and her breathing labored.

His breath tickled the shell of her ear as he nudged her hair away with his nose and gently pulled her lobe between his lips. "I tried to stay away. But you, young lady, are hard to ignore."

She wasn't used to this kind of attention. Her shoulders awkwardly twitched. Every motion was stiff compared to his competent ease. She had no experience with intimacy.

Holy shit! His warm tongue swirled over the place where her pulse raced, and his teeth scraped her throat. Her panties dampened as her eyes rolled back in ecstasy.

His palm cupped the back of her scalp and slightly angled her head. *My God!* This was beyond attention—this was blatant seduction!

Without taking his mouth from her neck, he gently coaxed the wine glass from her death grip and placed it on the counter. As he stepped closer, the warmth of his body burned through her clothing from chest to thigh. Her hands lifted and pressed into his shoulders.

Push him away! This is insane!

Her fingers bunched in the fabric of his shirt and held him tight. She shivered and tried to remain coherent, his words finally sinking in. "Wha...What do you mean stay away?"

Her head rolled back as his lips pressed against the curve of her shoulder. Warm, pillowy lips pressed over her flesh, gently sucking and kissing her skin. His tongue left a delicate trail of heat in its wake.

The hand cradling the back of her head massaged her scalp as kisses lingered down her exposed throat. Heat burst inside of her, unfamiliar and overwhelming, startling her.

She released his shoulders, forcing space between them, but he only stepped closer. She felt the hardness of his arousal poking at her belly and panicked, her mind objecting as her body molded to his in full agreement.

His tongue traced the soft spot below her jaw, and she moaned, gripping the back of the counter until her hands went numb. She needed to stop him, but what he was doing to her was very, *very* nice.

"You deserve someone your age," he whispered between nibbles along her collarbone. His words almost penetrated the sexual haze, but then he did this phenomenal little thing with his tongue, and she lost track of the conversation again.

"You can't be older than thirty."

He chuckled—a seductive tickle against her vulnerable neck, and she swallowed. "I'm thirty-six, and you, young lady, are veal."

Okay, thirty-six. That was a little older than she'd suspected. Yet, as he caressed her throat with his mouth, she couldn't think of one good reason why age mattered. "It's just a number. You look much younger."

She swayed against him and whimpered as he glided his soft lips over hers and whispered, "Kiss me, Kat."

She was done.

Her fine-tuned resistance melted away as he pressed his lips to hers with a groan. She hadn't kissed someone in years and was badly out of practice, but that didn't seem to bother him. The firm press of his body against hers increased as his tongue slid into her mouth. Her arms wreathed around his neck as he deepened the kiss. Tasting. Taking. Devouring.

A combination of expensive wine and sharp cologne created a taste that was uniquely Tyson. Her hands slid over his chest and neck to caress his smooth head while his firm grip glided down her back until his palms rested on her ass.

He gripped her and groaned. There was no mistaking the pleasure in the sound. His hands massaged through her skirt, and she savored every moment like a dream on the brink of a waking mind.

His teeth nipped at her lips as his tongue continuously dipped back into her mouth to steal another taste. His hips ground against hers, and her senses luxuriated in the complete attention being paid to her body. Every part of her being was affected by his touch.

As the kiss heated, his arousal pressed harder against her soft belly. He gave her ass one last squeeze, and his hands moved up to cup her hips. His thumb played under the hem of her blouse, gently gliding over her skin. Chills climbed over her shoulders, and her nipples pebbled as his touch dragged over her flesh.

Afraid he would feel her flabby stomach, she sucked in and held her breath. His grip tightened on her hips, choking a tight gasp from her as her feet left the ground, and he lifted her onto the counter.

Her skirt rode high on her thighs as he took up all the space between her knees. She let out a startled breath then moaned, as he continued to drug her with his incredible mouth.

He settled into the cradle of her thighs. If she looked down she'd see her exposed sex. Why hadn't she worn panties?

His lips moved to the corner of her mouth as his palms glided up her thighs. He dragged kisses lower, gently nipped at her jaw with his teeth as his hand coasted under her blouse, and finally cupped her breast.

Things were flying way out of hand, way too fast, but she didn't know how to make them stop, didn't really want to either. Her willpower had left the building, and her neglected hormones were having a party.

Cool air caressed her skin as he folded her blouse above the swell of her breasts. The backs of his knuckles slid over her lace-covered chest. Soft lips moved down her neck. Her breath shot out in a rush as his fingers pinched her nipple. His lips returned to hers in a plundering kiss that seared heat from her mouth to her nipples and all the way down to the space between her thighs.

Nipping her lower lip, he looked at her through those thick lashes with lust-filled eyes. His hand moved to the pearl buttons of her sweater and undid the two securing the cardigan at her neck. Her sweater slid off of her shoulders and down her arms. Anxious excitement battled against ingrained self-consciousness.

He tilted her upper body backward against the counter and pressed his erection against her. Bracing her hands on the counter, she waited for any signs of disappointment, but she saw none. His eyes darkened as he breathed deep.

Sliding an arm under her back, he lowered his head. Heat engulfed her nipple as his mouth closed over the tip, and he gently nipped her flesh through the silk of her bra.

She moaned. The fabric, now damp and heated from his mouth, clung to her flesh like a second skin. Her body rocked in his hold with each shallow breath. The hand at her back undid the clasp at her bra.

"You're so beautiful, Kat. Everything about you..." he continued as he folded the lace cups down, his breath teasing her freshly exposed skin.

Her blood ran hot, intensifying each anxious chill. Pleasure zipped up her spine and down to her core as his lips closed over the pale flesh of her breast, and he sucked one berry tip into his mouth.

"The way you look, your scent, the needy little sounds you make when you're aroused."

The intense, pulling pleasure had her arching off the counter as his arm slid farther under her back. The stuffed bunny fell to the floor triggering the sudden thought of Mia, reality hitting her like a bucket of ice.

What the hell am I doing?

As his mouth pulled her nipple between his lips, his palm skated to her upper thigh, playing at the lace edge of her stockings as he moaned in appreciation. Alarm bells sounded in her mind as she looked at the bunny lying on the floor, a taunting pile of floppy fluff telling her to stop.

His fingers trailed up her thigh and grazed her wet sex, jerking her gaze back to him. He froze as their eyes met. The gentle pressure of his knuckles against her delicate folds had her teeth digging into her lip as she held her breath. He didn't penetrate her. His finger stayed there against her, resting like a chess player holding their piece, debating their next move.

Slowly, he smirked—dimple as sexy as ever. "Why, Miss D'Angelo, you aren't wearing any panties."

She couldn't hold a single thought. She had never been this aroused in her life. The way he touched her body and the things he said in that husky voice—His palm opened and flattened over her sex. *Heat.*

"Tyson," she whispered as his thumb parted her

folds. "We…" She gasped as he grazed a particularly sensitive spot. "We have to stop."

"Are you sure that's what you want?"

His finger played at her opening without entering her, making her completely aware of how wet she was, leaving her breathless and dizzy. Good God, how long had it been since someone touched her there? And never before like this. Her body trembled almost violently. She feared she'd shatter if he didn't stop or finish this in the next second.

Confused and frightened by all the unfamiliar feelings racing through her, she shook her head. "I can't give you what you want."

"You don't have to give me anything, kitten." His finger slid inside, and her whole body coiled so tight she thought she'd break. Her head fell back as she cried out.

"Let me pleasure you, Kat. I want nothing in return. Trust me. It wouldn't be right for me to leave with you so aroused. I promise this is as far as we go."

His finger pressed farther inside, touching some hidden corner of her soul. Her spine curved, and her back lifted. Reflexively, her knees drew up and pressed against his hips as she shivered.

She couldn't think. He explored her in a way no one ever had. His other hand tightened over her hip. A wave of security shot through her at his gentle guidance. It was stupid to let something so simple make her feel cherished, but it did. He held her tightly as he moved his finger in and out and then added another finger. Her body tightened around him another notch.

"You're so tight."

She opened her eyes but found no trace of sarcasm or disappointment in his expression.

"Relax," he reassured, tightening his grip on her hip. "You're just as you should be."

The hand holding her hip relaxed. Fingers trailed up her belly, over her twisted bra, and around the swell of her breast. Leaning over her, he pressed his lips to her neck and continued to move his fingers in and out in a slow, easy slide.

Her channel stretched to accept him. Her arousal spread as he awakened parts of her that she'd forgotten. The rhythm increased in time to her rapid breathing.

It was as if he were filling her with bolts of energy with each stroke of his hand. Pressure built. Her knees worked over his hips. His tongue licked at her ear as her toes pointed. She felt as if she were going to burst but didn't know how. Fear and excitement for the unknown wildly churned in her belly.

Her body jerked as his thumb pressed down at the top of her sex. Reaching for some sort of anchor, she gripped his shoulders, fisting the soft material of his shirt, pulling him closer. Her back arched as her shoulders pressed into the counter. Was this normal? His mouth latched on to the exposed flesh of her neck, her taste buds memorizing his unique flavor. Never in her life had she imagined anything could be so frighteningly wonderful.

His thumb rubbed against her clit. Hot, delicious friction built, and he whispered, "Come for me, kitten." And as if on cue, her body shuddered from the inside out, unable to contain the built-up tension a moment longer.

Her toes pointed as her muscles locked and her back bowed. She vaguely registered one soft clop followed by another as her high heels dropped to the kitchen floor. He moved his fingers faster as she pressed her sex into his hand, riding out every extraordinary wave of pleasure. Her arms shook as she squeezed her eyes closed and cried out in a breathy whisper. "Tyson..."

He captured her moans with a kiss as her body quaked from the aftershocks of what could only have been her first true orgasm.

The first full breath she pulled shook her to her core. The pressure of building tears had her blinking and choking back a lump in her throat.

Don't cry. Do not cry.

She didn't want him to know that was the first time she had ever done that. A tear discreetly slid to her temple. She needed to save all this emotional crap for later when she was alone. As casually as she could manage, her trembling hand swept the hair out of her eyes and brushed away the trail of tears before he noticed.

One by one, her muscles unlocked as her body calmed. Tyson tenderly withdrew his fingers. Turning her chin, he softly kissed her and brushed his knuckle over her cheek. When she finally opened her eyes, he was looking at her in a way she didn't understand—as if she were precious.

She felt him pull away before he actually moved—sensed him—and then his arm slipped out from beneath her, and he took a step back.

Dazed, she waited on the counter, disheveled and spread out like a pagan sacrifice as she tried to understand what was happening. He looked at her with drowsy, lustful eyes, eyes that told her he wanted her, yet he was making his escape. She had no idea what to say or do.

He took another step, leaving a chill in his absence. Every muscle vibrated with tension. She folded her arms over herself, completely aware of her imperfect nakedness as the sexual haze faded, and he backed closer to the door. Memories of Jeremy backing out of her life appeared, uninvited.

Before she could find her words, he smiled and said, "Happy Easter, Kat. Sleep well."

Regret crept inside her like a snake through her veins. Her body jerked, and she clumsily pulled herself up to a seated position. She couldn't cover herself fast enough.

Used. That's what she was. "You're leaving?"

He stilled as if her objection had caught him off guard. She'd caught herself off guard. No need to drag out the inevitable.

"Did you expect me to stay?" he quietly asked with a genuine look of curiosity in his expression.

"Well, no, but..." She shouldn't have said anything. She should have just let him go. That's what guys did, right? They left. Her vision blurred, and she rolled her eyes as a throaty, humorless laugh bubbled past her throat. Perfect.

"Kat, if you want me to stay..."

She quickly swiped a hand over her eyes. "No. You should go."

"I didn't want—" He glared at her. "Are you

crying?”

"No,” she quickly lied, dashing away all traces of her tears. “I’m fine. You can go.”

With trembling hands, she fumbled to right her clothing. He stepped close but came up short when she jerked her chin and gave him a withering look. She didn’t need him coming any closer and confusing her again.

"Kat...I thought we were just having fun. I thought you were enjoying yourself. I never meant to get you upset.”

Her body twisted, and she dropped her feet to the floor. Her legs nearly went out from under her, but he was there, steadying her, surrounding her once more. She jerked her elbow out of his hands. She couldn’t bear his touch at the moment. Keeping her back to him, she pushed her skirt back down to her knees.

"Here,” he quietly said, handing her the green sweater.

She took it and protectively folded it over her crossed arms as she face him.

"Kat, this is crazy. I was only leaving—”

"Because you wanted to go,” she finished for him.

His eyes narrowed. “Because I thought you didn’t want me to stay.”

She was acting like a petulant child, and she wasn’t even sure why. Nothing made sense. Her body was sluggish yet pulsing with energy. Her brain was fuzzy. Tyson had just made her feel incredible, but her feelings were hurt at the same time. She was vulnerable and unsure if she wanted him to leave so she could cry or hold her while she did. Either way, the tears were coming.

Blanking her expression like a frost freezes a garden, she retrieved the last of her dignity and said, "You don't know the first thing about what I want."

His head jerked back, and he scoffed. "Do *you*?"

Well, he had her there. Molars clamped tight, she scowled at him. It wasn't fair that he looked so in control of his emotions while she was falling apart. With every passing second, she was more confused, more embarrassed, and resentful that she had no experience with such matters.

"Just go, Tyson."

"No," he said irritably, pinning her with a glare. "We're gonna talk about this."

Great. Now he's angry. Could you botch this up anymore? "There's really no need," she said with false calmness. She collected their wine glasses and dumped them in the sink. When she turned, Tyson was staring at her with a blank expression.

"What?" If he didn't leave soon she'd break and he couldn't see that. Nobody wanted to see that.

"I don't understand you. I didn't want to rush things. I figured…"

She tried to think how Jade would act in a similar situation. "Look, Tyson, don't make it more complicated than it is. You came over. Things got out of hand. We fooled around." *I had my first orgasm.* "And now you're leaving. No biggie." She was such a terrible liar.

"I don't want to leave with you angry."

"I'm not angry." *Maybe just a little.*

"Then upset," he amended.

She negligently shrugged a shoulder. "I'm fine."

His eyes narrowed. Emotions swelled inside her, beating at her like waves on a jetty during a full moon. *Leave. Leave. Leave.* She forced herself to breathe calmly and keep her expression blank.

He hesitated. "Are you sure that's what you want?"

"Positive." She remained perfectly still, waiting for him to go.

He let out a slow breath and rubbed his palm over the back of his neck. This would be a lot easier if he wasn't so damn pretty.

"Okay," he said in a reluctant voice. "I'll see you tomorrow?"

"Sure." *Not if I can avoid it.*

He nodded, a perplexed look clouding his dark eyes.

She held her breath until the door clicked shut behind him. The moment he was gone, her face crumpled faster than a pricked balloon as she gave into her tears.

~

The next morning Kat woke up like she'd been run over by a train. Muscles she didn't even know she had were sore. She looked at the clock and jolted upright. 9:45.

Scrambling out from under the covers, she nearly busted her ass as her leg got tangled in the sheet. Her panic only receded for a split second when she remembered it was a holiday and she didn't have work. She sighed, then gasped.

Mia!

She bolted out of her room. "Please be sleeping." Her legs had apparently been replaced with aching Jell-O. She dashed down the hall and peeked in Mia's room. Her heart plummeted when she saw the empty bed.

"Mia?" she shouted.

"Momma?" Mia called, calm as could be.

Rounding the corner to the living room, she let out a relieved sigh. Mia sat, in her pajamas, on the floor, watching cartoons with a brown bunny on her lap and a smile on her face.

"Morning, Momma. Can I have some milk?"

Kat shut her eyes and caught her breath. "How long have you been up?"

"You were sleeping, so I turned on the TV. Look!" She held up the bunny Tyson brought last night. "The Easter Bunny came back and left me more toys!"

That made her grin. "Oh no, sweetie, that's from Tyson. He dropped it off for you after you went to bed last night."

"Tyson was here?" She looked rather disappointed that she'd missed him.

"Yes. Only for a few minutes," she lied. "What do you say we get you some breakfast? What do you want to eat?"

"Cookies."

"No cookies for breakfast. How about scrambled eggs?"

"'Kay."

There was a knock on the door. She hated

waking up this late. Panic attacks and visitors were best when saved for the afternoon.

Mia jumped up and looked out the window. She winced as her daughter screeched, "Kiki!"

Why did she have such a hangover after only one glass of wine? Opening the door, grateful it wasn't anyone else catching her looking so rough, she let Jade into the house.

"Good morning!" Jade cheerfully placed a box of munchkins and two coffees on the counter and tousled Mia's hair. She looked at Kat and frowned. "Oh, you look like shit."

"Quarter," Mia said to Jade.

"Oh, sorry, Mia. How about some doughnuts instead?"

"Doughnuts!" Mia cheered, the sound piercing Kat's brain.

Jade handed her the box. "Here you go, kiddo. Why don't you take them in the living room so Mommy and I can talk?"

Kat filled a sippy cup with milk and walked it to the living room.

"Look, Kiki," Mia called, holding up her new bunny. "Isn't he pretty? Tyson got him for me. I named him Oscar."

Jade arched a blond eyebrow at Kat. "Oh, that's a nice name. Okay, you and Oscar have some dough-nuts and watch cartoons while Mommy and I have our coffee in the kitchen. Okay?"

"'Kay, Kiki."

Jade opened her mouth to say something as they entered the kitchen, but Kat held up a hand to stop her barrage of questions. "Wait. I haven't even peed yet. Let me go to the bathroom before the inquisition begins."

When she returned from the bathroom, she grabbed her coffee and sat across from Jade with a huff.

"Okay, spill," Jade said.

"Tyson came over again."

Jade sat up and quickly clapped her hands together. "I knew it!"

"Shh!" she hissed, peeking around the corner at Mia.

"I knew it," her best friend repeated in a hissed whisper.

"It's not good." Kat shook her head, pinching back the lid of her coffee.

"Says you. I'll be the judge of that. Tell me everything."

Scrubbing her hands over her face, she groaned. "He came over with the bunny and a bottle of wine, and we hooked up."

"Okay, I'm pretty sure your definition of hooking up and mine are totally different. Explain."

"We made out."

"And..." Jade waved her hand in a circular motion.

"And he saw my boobs," Kat grudgingly admitted.

Jade slapped her thigh. "Look at that! My girl's all grown-up! Anything else?"

She pressed her lips together, examining the chipped polish on her toes. Jade's gaze bore into her as a flush burned from the back of her neck to her cheeks. She struggled to make the next confession. She didn't have to tell Jade any of this, but she needed her friend's advice. Who else would she ask?

Looking around nervously, she whispered, "He used his fingers..." She motioned to her thighs, and Jade slapped her on the knee again, several times, in dramatic excitement.

"Ouch."

"Sorry. I'm just excited for you."

"Well, hit me again and you're gonna be unconscious." She delivered the empty threat while soothing her stinging thigh. "Jade, it was the first time I ever..."

"Oh. My. God."

"I know. And to top it all off, I have the world's worst hangover."

"Honey, you don't have a hangover, you have an orgasm-over." Jade laughed. "I can't believe it. What're you going to do?"

She sat back in her chair, protectively wrapping her arms around her stomach as she pursed her lips and shook her head. "I don't know." She sighed. "Part of me wants to see where things go, but another part of me is terrified of letting things go too far. Jade, he made me feel things—" she looked at her best friend, tears clouding her eyes.

Jade leaned over and laid a hand on her knee. "I know, sweetie, it's scary and new. But it's not the end of the world. You'll get a handle on it. Just take things slow and go at a pace you're comfortable with. If he can't accept that, then forget him."

"I don't know if I'm comfortable with *any* of this. I mean, he's my neighbor, and there's Mia to consider. I think it'd be better if I put some distance between us."

"Do you think Tyson would be okay with that?"

Kat scoffed. "Well, he's going to have to be."

"I think you should think about it before you make up your mind. There's no rush. I mean, I get that you want to keep everything nice and controlled in your neat, little bubble. And I understand you don't want to confuse Mia, but as far as she's concerned, you and Tyson are friends. Plus, Kat, the guy is like unbelievably hot. I mean, come on...."

She rubbed her hands over her forehead and growled. "I don't know. Every time I think of a reason to...whatever you call it...I think of three reasons not to."

"Well, you need to see what happens. And, sweetie, the 'whatever you call it' is called sex. You're an adult now. You need to learn how to use adult words. Now, tell me about this Dawson guy your mother's trying to marry you off to."

She rolled her eyes. "Ugh, that's a whole other issue I don't want to deal with. He's okay, I guess. Nice enough, likes kids, capable of asking questions, and not conceited enough to only talk about himself."

"What does he look like? Is he old?"

"Older than me, but no, not old. When I first saw him, he reminded me of Jude Law."

"Really? Wow, you're batting a thousand. We should go to Vegas."

"You do that, but you'll have to go without me. My life's a little busy right now."

Kat laughed as she stood to throw her coffee cup in the trash and move the wine glasses from last night back into the cabinet. "By the way, Tyson's thirty-six."

"No way."

"Way. And apparently, I make him feel like he's robbing the cradle."

"That's ridiculous. You're both adults, and *you* have a child, for God's sake. Besides, it isn't like he looks a day older than twenty-eight. It isn't right for a man to be that pretty."

"I know, right? You should see him without his shirt on. I can tell you one thing—he won't be seeing this body with the lights on. I don't know what I was thinking last night."

"Oh, stop. You're gorgeous." Jade walked to the counter and read the label on the wine bottle from the night before. "Nice. This is like a seventy dollar bottle of wine."

Kat almost dropped the dish she was holding. "Shut up! Do you think I should return it to him?"

"No. I think you should put it in the fridge so we can drink the rest of it next time I come over. Relax, Kat. The guy owns his own business. I'm sure he can afford to lose half a bottle of wine." She rolled her eyes, but Kat was still thinking of returning it to him. Seventy dollars was more than her monthly electric bill.

"Well, I've got to take off. Call me if anything happens. I want all the juicy details."

Jade went into the living room and said goodbye to Mia while she finished the dishes.

~

Later that afternoon, Kat sat at the kitchen table paying bills while Mia played with her new bunny in the backyard. Her gaze bounced from her checkbook to the window.

Running errands that morning had helped restore a sense of normalcy she desperately needed. Following her routine made her feel in control while soothing her frazzled nerves. She needed the structure in her day-to-day life.

At some point, while shopping in the dairy aisle at the market, she made a decision about Tyson. Mia came first, and it was in her daughter's best interest to have a sane mother, so she needed to focus on what kept her sane and avoid everything that left her feeling off-kilter. That meant no more making out with her hot neighbor.

It was for the best. She couldn't give him what he wanted and what he wanted terrified her. A disparaging laugh snuck out. She couldn't even say what *he* wanted. The pen nervously twitched between her fingers as she blankly stared at her checkbook.

"Sex," she whispered. "Tyson Adams wants sex." Confronting her fears should make her feel better, but it didn't.

At the top corner of her electric bill, she doodled the word *LOSER* and tossed her pen down on the stack of bills. Sitting back in her chair, she watched Mia bounce Oscar the bunny along the grass as she played and talked to the stuffed rabbit.

Mia's head turned toward the fence, and she smiled. She was so beautiful and carefree. Kat loved observing her play. Her daughter stood up and said something, and Kat's grin faded. She was speaking to someone. Mia took a step toward the fence and out of her line of vision.

The chair scraped along the kitchen floor as she bolted for the backdoor. Every thirty seconds, a child was kidnapped, and it took less than those thirty seconds for that child to be taken. Statistics were a deadly thing. "Mia!"

Her steps faltered, probably wondering why she'd snapped her name.

Tyson smiled, but she ignored him. "You know you're supposed to stay where I can see you."

Mia's grin slid into a frown. "I was talking to Tyson, Momma."

Tyson stood there, holding Oscar, his expression blank and his eyes observant.

"You know the rules. Now, go inside and play."

"But Momma—" she whined.

"Go," she repeated sternly.

"Kat," Tyson softly interrupted. "It was my fault. I—"

He was not going to override her authority again. "Inside, Mia." She pointed toward the house. Mia took Oscar back from Tyson and hung her head as she walked into the house.

When Kat turned back to Tyson, he was frowning. Defensiveness rose up inside of her, hot, like a groundless volcano. "I don't need to justify my parenting to you. She broke a rule, and there has to be consequences."

"Okay." He nodded, hands raised defensively. "I didn't know the rule. Now I do. Next time I won't approach her until you know I'm here. I'm sorry." He reached to brush a hand down her arm, and she stepped away. "What's going on, Kat?"

She shut her eyes and took a deep breath. "Tyson, I like you, but what happened last night can't happen again."

She needed to get this out, and then they could both put it behind them. "See, my life took a long time to get to this point. I like things neat and tidy. I have a routine for everything and a structure to our days and weeks that works. It works for me, and it works for Mia. My plate's already full, and anything more would just be a complication. I'm not the kind of girl you need in your life."

"Kat—"

"Let me finish. Please," she interrupted. "We're neighbors, Tyson. You're going to move into that house and make it your home. And even though I rent the cottage, it's our home, and I don't want to move. I love it here. *We* love it here. If we got involved and things didn't work out, I'd hate myself for having to take Mia away. I have to consider Mia first in all things. She's my sole purpose on this earth, and she wouldn't understand you being around and then suddenly not being around anymore when things don't pan out. It'd be confusing, and she could wind up getting hurt. Do you understand?"

"Can I talk now?" he asked, and she nodded. "Okay, first, I'm not an asshole. I'd never hurt Mia. Second, even if things didn't work out, I'd never make things awkward enough that you'd have to consider moving. Third, I don't want to rush you into anything. Things just got a little out of hand last night. I can be a very patient man, Kat. And fourth, you're lying to yourself if you think last night wasn't a big deal."

Eyes darting to the left, she mumbled, "It was just a hook up."

"I'm not a fool, Kat. I'm also not a teenager. I'm thirty-six years old, and I've experienced enough to realize when I'm dealing with someone who doesn't have a lot of experience."

Her mortification at his words must have been written clear across her face.

"Shit. That didn't come out right. I meant, last night I realized some things about you that I didn't know before. The more we got carried away, the more I realized how much your life's been solely about Mia. You did everything right, Kat. Please don't think you did anything to disappoint me." He rubbed his forehead and took a breath. "Kat, there are ways a man can tell when a woman is practically a virgin."

Her spine stiffened. She was not having this conversation. Not with him. She couldn't run away without making a complete fool of herself, so she put up a defensive front. "I have a child, Tyson. I'm far from a virgin."

"Tell me you've been with someone other than Mia's father, and I'll admit I'm wrong."

"It's none of your business who I've been with."

"I get that, but I'm asking anyway."

Her chin trembled as she glanced toward the house. "The day I conceived Mia was the first day I ever did anything more than kissing. It wasn't special, and it wasn't with someone I loved. It was in the backseat of a fucking Bronco, and afterward, he didn't even help me find my underwear. But, other than humiliation and a bruise on my hip from the buckle of the seat belt, I did get something out of it. I got scorned, but then I got Mia. So you can judge me all you want, but I am what I am, and my reasons only have to be good enough for me." By the time she got the last word out, she was shaking.

"Do you think I would criticize you for putting your daughter first?" he whispered. "Do you think I was making fun of your innocence?"

Shame welled up inside of her. She wasn't a nasty person, but she hated feeling cornered. Her frustration was more with herself than anyone else. Being non-confrontational caused more trouble than actual confrontation at times. Her mother walked all over her. Men got the wrong impression. "I don't know how to do this," she quietly confessed.

He let out a deep breath. "Last night, what we shared, it was something special. It might have been spontaneous and in your kitchen, but it was something intimate that had only to do with you and me. I know you aren't a virgin, Kat, but you might as well be. I felt you last night. I felt your surprise when you—well, let's say I understand how unfamiliar this all is to you."

How was it he saw all of her, no matter how much she tried to hide her flaws from him? She shouldn't be so transparent. Her insides quivered with every breath. It took all of her strength to stand there while he finished talking and not run into her home and hide.

"Please, Kat. Don't end this before we can see where it goes. I shouldn't have let things get so out of hand last night. I'm sorry. We can take things slow. Like I said, I can be patient. Let me take you out to dinner. Mia can come too if you want, but if you think it'll confuse her to be there, we can think of another solution. At least give me a chance to take you on a real date."

She blinked at him as twin tears fell down her cheeks. She wanted to say yes, but she couldn't. She cared about him too much for her own good. And she barely knew him. What would happen if he broke her heart? She'd be devastated.

She needed to stay firm. She wouldn't be able to be the strong mother she needed to be if she was moping around distraught with a broken heart.

Men walked away. That's what they did. Every single one of them. When the going got tough, they were gone. She had suffered enough from people turning their backs on her. It was a survivable kind of pain for an adult, but she wouldn't risk exposing Mia to that kind of hurt. She couldn't imagine explaining to her three-year-old that, unfortunately, sometimes people were just careless assholes with other people's feelings.

"I'm sorry," she whispered. "I just can't. My life doesn't allow room for dating."

She glanced up at him, catching the disappointment in his eyes. "Please try to understand and respect my wishes. You can continue to have a relationship with Mia, I know she adores you, but I think it would be better if you and I maintained a safe distance from each other from now on."

His head shook in defeat. "No."

She stilled. "No?"

He shook his head. "No. You go on ahead and lump me in with all the other men and boys who let you down, Kat. I'm not like them. I'm not afraid of taking things slow. I'll prove it to you. You can't scare me away with all your 'my life's complicated' crap."

"My life *is* complicated," she said, waving her hands defensively.

"So is mine," he snapped, and she flinched. He held up his palm. "Sorry."

In a calmer voice, he said, "You think you're the only one who has it hard? Everyone out there is fighting some sort of battle. It's all part of being a grown-up. If you're expecting it to get easier, I hate to disappoint you, but it's not gonna. Life's unfair, and it's hard, and there are a lot of assholes out there.

"I'm not a liar, Kat, so I'm gonna give it to you straight. So long as you're sitting here playing the martyr, nothing's going to change. You can go ahead and think I'm the bad guy, but I would never turn my back on the mother of my children or on my child when she needed me most. I'm not him, and I'm not your dad."

He leaned close to her ear and whispered, "I'm real, Kat. The way I feel about you is real. But that doesn't matter until you start seeing *me* and not lumping me in with all the other people who treated you wrong. I get that you're young, but you're no kid. When you're ready to act like a woman, I'll be more than happy to show you what it is to have a good man." With that, he walked away.

Shaken, she stood stock-still as he left. He was right about one thing. He was nothing like her father or Mia's.

He meant what he said. And yes, she was running. So what? So many parts of her life forced her to grow up. Maybe this was a part she wasn't willing to rush.

Chapter 8

"MIA, WHO ARE YOU TALKING TO?"

Kat carried a basket of laundry into her daughter's room and came up short. The blush that worked over Mia's round cheeks was followed by her little lips drawing into a tight bow. Only a child could form a look of such innocent guilt.

The antique wooden doll table was set with mismatched plastic teacups. Usually, Mia filled the chairs with her dollies, but today they were empty. "I was talking to Gorrum."

"Gorrum?" What the hell was a Gorrum?

"Uh-huh. You can't see him."

Wonderful.

"Gorrum, elbows off the table," Mia softly admonished in a tone that was so familiarly Kat's. The clink of tiny teacups and soft chatter filled the room as Kat folded little dresses and socks neatly into drawers.

"Can Gorrum stay with us for a while, Momma?"

The drawer slid shut. It looked like she'd be visiting the library in the near future. There had to be some developmental books on imaginary friends. "Sure, babe."

She left Mia and her invisible friends to their party and went to get the mail. The sight of Tyson's quiet house drew her attention. No cars in the driveway. No lights shining in the window. No music streaming from the backyard.

A strange sort of emptiness had stayed with her since she and Tyson decided they needed space. Not that it could be called space. Space was something a couple took when they needed time to think. They weren't a couple. They weren't even friends. He and Mia had more of a friendship.

Tyson had kept his word and respected Kat's wishes to ignore their chemistry for the sake of simplicity. Her life was again uncomplicated and simple. Totally simple. No complications what—so—ever. And she wanted to scream.

She was bored out of her mind. Never before did the idea of going to work, taking care of her home, tending to Mia, feel so...vacant. This emptiness wasn't there before the arrival of Tyson Adams, and she really wished it would leave.

Envelopes shuffled between her fingers as she scanned for anything good. The soft whoosh of a car pulling down the street mixed with the echo of children playing behind fenced-in yards.

Nothing but junk mail and bills. She shut the mailbox and stumbling to a halt. That must have been the car she heard. Tyson looked at her and his hand slowly raised in a sullen sort of wave. She mirrored the gesture. The ache that was becoming so familiar, the hollow feeling of starvation pulling on her heart, returned with a vengeance.

She couldn't make out the crease of his eyes or the set of his mouth, but his body language said it all. He didn't like this space in between them. She'd hurt him, and hurting others never sat well with her. Especially when the other person was someone she cared about. Maybe she should go talk to—

Shock was a funny thing. It had a way of short-circuiting the brain but making the eyes keen. Adrenaline let loose in her blood, tingling under her skin like little poking pins, as a tall woman with long braids down her back stepped out of Tyson's car.

Fingers trembling, lungs seizing, Kat's eyes stared unblinking. The woman looked at Kat. She was naturally beautiful with an air of grace and confidence exploited by her mature age. She was everything Kat wasn't.

Jealousy slithered through her gut, leaving a trail of hurt. So much for waiting. The envelopes clumsily fell from her fingers and dropped to the ground. Her gaze ripped away from the two of them as she scrambled to pick up the mail.

Hyperaware of how fast her eyes were blinking, she looked up, and they were gone—into his house, a place she'd never been. *Not your business.* Slow, deep breaths cut to the bottom of her lungs as she quickly moved inside.

The phone rang, but she let it go to voicemail.

She shut her eyes and tried to get a grip. *This is why you can't fool around with the neighbor.* The chances of things not working out were too high. There would be too many women coming and going over the years.

Once her emotions were somewhat under control, she picked up the phone and dialed the code for her messages.

"Katherine, hi. Dawson Price. Your mother gave me your number. I'd like to get together with you, take you out to dinner if you're interested. Call me, and we'll set something up. Hope you're doing well. Take care."

He rattled off his number, and the message cut off. The pen and notepad sat just next to the stove on the counter, taunting her. Her molars ground tight as she imagined Vivian's joy when giving Dawson her phone number.

As the polite mechanical female voice detailed the message options, Kat's thumb slid over the keypad. Without needing to look, her thumb found the number three and pressed. "Your message has been deleted." She tossed the phone on the counter.

Since she was a child, Kat had been raised to do as she was told and not make waves.

Do as I say, Katherine.

Don't be difficult, Katherine.

It's impolite to argue, Katherine.

She had been molded into a proper little puppet, incapable of standing on her own. But when one string started to unravel and she wasn't so perfect anymore, her parents had cut her down and left her behind.

It became her mission in life to prove her parents wrong and survive without their help. But her mission had made her life one long, exhausting line of overcompensating.

No matter how much she told herself she didn't need her parents' approval, she still hungered for it. But giving Dawson her phone number was going too far.

Her skin grew clammy as she acknowledged deleting Dawson's message without copying down his number. But her mother had no right to go over her head like that, complicating her life more than it already was. And the act of rebellion felt good at the time, but now she was nauseous.

~

Mia pouted the day Tyson's house was sided in yellow instead of pink, but the color looked phenomenal on the old colonial. Even Gorrum—who was 'showing up' more and more—agreed yellow was the best choice. The house looked completely different. It was breathtaking.

Much of its historic charm had been restored while also incorporating state-of-the-art amenities. The day Tyson's crew carried in an enormous Jacuzzi tub, Kat had longingly stared. Tyson's company would no doubt enjoy such luxuries.

Spring was in full bloom, and he'd begun to work on the yard. The old, rundown fence in the back was replaced with a white picket fence. His driveway was full of shrubs and flowers waiting to be planted, and he was doing most of the remaining labor. It was obvious he took great pride in his house, and it seemed to mean something to him that *he* be the one to make it a home.

Sometimes floodlights glowed from the backyard late into the night. In the mornings, when she dropped off Mia at Mrs. Bradshaw's, she would occasionally see him jogging through the neighborhood in a pair of loose gym shorts, and her body would tighten, reminding her of all the reasons they needed to keep their distance.

Days passed with dull repetitiveness. She worried that Mia's invisible friend was a sort of coping mechanism for something missing in their life and tried not to beat herself up too much about what that something could be.

At least one thing stayed constant—her mother was still a tyrant and insistent on pushing things with Dawson. With all the bleak, unrelenting emptiness dulling Kat's moods, she thought it wise not to mention his deleted message to her mother. But, as it turned out, she would have been better off telling the truth. A week after Dawson called, her mother surprised her by doing the same.

"Hello," she answered as pleasantly as she could manage after recognizing her mother's number on the caller ID.

"Oh, your phone does work. Interesting. I assumed you were having trouble paying your bills after I spoke to Dawson Price tonight at a benefit. Imagine my surprise, Katherine, when he informed me that he called you to ask you to dinner almost a week ago, and you never returned his call."

Shit. "Mom, I—"

"Don't you dare waste another one of your excuses, or lies, on me. I was humiliated. I stood there, singing your praises, telling Dawson how upset you were that he never called when to my shock, he informed me it was the other way around."

"Why did you tell him I was upset he didn't call?" she snapped.

"Because any normal girl would be! Any normal girl would jump at the opportunity to have someone like Dawson Price show interest in her. Any girl in your situation would be grateful to have a man like that willing to tolerate and overlook her past."

"Stop calling it *my past*! I hate when you say that. My mistakes gave you Mia, so stop holding it over my head."

"Yes, the one silver lining was Mia, but a scandal is still a scandal, Katherine. You have no idea what it was like to be judged by our friends, knowing that they were whispering about you and looking at us with pity. It was humiliating! We were ostracized, and you never seemed to be one bit repentant. Mia wants for nothing because of our generosity."

"You have no right—"

"Now, here's what's going to happen, Katherine. I covered up my faux pas by explaining to Dawson that you lost his number. He was forgiving enough to give me his card to pass onto you. Tomorrow, you *will* call him and apologize for not getting back to him in a timely manner. And if he's kind enough to ask you out again, you *will* go. Do not cross me on this. I've been patient, but my patience is ending. I'm not sure your father could forgive yet another disappointment. Do we have an under-standing?"

Frustration choked her. A thousand nasty, hurtful words rested on her tongue. She wanted to scream them into the phone. She wanted to hang up and never speak to her again. But she couldn't.

Other than her parents, Mia had no family. They had Jade, but Jade had her own family. Mia needed family. She needed something larger than Kat. So despite all of the things she wanted to say, all she said was, "Give me his number."

The last of the dishes were washed, and Kat was drying them with a cloth when there was a soft knock at the door. Heart stuttering, she quickly wiped off her hands and pressed her palms to her stomach. A strange wistfulness came when Mia yelled.

"Tyson! Can I open the door, Momma?"

"Go ahead." Sublime anticipation prickled her skin as she slowed her breathing.

A yipping bark sounded, and Mia squealed. The counter pressed into Kat's hip as she jumped back to make way for the scampering, four-legged ball of fur that came barreling into her house. Its leash swung like a wild kite tail as the dog jumped, pressing two soft brown paws into Mia's chest. Her daughter gig-gled with enchanted affection as the puppy licked her chin.

"A dog!"

Tyson sauntered in, wearing the grin of a proud

father. "What do you think, Mia? He definitely likes to run."

Mia fell to the floor in a fit of laughter as the beagle squirmed with uncontained excitement and nudged her neck with its black nose. "He loves me," she giggled with conviction.

"Look's that way." Tyson crossed his arms and eased his hip against the counter next to Kat. Never taking his gaze from the display of newfound friendship rolling out before them, he asked, "How are you?"

The revelation that he'd not come to visit *her* settled like a cement boulder in her chest. "I'm good."

Through sidelong gazes, she watched him observe Mia and the dog. Turbulent emotions swirled in her chest. There was no longing in his glances, nothing that said how much he missed her. The uplifting anticipation that accompanied his entrance faded into nothing more than cold and hollow reality. He was over her.

The dog pinned Mia, and Tyson stepped in. "That's enough, Trix."

His firm hand gripped the leash, and the dog immediately recognized the authority of its owner and settled. The dog's tongue lolled to the side of its mouth like a piece of ham. Tyson reached into his pocket and pulled out a treat. The dog caught it with a succinct snap and happily wagged its tail.

"Good girl."

Was it wrong that she was jealous of the way he complimented the dog?

"It's a girl?" Mia asked.

"Yup. Her name's Trixie. Do you like her?"

Mia nodded. "Isn't he great, Momma?"

Pushing all worries aside, Kat smiled at her daughter's excitement and laughed. "*She*, Mia. And yes, she sure is great."

Her daughter faced Tyson. "Since it's a girl, are you gonna paint her doghouse pink?"

Fingers curled over her lips, Kat held in a giggle, as Tyson seemed suspended in the air for a moment.

"Uh, I was thinking it'd be nice to match the house. You like my yellow house, don't you, Mia?"

Huffing with defeat, Mia sighed. "I suppose yellow's okay. But Trixie really would've liked pink." The fact that dogs were colorblind was clearly not in her daughter's expansive bank of knowledge.

"I got her a pink collar," Tyson said, and Mia nodded in approval. "Besides, if we make it yellow, we can start building it this weekend—if that's okay with your momma."

Kat nodded, not seeing an issue with their schedule.

"Okay!" Mia and Trixie raced into the living room, and the tickling game of chase continued. They watched for a few minutes in thoughtful silence.

"Am I nuts getting a puppy?" Tyson whispered beside her.

The same unsatisfied yearning resumed at the soft expression on his face. His lips barely curved, but the dimple was there. "You're not nuts."

The heat of his arm brushed her skin. Shutting her eyes, she inhaled his scent, and the slightest sigh tickled her throat. When she opened her eyes, he was watching her with unblinking observation. "I miss you, Kat."

Pressure built in her chest, and her head lowered. It was the one thing she wanted to hear but also dreaded he'd say. "Tyson—"

"Nothing more needs to be said. I just want you to know I think about you when you're not around."

Her gaze focused on a hangnail she used as a distraction. "I think about you too."

"How long we gonna keep this up?"

Her head slowly shook. "It's not a matter of keeping something up. Nothing's changed."

"Exactly. So how long do you plan on ignoring it?"

She sighed and dropped her hands. "Ignoring what?"

"The fact that I want you."

In a breathless tenor, she whispered, "No."

Warmth from his finger trailed down her arm. "That didn't sound too convincing." Undisguised amusement tinged his voice.

She filled her lungs and stepped away. When she met his gaze, all traces of humor were gone. "We have to stop doing this to ourselves, Tyson. A matter of time won't change my circumstances."

"Your circumstances have nothing to do with us."

"They have *everything* to do with us. They're the reason why there is no us, and there never will be. I'm not interested."

"Bullshit. I see the way you get all nervous around me, the way you peek out the corner of your eye watching me. Your voice goes all breathy, and your freckles darken over the pink in your cheeks. That's not the behavior of someone who isn't interested, Kat."

Her brows lowered, shuttering away any of the softness he'd just referred to. "And what about you, Tyson? What have you done that qualifies as the behavior of someone interested?"

Defensively, he pulled back and said, "What are you talking about?"

"I'm talking about the woman you brought to your house the other day. Parading your booty calls in front of me certainly isn't working in your favor."

He scowled. "Booty calls? Kat, I don't—Oh my God, are you talking about Gloria?"

"How should I know her name?"

"Tall, thin, hair down to her butt?" He didn't sound too impressed.

"Yeah, that sounds about right."

His soft lips pressed together, forcing his dimple deep as he tipped his head back and made a snick with his tongue against his teeth. "That's Gloria."

Like the name made a difference. She stared at him in vacant stupidity.

"She's my sister, Kat." He laughed. "And she is so not the kind of woman I'm into." He blew out a long breath, the predatory set of his shoulders causing her to step back.

Her butt hit the lip of the counter as he crowded her front. She glanced over to where Mia played, making sure her daughter wasn't watching.

His lips tickled her ear, sending chills skittering beneath the collar of her shirt. "Let me explain to you the kind of woman I want, kitten." His lips pressed into her neck as his warm breath whispered over her skin. "She's smart, cute, soft, brown wavy hair, cut to about here." Calloused fingers glided along the wing of her collarbone, and her breath hitched.

His mouth moved to her other ear, and he went on. "She's sweet but feisty in an endearing way. Prickly, you know the type? But my favorite thing is when she's aroused because she goes all soft in my arms and looks at me like I'm the only man who can give her what she needs."

Her chest rose with shaky breaths as he stepped back, and she recognized the familiar unshrinking determination in his eyes. Hands gripped to the counter, she held herself in place, so she didn't do something undignified like propel her body at him.

He winked. "You see a woman like that around, Kat, you let me know." He whistled. "Trixie, come on, girl."

It was too much. Her panties were wet because he'd told her a secret. She had no control over her body when it came to this man, and he simply strolled out of her house with all the calm in the world.

∼

The following day, Tyson built a foundation under the tree Mia declared the perfect location for the doghouse. In the process of framing out the structure, he invited Mia over to help him hammer in nails and announced that they would be painting the following Saturday or Sunday.

That night, after dinner and a long conversation about Trixie and her new pink dog bowl, Kat gave Mia a bath, read her a story before tucking her into bed. As she was about to curl up on the couch with a book, the phone rang.

She didn't recognize the number. "Hello?"

"Katherine? It's Dawson."

She'd dreaded this call. Since the disastrous conversation with her mother, she'd called Dawson and left a message. She was an idiot for assuming he might not call back. Vivian was probably riding him as hard as she was riding Kat but in a much more flattering way.

"Hi, Dawson."

Their conversation was short and formal to the point of tedious. Dawson spoke with polished ease that gave away nothing about the real him. However, his unfailing politeness made him difficult to dislike.

Within a matter of three minutes, their date had been scheduled, and the phone call had ended. If only the actual date could be over with that quickly.

Chapter 9

KAT PULLED her hair into a chignon at the nape of her neck. Dawson would be there to pick her up in twenty minutes to take her to an Italian restaurant in the city that he promised made the best homemade wine in the world.

Jade had picked up Mia from Mrs. Bradshaw's that afternoon for a special sleepover at her house. Mia was over the moon at the idea of sleeping at Jade's and barely spoke of anything else for the past two days.

Kat wore a simple black dress cut to just above her knees and strappy sling-back heels. Slender, silver chain earrings barely brushed her shoulders. When she answered the door, Dawson grinned as he looked her over from head to her toe.

"Wow, Katherine. You look great."

Don't fidget.

"Thank you." Blind dates were so awkward. "You look nice too. Would you like to come in for a minute?"

He looked at his very expensive watch. "Well, our reservations are in thirty minutes, so we should get going if we don't want to be late, but how about when we get back?"

"Okay, let me grab my purse." She dashed to the counter to retrieve her purse and turned on the porch lights.

Dawson took her arm and walked her around to the passenger side of his BMW. He opened the door and helped her inside. As he walked around to the driver's side, she looked to her right and saw Tyson standing in his front yard.

She sucked in a breath and held it as her mind comprehended what he must be assuming. He was completely motionless as he stood there watching her. Although he couldn't see her through the darkened window, his stare burned right through the glass.

A lump formed in the pit of her stomach as the engine rolled into a soft purr only a high-end sports car could mimic.

"Everything okay?"

Kat presented her best fake smile. "Everything's fine."

The leather-scented air chilled as the vent blew over her skin, but the air temperature had nothing to do with the cold feeling in her chest. Dawson backed out of the driveway. As they drove past Tyson's home, she stared at the gearshift.

～

Tyson did a double-take. His eyes had to be deceiving him. There was no way Kat, in a sexy, little black dress, just climbed into a BMW with some guy. By the way the man held the car door and the way she was done up, it appeared as if she were going on a date. But that couldn't be right. Kat didn't have room in her life to date.

Or perhaps she didn't have room in her life for *him*.

He slammed his shovel into the ground and vigorously dug a hole for one of the shrubs. Was it his age? His race? Or him in general? Thirty minutes and two planted boxwoods later, Tyson still wasn't sure what the problem was. Well, other than the fact that jealousy coated his stomach like acid.

The sun had set, and he was planning on working well into the night when his cell phone vibrated in his pocket. He was in no mood for social calls. He plucked off his gloves, stabbed his shovel into the ground, and reached into his jeans, opening the phone without looking at the display.

"Adams," he barked.

"Baby? You okay?"

"Hey, Ma." He took a calming breath leaning his foot on the spade of the shovel. "Yeah, I'm okay. Just finishing up some yard work. What's up?"

"I was calling because your father bought a new grill, and we're planning on having you kids over for a picnic on Mother's Day, but the darn thing has to be put together. And, well, you know your father…"

"I can come over this week to do it. Don't let Dad touch it until then."

"Thanks, baby. I knew I could count on you. So how's the house?"

"It's getting there." He tossed the shovel into the bed of his work truck and hefted his body up to sit on the tailgate.

"You sound overwhelmed. You sure you're okay?"

Did he really want to whine to his mother about his life? "I don't know, Ma. Do you ever feel like no matter how hard you try, you're still always coming up short?"

"Aw, Baby, owning a house is hard work. You'll get there. I know you will. It takes time, like any other project."

Ty laughed at his mother's unending belief in him. "You have such faith. But actually, I was talking about a girl."

"A girl? Well, my stars, Ty, who is she?"

"She lives around here. Her name's Katherine—goes by Kat. She's got a daughter, and she's an amazing mother. And I can't get her out of my head."

"Where's her baby's daddy?"

"Gone. A fool, if you ask me. He met his daughter once, three years ago, and now he lives in Japan or something."

"So, what's the problem?" his mother teased, and he smiled.

"I wish I knew, Ma. I wish I knew."

He detailed the Kat situation to his mother over the next twenty minutes. It wasn't like he was gaining any perspective. She was completely biased and couldn't understand why any woman wouldn't want her son. Still, even at his age, it felt good to have sympathy from his Momma.

The easy way their conversation flowed made him think about how Kat had described her relationship with her parents. Having such a healthy relationship with his parents made it hard to comprehend a different dynamic.

Of course, Ty had the privacy to live his life as he pleased, but he always had the reassurance his parents were there with whatever support he needed—be it emotional or otherwise. Kat had nothing like that. She'd said that her mother was critical of everything, from how she raised Mia to the way she dressed. He saw nothing wrong with either.

It was hard to even imagine what her parents could use for ammunition. Especially considering where he grew up in the city and the real external issues, families struggling to cope with hunger, eviction, drugs, and gangs.

It didn't matter anyway.

She made her stance loud and clear. Her personal life was none of his concern. However, he couldn't ignore the niggling that she'd lied to him and was, at that very moment, getting close and comfy with some pompous yuppie in a BMW.

The restaurant had waterfront seating, which was very romantic. Dawson addressed the wait staff with polite indifference. He opened doors, pulled out chairs, and frequently asked if she was warm enough. As a date, he was charming. As far as chemistry went—zilch.

Kat made sure to smile at all the right places and nod when needed. The shell of her was there, fancied up and filling space, but her mind was elsewhere.

After the look of shock had faded from Tyson's face, she still recalled how his glare smoldered with resentment when he stared at her in Dawson's car. Although she was now sitting in a restaurant miles away from Tyson, the sickening shame of how she misled him lingered. The memory played in her head like a gigantic wheel, over and over, until it seemed to leave a groove on her brain.

She cleared her throat and focused on Dawson. Her date.

"...but once you get involved in that level of arbitration, things start to get a little sticky, if you know what I mean."

Kat made an agreeable sound and smiled. What the hell was he talking about?

His mouth formed a smiling "o" as he breathed a laugh. "Listen to me, going on about boring business. Let's talk about something else. What would you be doing right now if you weren't here with me?"

Nothing.

"Probably just relaxing with Mia at home or sitting out front with Jade since it's such a nice night."

"Jade?"

"My best friend."

The conversation was easy. Dawson had a decent sense of humor and asked good questions, so there weren't any awkward silences. He asked a little bit about Mia but didn't pry. The food was good, and the wine was spectacular. After Kat's second glass, she switched to water because she could already feel herself getting tipsy.

By the time dessert came, the conversation got a little more personal.

"Are you involved with anyone at the moment, Katherine?"

Intimate questions were the worst. She was awkward, to begin with. Throw personal in the mix, and she was a plain disaster.

"Um, no. I don't really date."

His hand slid over hers, and he did that thumb-rubbing thing again. Kat didn't want to be rude and pull away, so she tolerated it. His touch was pleasant but empty.

When she was a little girl, and they would play at Jade's, her parents kept a kerosene heater in the basement. It kept the room usable all year long but never really heated the space. If they stood close enough, their skin would warm pleasantly on one side, but the direct heat to one part of her body only made the chill on her other side more prominent. Dawson was like a kerosene heater, warming one spot of her but leaving the rest cold.

When the check came, Dawson covered the bill, and they continued to talk while he finished his wine. "I'd like to see you again. How do you feel about going on another date?"

"Tonight was nice."

"That's not exactly an answer," he teased,

bravado camouflaging the hint of doubt showing in his eyes.

Why did people have to put her in such uncomfortable situations? "Sure. Another date would be nice," she agreed, pressing the words past her plastic grin.

His posture eased, and he seemed satisfied.

The drive home was made quietly, listening to the music. The world sped by dappled in silver shadows of moonlight. She stared out the window as the expanding reflection of headlights traced over trees and curbs.

The weight of Dawson's hand pressed into her knee, and she tensed. His thumb swirled over her skin, and she gazed down at her knee through her lashes. The only thing she felt was gratitude that she had shaved that day.

"I like that dress," he said as his eyes followed the road.

She really wasn't being all that fair to Dawson. He'd done nothing wrong. She could at least go out of her way to be a little nice to him. Turning from the window, her back pressed into the cool leather of the seat. "Thank you."

He had a nice profile. His features were sharp and flawless. The shadows of his lashes swept low as he blinked. They weren't as full as Tyson's. And rather than dark eyes, Dawson's were pale.

"Where's Mia tonight?"

Mia was a topic that was always comfortable. "Oh, she's sleeping at my friend Jade's." She inwardly winced as soon as the words left her mouth. *Wrong thing to say.*

Whorls gently glided over her skin as his thumb moved up and down the top of her thigh. A shiver tiptoed up her spine. It gave her the chills, but not the way she got chills when Tyson touched her. She silently reprimanded herself for making the comparison.

His stroke changed from up and down to side to side. The angle left his fingers pointing toward the inside of her thigh. Breathing as little as possible, she drew her knees together, hoping to block him off from further touching, but when she inadvertently clamped his fingers between her thighs, her knees jerked apart. If he noticed, he didn't say anything.

His fingertips lightly drummed over her skin as they pulled into her driveway. He shut off the car. The engine quietly hissed and pinged in the absence of the music. It was quiet except for their breathing. The shift of his jacket against the firm leather seat was audible. The uncomfortable stillness was too much. Her hand reached for the door.

"Did you want to show me your home?" His voice was so low and close she could almost make out each rumbling note.

"Uh, sure," she lied. She'd made it this far. She just wanted the night to be over so Vivian could get a good report and get off her back. Her feet were killing her, and all she wanted to do was get in her pajamas and go to bed. *Alone.*

"Stay put. I'll get your door."

The door clicked open, and the warm sultry night kissed her skin. She took the hand he offered as he walked her to the door. The thumb was moving again. *Didn't this guy have any other moves?*

She gently tugged her hand back to dig out her keys and briefly glanced at Tyson's. Dark. If it were at all possible, her mood deteriorated a little more.

She flicked on the lights and hung up her purse and wrap. Hospitality was her mother's forte. It had been drilled into Kat since she was a child that all guests should be made to feel welcome. Being that Vivian had assigned herself executor of this date, Kat needed to follow protocol. "Would you like something to drink?"

"Do you have any wine?"

"Uh, let me check."

She opened the fridge and looked around. Her gaze settled on the bottle Tyson brought over Easter night. The bottle slid off the shelf with a smooth scrape and a splash of remorse. The wrongness of giving another man Tyson's wine was undeniable, but she had nothing else.

Her palm cradled the chilled base. "Is this okay?"

"That's fine."

Kat retrieved two glasses and poured the wine while Dawson appraised her cottage. Should she put on music or something? *No, too suggestive.*

"Would you like ice?"

He declined with a shake of his head. She didn't want to look stupid, so she didn't add any ice to her glass either. Her sandals clicked over the hardwood as she handed him a glass. She needed to regroup. If she had a team, they'd be in a serious WTF huddle.

"Will you excuse me for a second? Make yourself comfortable."

She went into the bathroom and sat on the

toilet seat. How was she going to get him out of there? She needed to think. She didn't want him to get the wrong idea. She also didn't want him telling her mother she blew him off again.

She was so bad at this. Why didn't she bring the phone into the bathroom? Jade would know what to do. Maybe she could fake a headache, or was that too cliché?

She flushed the toilet and washed her hands. When she came out of the bathroom, she found Dawson sitting on the couch. His suit jacket lay over the arm of the chair, and the top button of his collar was undone. *Not good.* He looked comfortable, reclined with his ankle crossed over his knee and a wine glass dangling in the hand draped over the arm of the sofa.

Her wineglass sat on the coffee table. *No coaster.*

Kat sat down on the other end of the sofa and picked up her wine. She took several sips and placed it back on the table *using* a coaster. She shot him a darting, bland smile. He uncrossed his legs and placed his glass on the table as well.

"Dawson—"

"Katherine—"

He softly chuckled, and she said, "Sorry, you go."

"I was going to tell you how pretty you look tonight." His body twisted toward her, and he picked up her hand. The position left her slightly uncomfortable, but she kept her expression serene, so he wasn't offended.

"I like it better when you pick out your own clothes. I could tell the last time I saw you that your mother helped you choose what to wear. I prefer a woman your age to dress her age, not her mother's." His voice was low and getting huskier with each word. "Vivian's a lovely woman, but she has nothing on your beauty."

She didn't comment. He lifted Kat's hand, and claustrophobia set in. When he lowered his head toward hers, she pulled back, but the couch arm blocked her full retreat.

"Don't be shy, Katherine," he said, tugging her hand and pulling her closer. "I'm just going to kiss you."

Her eyes widened as he came closer. The scent of wine mingled with cologne filled her head. She jumped as a loud knock rattled the door. He froze, and the knock impatiently sounded again.

"It's a little late for visitors, isn't it?" he asked, not really disguising the tartness of his tone.

"I don't know who that is. I wasn't expecting anyone." She scooted forward, and his hold on her hand tightened, not painfully but firm enough to stop her from standing.

"Ignore it. They can come back tomorrow."

"I can't ignore it. What if something's wrong?"

The knock sounded for the third time, louder than before. Dawson released her hand and stood as she went to answer the door. He irritably brushed the creases from his slacks.

Relief swamped her the minute she recognized Tyson through the window. "Tyson," she said as she opened the door, his body filling the entrance. He held a large flashlight in his hand, jaw tight and brows low. She was taken aback by the formidable glint in his eye.

"Hey, Kat," he stiffly greeted. "Sorry to bother you. I came to see if you have any batteries. I have a pipe leak, and my flashlight died."

"Is everything okay, Katherine?" Dawson called from the living room.

Kat slowly winced and gave Tyson an apologetic look, then turned to Dawson. "Everything's fine. It's my neighbor." She turned back to Tyson. "Come in. I think I have some batteries in the closet. What size do you need?"

"C's." He followed her toward the living room.

She didn't know how he was doing it, maybe it was her own turbulent emotions, but she felt his gaze on her skin, possessively marking her in some way. Her shoulders pulled tight as if weighted with the heavy down of angel's wings, but nothing removed the sensation of him all around her.

"Dawson Price, this is Tyson Adams. Tyson's my neighbor," she explained. "Dawson's a friend of my parents."

Tyson's eyes slowly moved, thoroughly taking in the scene, Dawson's collar undone, jacket off, and the wine glasses. She mentally groaned when his gaze snagged on the bottle of wine. He picked it up and pointedly studied the label. "Oh, one of my favorites." He glanced at her with accusation. "Am I interrupting?"

Dawson cleared his throat. "Well, actually—"

"No, not at all."

"Oh. Good. I'd hate to interrupt a *date*. You look nice, Kat. Where are you two coming from?"

Her lips tightened. She hated herself in that moment, hated that she was such a phony, hated that she was such a coward. She gave him a pleading look, mentally begging him to please not do this, but he tilted his head. One dark brow rose, and the inquisition was on.

Please, don't make me say it.

His expression was smooth, but the stormy glint in his eyes was merciless. He wasn't leaving without some answers. Damn him.

"I took Katherine to dinner in the city. Antonio's. Have you heard of it?" Dawson said with a self-important sentiment. It was a defense mechanism. His sudden snobbish overcompensating for some insecurity he harbored. She knew that trick, used it all the time. He was trying to intimidate Tyson, and she resented it.

"Actually, I have, but I can't say I've ever eaten there."

"Pity. The setting's spectacular, and the building's extravagant. And the food's delicious. Katherine enjoyed herself very much."

He sounded like a pompous ass. And *very much* was pushing it. She hated when people bragged. It screamed lack of confidence.

"Well, thank you. That's quite a compliment." Tyson's lip deviously curled. He wore the same triumphant expression he often did when he'd pushed her buttons.

"I beg your pardon?" Dawson asked.

"While I've never eaten there, I did, in fact, design the building. I've heard it described as many things before, but never as, what was it you said?

Spectacular and extravagant? That's very kind of you. And I'm glad to hear *Katherine,*" he dragged the name out, "enjoyed it."

Ha-ha! Score one for Tyson. Kat pressed her lips together and moved toward the kitchen.

Dawson looked confused and slightly disgruntled, so she helped him out. "Tyson owns Adams Construction. He designs and builds everything from homes to commercial properties."

A muscle in Dawson's jaw ticked, and he smiled tightly, his eyes narrowing as he continued to take the other man's measure. "Well, it's getting late. I should get going. It was fun, Katherine. I'm glad *you* contacted me. Call me again sometime."

He just had to slip that in. He retrieved his jacket from the sofa. Tyson had the grace to pretend he found her bookshelf incredibly interesting. Dawson leaned close. "Next time," he whispered.

Body stock-still, she held her breath as he kissed her cheek. No one said a word as he left, and the flash of his headlights dragged across her windows. The silence was deafening. If she shut her eyes, she could probably feel Tyson seething behind her. This was not going to be good.

Kat stared at the door, too afraid to face him. Tension rolled off of him in waves, choking the air from the room, so she jumped right into distraction mode without sparing him a glance. "I'll get you those batteries." Her feet made a beeline into the hall.

She was at the closet when she sensed him behind her. She wished she could wiggle her nose like the witch in *Bewitched* and escape whatever judgment was coming. Her muscles clenched at the premonition of an oncoming fight. Her neck draped as her head limply hung over her chest. With drooping shoulders, she sighed. "I—"

His voice cut through the air like a whip. "What the hell is going on, Kat? Or should I call you Katherine?"

She pulled every bit of reserved energy she had for the oncoming battle. He had her cornered, his big body blocking her only escape. "Do you even *need* batteries, Tyson?"

"Fuck the batteries! I want an explanation." Crowding her closer toward the wall, his voice filled the cramped space with a resounding blare, and she flinched.

"Don't talk to me like that! And I don't owe you anything."

"How should I talk to you, Kat? You lied to me. You said you didn't date. Period. And here you are, with your hair done and makeup on, drinking *my* goddamn wine, with some prick!"

"He's not a prick."

He stepped closer, and her back arched over the shelving. He crowded her, his hands on the lip of the highest shelf, caging her in with the hard line of his body. She should have been scared.

His eyes smoldered with stormy passion. No one had ever looked at her with such raw possessiveness. The propelling impulse to push him past his limit hit hard. He took her from zero to sixty in less than a second.

She panted as he leaned close, drawing in an audible breath. "I can smell him on you. Did you let him touch you? Kiss you?" he growled, hot breath hitting her neck.

"Tyson, stop it. It's none of your business anyway. You're my neighbor, that's it."

"I am your neighbor," he whispered, thigh pressing tight between her own, parting her knees. Her skin tingled as the proof of his arousal nudged her hip. "Because you told me that's all I could be to you because your life was too complicated to date anyone. Now, which is it, Kat? You either aren't dating, or you are. Or is it that you just don't want to date *me*?"

Her first instinct was to run, but there was nowhere to go. "I don't know."

"You know. You don't want to say. Is it because of our age difference?" His breath held for a moment. "Is it because I'm black?"

"No!"

"Then what is it?" he snapped, losing patience. "I've respected your wishes and given you your space. I figured if I were patient, you'd come around. But you barely even speak to me anymore. I expected us to at least be friends. What I didn't expect was to see you inviting some guy into your home."

"Nothing happened!" Her frustration gave way to panic. She couldn't take him being mad at her. She didn't know why his opinion mattered so much, but it did. "My mother fixed us up. She introduced us on Easter, and he called a few weeks later, but I blew him off because I wasn't interested —in dating him or anybody for that matter. Then my mom twisted everything up, and we had a huge fight, and she made me call him. What was I supposed to do?"

His head tilted quizzically, and their breathing was the only sound. A responsive throb to his nearness started low in her belly. She wanted to push him away, and at the same time, she wanted to pull his gorgeous face down to hers and kiss his tempting lips like crazy.

The electricity arcing between them was dangerous, and she was the kind of girl who never played with matches.

Finally, he broke the silence. "If he asks you out again, will you go?"

"I don't know," she replied honestly.

"Yet, if I ask you out again, you'll say no. Why is that?"

"Tyson—"

"Why?"

"I..."

"Answer the question!"

"Because I like you so much, it scares me!" she yelled. "I like you more than I've ever liked anyone! When you kiss me, I get chills, and when you look at me, my stomach fills with butterflies. The way you are with Mia makes me ache with a sort of happiness I've never experienced before. When you touch me—"

Her words silenced as he growled and fused his mouth to hers. Unlike the soft patient kisses she remembered, this time, he devoured her like a man denied too long. His tongue speared into her mouth, searing her own, his entire physical being demanding she kiss him back. He claimed her, marked her.

Her heart wildly beat behind her ribs like a caged hummingbird. His hands cupped her ass, supporting her, and she crawled up the wall of his chest, gripping the fabric covering his shoulders in her tight fists.

The slide of her dress tickled her thighs as he tugged at the material. She moaned as he squeezed the soft curve of her bare thigh. The ground gave way as he lifted her to him, his large hands cradling her ass.

Her body immediately reacted to the contact. Strong arms snaked around her back, pulling her closer against the hard line of his body. His teeth scraped along her lower lip, sensually teasing her mouth as his lips slanted over hers.

The room blurred as he spun them around, carrying her from the cramped closet. Objects clattered to the floor, and the cool, flat wall pressed into her back. Right there in the hall, he ravaged her mouth.

The complete weight and contact of his body had her arching into him, legs around his waist, and his arousal strained against his jeans. He tilted his head to get a better angle on her mouth. She moved her tongue over his, and he groaned in pleasure.

Her dress rode up over her hips as his large hands slid under the delicate lace of her panties. The skid of his work-roughened fingers was marvelous as they caressed the soft, exposed skin of her ass. He squeezed her bottom almost painfully and firmly pressed himself into the cradle of her thighs. Her hands coasted over every hard muscle and ridge she could reach through his clothing as she clung to his solid form.

Needing air, she ripped her mouth away and leaned her head against the wall, gasping for breath as he pressed a trail of hot, wet kisses down her neck. They were both breathing heavily.

In between kisses, he mumbled broken words of lust and wasted time. "I tried to stay away—" He bit her earlobe, his mouth kissing a trail along her jaw. She arched her neck, giving him access. "What you do to me—" His lips connected with that magic spot on her collarbone. "God, Kat, I can't get enough of you."

Their hips ground together. Her breasts ached as she slipped her fingers beneath his collar and dug into the smooth skin pulling tight over his broad, muscled shoulders. He breathed her name against her. The cool weight of her hair slipped over her shoulders and out of its bun. One shoe fell to the floor with an unceremonious clop. His lips found hers again, and she moaned.

The ache that he slowly kindled ignited into a white flame, charring every shred of common sense she had left. The last of her good intentions fell away as his hand closed over her breast.

"My bedroom—" she breathed as he continued to ravish her. She gasped, "Tyson...my bedroom."

His palm slid low on the center of her bottom and his fingers pressed over the silk covering her slick sex.

The strength of his arm was banded around her waist. Teeth scraped the sensitive spot on her shoulder, biting and then soothing the sharp sting. Wet sucking kisses pulled at her tender throat.

Clawing at the fabric of his shirt, her fists bunched the fabric, longing to feel more of his skin on hers. The material gathered at his upper back, and her palm moved low, pressing over his heated flesh. The muscled tension that vibrated under her touch stoked the flame burning deep in her belly.

She was pinned, pegged, spread out against the wall as he ground his hard body against hers. "Please, Tyson," she begged as he pressed her more firmly to the wall and stilled.

His face pushed into the curve of her neck. Labored breathing echoed between them while he held her tight as if trying to regain his control. At that point, she was beyond caring about control.

"Kat—" he panted. "We have to stop."

She whimpered in frustration as she dragged her forehead against his shoulder. Why was he doing this to her? He started this. He should finish it. Damn this man for coming into her life and turning her world upside down. She squeezed her eyes closed, rejected, determined, and weary all at the same time.

The fast pounding of his heart rested under her ear as they breathed together. Seconds shifted into minutes until she finally gave an unconvincing nod against his shoulder and slowly released her hold on his shirt.

Her palms flattened over his biceps. His intimate hold on her ass gave way as his hands curved around her back, still supporting her weight and lifting her higher over his hips, but in a less sexual way.

She placed her cheek against his shoulder. He laid his head along her shoulder as well. They stood locked together, him tenderly holding her, heads on each other's shoulders—yin and yang.

Eventually, he moved his palm in soothing patterns up and down her back, slowly rocking and lulling her away from the sexual hysteria that had almost swallowed her whole. Gratitude that he knew when to stop even when she didn't bloomed into tender affection for this man.

She didn't understand the way her body reacted to him. Nothing compared to the effect he had on her. It was as if, when he touched her, she forgot who she was and let go of all her idiosyncrasies and insecurities. In the moment, it was liberating and addicting, but once she regained her bearings, it scared the ever-loving crap out of her.

"Tyson," she whispered.

"Shh, just let me hold you."

She nodded and shut her eyes.

His palm ran soothing patterns over her back for what felt like hours. Everything between them had changed. As he held her in his arms, she realized that she wasn't strong enough to deny the sexual pull between them any longer.

~

Tyson needed to think. All he wanted to do was bury his cock into Kat's heat—right there, in the hall of her dainty cottage—but he needed to think.

God, this place was small. He felt like a giant in a dollhouse.

Every time he touched her lush, tight body or kissed her timid little mouth, he was reminded of how inexperienced she was. He had to slow the fuck down. He couldn't mess this up. He *wouldn't* mess this up.

Slowly easing his grip, he allowed her slight body to slide down his front—*Sweet Jesus*—until her feet softly landed on the floor. Sleepy, vulnerable eyes questioningly gazed up at him. His thumb coasted over the crest of her cheek. So smooth.

She needed to be taken slowly, tenderly. He wanted to get it right the first time. Slowly build that emotional connection, so the experience was more than two bodies writhing against one another, seducing her mind as well as her body. Depth mattered to him, and he didn't want something shallow with her.

"What do you say, while I go let Trixie out, you make us a pot of coffee? I take it Mia's away for the night?"

She nodded. "She's at Jade's."

"Good. I'm gonna run home for a minute. You need anything?"

"No. I just want to change my clothes, and then I'll make coffee."

The moment he completely withdrew his touch, he caught a flash of disappointment in her eyes.

Good. Progress.

"I should only be a minute. I left some food on

the counter. God knows what that dog's been up to since I've been gone."

She laughed, and he fought the urge to stay. She probably needed a few minutes to regroup, regain her bearings. Besides, he needed to have a serious talk with his dick about manners before she noticed how aroused he still was.

Kissing her temple lightly, he squeezed her shoulder and turned away. Well, this night sure ended differently than he'd predicted. Adjusting himself, he headed down the sidewalk to his house.

When the sleek BMW returned, and that guy followed her into the house, it was like having an anvil dropped on his head. He'd stared, dumbfounded, and then his fist was pounding on her door, still holding the flashlight he'd been working with earlier.

Warning bells clamored when he spotted the bottle of wine *he* left for her. That was his goddamn wine. He became a territorial animal ready to mark his claim.

Tyson unlocked his front door, and Trixie charged. "Whoa, girl. Easy. Did you get my sandwich?"

The dog had the grace to look repentant.

"Wonderful," he mumbled as he entered the kitchen. He came up short at the yellow *Wonder Bread* wrapper shredded on the floor next to the spilled trashcan. "Trixie!"

The dog's head tilted in curious shock, ear cocked as if she couldn't understand what she'd done wrong. Slowly, she bowed and spat out the gnarled paintbrush. The wooden handle was chewed to a nub.

Tyson sighed. "You're going to doggy charm school."

As he used the dustpan to scrape up a mixture of coffee grounds, eggshells, and other garbage, he thought about Kat's date. The guy was an arrogant douche. He'd seen the kind a million times. All glitz and shine firmly rooted in Mommy and Daddy's pocket. He'd be shocked if a guy like Dawson Price ever put in a day of hard labor in his pampered, silver spoon life.

Tyson was different stock. He was clear on the score. He didn't come from money. His parents were average, hardworking, middle-class citizens.

He fit a new trash bag into the can and shoveled up the pile, sending Trixie a glare. "You're lucky you're cute."

The dumb dog wagged her tail.

"You're pathetic." Bending down, she scratched under her ear, and she rolled onto her back, asking for more. The tap, tap, tap of her tail filled the room. "No can do, pup. My other girl needs me right now. You behave."

He tied off the bag in case Trixie tipped the canister again. Snatching the ruined paintbrush off the floor, he left a piece of rawhide in its place.

As he washed his hands, he tried to pinpoint what exactly bothered him about Kat's date. Perhaps it was his highhandedness. *Katherine enjoyed herself.* Men like that were so transparent. She could do better. However, pushing her to do better might take him out of the equation altogether.

He stood at the edge of her driveway and watched the window. Under the soft glow of light in the kitchen, she carried a pot of coffee to the table and placed it on a potholder like his Gran used to do.

A smile pulled at the side of his mouth when she neatly positioned two cups, a bowl of sugar, and the creamer before stepping back and examining the arrangement. A soft frown knit across her brow, and she leaned forward to tweak the display. Stepping back again, her shoulders lifted and fell, and she combed a hand over her hair.

She looked like she could use a few more minutes, so he carried her trashcans to the curb. His Momma always told him what matters in a good man is, if, after thirty years, he still took out the trash. Kat reminded him of his Momma in some ways—sweet, strong, and nurturing.

She might be as skittish as a kitten, but she had the determination of a lioness.

Kat knew how to love, but he wasn't sure she knew what it was to be loved—without conditions. All he was asking for was the chance to show her such things were possible. It was a damn shame a girl as sweet and big-hearted as her jaded at twenty-one. Even if he wasn't the man for her, he had to keep her from settling for men like Price.

He leisurely stepped onto the porch and knocked at the door. It'd be a mistake to rush her. Slow and steady won the race, and sooner or later, she'd notice the difference between those that loved her only when their expectations were met and

those that simply cared with nothing but good intentions.

174

Chapter 10

THE MOMENT she opened the door, her body tightened. How was it this beautiful man kept returning to her? Breathless, she smiled. "Hi."

"Hi."

An awkward moment of silence stretched, when all she could picture was their groping bodies in the hall only minutes ago. "The coffee's ready."

"Great. Thank you." He settled into a seat at the kitchen table. "We need to talk, Kat."

Her hands trembled as she reached for the cups and steadily poured the coffee. "Okay."

Changing into sweats and a tank had only removed a fraction of the tension. The sensation of his lingering touch still tingled all over her skin and deep inside her body. Things, of course, needed to be discussed, but she had no idea how to go about discussing them or what she should say.

"I made decaf so we can still go to bed." She winced. "I mean, so we aren't up all night." *Damn it!* "So we can *sleep.* Me in my bed. You in yours. Apart. Not together."

Please stop talking.

His hand settled over hers, and she held her breath. "Kat, relax. It's okay. We're gonna talk, and then you'll go to bed, and I'll go home."

Sucking in a choppy breath, she nodded.

He picked up the mug Mia painted and laughed. She loved that soft, deep laugh of his. "This is cute." He admired the artwork. "I'm wondering what my doghouse is going to look like."

She laughed. Mia was a fine painter for a three-year-old, but like any other three-year-old, her strokes were sporadic and patchy. "You knew what you were getting yourself into the day you let her doodle all over your blueprints."

His patience and tolerance with Mia were what she found most attractive. And being that he was drop-dead gorgeous, that was saying a lot. It meant a lot that he continuously encouraged her daughter's abilities and accepted her limitations, never once causing Mia to question herself.

They doctored up their drinks and quietly took a few sips. She waited for him to begin because, aside from small talk, she had no idea what to say.

"Do you plan on seeing him again?" he calmly asked.

She shut her eyes and thought for a minute. Her instincts told her no, but she couldn't deny the hold her parents had over her. She came from a lifetime of manipulation. It was exhausting, but ignoring her parents' demands only made life more difficult.

"My mother's a tough person to handle." She

didn't trust her mother not to use Mia as leverage in order to get her way. Kat had always done everything in her power to protect Mia's feelings and maintain a wholesome image of Vivian in her daughter's eyes. "I need to keep her happy for Mia's sake."

"Would they treat Mia differently if you didn't do everything they asked?"

She shook her head. "I don't know, but Mia likes spending time with them, and I don't want her to lose that. I think she needs other family in her life."

He stretched, and she was distracted by his overwhelming presence. Shock still rocked her that she had asked him to take her to bed. *What the hell would you have done then, genius?* Her brain went haywire every time he looked at her. If he touched her—done.

Those dark eyes leveled her as he tipped his glance in her direction. "Do you like him?"

She sighed, internally forcing herself to be honest. "He's a nice enough person, but I can't say that I'm *attracted* to him. After dinner tonight, he asked to see the inside of my cottage, and I didn't know how to tell him I was tired without seeming rude. I didn't want it to get back to my parents that I blew him off again."

"Kat, when a guy asks to see the inside of your home after a date, it isn't because he wants to know how you decorate. Women turn down guys all the time. I'm sure you wouldn't be the first to shoot down the remarkable Dawson Price."

"I know." She moaned and dropped her head

into her palms. "I'm so bad at this stuff. I was hoping he'd get the hint and leave."

"Next time, try saying no if you're not up for company."

She laughed without humor, thinking of how Dawson would have kissed her—invited or not—had Tyson not interrupted their evening. She nodded. "I'll try that next time."

"And if they don't understand 'no' or pressure you, then they're an asshole, and that's when you call your big, strong neighbor over to kick his ass."

She giggled and smirked at him through her fingers. How could he be so calm talking about this? This man, from what she understood, wanted to be her boyfriend, yet he was giving her tips on dating other men. "Why are you telling me this?"

"Because I care about you, and I don't want you to get hurt." He pulled her hands from her face, holding on to her fingers. "Do I want you to date other men? Hell, no. But I want you to be happy. From what I know of your parents, they aren't the most nurturing people. I'm sorry if that offends you, and I can almost understand why you want to please them by dating someone they like, but if you don't like this guy, then you need to tell your parents that and call it a day."

"I don't really feel any way about him, to tell you the truth. I don't really know him."

His jaw twitched. "Did he kiss you or touch you in any way that made you uncomfortable?" More importantly, had *he*? He didn't want to cross a line but he also wanted her enough to throw subtlety out the window.

"No. He was about to kiss me when you knocked at the door. Other than that, he didn't touch me, aside from holding my hand or putting his hand on my knee on the drive home."

He made a derisive sound.

She looked at her lap and mumbled, "And I'm really sorry about the wine. I asked if he wanted something to drink, and he asked for wine, and yours was all I had."

They sat quietly for a couple of minutes. She silently scoffed at the idea of Dawson ever making it to her bedroom. She barely knew the guy. It wasn't like she was an expert on the makings of Tyson Adams either, but for some reason, with him, it was different.

She felt safe around Tyson. It was her own behavior she had to worry about. But every time they moved forward, he slowed them down, reminding her she shouldn't go too fast. She couldn't imagine Dawson doing that.

"What are you thinking about?"

"How different you are from other men."

He nodded. "Different can be good."

Drawing in a deep breath, she asked, "So what happens now?"

"Well, you're a grown woman, and I can't tell you whom you can and can't date, but I would like a chance to date you to at least even the playing field. I want to take you out to dinner and maybe a movie. I want to spend time with you and with Mia, and sometimes with just the two of us. I get that you're in a tight spot with your parents and Mia. If you choose to go out with Price again, well, I can't stop that, but at least give me a fair chance. I missed you these past few weeks."

Dark eyes stared into hers, showing nothing but sincerity. Her chest filled with warmth, but there was still that ever-present skepticism when it came to trusting others. "Why are you being so understanding?"

"I told you. I can be a patient man, but Kat, even my patience has its limits. I won't be taken advantage of. If you date this guy, I can deal with that, but once things get involved, you're going to have to make a choice. Do you understand what I'm saying?"

She nodded.

"On that same note, if our relationship moves to the next level, I expect anyone else to back off. I do not share well with others. Especially what I consider mine."

Her stomach dipped and filled with a delicious, woozy sensation. Casually, she scratched her arms to hide her pebbled nipples. The possessive gleam in his eye and confident tone of his voice made her a little punch drunk and dizzy. *His*. What would that be like? "I understand."

"Good." He stood up and placed his mug in the sink. "It's getting late." Bending, he brushed his lips across her temple, and her body sparked to life. He must have noticed because he chuckled. "Try to get some sleep, and we'll talk more tomorrow." He gently slid a piece of hair behind her ear. "Goodnight."

Every time he left, the urge to call him back grew stronger. "Goodnight."

Chapter 11

THE NEXT DAY Kat was planting flowers out back as Tyson and Mia painted the doghouse. Mia was covered with spatters of yellow paint, and every few minutes her laughter rang through the air like little bells tied to the tail of a kite. When Kat's gaze snagged on Tyson's, he'd send her a smoldering look that made her blush from a hundred feet away.

After all the flowers were planted, she walked over to the fence and yelled, "How about some lunch?"

"Momma, do you see our doghouse? Do you see it?"

"I see it, babe. You're doing a great job. Are you hungry?"

Tyson hollered back, "Lunch sounds great. How about fifteen minutes?"

"Okay." She headed into the house to fix a meal.

Several minutes later, they came tromping into the house covered from head to toe in yellow paint, looking like they had rolled in sunshine and pollen.

Mia's old T-shirt and cotton shorts would likely end up in the trash before the laundry.

Tyson wore a threadbare Adams Construction shirt and a pair of jeans used for messy projects. The denim was stained with different shades of paint, dried putty, and had a tear at the knee. He looked utterly delicious, so she took a moment to admire the way his muscles pressed against the thin fabric of his shirt.

"Wash your hands before you sit down, Mia."

"'Kay, Mommy." Mia scampered into the bathroom.

Standing by the kitchen sink mixing a glass pitcher of pink lemonade, Kat casually breathed in Tyson's warm, sunbaked scent while he stood next to her washing his hands. Mia sang in the bathroom, her words offbeat and concise over the soft sound of running water.

He shut off the faucet and dried his hands. The hair on the nape of her neck was lifted away as his warm lips pressed into the sensitive curve of her shoulder. Spine arching like a cat, she shivered.

"What's for lunch?" Mia asked from the hall as Tyson stepped away.

Slightly off-kilter, she had to think what she'd just prepared. "Turkey sandwiches and apple slices."

Tyson carried the pitcher of lemonade to the table, and Kat pulled out three cups and filled them with ice. Mia talked, without pause, about Trixie and the doghouse. After lunch, Tyson helped clear the table and did the dishes while Mia played in her room.

"How's your day going?" he asked.

Her blood warmed like melted butter. He probably didn't realize how much she loved when he asked simple questions like that. "Good. How are you making out? Ready for a drink yet?"

He chuckled and came up behind her as she dried the dishes at the sink. Mouth close to her ear, he whispered, "I'm good. Could be better with a kiss."

His breath tickled her neck, and she shivered. She twisted the towel in her hands. "Tyson..."

"One kiss."

She sighed. "Mia's—"

"In the other room playing. I can hear her singing. She's totally engrossed in her own world. Come on, Kat. Turn around and give me a kiss. You don't even have to use your tongue."

Lips parted, breath coming quick, she debated. It wasn't easy, considering how he kept dragging his lips over the sensitive skin of her neck. He wasn't kissing, wasn't opening his mouth, just dragging his lips, and holy crap, did it feel good.

She cuddled into the space of his arms against the counter. A half smirk pulled at his mouth, and there was that adorable dimple. She looked into his eyes, but he made no move to lower his mouth to hers.

"Ty..."

"Yes," he slowly answered, his voice reverberating from his chest.

Mia continued to sing from her bedroom. The heat of his body warmed her front, and she swallowed. "I can't reach you."

"What if..." He slowly lowered his head. "I got...

real...close...like...this." His lips were only a breath away from hers.

Head tipping the slightest bit, she extended her neck and pressed her lips to his. His arm snaked around her back and pulled her flush to his front. She breathed in deep. The kiss was only a meeting of lips, but it was incredibly sensual and intimate.

With a whispered smooch, she pulled away, and he removed his palm from her back. His tongue briefly tasted where her kiss had touched, and then he bit down on his lower lip. "Mmm. Very sweet." He stepped back, and she exhaled, totally aroused.

"Mia," he called, keeping his eyes on her mouth. "Come on. We've got a doghouse to finish painting."

It was a perfect Saturday. The warm weather lofted through the opened windows sending the curtains dancing about, pouring the beauty of the day into her home. Children's voices carried over the grass-scented breeze. Birds chirped, and the hum of a lawnmower echoed in the distance. It was the symphony of springtime.

Kat worked around her house, dusting, and then remaking the beds with fresh linens as she breathed in the peacefulness of the late afternoon. She was rinsing out a mop when a sound clashed with the otherwise tranquil day. The moment she recognized the noise as Mia's cry, she went out the front door and sprinted toward Tyson, who was already holding Mia in his arms and heading her way.

At that same moment, a BMW pulled up to her curb. Her body tensed, but she kept jogging toward Mia. "What happened?"

Tyson held onto Mia as the three of them turned back toward the cottage. "She got a splinter." His gaze was distracted as Dawson stepped out of his car.

"Momma!" Mia cried and reached for her. Kat took her in her arms, heedless of the wet paint covering her daughter's hands and clothing.

"Shh, it's okay, baby," she soothed as they walked up to the front porch. She perched Mia on a rocking chair and investigated the splinter. It looked like the kind that hurt the moment it pierced the skin. Mia's tender, pink flesh swelled around the shard of wood.

Kat was mindful of Dawson standing at the curb but found it easier to immerse herself in her daughter's needs than acknowledge her uninvited guest.

Once she calmed Mia's tears, Tyson quietly said, "You have company. You want me to go?"

Before she could answer, Mia sniffled and cried, "Don't go, Tyson."

Dawson stepped onto the porch holding a bouquet of flowers at his hip, and her daughter cowered into the rocker as she loudly whispered, "There's a stranger here, Momma."

Taking a fortifying breath, she patted Mia's knee, wondering what the hell happened to her quiet afternoon. "Dawson," she greeted, standing up with a tight smile in place.

"Is this a bad time?"

Kat looked down and remembered that she was in her cleaning clothes, cotton capris, and an old, snug-fitting T-shirt that said *Got Milk?*, which was now covered with smears of yellow paint. She cringed. "No, not at all. Mia got a splinter."

"Oh." There was no softening in his expression toward her daughter, no attempt to offer condolences for—according to a three-year-old—the absolute devastation of getting a boo-boo. If anything, he seemed to look right through everyone but Kat. He probably wasn't used to being around children.

She attempted to include the others in the awkward moment. "Mia, you remember Dawson. He ate at Grandma and Grandpa's with us on Easter."

Mia leaned back in her chair and hid behind Kat's butt as she scrutinized Dawson with a distrusting, shy expression.

"Hello, Mia. It's nice to see you again."

Her daughter didn't reply.

He looked at Kat. "I came by to apologize for leaving so abruptly last night."

Her gaze darted to Tyson, who waited beside Mia, silently watching Kat. Talk about uncomfortable.

"These are for you," Dawson said, holding out the bouquet of wildflowers.

"Oh, how thoughtful. Thank you, Dawson." The scent of tiger lilies tickled her nose as she took the flowers.

"Can I smell?" Mia asked, and she held them under her nose. She sniffed and gave a diluted smile.

When the silence lingered, she offered a quick explanation. "I'm sorry. Mia was painting and got a splinter right before you pulled up. Let me put these in water and grab some peroxide and tweezers, then

I'll be right back." She scurried into the house like a big fat chicken.

Pulling a vase from the cupboard, she filled it with water. When she shut off the faucet, the porch was as silent as a graveyard. Dawson and Tyson were looking anywhere but at each other. Dawson appeared extremely interested in her gutters, and Mia wasn't making a peep from her spot on the rocker. She quickly stuck the flowers in the water and left them on the counter.

Digging through the bathroom medicine cabinet, she searched for the stuff for Mia's splinter as someone called her name.

Shit. Dawson.

Gathering the peroxide, tissues, a needle, and tweezers against her chest, she found him standing in the kitchen. This was obviously not what he was expecting to find when he decided to pay her a visit.

"Look, I can see this is a bad time..."

Her shoulders drooped in resignation. "I'm sorry. Things are kind of a mess right now. Not that things are typically calm around here. As a matter of fact, I should've predicted something like this would happen the moment I realized how freakishly quiet the first part of the day was." She took a breath. He should understand. At her parents', he said he wanted a family. This was parenthood. "That's life with a three-year-old. You sure you want all those kids?" She nervously laughed.

"Katherine." He smiled and took a step toward her. "It's fine, really. I wanted to make sure we were okay and that you weren't upset that I left last night—"

"Oh, no, I'm totally fine," she blurted.

He laughed without humor as her words unintentionally told him his leaving didn't affect her one way or the other.

"Well," he said. "While I'm here, I may as well ask you out again. What are you doing Tuesday?"

The front door opened and slammed shut as Mia sprinted by and ran toward the bathroom. "I gotta go pee-pee!"

Kat winced as the bathroom door slammed. This day just kept getting better. She sighed.

Dawson was frowning and inspecting a smudge of yellow paint on his pants. Mia must have bumped him. Great, all she needed was this getting back to her mother. Not only would it emphasize—in Vivian's mind—how much more complicated Kat's life was, but she would also start obsessing over Mia's untamed behavior and how she needed more discipline. If Dawson's expression were anything to go by, he'd no doubt agree with her mother.

"I'm sorry." She took a step toward him but came up short. There was nothing friendly in his tight smile.

"It's okay."

Yeah, that was convincing.

"I can ask Tyson for something that will get it out—"

"That won't be necessary," he said, and she got the impression he was irritated with not just the paint but also her and her not-so-tidy life. "Why don't I call you later, and we can talk when things are a little calmer around here."

"Well, that may not be until Mia's in college."

She laughed uncomfortably, and then quickly sobered. *Definitely not in the mood for sarcasm.*

Ignoring her joke, he asked, "How about sometime after eight?"

She did an odd, slow, shake, nod thing with her head. He nodded and took a step closer as if he intended to kiss her goodbye. She braced herself—

"Momma, I pooped, and I need help wiping!"

Smothering a laugh, she hid a smirk as Dawson froze. Saved by the bell. "Sorry. I gotta go help her before she makes more of a mess.

"Right...eight-fifteen then?"

Hedging toward the bathroom, she nodded. "Sure."

"I look forward to it, Katherine."

~

After Kat helped Mia in the bathroom and cleaned her up, Tyson came into the kitchen and sat at the table with them.

"This may sting for a second," Kat said as she wiped Mia's splintered finger with a tissue dipped in peroxide.

"Ouch!" Mia yelled and started to cry as Kat blew on her injured digit.

"I'm sorry, honey, but we have to get it out." She picked up the tweezers and held Mia's finger. Mia squirmed and tried to pull her hand away. She started to cry again as Kat plucked at the splinter.

"Ouch! Don't!" Her hand plunged into the protection of her lap.

"Here, why don't you hold her on your lap while I get it," Tyson offered.

She moved Mia to her lap and held her as he looked at the splinter.

"This isn't so bad," he told her in a gentle voice. "I get splinters all the time." He tenderly cradled her hand inside his large palm as if it were a baby dove.

"You do?" Mia sniffled, a big crocodile tear rolling down her cheek.

"Sure. The trick is to shut your eyes and think of your favorite color while someone pulls it out."

"I like pink," she said, watching Tyson.

"Okay. Shut your eyes and think of all the pretty things that are pink while I fix your boo-boo. No peeking until I say so. Okay?"

"Okay." She braced herself and squeezed her eyes shut.

He picked up the sewing needle from the table and held Mia's tiny, pudgy finger between his thumb and index finger, and gently plucked at her soft skin.

Kat was speechless. She couldn't look away from the way he held her daughter's hand. Her throat was suddenly tight as she rubbed Mia's knee, soothing both their nerves.

"I like pink cotton candy best. Well, that and bubblegum," Tyson softly told Mia as he continued to work out the shard.

Kat kissed the back of her head and whispered brave words of encouragement.

A few minutes later, Tyson said, "There. Good as new."

Mia opened her eyes, and he placed a kiss on her boo-boo. She inspected the finger and smiled, jumping off her lap and throwing her arms around Tyson's neck. "I love you, Tyson."

Kat's heart sputtered in her chest as her eyes met his over her daughter's shoulder. His strong arms around her little body as he whispered, "I love you too."

Overwhelmed with sentiment she wasn't prepared to feel, she jerked her gaze away and focused on gathering the items they used to remove the splinter. The tender moment touched her someplace deep in her heart. Mia loved him? Perhaps love wasn't such a strong word to a three-year-old. Shaken, she frowned and returned the items to the medicine cabinet.

This was the rapid attachment she feared. If Tyson's life got too busy for them, Mia would be devastated.

She wouldn't be the only one.

That night Mia was so exhausted, she didn't even make it through the first two pages of her bedtime story. Kat covered her, kissed her forehead, and shut out the lights. Shutting the windows and locking the doors, she left the hall light on and reluctantly grabbed the phone.

As soon as she changed into her pajamas, the phone rang.

"Hello?"

"Katherine?"

"Hi, Dawson."

"How are you? Am I catching you at a better time?"

"Perfect. I just got Mia off to bed, and she's sound asleep."

"Good."

She pulled back her covers, thinking this conversation wouldn't last more than a few minutes. It was really just a courtesy call. "Things were so chaotic today, I don't remember if I thanked you for the flowers. That was very thoughtful of you."

"You're welcome. I guess it's hard, sometimes, doing everything by yourself."

"It is, but Mia means the world to me, so I don't mind too much."

"She didn't seem too fond of me." He laughed.

"No, you caught her at a bad moment. She's usually friendly to everyone. Please, don't take it personally."

"What was she painting?"

"Oh, she was helping our neighbor paint a doghouse for his new puppy."

"Tyson, right? He seems to be around a lot. Are you that close with all your neighbors?"

Nope. "We have a couple of neighbors we're friendly with. Mia's very fond of Tyson." She crawled quietly into bed.

"And what about you? Are you okay with them being so close?"

Her hand paused as she reached for her glass of water. "Why wouldn't I be? He's great with Mia."

"I mean," he paused and obviously reconsidered his question. "What's your relationship with him?"

None of your business. "We're friends." She'd yet to define their relationship in her own mind, so she could hardly explain it as more than that, even though it definitely was. Other friends didn't pin her to the wall and grope her. She wasn't complaining, of course.

"Okay." He let the topic drop. "Are you free Tuesday night?"

Her eyes closed as she considered ending this charade and disappointing her mother. She'd never hear the end of it, but how much longer was she supposed to entertain this guy? He was good-looking, and nice enough, but she couldn't see past the fact that he was a colleague of her father's, which stifled any possible attraction. Besides, her attention was elsewhere.

Make an excuse.

"Um, I don't have a sitter. Going out on weeknights can be a bit confusing for Mia."

"Oh. I asked because I have tickets to the ball game. Club seats. Do you like sports?"

"I haven't been to a game since I was a little girl." Hopefully, he didn't buy the tickets for her.

"It's quite an experience. There's an open bar and a buffet of fresh seafood and appetizers."

"That sounds nice, but like I said, it's a little difficult to get a sitter on such short notice and on a weeknight." So he wouldn't think she was blowing him off, she lied, "But I could try. What time would you want to leave?" So long as her mother believed she put in a valid effort, she could get out of this.

"The game starts at five. I thought I'd pick you up around four, so we arrived a little early. It'll probably last three hours, so I could have you back by eight-thirty, nine o'clock."

She was quiet. Kat rambled when she was uncomfortable, and there was a good chance she'd ramble herself right into a corner.

"May I make a suggestion?" he asked.

"Sure."

"Why don't you ask your mother to take Mia overnight? I'm sure she wouldn't mind if she knew I was treating her daughter to a night out."

"Um, that's an idea." Did he know her mother at all? Vivian did not do sleepovers. *Perfect.* "Why don't you let me get back to you tomorrow with an answer?"

"Sure," he sounded quite confident. "And just so you know what to expect, the guests in the box are usually a little more formal than fans sitting in the stadium seats."

"So leave my big foam finger home?"

He didn't laugh. "Whatever you'd wear to a bar should be fine."

That gave her a chuckle. "Sorry to disappoint you, but I don't go to bars."

"Ever?" One would think she admitted to kicking puppies by the shock in his voice.

"Nope. I went to one on my twenty-first birthday, but that was it. I really don't have much of a social life, what with Mia and all."

"Where do you go on dates?"

Silently laughing, she rolled her eyes. "I don't. My date with you was my first one since I had Mia."

"You haven't dated since you had Mia? How's that possible?"

That was her—the social butterfly of the new millennium. "Oh, trust me, it is."

"Well, I'll have to deliver a good time then." His voice dropped an octave, taking on gravelly quality he didn't usually have.

Her unsure laugh filled the silence. *Let's see if Vivian even agrees to babysit—*

"How long has it been?"

Her motions stilled. Was he asking when she had sex last? No. "How long since what?"

"Certainly not since Mia…"

She gaped. Definitely asking about more than bar hopping. Literally speechless, she tried to think of a response to such a question.

"Don't worry. We can take it slow."

Take it slow? What happened to politically correct Dawson Price? *There was nothing to take!* "Um…" She was at a loss.

He gave a husky laugh. "Well, I'll let you get your rest. Call me tomorrow after you talk to your mother. And Katherine?"

Thank God this conversation was ending. "Yeah?"

"Sweet dreams."

She inwardly groaned. So. Weird. "Goodnight." She quickly ended the call.

Chapter 12

SUNDAY, right on schedule, the luxury Mercedes SUV pulled to the curb, and Kat walked Mia out the front door to greet her mother. Once she had Mia buckled, she sighed and prepared to do something she hated—ask her mother a favor. Well practiced at Vivian telling her *no*, Kat didn't expect much. "Do you think Mia could spend the night at your house on Tuesday?"

Her mother's manicured eyebrows lifted as far as the Botox would allow. "Well, that depends. Where will you be?"

"At a ball game."

"A ball game with whom?"

The woman does nothing without somehow serving herself. Through clenched teeth, she smiled. This was where her plan fell, though. "Dawson."

Vivian's face lit with approval. "Really? Well, that's wonderful. I knew you two would hit it off. I suppose Mia could come for a visit. Will you be dropping her off?"

Resigned, Kat muttered, "Yes, around three o'clock."

"Okay, dear. I'll arrange my schedule. I'll have to postpone my appointment at the salon." She never agreed to anything without letting Kat know there was a sacrifice.

Tyson was in front of his house. She had to force her face to remain placid as her heart kicked up a beat. *Time to go, Mom.* Kat blew a kiss to Mia. "Bye, babe. Be good for Grandma and Grandpa."

"Well, I won't keep you. I'm sure you want to go shopping for your date. You run along now." Vivian beamed, and she wanted to remind her it was a date and not a betrothal, but her mother's expression tightened, her gaze on the rearview mirror. Tyson was walking in their direction.

"And Katherine..." her mother said before she put the car in drive. "Lock your doors."

She rolled her eyes.

As her mother's car disappeared around the corner, Tyson approached. It was ridiculous how excited his presence made her. The closer he came, the more she admired his swagger. "Alone at last," he said, leaning in to brush his lips across hers. She was taken off guard as he hugged her tight, but Mia wasn't there, so she guessed it was okay. "Was that your mother?"

Shivers raced up her arms as he released her. "Yup. The one and only."

"She's not what I expected. She's pretty."

She laughed. "You imagined my mother was ugly?"

"No, I guess I just didn't picture such an attractive woman, but that was dumb, considering you're her daughter and how pretty you are." Her cheeks heated as he tucked a piece of hair behind her ear. "Did you have coffee yet?"

"Yes, but I could use some more. Want a cup?"

"Sure." He followed her into the house, and her belly did cartwheels the entire way there.

Suds rolled over her hands as she washed out the coffee pot while Tyson wandered around her living room checking out books and DVDs.

"We could watch a movie," he suggested. "Is this all you have as far as movies go?"

"I usually keep anything that isn't PG in my room. What kind of movie do you want to watch?" She really did have errands to run, but a movie on a Sunday sounded so tempting.

"What do you have?"

"Go look. They're on a rack next to the dresser."

He disappeared down the hall. "You alphabetized your movies?" he shouted from the bedroom.

"Shut up!" She laughed.

He returned holding an action flick and a romantic comedy. "Your room's pretty. Which one?" He held up two DVDs.

"Thanks." She considered his movie choices. "Oh, well, that depends. Do I want to be a good hostess and choose the movie with explosions I know my guest would probably prefer, or do I want to be selfish and choose option B, which happens to be one of my all-time favorites?"

"This is one of your favorites?" he asked, holding up the chick flick. "I never saw it."

"Absolutely. Makes me cry every time."

"Oh, God." He rolled his eyes and made a terrified expression.

She laughed. "Surprise me. You choose."

She put away the mugs, returned the coffee pot to the machine, and filled the filter trap with grounds for the following day while he fiddled with the television. She joined him on the couch, fluttery butterflies abuzz in her belly.

He pulled her back against his chest and wrapped his arms around her shoulders. The sensation of being held was so novel and cozy, the guilt of selfishly loafing around set in, and she tried to think of something else. She rarely took time like this for herself. As they got comfortable, she pulled the blanket off the back of the couch and covered her legs.

"This is soft. Where'd you get it?" His long, fingers dragged over the blanket.

"I made it."

"Really?" He sounded genuinely impressed.

"Yeah. When I was pregnant, I taught myself to crochet. I can make you one if you want."

He kissed her head, and she drew insurmountable pleasure from the simple act. "I'd love that, but you don't have to. You're already busy."

The DVD menu came on the television. She recognized it right away. "My favorite!"

He hit play. "But you're not allowed to cry."

"I won't if you don't," she agreed, and he snorted.

The steady thud of his heart beating slowly against her ear coupled with the sound of Christmas carols playing from the television filled her with a new yet nostalgic sort of bliss. "I love Christmas," she sighed.

"Me too." His fingers idly toyed with her hair, sending an occasional chill down her spine.

She loved how strong and tightly knit the family was in this movie. She always wished that she were a part of a big family like that. It was hard not having any brothers or sisters. It upset her that Mia would probably grow up as an only child as well and someday have the same longing for family.

Tyson was a good cinema buddy. He didn't chatter the way her usual movie companion did, and he never did egg beaters across the couch when the plot slowed. She'd forgotten how peaceful a little grown-up time could be. Two hours later, as the last scene cut away, she sniffled into the blanket and wiped her eyes.

"Hey, you okay?"

"Yeah." Struggling not to ugly cry, her voice came out in a croak. But wailing into a pillow would be completely unacceptable. So she fought back her tears. They should have watched the action movie. She was more emotional than usual for some reason, and this movie put her over the top. She couldn't cry in front of Tyson.

"Hey, Hey, come here."

Her face pinched as he tenderly pulled her close. She wasn't sure if it was the sad ending to the movie or her joy that he'd come into her life that undid her, but either way, she lost the battle.

"Aw, kitten, don't cry," he soothed as he held her tight.

"I'm sorry." Damn it, she couldn't stop the snot and tears from leaking from her face. So much for keeping it classy. "I'll be done in a minute. Just ignore me." She hiccupped. "Cover your ears and look away."

A deep chuckle rumbled through his chest. "And this is what your favorite movie does to you? You're a mess!"

"It's a great movie! They all love each other so much." She managed a tear-filled laugh. She was making an ass out of herself. Glancing at his shirt, she moaned. "Oh... I got boogies on your shirt."

"That's okay. They're boogies of love." They both laughed. "Come here."

Tyson adjusted their position so he could see her face. His eyes were sympathetic, but his mouth pursed, probably smothering another laugh. She was never a cute, little delicate crier. Nope, she usually broke out in hives, got a red runny nose, and bloodshot eyes the moment the first tear fell.

Tucking her hair behind her ear, he kissed the tip of her red nose. Bunching his shirt around a finger, he wiped her eyes. He was so kind and gentle with her.

Without thinking, Kat leaned in and pressed her lips to his. She feathered one slow, soft kiss after another over his mouth and breathed him in. He remained still as she played and experimented, tilting her head to shyly slide her tongue along the seam of his soft, full lips.

"Mmm," his voice rumbled as he chuckled.

Knees supporting her, her palms pressed into his shoulders. He was so strong and sturdy. Licking over his lower lip, she hummed as his chest expanded as he drew in a deep breath.

The weight of his hand pressed into her ass, sending shock waves of pleasure to her core. His head tilted, and he took control of the kiss, her body firing to life. The gentle tug of his fingers sifting through her hair sent chills down her spine.

She pulled his ears between her fingers as her lips worked their way from the corner of his mouth to his strong jaw. The scent of his shaving cream made her sigh. He smelled so good, clean, and male.

Since she loved when he kissed her ears and neck, she attempted to repay the favor. Her lips closed over his lobe, and he moaned, hands tightening on her hips as he settled her more over his lap, dragging her sex across the bulge pressing at his zipper.

She pulled on the skin of his neck, sucking hard. His head tipped back as he groaned again, his fingers tightening another degree. "That feels so good. I love your mouth on me."

Her lips curved against his skin as she smiled. Who knew she had the ability to arouse him the way he aroused her? It was empowering.

Her hips slowly started to rock. A delicious friction bloomed between her thighs. His mouth found her, as he lifted and turned her. Her back pressed into the cushions as his weight settled over her.

His hand dragged along the underside of her thigh, lifting her knee as he pressed his erection into the apex of her pants. He squeezed the back of her leg and ground his body into hers. Her hands smoothed down the back of his head as she held him to her, kissing him deeply.

He never tried to undo her pants or slip a hand under her shirt. It was all about kissing, that sweet groping over clothes, grinding into one another that was the essence of true making out.

They twisted and rolled, her nipples straining against her clothing, his hard arousal digging into her thigh. They needed more room.

Breathlessly, she pulled back and nudged him into a sitting position. "Let's go to my room." He stared at their clasped hands and hesitated as if weighing his options.

Please don't reject me now.

Hesitantly, he stood, and her gaze remained on the ground as she led him to her room. The short walk dragged out her thoughts and trepidation as if it were a mile. When they reached her room, she placed a soft kiss on his jaw.

"What are we doing, Kat?" he whispered.

"I don't know," she whispered back, as her mouth made a slow drag down his neck. "Show me what to do."

"To what point?" His voice was thick, as though she were causing him pain.

Her cheek nuzzled against his chest as their fingers laced to their sides. "As far as it's safe." She timidly looked at him, begging him not to throw her request in her face. She trusted him, and she hadn't trusted another person in such a long time. "Show me, Tyson."

He leaned down and skillfully kissed her, taking complete control. His fingers plucked at the hem of her tank top, slowly lifting it over her head, breaking the kiss. His eyes devoured her body, heating her skin, as she stood before him in white drawstring yoga pants and a cotton bra.

Trying not to shrink from his scrutiny, she met his gaze and forced her hands into fists, refusing to cover herself. This was her. She wasn't perfect, and she wasn't rail thin, but she was real, and this was the only size she came in.

His thumb trailed over her cheek and down her jaw. Chills skated over her flesh as his forefinger trailed to the valley of her breasts. The backs of his knuckles curved over the slight swell, and goose-bumps crested her shoulders. "You take my breath away, Kat."

"I want to touch you too."

His hand fell away as he pulled his shirt over his head, dropping the garment to the floor. Her palm lifted to his chest.

His nipples were deep brown and flat, while hers were delicate and pink. Her feminine softness against his strong, hard maleness was perhaps the most erotic contrast of all. He was a beautiful man, so chiseled and hard. She traced the lines of his muscles and noticed that in the deep valleys of each bulge where shadows darkened, begging to be licked.

"You're so fit and solid. It makes me want to cover myself and hide."

Her gaze moved to the bed. Maybe if they just moved and she could get under the covers—

"Women aren't supposed to be solid, they're supposed to be soft, like you, kitten. I love the way you look. Don't hide yourself from me." He gently unwound her arms from her belly and pressed his lips to her neck. "You're beautiful just the way you are."

Kisses feathered across her shoulder as the strap of her bra slid down her arms. The weight of his fingers closed around her wrist. He turned her to face the bed.

Knuckles dragged seductively up and down her spine and the clasp of her bra released. Her head lowered as his lips pressed against the nape of her neck, kissing softly as the garment fell to the floor.

Crouching low, he kissed the base of her spine and slid his tongue upward. Sweeping her hair off her shoulders, he slid his touch down her arms and gently captured her wrists, lifting her hand. Open-mouthed kisses trailed across her skin to the tender inside of her elbow, the pulse at her wrist, and he placed a kiss in the center of her palm. She visibly shook with need.

"Lie down." He eased her on the mattress. The bed dipped as he leaned over her. A touch of fear threatened to interrupt the moment, but she reminded herself that this was Tyson. So long as he continued to look into her eyes, she felt safe.

Kissing her deeply and slowly, the firm press of his chest, flesh on flesh, dragged over the sharp points of her nipples, and she moaned. His lips traveled toward her breasts as he slid lower. Calloused hands cupped her breast as his warm mouth closed over her nipple. A gasp escaped as his lips pulled tight.

While his mouth did wonderful things to one

tight peak, his hand held her other breast, his thumb and forefinger moving back and forth over the pebbled nipple. The scent of their bodies blended. Her hands gripped his arms as he released her and blew cool air over her wet skin.

His fingers tugged at the strings of her pants, and her stomach flipped in anticipation as her clothes loosened. As she lifted her hips, he gently tugged, and the worn cotton pulled over her thighs. Silk lifted as her panties slid away.

His mouth returned to her breasts, his breath softly teasing her skin, adding yet another delicious sensation as his fingers ran over the dewy nest of curls covering her sex. Excitement rolled over her, through her as the press of his work-roughened finger skimmed over her delicate opening. Her heart raced, and she swallowed back the taste of fear.

She trembled with building anticipation as he moved his finger. His mouth nipped and pulled at her nipples.

Body tight, she held him to her as he kissed his way down her belly, shifting his position on the bed so he could suck on her hip and lick the crease of her thigh. No one had ever kissed her there.

Liquid heat pooled between her thighs as her skin tingled from the tops of her ears to the tips of her toes. She writhed as he held her hips, pressing her ever so slightly into the soft mattress.

"Open for me, kitten."

Warm breath fanned over her sensitive folds. *Dear God.* It was the most intimate position she'd ever been in. She was completely exposed. His soft mouth teased the top of her sex, and she was assaulted by indescribable pleasure.

His thumbs separated her slit as he licked at the opening of her sex. Her oversensitive flesh wept as he sipped from her. Her body drew tight like a bow as his thumb nudged her clit.

She let out a hoarse, startled cry at the intense sensation of his tongue softly licking her as his fingers expertly penetrated. Her muscles tightened as his lips closed over the tight bud.

Flashes of the last time he'd touched her there broke into her mind and mingled with images of the present. Pent-up energy tightly coiled beneath her skin. The waves built faster and faster. Her lungs struggled to breathe as she swallowed great gulps of air. Fisting the blankets, her muscles drew taut as an orgasm swelled inside of her.

She gasped as her head moved from side to side. Deeper, faster, he worked her over as the waves continued to build. And then he found that magical spot someplace deep inside of her. Fingers firmly pressing upon that secretive place of pleasure, his mouth sucked hard, she shattered.

Her legs tightened as her back bowed, pressing further into his touch. Her body racked with shudders as the sheets clung to her dewy skin. Never had she been so aware of her flesh, her bones, her blood rushing through her veins. The throb of her heartbeat pounded between her thighs. Moans reverberated off the walls as she swelled beneath his tongue. There was nothing better than that moment when every part of her simply let go.

As her quaking muscles trembled into slow

quivers, he gently pulled away. He placed kisses on her inner thighs and the most sensitive points of her knees. She lay motionless, aside from a spontaneous spasm every few seconds that came in the aftermath of her climax.

He lay beside her and drew her close. Muscles were too weak to move on their own. Wrapping her naked body in his arms, he kissed the back of her shoulder. She sighed in complete contentment and ignored the distant echo of clamoring concerns.

His chest pressed into her with solid reassurance. The strength of his body was the only reminder that she still existed. His breathing leveled out and, though his hold grew lighter, the cocoon around her seemed to tighten.

Her thoughts slowly swam to the surface of her mind.

"Sleep, kitten," he whispered as his body nestled more into hers.

Eyes wide, Kat stared at the wall of her bedroom. Her mind counted cracks in the plaster so as not to count all the ways she was losing her heart to this man. Never in her life had she experienced such pleasure, but it wasn't just pleasure. It was conversations. It was common courtesies. It was his soothing company. No one, before Tyson, had ever shown her such tenderness.

She was no virgin, but what she was sharing and building with him was so much more than sex, so much more than anything she'd ever experienced before. The closeness, the opening of her soul, and bearing of secrets, it was new territory she hadn't anticipated crossing.

She'd worried about sex, about consequences, and morning-after awkwardness, but her slow, lust-muddled mind never considered there might be bigger things to fear.

She wasn't ready to bare all, but he was driving her there. There was some unnamable part of her, perhaps her mind, perhaps her heart, perhaps her fears and worries, and doubts that he saw. It was as if he could see into her soul.

She wasn't ready to trust another person that much. It was disconcerting to know he'd seen her so vulnerable, saw how desperately she needed to be touched, how starved her soul was for the most minimal affection. He cracked her open and exposed the emptiness inside. She defensively wanted her secrets back, didn't want anyone to know how incomplete she was.

He'd fallen asleep, and all she could do was lie there, frantically following one insane thought to another. There would be no meaningless sex between them. He would demand all of her, mind, body, and soul. Sharing her body was a hurdle, but sharing all those other parts seemed like an impossible mountain to climb.

Chapter 13

KAT'S SHOULDERS pulled tight as her fists clenched at her chest, and she shivered. Her front was freezing, but her back was burning up.

Just pull the blanket up. No. Too cold to move.

Slowly, opening her eyes in a series of widening blinks, she admired the pretty pink hues of sunlight reflecting on her wall. It was almost dark, marvelous shades of burnt amber and violet piercing the curtains as the sunset.

Sunset?

"*Mother fucker!*" Bolting off the bed, her foot snagged on a pillow, and she fell to the floor with all the elegance of a cord of firewood being dumped.

Her mind snapped into overdrive as she shot to her feet and saw Tyson lying across her covers barefoot, in nothing but jeans. This was so not good. Eyes wide, she breathed fast, thinking of the quickest way to get him out of there.

He cracked open an eye and frowned. "What was that? You okay?"

"You *have* to go! *Ohmygod*, you have to go!"

She scooped up his shirt and socks and threw them at his legs. Grabbing his left shoe, she frantically searched for its mate, like a dog twirling in repetitive circles before it sits.

"Kat, *what's* wrong?"

"My mother's going to be here any minute with Mia!" She anxiously continued to search for the shoe and didn't waste any time looking at him. *No time for distraction!* How hard could it be to find a size thirteen shoe? It was the size of a canoe, for Christ's sake. "*Where the hell is your other shoe?*"

"Baby, calm down, my shoe's right there. So what if your mother comes here? You're a grown woman. This is your house. You're allowed to—"

"*You don't know my mother!*" Her voice shrilled, as she tossed him his other shoe and winced when it nearly landed on his crotch. "Sorry."

She snatched up her shirt to shield her private parts and hastily found the rest of her discarded clothing. Doing an unattractive one-legged hop, she jumped into her pants, foregoing her underwear.

Readjusting her inside-out tank top, she slid it over her arms and popped her head through the collar like a whack-a-mole popping from its hole. She wouldn't be surprised if he tried to club her as she bordered hysteria. "Get dressed!"

His face darkened like a thundercloud as he stared at her. He could think whatever he wanted. He didn't have to answer to Vivian.

Neither do you. Oh, shut up.

Her fingers frantically combed through her bed

head as he shook his head and sat up. "I think you're overreacting—"

"Tyson, please, don't make an already complicated situation worse. I don't feel like answering questions or getting the third degree. Mia will be here. I don't want her wondering about us yet."

He stood staring at her but said nothing.

It was a copout, using Mia to push him out, but there wasn't time to explain what a psycho her mother could be. Swallowing back the heavy sense of guilt, she focused on fixing the bed.

Looking disappointed and resigned, he started moving. Once his shoes were on, he rolled his eyes, pecked her on the cheek, and left. An unsatisfying relief washed over her at the sound of the door shutting behind him.

Not five minutes after he left, her mother arrived with Mia. Kat was still flushed from the exertion it took to try to look like everything was normal. She forced herself to slowly walk out to Vivian's car. "How was your visit?" Her mouth curved into a nervous smile, and Vivian frowned.

"Katherine, what is going on with your hair?"

A hand nervously fluttered to her head and patted down her frizz. "I...I was vacuuming, and the vacuum jammed. I had a hard time unclogging it."

Vivian's lips pursed as she made no comment, vacuuming being something her mother never discussed.

Mia jumped into her arms. "Look what Grandpa gave me."

Kat ignored her mother's critical stare and

showed great fascination with the small model schooner Mia held. "Wow. Very cool."

A disapproving sniff came from Vivian's direction. "Okay, Mia darling, give me a hug goodbye." Mia leaned off of Kat's hip and hugged her mother. "Katherine, I'll see you Tuesday."

The mention of Tuesday made her inwardly cringe. This was the last time she was doing this. She didn't like Dawson that way, and it was pointless to encourage him or her parents, for that matter. "Thanks, Mom."

"Please do something decent with that hair by Tuesday. And get some rest. Your eyes look tired."

Galvanized by years of practice, she didn't respond. Her mother pulled away, and she let out a long breath. "Okay, kiddo, let's get you in the tub."

That night she lay in bed, the scent of Tyson on her sheets, as guilt ate at her like acid. It was completely juvenile to chase him from her home, and she needed to apologize.

At one in the morning—still awake—she considered walking to his house. She would've called, but she didn't know his number. By one-thirty, she threw on a sweatshirt and slippers. She got as far as the front porch before reconsidering the dark and deserted street. He was probably asleep. Deciding to apologize in the morning, she tossed and turned until well after two.

When the alarm went off at five, she hit the snooze until six. When she finally got out of bed, she had to rush. Mia was a ray of sunshine next to Kat's run-over zombie thing she had going. Sluggishly opening the cupboard, she was reminded that she hadn't gone to the market. Instead of getting Mia a quick bowl of cereal, Kat took an extra ten minutes to make pancakes.

By the time she got a shower, it was six-thirty, and, of course, she was out of conditioner. Filling the bottle with water, she repeatedly dumped it over her head until her hair became somewhat soft and manageable. Instead of blow-drying her hair, which was necessary, she threw some product in the tangled mess and prayed it wasn't a humid day. She couldn't be late for work.

At seven o'clock, she left the house—on time—but left clothes on her floor, dishes piled in the sink, makeup scattered all over the bathroom, and on top of everything else, she forgot Mia's bag of toys. Speeding home, she grabbed the bag and sped back to Mrs. Bradshaw's.

She was in such a hurry after leaving Mrs. Bradshaw's for the second time that she forgot to buckle her seatbelt. As she entered the metro section of New Castle, she hit every red light and nearly had a panic attack when she spied the gas gage ticking on E.

As she eased over an intersection at a stop sign, lights flashed in her rearview. "Son of a bitch." Flicking her signal, she pulled to the side of the road.

Wasting precious minutes, the officer moseyed toward her window. Kat shut off the engine because if she ran out of gas, she was going to lose it. Prepared to flirt, she glimpsed her reflection and immediately aborted that plan. It was *not* good. Her hair was half-dry frizz and half-damp snarls, and no amount of makeup was going to cover the bags under her eyes.

Resigned to being late, she patiently handed the officer her license and registration. Tapping her fingers on the steering wheel, she waited for him to write her a ticket and tried not to stress about the expense.

He handed her the slip of paper and pointed out that her inspection was up in a few weeks. She smiled tightly. "Thank you." *Officer Dickhead.* Shoving the ticket in her purse, she buckled her seatbelt—a hundred-dollar oversight she wouldn't overlook again.

By some miraculous magic, she beat her boss to the office. As he entered, he frowned at her, his bushy white brows spreading a fat shadow over his crinkled eyes. "Kat, are you feeling all right this morning?"

"Just running a little behind today," she said in the calmest voice she could manage. "Go ahead in your office, and I'll bring you your coffee as soon as it's done brewing."

His eight o'clock arrived before the coffee was finished perking, and he had to start his session without it, which was all her fault. She checked the messages and sorted Saturday's mail. At nine o'clock, she brought Dr. Stevens his coffee and he, again, frowned at her appearance. "Maybe you should go home for the day."

She couldn't miss a day's pay. "Oh, no, Dr. Stevens. I'm okay. I promise."

He didn't appear convinced. When his next appointment arrived, she took a few minutes to rest her head on her desk. Wearily, she rubbed the back of her neck, trying to work out the tension knotting there.

For her to look bad enough that her boss questioned her health was pretty low on the scale of vanity. Add another check in the column of confidence-building moments in the sorry life of Kat D'Angelo. She visited the bathroom with her purse and winced at her reflection. She looked atrocious.

Wetting her palms, she attempted to tame the wild mess that was her hair. She pulled the snarls as tight as she could then secured them in a ponytail with a rubber band from her desk. It took care of the frizz but made her puffy eyes more prominent. She had no makeup with her aside from lipstick, so there wasn't much of an improvement.

Digging in her purse for some Motrin, she stumbled across the ticket from that morning. As her gaze settled on the total, she almost vomited. *A hundred and fifty dollars!*

Her vision blurred as she continued to search for anything that might relieve the tension headache, now shifting into a migraine. How was she going to afford that fine? She could fight it, but then she'd lose a day of work in court, and she'd probably lose the case anyway. She *hadn't* come to a complete stop, and she definitely wasn't wearing her seat belt.

She worked in complete silence, sniffling away. Luckily their office didn't get a lot of foot traffic, and her desk partially faced the wall, wiping her eyes before each tear fell. By the end of the day, her eyes were raw, red-rimmed, and marked with bags. Her face was splotched with hives. She pulled the rubber band out of her hair and grimaced at the clump of hair that came with it.

I just want this day to be over.

As she pulled onto their street, her car slowly crawled past Tyson's house. It was dark, and no cars were in the driveway. Mia seemed to detect something was off and walked quietly into the cottage.

"Mia, Mommy doesn't feel good. Why don't you go play so I can lie down?"

Curling into a ball on the couch, she rested her eyes for a bit, but the headache didn't ease. When she opened the pantry, she cursed, reminded for the second time that she hadn't gone to the market. It was obviously not the day for a routine. Grabbing a can of tomato soup, she heated it. After dinner, Kat took the trash out and noticed Tyson still wasn't home.

For as tired as she was, sleep seemed elusive. Tyson hadn't stopped by or called. Not that he could have without knowing her number. A sad sigh slipped into the darkness. This wasn't Ty's fault. It was hers. She should have never wasted the day yesterday. If she had just gone to the market and done everything she needed to do, her day could have gone much smoother. Tomorrow, after work, she'd just have to go to the store with Mia and stay up a little later catching up on chores.

Her face pressed into the pillows, the faint scent of Tyson still clinging to the linen. That right there was the first thing that made her smile all day.

~

"These look great, Ty."

Tyson took the plans from Imani as she stood from her chair at the conference table and stretched. Long arms extended toward the ceiling as the sharp angles of her face contorted in a yawn.

They'd been back and forth over the layout for the renovations to her secondary home for the past six months. It was a relief to finally produce something she was happy with because Imani Jones was no easy woman to please.

She made a show of looking at her diamond-studded wristwatch. Her short, black hair took on a glossy sheen as she tipped her head and rolled her shoulders with the grace of a sleek panther. "Wow, it's almost ten o'clock. Tracy, you can go home."

Her personal assistant looked relieved and quickly gathered the coffee paraphernalia from the room and left.

Imani rested her narrow frame against the conference table and leaned back, arching her long spine and pressing her palms into the expensive cherry wood. She sighed, her tapered legs crossing, as she rolled her shoulders, relieving the day's tension. "Did you eat, Ty?"

Sidestepping her offer with an air of disinterest, he stood and retrieved his blueprints. Hoping to catch Kat before she went to bed, he rebuffed what was more than a dinner invitation.

As he drove home, he forgot about Imani and thought about the way he left Kat. Her fear of her mother's judgment was ridiculous. He couldn't wrap his brain around a grown woman reverting back to such childish fright. It was irrational, and he'd tried to reason with her, but the middle of her panic attack was not the time for lectures.

He cared for Kat, that much was clear. They were rounding the bases at a teenager's pace, but he liked that. He couldn't remember the last time he'd actually *made out* or felt up a girl, under the shirt, over the bra, and experienced that sharp longing.

He turned onto the bypass and adjusted his cock in his pants. Sooner or later, he was going to need some satisfaction. Jerking off in the shower, imagining Kat's sexy ass and plush spread thighs could only take him so far. It had become a fascination of his, Kat's sexual awakening. He was thoroughly enjoying the slow journey and couldn't wait to take the next step, but each time he pulled back, the reward increased in value. He wanted her, and sooner or later, she'd be his.

~

Kat woke up on time but was still moving at a slugs pace. Her period arrived in the middle of the night, and, of course, she was almost out of tampons. Still out of cereal, she had to make pancakes again. If she didn't get to the market soon, she was going to run out of pancake mix as well. Slow but steady, she dressed for work and got Mia ready for the day.

After loading Mia into the car and climbing behind the wheel, she started the car and backed out of the driveway. When she put the car in drive, it died.

I forgot to get fucking gas!

The steering wheel smacked against her forehead. Complete defeat swamped her, extinguishing her last flicker of forced enthusiasm. She could not do another day like the day before. Keeping her head on the wheel, she growled and began to cry.

"Momma?" Mia's small voice came from the backseat.

"What, baby?" Kat tried to compose herself. It wasn't happening.

"What are we doing?" Her question only made her feel like more of a failure, wringing out another string of shuddered sobs. "What's wrong, Momma?"

Taking a deep breath, she wiped her face. *So much for makeup*. How had something as simple as getting to work avalanched into something she could no longer handle?

She rubbed her temples and tried to think of what to do as she saw Tyson climbing into his work truck. Guilt and fear added to her upset.

She was so tired of feeling guilty, tired of trying to keep everyone happy, tired of coming up short when it came to being an adult. She just wanted to say *fuck it* and let someone else deal with all the crap that needed to be done.

His truck slowed next to her little car as he leaned out the window. "Did your car break down?"

"I ran out of gas."

He said something she couldn't make out and pulled to the curb. As he walked toward her car, Kat instructed Mia to stay put and got out as well. The moment Tyson saw her face, he scowled. "Are you okay? What the hell happened?"

Upset that she looked bad enough to get a reaction like that two days in a row, she welled up and choked out, "I had a really bad day."

He laughed. "It's seven a.m."

She wished she could find the humor in her ridiculous statement. Her attempt at laughter came out as a jagged sob. "It's been going on for thirty-six hours."

"Aw, come here, kitten. Don't cry." He pulled her into a hug.

She clung to his strong form, greedily taking the offered comfort, knowing it was dangerous to depend on him for such things. His palm soothed her back as his lips pressed into her hair. She needed to pull it together, but a gate had opened, and she was pretty sure the hinges and latch washed away.

"What happened?"

"Everything," she mumbled into his shirt. He always smelled so good.

"Do you want to talk about it?"

"No."

"Okay."

Still, her words followed a shuddering breath. "It all started after you left. I felt really bad for blowing you off, and I was going to call, but I don't even know your phone number," she blubbered. "I couldn't sleep, and I thought I'd walk over to your house to apologize, but it was the middle of the night, and it was dark. I got scared and went back in like a big fat chicken, but I still couldn't sleep. The next morning I overslept and turned into a frizz ball. I forgot Mia's Dora bag and was already late from the pancakes. By the time I was almost at work, I got pulled over and got a hundred and fi—fif—fifty-dollar fucking ticket, which I don't have the money to pay. I scared my boss and didn't have his coffee. A clump of hair fell out, and I had to feed Mia tomato soup. Then I got my..." she caught herself, a little late, but at least before she started talking about her cramps and stuff no man wanted to hear about. "Everything just sucks, okay? And now I'm out of ga—" Hiccup. "—gas."

Gibberish continued to spew from her lips in the form of nonsense words and syllables that didn't even make sense to *her* as she started to bawl.

"Okay, okay." He patted her back and pressed her head to his shoulder. He twisted around, and the car door squeaked. "Okay, Mia, out of the car. Mommy doesn't feel good."

Shifting her under his arm, he scooped Mia up with his other arm, settling her on his hip, and walked them back inside. One-handed, he directed her to bed and covered her, all while holding Mia.

"I'm going to take Mia to Mrs. Bradshaw's, then I'm going to move your car. I'll be right back," he whispered as he pressed a kiss to her damp cheek.

Too emotionally exhausted to object, she merely nodded. She couldn't take any more. She just wanted someone else to deal with all the stress, the groceries, the chores, the cooking, and gassing up her car. She rarely gave into moments of self-pity, but right now, the pity parade was in full swing, and there was no calling back the weariness stomping over her.

She must have dozed because when she woke up a little while later, Tyson was rubbing her calf through the blanket as he sat on the edge of her bed.

"That was fast," she groggily said.

"You think? It's eight-fifteen. That Mrs. Bradshaw can talk."

"*What?*" Her body tensed as it fought with her need to get up. She could not believe she went back to bed. What was she thinking? The entire episode played back in her head like an out-of-body experience.

"Relax, relax. Everything's fine." He eased her back down on the bed.

"I have to call Dr. Stevens—"

"Already done. When I dropped Mia off, Mrs. Bradshaw said she had the number and called to let him know you wouldn't be coming in. I also filled your tank. I called my crew and told them I wouldn't be on the job site until noon, so is there anything else you need? I'm at your disposal."

Dumbly, she blinked. "Why are you doing all this?"

"What do you mean?" He frowned. "This is what friends do."

"But after the way I threw you out the other day and—"

"Don't worry about that now. I may not completely understand your relationship with your parents or this hold they have over you, but it's not my place to tell you how to run your life. Forget it. It's over." He tucked the blankets up closer to her chin. In a soothing voice, he asked, "Do you feel better?"

Kat eyed him doubtfully. No one was *that* understanding. "A little. Thank you." He'd never know how grateful she truly was for his help.

"Is there anything you need?"

Yeah, tampons, groceries, a hundred and fifty bucks to pay a traffic ticket— "No. You should go to work."

"Kat, you know... it's okay to ask me for help. I care about you. I don't want you to shut me out. You can talk to me."

"Thanks. I'm fine. I just had a really bad day yesterday, and I'm still recovering. On top of that, I didn't get any of my errands done on Sunday, so my routine's all messed up. Now that I have the day off, I can run to the market and grab what we need for the week. I'll rest a little, and tomorrow I'll be as good as new." She had no other choice. These moments of indulgent weakness were not allowed in her life.

"Are you sure?" His expression said he didn't believe her.

She pushed for her most convincing smile. "Yeah, I'm sure. Thanks again. You really saved me this morning."

She wasn't used to others taking care of her, and she was starting to really like the feeling, which was dangerous.

"Well, how about after work tonight I swing by with a pizza, so you don't have to cook?"

"Oh, that would be—shit."

She looked at him, shame smothering her all over again. She was such an asshole. "Today's Tuesday. I can't."

"Why?"

"I, uh, have plans."

His brow lifted. "Plans?"

"I have... a date," she muttered, avoiding his gaze.

He stiffened. "I see. With Dawson?"

"Yeah, he called to ask me out the other night. He's taking me to—"

"I don't need the details."

His curt tone caught her off guard. "You said you were okay with this." An awkward silence stretched between them. Was he having second thoughts? "This will probably be the last time I see him. We could do pizza another night," she weakly offered, trying to break the tension.

Rather than answer or even acknowledge her olive branch, he said, "Well, if you're okay, then I better head into work."

A sad, unwanted sense of loss filled her. She wanted him to understand. "Tyson—"

He stood. "I gotta go, Kat. Feel better."

"Tyson, please." She sat up but stilled when he held up a hand.

"Save it, Kat. These are your choices, and you have to live with them. But I don't."

She scoffed. He said he understood. He said he could be patient. "Then why did you say you'd wait?"

"I thought things changed," he snapped, and she shrunk against the headboard. He never spoke to her like that. He exhaled a harsh breath, scrubbing his hand roughly over his face.

"Look," he said in a calmer voice. "I...I want you to get it. I like you. Being with you isn't some bullshit way I pass my time. I enjoy being around you. I like hanging out with Mia. And I like when it's just you and me.

When I'm at work, you're never far from my mind. But I have *no* idea how *you* feel. You don't talk to me. I think I have you figured out, but then you send me a curveball, and I'm confused all over again. It's frustrating."

"I like spending time with you too."

"We spent the whole day together Sunday. I thought we finally got to a point that we were ready to face this thing between us like adults, but then your mom shows up, and I feel like I'm a teenager again, expected to shimmy down the fire escape before your parents walk in. What am I supposed to think, Kat? I'm not a fucking kid anymore. I want more than this. And I'm not talking about sex. I'm talking about an emotional connection where we actually communicate with each other and don't sneak around because you're afraid Mommy and Daddy won't approve."

She looked at the carpet. Everything he said was true. "I'm sorry," she whispered.

A few seconds ticked by. "I appreciate your apology, but what are you actually gonna do about it, Kat? How many more dates until you tell your parents no?"

"I tried to get out of it—"

"No one has a gun to your head. Maybe if you stuck up for yourself a little more, your parents would respect you more as an adult."

That hurt.

Arguing was pointless. She'd tell her mom it was over with Dawson and face the consequences. But tonight was already arranged. Her mother had rearranged her schedule to babysit, and Dawson had already purchased tickets.

"Say something!" he said.

She shrugged, hating that her choices were upsetting him. "You're right. I have nothing to say. Everything you said was true. I don't know how to say no."

"Goddamn it, Kat, fight back! I just insulted you!"

"I don't know how!" she shouted, unshed tears burning her eyes. "I can't just yell at someone. I'm not made that way. Words hurt, Tyson. And words said in anger can never be taken back."

"Fine, you don't want to fight. At least take a defensive position. Stick up for yourself."

Her thoughts quieted, and her mind tucked itself away in some dark corner like a child hiding with a blanket.

He sighed and shook his head. "Kat."

She stared at the little daisies sewn into her comforter. "I'm sorry."

"I don't want another apology," he said in a softer tone. "Tell me one thing you like about yourself."

"Mia."

"Something else."

She shrugged.

He took her hand and tugged her off the bed. "Stand up." She stumbled after him as he crossed the room. "Look."

She gazed at her reflection in the mirror.

"What do you see?"

He stood behind her, a dark image of strength and confidence, with her a slight and pathetic picture of nothing special. Her eyes had smudges of black makeup under her lashes, and her hair was sloppy. Her clothes were wrinkled, and her posture slumped. "I see me," she mumbled.

"And what's you?"

"I don't know."

"Tell me something about your reflection you like."

There wasn't anything. Her gaze lowered and focused on a small dish holding her cheap jewelry, but his fingers pressed under her chin and lifted her head.

"No, look at yourself. Forget about everything you've been told and see the girl I see."

She stared at her reflection. Her eyes focused on the spattering of freckles cresting her cheeks, the curve of her lips, and the elasticity of her skin. She didn't have wrinkles. That was a plus.

No matter how much she straightened her hair, a little wave always formed by her temple. Her throat was slightly concave at the base, just above the V of her collarbone. It was all so overwhelmingly ordinary.

Her brows were dull and dusty brown rather than sharp and angular the way women wanted them to be. There was nothing sharp about her. And under her clothes, it was worse.

Her shoulders were rounded, and her breasts were lifeless without a bra. Scarring from pregnancy stretched thin silver lines over her hips. A pouch of baby fat that no amount of sit-ups could cure showed beneath her belly button. Her butt was flabby and too wide. Her thighs were dimpled where they should be smooth, and her knees were incredibly knobby. She'd probably have nice hands if she didn't bite her nails.

"Do you know what I see?" Tyson whispered.

With shimmering eyes, her gaze met his in the mirror.

"I see a beautiful woman who's too afraid to show her strength. I see soft, gorgeous hair that always has my fingers itching to run through it. A neck that's made for kissing. Bee stung lips that could bring a man to his knees."

Her breath trembled in her lungs as his words pierced the vulnerable bubble she hid within. She wasn't strong. She couldn't even stand up to her parents.

"Your eyes are so expressive, Kat. I love looking into them, hoping to catch a glimpse of some secret you're trying to hide. And that little feisty temper of yours, it shows when your face flushes, taking your freckles from the soft shade of sand to fiery cinnamon."

His palms slid over her hips. "Your breasts are the perfect size to fill my hands, and your hips flare as a woman's should. You're soft and cuddly and fit perfectly against me. And your ass—mmm, mmm, *mmm*—I love that ass.

"There isn't one thing about you I don't like, except for your inability to see the value in yourself. Stop listening to people who do nothing but hurt you, Kat. They're a bunch of idiots. The day you stop giving them the power to hurt you is the day all their condescending comments go away. But *you* have to make them stop, or they never will."

Her body shook, as she feared one whispered

word would break her. She wanted to call him a liar, but the look in his eyes showed nothing short of sincerity. Whether she possessed the beautiful traits he listed or not, it didn't matter. He saw her that way. Same as she saw her daughter as the most beautiful child in the world, Tyson saw her as pretty.

It hurt. It actually physically hurt to accept his opinions. Like a backward birth, she shoved everything she thought about herself into the depths of her mind, but her flaws didn't want to fit anywhere but the forefront of her brain.

He ran his fingers down her arms and leaned over her shoulder to kiss her cheek. "You do what you have to do, Kat. But the girl I just described, that's the one I'm waiting for. Fuck 'em, Kat. You just gotta learn to say fuck 'em." He stepped away, and she steeled herself to stay calm in the absence of his strength.

What kind of message was it sending her daughter when Kat couldn't defend herself from people that took advantage? She protected Mia, but it cost her greatly. Same as she protected her daughter, she wanted to protect Tyson. Why? Because no one else saw her as he did, and if she didn't learn to stand up for herself, he wouldn't stand by waiting forever.

~

Tyson barreled into his work trailer and slammed the metal door. Throwing his sunglasses on his desk, he groaned in frustration. He'd left Kat with a whole pile of crap to think about, but only Christ knew if any had sunk in. He wanted to find her parents and strangle them.

At first, he thought, sure, a little low on the self-esteem scale, he could manage that. He'd treat her nice and be a good friend—all easy objectives with a sweet girl like Kat—but perhaps he'd bitten off way more than he could chew.

He was not giving up. He liked her. Fuck, he might even be falling for her. Those small glimpses of her natural self when her insecurities weren't crowding in, were enough to make him beg like a fifteen-year-old boy. She did something for him in a way no other woman or girl ever had.

It could be the way she looked up at him with those soft, trusting eyes. Or maybe it was how sweet she was as a mother that triggered some male biological clock in him. She was sexy as all get out, but it was so much more than that. It didn't matter. This would never work if she didn't start believing she was good enough to have a happy life.

It was like watching someone quit when victory was only a breath away. If she could just stand up to the bullies in her life and start worrying about what *she* wanted instead of what others thought, things would start to change.

There was a light knock on the siding followed by the squeak of the door. Ready to explode, needing a target, he scowled at the intruder.

Eric, an apprentice electrician on his crew, didn't seem to notice his mood, so Ty gave him a preview. The kid was supposed to be off-site. "I thought I told you to clean up that shit and go to the Hoyt property!"

"I know. I'm heading there now, but there's a woman here looking for you."

His heart stuttered with excitement as he thought of Kat. Eric jumped out of his way. Disappointment smothered his hope as his sister, Gloria, waited outside the trailer. "What are you doing here?"

Eric fled without another word. Ty really shouldn't have snapped at the kid like that.

"Geeze, Ty, nice to see you too." She stepped into the cramped office and dropped her oversized, knockoff pocketbook on the table.

Gloria liked to think she was classy and bourgeois with her knockoff *Louis Vuitton* accessories, but she thought nothing of pulling a bottle of hot sauce out of that designer bag in a nice restaurant.

"Sorry. Rough morning. What's up?"

She tapped her neon claw on the table and made herself at home in a metal folding chair. Apparently, this was going to be a long visit. *Great.*

He eased into the upholstered chair behind his desk. The permanent scent of coffee and blueprint ink that always filled his trailer had him looking to the coffee pot. Of course, no one made coffee. Why would they? Boss was a little late, and they all thought it was a holiday.

"Can't a girl come and visit her brother once in a while?"

"Sure, a normal sister can. You, on the other hand..."

"Boy, you *are* in a mood." She dropped the diva façade and slouched. "Darrel lost his job again."

"Aw, Christ G, I'm sorry."

"We'll be all right. We got our savings. It's just..."

"If you need a loan, you know I'll spot you."

"No, it's not that." She squirmed and pursed her full lips. "A man needs to work, Ty. I can't go through this again with him. It's not that he doesn't do his part, but during the workdays, Davis is with Mommy. That's a lot of time to sit around. And not for nothing, but eventually, our savings'll run out. I got financial aid, but school ain't cheap. I need books and shit. Eventually, if he doesn't get work, I'm gonna have to get a second job, and I don't know how I'm gonna manage that with college, findin' time to study, working at the grocery store, taking care of Davis, and worrying about Darrel."

"Can't he go back to the mill for the time being until he finds something else?"

"He hates that fucking place."

"Well, how much are your books? I told you I'd pay for your school. You wouldn't let me do that. Let me at least buy your books, G. I want to."

Her lip quivered, and a sheen of tears covered her dark eyes. "Don't you get it, Ty? It's about my husband's pride. I can't take your money. He'd see that as a slight on his ability to take care of his family. That's exactly why he needs to work. He needs to contribute, feel like he's pullin' his weight. He needs to feel like a man," her voice had gone more frantic and emotional with each pleaded word.

"Well, if you won't take my money, what is it you want me to do?"

She looked up at him, eyes clear, hysterics put aside, and broadly smiled. Tyson had the sneaking suspicion this conversation was a prepared dialogue, and Gloria couldn't be happier with his lines. Before she even asked, he knew he'd been played.

"I want you to give him a job."

He groaned and waved his hands, as far removed from the conversation as he could physically get in the tight trailer. "No, Gloria. No, no, no, no, *no*. I've seen Darrel try to fix stuff around the house. Most of the time, you're calling me over to *fix* his botched repairs—"

"Come on, Ty! He doesn't need to do anything with big tools. Give him a broom or somethin'. Let him get your coffee. Whatever. Just don't let him sit home all day."

"You don't want him sitting at home all day because you're scared he'll get bored and try to fix something of *yours*!" He shook his head. "The man is a card-carrying member of the *duct it or fuck it* club. He's a liability."

His sister pursed her lips and took a breath. "Please, Tyson? Don't make me beg. You know I'm too pretty for that."

He laughed, then scrubbed his palms over his face with a groan. "I should've never gotten out of bed today."

"Is that a yes?"

He was glad she was finishing her degree, and he didn't want their finances to get in the way of her progress. If she wouldn't take his money… "Yes," he moaned.

Gloria squealed and did a little touchdown dance from her seat. "Ooh, I knew I could count on you!" Kicking up her feet, she made herself at home. "Now, tell me what's got your panties in a bunch?"

He made coffee and gave her the details of him and Kat. As he talked, she did a lot of head shaking and disapproving *mmm, mmm, mmms.* When he finally finished, ending with how he had left Kat that morning, she said, "Mommy told me you had it bad, but I didn't realize it was *this* bad."

"I do not *have it bad.* I care about her."

"Boy, your emotions got you as overwhelmed as a hungry baby in a titty bar. I've never seen you so unsure. It's kinda funny."

"Since you're so smart, you tell me what to do."

"Fine." She adjusted her shoulders and lifted her chin, taking on her diva persona. "You say you care about this girl? Then why are you gonna sit around and wait for this fool Dawson to hurt her? Aren't doin' anyone any favors there. You got to look out for her. That's what real men do. Since when are you the type to sit around and wait for things to come to you? I get that you're trying to be all patient and sweet, but Ty, be a *little* creative. Do something nice for the girl."

"I was going to bring her pizza tonight, but she had a *date!*"

"Oh, pizza... Well, why didn't you say so?" She rolled her eyes. "Come on, Ty. You can be more creative than that."

"She isn't like other women. She likes being home. She gets all tongue-tied when she's around people she doesn't know. Plus, she's impressed with people's character, not what they can do for her or what they have. She isn't materialistic at all. I love that about her."

"Excuses, excuses." Gloria shook her head. "Ty, if you want to win the girl, you got to be the better player. Put your game face on and start using strategy. While this fool's out there taking her to all these places she's never been, you have the advantage of knowing where she wants to be. Bring the game to her home court. And for God's sake, think of some creative plays. I swear to God, all you men are the same, boo-hoo, my woman don't pay me any attention. Well, maybe if ya'll stopped pouting and started thinking romantically, you'd see a different outcome for once."

"You think she wants romance?"

"*All* women appreciate romance. And romance is *not* fancy things. Romance is a look, a genuine smile, heartfelt words, and everyday kindness. Romance is bringing the trashcans up from the curb. That's the kind of love a woman wants because that's the kind that lasts. Flowers die, jewelry tarnishes, and chocolate melts. Give her something meaningful, Ty. Trust your instincts. All joking aside, you really want this girl? Then let her into your heart and show her the kind of man you truly are, and you'll get her."

She had no idea how badly he needed to hear that. "Thanks, Gloria."

KAT WAITED in the kitchen for Dawson to arrive. Wearing a yellow cotton sundress with eyelet detail along the hem and a pair of espadrille wedges, she gave up her hope that the game would be rained out.

Motrin in full effect, she cleared her throat and straightened her shoulders. For the first time in two days, she was feeling pretty good— except when she thought about the look on Tyson's face as he left that morning.

"This is the last time," she told herself. *Just get through tonight, and then you never have to go out with him again. Vivian will just have to deal with it.*

The BMW pulled up, and she grabbed her purse and her short-sleeved white sweater, in case there was a chill. She blocked the door and quickly pulled it shut behind her.

"Hi. You look great."

"Thank you." *Let's get a move on.* "Shall we go?"

He walked her out to the car, and this time she

was grateful there was no Tyson to witness the act. She'd called her mother that afternoon in an attempt to justify why she should cancel the date, but Vivian trampled every hedged excuse and barreled right into a lecture on remembering her manners. It had been an exhausting conversation.

"Ready?" Dawson asked as he started the car.

"You bet."

The club box was incredible. A balcony with a dozen plush velvet seats overlooked the field. Tall bistro tables and high-backed bar stools sprinkled the room. Fully stocked, top shelf alcohol beckoned more than the raw bar piled high with various seafood. Filet mignon kabobs, portabella mushrooms, and little puffed pastry things were served by a white-gloved wait staff. Instead of the sounds of the game, the room echoed with quiet conversation and soft music.

Dawson was polite and attentive. After obtaining a vodka tonic for himself and a much-needed glass of zinfandel for her, he introduced her, one by one, to his colleagues. It was all very put on and silly. The game had yet to start, but these people might as well have been at a bar, for all they seemed to care about the sport.

"Are you enjoying yourself?" he asked, close to her ear, as she took a bite of beef from a skewer.

She chewed and nodded, covering her mouth with her fingers. "This is nice."

Shifting, he met her eyes and smiled. "I'm glad you like it." Something hid in his gaze, something she didn't want to decipher.

"Here, try this. They're decadent."

She eyed the pastry he offered. Her hands were filled with a kabob and wine.

"Open," he whispered.

She looked around and back at him to see if he was joking. Nope. Dead serious *and* a little creepy. He edged the pastry closer to her lips, and she reflexively opened.

"Mmm," she said with questionable conviction. Did he think she was a helpless baby bird? Or maybe she was closer to a momma bird because the idea of being hand-fed in public made her want to regurgitate.

When was this game starting?

She desperately needed a distraction and decided—*tonight*—she was a baseball fanatic. *Go, team! Who's playing?*

Holding her wine glass to her chin, she avoided any other feeding episodes. Every time he raised his fingers with a piece of food, she took a long sip. She was getting buzzed, but maybe that was for the best.

"You have a spot of raspberry on your lip."

Her napkin was gone, but there were more at the bar. He clasped her wrist. "Allow me."

Mayday! Arching back, her eyes went wide as he leaned in, brushed his lips to hers, and swept away the spot of jam with his tongue.

His eyes were heavy as he pulled away. "Delicious."

"Excuse me." She placed her glass on the table. "I have to visit the ladies' room." *To throw up.*

As spacious and impressive as the box was, there weren't many places to hide. The remainder of the evening passed in a mingling dance around the room, Dawson always in her peripheral, and she always ten steps ahead, escaping before he could catch her. She never did get a chance to relax and watch the game.

Once they were in the car, he drove with his hand on her knee again, and she mentally searched for the courage to ask him to stop touching her, but the words never made it past her lips. She was completely irritated by her debilitating shyness in situations like this.

"Would you like to come to my place for a drink?"

"Uh," she stalled. "I have to be up early for work in the morning."

He didn't make a verbal response but gave her knee an affectionate squeeze as he took the off exit toward Upper New Castle.

Almost home.

When they pulled into Kat's driveway, he shut off the car and was out the door before she could say goodnight. Her door opened. "At least let me walk you to the door."

"Oh, you don't have to."

"I insist."

Eyes on the ground, she pulled her house keys from her purse and inserted them in the lock. Without asking, he turned her body and kissed her. A startled sound escaped her throat, and she was pretty sure he misinterpreted it as excitement.

Firm lips pressed against hers as his hands pulled her hips. "Dawson," she broke the kiss.

"Katherine." His tongue pressed into her mouth

as he adjusted his stance, forcing her to take a step back. The cold door pressed against her shoulders.

Fuck, fuck, fuck.

She tried to deter him. His mouth moved to her throat in an aggressive pull of soft flesh. "Dawson —" His hand cupped her boob.

What. The. Fuck.

Hot breath teased her ear, sending chills down her body in the most unpleasant way. "Dawson, stop—"

"Shh..." His other hand grazed her bottom, continuing downward to the hem of her dress, which he slowly lifted.

Okay, that's it!

She shifted away, but the door gave her little space to move. Her hand gripped his wrist closest to her chest. "Dawson, you have to stop."

Breathing heavily with booze on his breath, his gaze rested on hers, unfocused and hooded with desire. Her dress fluttered out of his grip, but his hand still cupped her breast.

Breasts were a funny thing after having children. It took a lot of special attention to remind her that they were actually an erogenous part of the body. He might as well be fondling her elbow for the lack of skill he applied.

"Spend the night with me, Katherine." Boozy breath fanned her cheek. "Tell me you don't want to. Tell me you don't miss having a man in your bed."

I don't want to. "I can't."

"Come on, Katherine, you want this. I know you do."

"Really, Dawson," she said, trying to sidle herself out of his hold. "I can't. Let's just say goodnight and not spoil the evening."

"You know your pussy's wet right now."

Okay! Time to go home, buddy! She stopped trying to be polite, broke his hold with a stern shove of her fingers against his. "I think you've had too much to drink, Dawson. Go home before things end badly."

His stance shifted from relaxed to tense. Finally registering that he wasn't getting anything from her, he shot her a derisive sneer. "You know, if you're going to play the chaste virgin, you probably shouldn't talk about your kid so much." He looked in her eyes and enunciated, *"Mom."*

She stiffened. "Wow, drunk *and* an asshole. Goodnight, Mr. Price." She grabbed for the doorknob as he swatted her wrist away and roughly pushed her against the cold surface, his larger body pinning her in place. She gasped, heart thundering as her brain tried to process what the hell was happening.

He twisted her wrist behind her back at a sharp angle, and her eyes watered. "Smart mouth for such a prude. You think you're better than me, Katherine?" The cramped position had her chin angled uncomfortably, her breasts crushed against the door. His grip tightened, forcing her to whimper and rise to her toes. "What makes you so fucking special, huh?"

He jerked her, and a panicked sound left her throat. *Scream. Scream!* "I'll scream," she threatened in a weak voice.

He snaked his other arm between the door and her abdomen. "No, you won't." The material of her dress bunched in his fist.

This is not happening! Tears blurred her vision. She opened her mouth to scream, but all that escaped was a croaked plea. "Stop."

He roughly squeezed her thigh, and she cried, fearing how far he would take this. Her neck twisted, eyes searching through the blurred darkness for Tyson's house. The windows were pitch black. No car in the driveway. Without Tyson there, true terror took over, and she began to shake violently.

"You're not special. You're the opposite of special. Your own family doesn't even want you. Your mother practically was selling you off to the highest bidder."

Words slipped out in a panicked sob, "Please stop—"

"*Shut up!*" Her face jostled against the door as he shoved her. "I would've been nice to you, Katherine. But on second thought, what do I need with someone else's damaged goods? You're probably as loose as an old glove anyway."

Something broke inside of her. He was going to do whatever he wanted, and her mother would continue to plead for his time. Maybe Vivian knew this was the sort of man he was and thought this was what she deserved. Done, she swallowed back her hurt and let her anger free.

Gritting her teeth, she growled, "Fuck. You." Her elbow jabbed into his side with as much force as she could muster. The shock was enough for him to slacken his grip on her wrist. Twisting, she shoved him with both hands knocking him back a step. *"Don't touch me!"*

Pivoting, she frantically jammed her key still hanging in the lock all the way over. The door opened, and her purse slipped out of her hand. Ignoring the spilled bag, she rushed into her home and slammed the door, immediately twisting the deadbolt into place. "Get off my property before I call the police!" she shouted over her roaring heartbeat. Her ribs rattled like wind chimes, she was trembling so fiercely.

"You're a fucking charity case," he yelled. "Your mom's better off campaigning pedigrees. I'm out of here."

Shutting her eyes, she pressed her forehead to the door. Lights glinted across the windows as tires squealed.

I hope you crash.

Positive he was gone, she unlatched the door with trembling fingers and scooped up her spilled belongings.

Shutting the door, she relocked it and flicked off the porch lights. Her back slid down the wall until she landed on the floor, her entire body convulsing with adrenaline.

Her mind refused to replay her evening as if unconsciously defending her sanity. Soft prattles of raindrops hitting the windows captured her attention as thunder rumbled somewhere in the distance. The glass flashed white as lightning streaked the sky, and she flinched.

Numb, she forced her body off the floor and stared out the window. Wind whistled against the glass as her flag out front flapped wildly, snapping tight like a sail. Hand on the knob, she unlocked the deadbolt, and she stepped onto the porch. A gust of wind tore through her yard, chilling her thighs as her dress whipped in the breeze.

She turned to the left. Tyson still wasn't there. Hair twirled and took flight around her face as she eased into the rocking chair. The vacant chair beside her creaked and rocked on its own as wind chimes sang chaotically in the distance, and soft drops fattened and pelted the leaves. The sky rumbled like a stampede of horses racing on the clouds.

She shut her eyes and breathed in the damp scent of hot, spring rain. The storm was a comfort, its strength and power a reminder that there was always something bigger out there, bigger than her, bigger than bullies.

A glow bloomed at the corner, and Tyson's headlights sliced through the puddles as he pulled slowly down the street, bringing a sense of calm she desperately needed. Her skin tingled as chills crested her shoulders, and understanding took shape. She loved him. It was that simple.

She stood, but he wouldn't see her through the rain. Opening the door to her house, she reached a hand in and quickly flicked on the porch light. He was standing by his car, in the rain, looking right at her. Time stood still as his presence grounded her.

Her chest lifted as her breath quickened. She stepped into the storm, and the sopping ground splashed her bare legs as her clothing dampened and her body shivered.

Tyson.

The mere thought of him, his scent, his strength, his voice jerked her body into motion as she shot into a dead run. "Tyson!"

Water doused her hair and saturated the thin material of her dress. Time moved in slow motion. The sky lit above as a bang of thunder rent the air.

Her name echoed over the roar of pouring rain as he raced toward her. "Kat?" She heard the worry in his voice, saw the panic in his step, but her voice could only form one word.

"Tyson!" She barreled toward him, propelling off the ground at the last second as she crashed into his strong hold. Lifting her feet, she locked her legs around his waist as her slick arms wrapped tight around his neck, and she sealed her lips to his. He was so warm. She sobbed against his mouth, never before more grateful to see him.

"Are you okay?" He frantically brushed her wet hair away from her face.

"I'm sorry," she cried, kissing down his jaw.

"Sorry for what?"

"Dawson. He's such a jerk. I should have never gone out with him."

His body tensed. Wedging his fingers under her arms, he eased her away from his chest. She blinked as hard drops stung her face. Those full lashes lining his eyes spiked, so long tiny droplets clung to the edge of each point like a diamond. His eyes searched her face. "What happened?"

Shaking her head, her voice challenged the pounding rain. "I want you, Tyson. I just want you."

His nostrils flared as something possessive

flashed in his dark eyes. Jerking her chest to his, his mouth crashed down on hers. She kissed him with everything she had, gave him all of her passion, showed him every bit of her desire.

His hands gripped her ass, anchoring her to his body as his arousal dug into her sex, and she ground her body against his. Breaking the kiss, he held her tight and walked quickly through the rain. It was louder beneath her porch, drops pelting the gutters and beating on the roof.

He pivoted, and his lips were on her again. He lowered her to sit on the banister and stepped into the space between her thighs. His mouth worked from the corner of her lips, down the column of her throat. He paid homage to that sweet spot at the curve of her shoulder and licked along the wing of her collarbone before losing himself in the valley of her breasts.

The strap over her dress was yanked down her arm. Her wet clothing peeled back from her skin. She shivered as his heated mouth closed over the tip of her tight nipple. She arched back and moaned.

Open palmed fingers splayed against her spine as his other hand twisted in her hair. Teeth scraped to her jaw in a soft bite, nibbled, driving her crazy with those teasing kisses as his hand shifted to her breast.

His mouth found hers as she linked her hands behind his neck. The bulge of his arousal settled directly against her sex as he rocked forward. Tight waves of heat pulled low in her body as the friction built. His hips snapped forward, harder and faster. Pressure built. Teeth nibbled. Fingers pinched and plucked, and then she broke—he made her come without even penetrating.

His brow pressed to her chest as his breath beat against her damp flesh. "That's it, kitten. I got you. Give over to me."

She trembled and chills raced over her wet skin as the muscles in her calves slowly unlocked. His mouth found hers, and as he kissed her deeply, his touch gentled. Hands coasted over her body, soothing and lightly petting. The scent of Tyson and damp earth filled her lungs as he tenderly pulled away and looked into her eyes.

She reached for the top of her dress twisted around her ribs.

"Leave it." Pulling her head to his shoulder, he kissed the top of her hair. Fingers trailed down her spine as his heartbeat pounded in her ear. "Tell me why he's a jerk."

She didn't want to think about how rough her night had actually been. "I don't want to talk about it."

A grunt rumbled in his throat, but he didn't press her on the subject. He held her in silence as the rain slowed to a gentle prattle.

"I'm not very good at this," she admitted. "I'm probably going to mess up again."

"Sometimes things take more than one try, Kat. But if it's worth having and you want it bad enough, you don't stop trying until you get it right."

"I want to keep trying."

He kissed her temple. "I'm glad, kitten."

She shut her eyes and curled deeper into the warmth of his chest. "What happens now?"

He sighed. "Well, if I'd known this was going to happen, I would've planned my week differently."

She eased back and looked at him. "What does that mean?"

"I have to go to Washington tomorrow to break ground on a job. I won't be back until late Friday night."

Disappointment flooded her. "Oh."

"But you can call me."

She smiled. "You'll have to give me your phone number. What kind of job is it?"

"A client's having a second home built. We just finalized the paperwork last week."

"Will you be going there a lot?" She just got him and didn't want to let him go.

"On and off. More so in the beginning and the end, but I'll assign a foreman to oversee most of it. But we'll have the weekends."

Her gaze met his. "Then maybe we should start thinking about that date you promised."

Chapter 15

AFTER A LONG WEEK of jitters and anticipation, Saturday was finally here. As Kat, Mia, and Jade turned the corner, the sound of a lawn-mower had her heart jumping into overdrive. Jade sent her a sidelong glance.

"Momma, Tyson's back!" Mia cheered. "Hi, Tyson!"

The mower silenced as they paused at the edge of his property. He wore work boots, jeans, and a bandana—but no shirt. Removing his canvas gloves, he clapped them against his thigh and smiled, stealing her breath. Snippets of grass misted in his wake as he sauntered toward them. "Hello, ladies."

Pent-up tension eased in a rush as she met his gaze. God, she'd missed him. "Hi." It was difficult not to throw her arms around him, but she had to be mindful of Mia.

"We went to a birthday party!" Mia said by way of greeting.

"Did you?" He crouched to her level. "And whose birthday was it?"

"Dr. Stevens'. I made the cake!"

"Oh, well then, I bet it was delicious. Did you save me a piece?"

Mia looked at Kat, and she shook her head. "We forgot," Mia apologized.

Tyson dramatically pouted. Trixie barked from the backyard, and her guilt vanished as she ran after the dog.

"Nice party?" Tyson asked as he stood up.

Her stomach did a cartwheel as she mutely nodded.

"The party was okay," Jade answered since Kat had lost her ability to speak in more than juvenile twitters and giggles. "It was your run of the mill, sixty-eight year old's birthday bash—amateur beer pong tourney, topless women in hot tubs, keg stands at every corner—you know what it's like at those senior citizen shindigs. I'll tell you, that Mrs. Bradshaw can really throw back the shots."

He laughed. "Typical." His smiling eyes turned to her. "And what are your plans tonight, Kat?"

Gaze drilled into hers, full of dark secrets and intentions, she could easily agree to anything he asked. "Just hanging out at home."

"That so?" His slow, intense regard was a weighted caress. "How'd you like to have dinner with me?"

Like a dip of a rollercoaster, her belly whooshed as every butterfly spun into a summersault. "I'd love to, but it would have to be someplace Mia can go."

"I'm free tonight," Jade chimed in. "Mia and I can have another sleepover."

A slow, satisfied grin worked over Tyson's face. "Now see that. What a nice friend. Thanks, Jade. I'll pick you up at seven."

She smiled tightly, trying not to appear too anxious. "Okay."

~

At seven o'clock sharp, there was a soft knock at the door. Kat didn't know where they were going, so she wore black capris and a white halter-top and dressed it up with strappy sandals. When she opened the door, Tyson held a bouquet of lavender roses, but her eyes were more fixated on the forest green suit jacket he wore over a fitted, black t-shirt.

"Good evening, beautiful." That deep, husky voice rolled through her, sending quivers to the depths of her belly.

A seductive half-smile highlighted his dimple as he stepped through the door and brushed a soft kiss across her lips. Her panties were about to spontaneously combust.

"These are for you," he whispered against her mouth.

Pulling in a long, slow breath, she steadied her nerves and poorly disguised the effect he was having on her. He smelled magnificent. Thrills of anticipation rocked her composure. She'd never survive this man.

Voice hoarse, she whispered, "Thank you." She spotted the flowers from Dawson, still fresh in a vase on her kitchen table. "Let me put these in some water."

She picked up Dawson's flowers, walked to the trashcan, and dumped them into the container without ceremony. Tyson chucked and crossed his arms in a casual pose, observing her as she arranged the *new* roses.

Pleased, she replaced the vase on the table. "Am I dressed okay? I didn't know where we were going."

"You look perfect. We're going to a quiet little place nearby."

She grabbed her purse and shut out the lights. He held her hand as they walked toward his driveway. It was a path she'd taken a thousand times, but never with such meaning behind each step.

"I hope you're hungry," he said as they passed his driveway.

"We're eating here?"

"Do you mind? It was my first chance to really cook in my kitchen." He opened the door, and mouthwatering aromas greeted them.

"You cook?"

Deep cherry woodwork and spacious granite countertops were set in soft lighting. Lots of natural materials and autumnal tones blended with brushed copper accents. The lights were dimmed, and a female blues singer vocalized sultry classics from hidden speakers throughout the house.

Removing her purse, he placed it on the counter. "I do all right. Come with me."

Her breath left in a whoosh as they entered the dining room. The long, formal table was draped in white linen and set with red glass dishes that glowed amber in the candlelight. A bottle of Champagne chilled in a silver ice bucket next to two ruby stemmed champagne flutes.

Holy crap. Remember this because it's doubtful anyone will ever do something this romantic for you again.

"Are you impressed?"

She was breathless. "Very."

He pulled out her chair and poured champagne. "I have to check on something in the kitchen. Make yourself comfortable."

Her cheeks heated as she grinned at the incredible presentation, unsure if she'd ever seen something so spectacular. Sure, her mother was the queen of overdone dinner parties, but this was different. This was intimate and thoughtful, and—dear lord, if he didn't return soon, she was going to cry like a big ninny.

The kitchen door swung open as he returned with two plates. "I thought we'd start with salad."

Colorful lettuce leaves mixed with cranberries, walnuts, pear wedges, and crumbles of cheese. She laid her napkin, thinking the salad was a meal in itself. "There's more?"

"There's more. Dig in."

As they ate, she asked him about the house, and he described some of the amenities added during the remodeling, such as his built-in sound system and the heated tile floor in the master bath. It seemed Tyson was a man who enjoyed life's comforts.

After the salad, he brought out two red martini glasses filled with a raspberry sorbet he called an intermezzo. It was cool and refreshing and tickled her tongue. The length he'd gone to prepare such fine touches swiftly overwhelmed her.

The main course was lobster tail nestled against a plump cut of filet mignon. She stared at him.

"What?" he laughed, sitting down.

She shook her head. "You're unbelievable. You did all of this yourself?"

He actually blushed. "Well, I called my sister about thirty times this afternoon, but I did all the work myself."

She shook her head. "Tyson... This is the nicest thing anyone's ever done for me."

He squeezed her hand. "Well, that, Kitten, is a pity. You're always going out of your way to put other people's comforts before your own. You deserve to be treated more often."

She was completely overwhelmed by the emotions welling in her heart. She hadn't prepared for this. "You're gonna make me cry. And I think you've seen me do that enough."

He laughed. "I'm okay with tears of happiness. It's the other sort that rips me up. Here, taste the lobster. Dip it in this. I got the recipe from a chef I designed a kitchen for last year."

The lobster, like everything else, was out of this world. By the time she finished half her entree, she was ready to burst.

"I still have one more thing," he said as he disappeared into the kitchen, returning a moment later with a glass dish.

"What are these?" She breathed in the sweet fragrance. Maybe she wasn't full.

"They're baked pears. I soak them in rum and

bake them in a caramelized brandy sauce. It's an old family recipe. My great-great-grandfather used to work for a family that owned a plantation and grew apples and pears. Every year, they would steal some of the bruised fruit that fell out of the bushels and put them in jars of alcohol. During the holidays, they'd pull out the jars, eat the pears, and get piss drunk." He laughed.

She tasted a piece of the warm fruit and moaned in appreciation. The sweet brown sugar complemented the spiced flavor of rum as a trace of cloves hit her tongue. The effect of the alcohol-saturated dessert was slow but potent, leaving her quite relaxed.

"Where do your parents live?" he asked, settling back in his chair.

She sipped her champagne, the bubbles tickling her like a coming sneeze. "Parkside. When I was little, we had a regular house, but after my dad's first term as Mayor, we moved into a much bigger home."

"How long has he held a position in office?"

"He's always been involved in politics. Over the years, he just moved up the ladder one election at a time."

His gaze was soft, never seeming distracted. He had great communication skills, the ability to hold a person's eye contact without appearing to stare. "You don't sound all that impressed with his success."

She shrugged. "My dad and I aren't that close. Since Mia, he barely speaks beyond common courtesies. We have a very superficial relationship."

Realizing her father wasn't a topic she cared to discuss, he moved on to a topic that would put her at ease. "Mia's an incredible kid. She was hilarious when we were painting the doghouse. She had all sorts of advice for me."

Kat laughed. That was her daughter. "Oh, I'm sure she did. Mia's a self-proclaimed expert on all things."

"You know," he said with a smirk. "She told me her mother's an artist too."

Her cheeks heated. "No."

"No?" His dimple winked. "I heard you used to paint portraits."

Painting was a pastime she rarely had time to enjoy anymore. She'd all but forgotten her talent. Her art supplies sat, neglected in a dark corner of her bedroom closet, and she should probably throw them away. She wistfully sighed. "I used to paint, but since having Mia, I really haven't had the time. I don't even know if I still could. I'm extremely rusty."

"You know, in the newspaper, I saw the community center's offering a watercolor class. It's only ten dollars because volunteers are running the program."

The temptation of taking up the old, cathartic hobby was temping. And ten dollars wasn't much. "I didn't know that. When?"

"It starts next week. I think it's a three-week summer program, and there's a second series of classes in the fall. You should do it. It's only one night a week."

She weighed the pros and cons in her head. "It

would be tough to arrange a sitter on such short notice. I have a feeling my Mom isn't really happy with me right now."

"I could watch Mia."

"No…" There really wasn't any reason why he couldn't. Kat trusted him. Mia adored him. But she didn't want to impose.

"Why not? It would be fun. The classes are only two hours. You'd get some time to yourself, and Mia could advise me on life."

Kat laughed. "Two hours with a three-year-old isn't as easy as it sounds."

"I know, but I think I'm up for the challenge. Come on, Kat, do something for yourself. Take the class. It's only ten bucks and only three weeks."

She mentally calculated her finances. She had some old books she could trade in at the used bookstore. They would probably add up to ten dollars. Was it really that complicated? Her teeth pressed into her lower lip, and she smiled. "Okay."

He grinned. "That's my girl."

His girl.

They sipped champagne, and the conversation turned to family. "Tell me about your sisters," she said.

A fond expression crossed his face. "Which one?"

His youngest sister had passed away. Maybe she shouldn't have asked about his family. "We don't have to talk about them if you don't want to."

"No, it's okay. I don't mind." He took a deep breath and leaned back, his expression thoughtful. "Phia and I were closest. I'm closer in age to Gloria, but she always moved with a different crowd. Sophia was more like my little sidekick. She followed me around when I was a teenager and used to drive me nuts."

He gave a sad smile. "When she became an adult, we really got close. She'd come over to my apartment every Sunday at the butt crack of dawn to drag my ass out of bed to go to some flea market in the middle of nowhere. She always found these odd, tucked away markets, the kind that looked like they came in with a band of gypsies the night before."

"I love places like that."

He sighed. "I never did, but I sort of miss them now. We'd browse the booths for hours but never really buy anything. She usually found some piece of junk she *needed* to have. Her apartment had more decorations than a Christmas tree."

"She sounds interesting. Eccentric."

"She was that. She was good, you know? Never really got mad at anybody, had a way of telling you how it is without being too pushy. She was a cool girl. I'm sorry she never got to have children or a husband. She would have been a great mother and wife." His thumb glided up the side of his glass, his gaze seeming to be stuck on a distant memory only he could see. "I miss her."

Her chest tightened with vicarious grief. His voice had gone hoarse as a glassy sheen of tears glazed his eyes. She leaned forward and gently clasped his hand. "I'm sorry you lost her."

He nodded and cleared his throat. "Gloria is completely different. She's like a thundercloud, always moving, loud, moods powerful enough to clear out a room. You'll see when you meet her. People either love her or hate her."

It struck her as odd that they might know she existed. "Does your family know about me?"

"I've talked to Gloria and my mom about you," he said, his cheeks darkening.

"And what did you tell them?" Insane curiosity had her sitting a little straighter.

"I told them I had my eye on a hot little woman nextdoor."

She giggled. "No, you didn't."

"Sure, I did."

"What did they say?"

He laughed. "My momma told me it was only a matter of time before you realized what a catch I am. Gloria... She told me I was an idiot, but in her own twisted way, she said it with love and wished me luck."

The conversation turned to work. He inquired about her job and other parts of her life. She loved hearing how he started Adams Construction with only a thousand dollars in his bank account and the determination of a thousand men in his heart.

She told him about the night she had Mia and how hard she fought to keep her, the promises she made to always protect her, and how instantly and completely she fell in love when she held her that first time. Conversation flowed as if they'd known each other for years.

"Do you dance?" he asked.

"Only in my kitchen when no one's looking."

"Dance with me." He smoothly pulled her to her feet, fitting her into his hold.

They swayed as the singer crooned words of love accompanied by soft piano and the plunking melody of fingers scraping along the strings of an acoustic guitar. It was warm, wrapped in the lyrical, bluesy mood of the song and Tyson's arms.

Her eyes closed as she leaned into him. "This is nice."

They leisurely rocked back and forth, his fluid baritone sometimes mixing with the words. *Peace.*

As the song ended, he continued to hold her. Her fingertips traced slow, lazy circles over his lower back. She was getting braver when it came to touching him. They held each other, swaying in the comfortable silence.

"Stay with me tonight?"

Easing back to look in his eyes, the answer came to her with little hesitance. "I'd love to."

Chapter 16

TYSON LED her up the stairs, and she was sure her palm was sweating. They walked through the house in silence. When they reached his bedroom, he released her hand and held the door. Taking a deep breath, she entered.

The snick of the latch reverberated in her bones. Her heart raced. She was already out of breath yet not moving at all. Blurred visions of the unknown flashed through her mind.

"You okay?" he softly asked as he switched on the bedside lamp.

"Mmm-hm." She toed off her shoes and neatly set them by the door. The plush carpet tickled her toes.

The furniture was masculine but not lacking in detail. She slowly walked to the side of the bed as he silently watched her.

He placed his shoes by the door as well, and she liked the way they looked sitting next to hers. She wondered if he always put them there or if he'd done it because she had. Maybe he was nervous too. He moved to the other side of the bed and smiled.

"I'm scared," she whispered.

"We don't have to do anything you don't want to do, Kat."

She wasn't backing out. Her hands swept below her hair to the tie of her shirt. Her fingers were practically useless, she was shaking so badly. Finally, the fabric fell away.

His chest rose as his eyes widened. "Don't stop," he whispered.

With a steadying breath, she undid the button of her pants and slid down the zipper, each ticking tooth ratcheting up her arousal a little more. Bending at the waist, she pushed her top and pants to her ankles and stepped out of the material. *Might as well go for the gold.* Her thumbs slid under the string of her panties and removed them as well.

Her breath echoed in her ears. She shut her eyes. *Stand up. He's going to see you anyway.*

A slow exhale passed her lips as she unfolded her body. His Adam's apple bobbed under the smooth skin of his throat as he swallowed. Unblinking, dark eyes moved as his gaze traveled from head to toe. No one, not even her doctors, had ever seen her so bare.

"Now you," she rasped.

He crossed his arms at his belly and pulled his shirt over his head, revealing his sculpted abdomen and chest. Her self-esteem always stumbled whenever she saw his body.

His hands went to his belt as he slid the leather through the catch. Her attention locked on his fingers as they slowly slid down the zipper. Bending gracefully, he returned to his full height utterly and completely naked. He was magnificent. Cut like a chiseled statue.

His erection proudly stood, dark and full. She didn't remember a man's body being so...intimidating. She knew in that moment there'd be no comparison between this time and her first.

He pulled back the duvet, exposing ivory satin sheets. She sucked in a breath as a terrible thought occurred to her. "Tyson, I don't have anything with me."

"Don't worry. I have something. We'll be safe. I'd never do anything that put you in jeopardy, Kat."

As he walked around the bed, her body tightened. His lashes lowered as his hand trailed over her hip, up and around the gentle swell of her breast. Stepping closer, he pressed his mouth to hers in a slow, devastating kiss.

The heat of his cock scorched her belly as his arms wrapped around her back, cocooning her in his warmth. His mouth slowly pulled from hers, and she went up on her toes, not wanting the moment to end.

An amused chuckle rumbled from his chest. "Come on."

He returned to the other side of the bed and dimmed the light. They slid onto the bed, and cool satin whispered over her skin as he drew the sheet over their legs.

He pulled her into his arms. "You still okay?"

She blew out a shaky breath. "Yes."

"Good." His lips found hers, and she sighed as

he eased her onto her back. His mouth moved over hers with slow, drugging, seductive strokes. His solid body pressed into her pliable form, reminding her how strong he was. Skin rasped against skin as his fingers gently curved around her hip.

His mouth left hers in a gentle exploration toward her breasts. He kneeled between her thighs, his body slightly lifting. His lips pulled at her nipples as a fiery heat built inside of her. Her fingers pressed into his shoulders, her knees tightening at his sides. "You're so beautiful, Kat," he rasped. "You haunt my thoughts. I find myself constantly daydreaming about your sweet breasts and your plump little ass and all the ways I can make you come. I want to make you feel like you've never felt before."

Maybe it was the alcohol, but at that moment, that sounded perfect to her. He entwined his fingers with hers as his arousal grazed her sex. She momentarily stiffened until his lips slowly ran back and forth over her hardened nipple.

"S'okay, baby. Relax."

Breathing out, she forced her body to loosen. His warm mouth closed over her nipple, and pleasure shot through her body. She arched into him, his heavy erection pushing between her thighs.

Her heart raced. "Ty?"

His mouth kissed and suckled along her jaw. "Yes?"

"Should we...Should you..." Her brain and mouth were not communicating. "Condom?"

His face lifted from the curve of her shoulder, eyes drowsy. "We're not there yet. There's no rush, kitten. Do you want me to stop?"

"No," she answered quickly. "I just...wanna be safe. If I got..."

The fear of another unplanned pregnancy was almost enough to completely extinguish her desire. She wanted this. But she couldn't afford another child.

"I got you. Don't worry. I won't do anything without using one. Trust me. I promise I won't forget."

His words relieved her, and she exhaled as his hand trailed down her belly and over her hip to her swollen folds. Thighs parting, a wide finger slid deep into her core. She sighed as his thumb teased, intensifying her pleasure.

Her breath quickened as his strokes intensified. His teeth nipped at her curves as he added another finger and moved his hand deeper, in and out, stretching her. She writhed against him as the pressure built, and she crested over a precipice of sensation.

"Come for me, kitten," he rasped against her nipple as she shattered.

Her muscles locked as every nerve in her body splintered outward. The whisper of a wrapper tearing vaguely registered. Still reveling in the force of her orgasm, she jerked with sensitivity when his hands pressed her thighs farther apart.

The broad head of his erection nudged at her opening, the tip easing into her small channel. Her mind struggled to remain present as so many sensations assaulted her.

"Put your arms around my neck," he said, keeping his touch tender and paced.

Her hands slid over his shoulders. Taking

shallow dips, he inched his hips closer, each thrust eased by her arousal. "Tyson," she whimpered. Groggy from her orgasm, body slick, mind slow, she tensed.

"You can take me, Kat. Just breathe."

Taking a deep breath, she trembled. There was such a difference between her first time and this time. Why had she only considered the emotional differences? He pressed further, and she gasped. He pulled back, and the pressure eased.

Fingers grazed her clit as the blunt end of his cock worked deeper into her core. The dual stimulation relaxed her body. The pressure built, as did her arousal, as he slowly, fluidly thrust. Each plunge a bit deeper and unexpected, a bit more desired.

Her mind shied from the overwhelming connection. Body to body gazes locked, heartbeat to heartbeat, he pushed forward to the hilt, and she gasped. Everything stilled.

His voice was strained as his focus rested on her, eyes heavy with desire. "I've wanted to be in this moment for so long."

The heaviness transcended from throbbing need to pleasure as she wrapped her legs around his hips. "Tyson."

Rising, his lips brushed hers as he drew back and thrust, his strokes steady and hard. The beating of her heart echoed in her ears, reverberated in her sex. The tempo of their bodies coming together, flesh against flesh, fueled her need.

Arching, she rocked her hips, matching his rhythm. His whispered words of encouragement doubled her confidence. Hands, no longer passive, moved to his strong back as she clung to him, wanting more. He moved his hips harder, rotating and thrusting faster until she cried out in pleasure.

"That's it, kitten. Don't be shy with me. Let me hear you. Let me feel you let go." His mouth pulled at her collarbone as he softly spoke. "Feel the way your body grips mine? Perfect. There isn't anything about your body I don't love." He drove deep and arched back, moaning deep.

The pleasure filled hidden parts of her soul that had been empty for so long. Her gaze never left him. She was mesmerized. Her heart swelled as blissful emotion threatened her composure. His desire, tenderness, and composure overwhelmed her senses.

His muscles tightened as her body constricted around him, milking him. Her cries danced with his deeper moans as his body pulsed. He kissed her with unparalleled passion. Timidity gone, she met his kiss with unrefined passion, gasping and shivering from so many intense awakenings.

His mouth tore from hers as his arms slid beneath her, lifting her to him. She gripped his slick shoulders, pressing her nails into corded muscle. She hadn't expected it to be this powerful, so amplified compared to everything she knew, so real.

Tender, lingering kisses accompanied the occasional shiver of lingering pleasure mixed with the intimate moment. Slowly, he shifted, and her sensitive body noted every place his touch withdrew. Shutting her eyes, she waited for him to come back to her, savoring the many ways she felt altered, not just physically but emotionally.

He lay back down and pulled her body to the crook of his arm. Cool satin settled over her limbs. Emotion exploded inside of her, and she fought to hold it in with all her might. She was, without a doubt, in love with him.

~

They sat in Tyson's bathtub, which was three times the size of Kat's.

"You painted your toenails," Ty said.

"Anything to make them look less like Fred Flintstone's," she joked, wiggling them in his face.

"I never realized Fred had such sexy feet." He laughed and bit her big toe.

She yelped, splashing water along the porcelain walls. Settling, she smiled. "This is nice, Tyson. You really do extraordinary work."

"This room wasn't half as beautiful until you stepped into it."

Snorting, she rolled her eyes. "Cheesy, but I like it."

His fingers massaged her instep. "What are you doing today?"

"Well, Jade's dropping off Mia around eight, and then my mom's picking her up at nine. I have to go to the market and—Oh! That reminds me. How much do I owe you for filling up my tank last week?"

"Don't worry about it."

"Tyson—"

"Kat, I said don't worry about it. You're my girl. I'm allowed to pay for your gas if I want."

Her cheeks heated under the already humid air. "Is that what I am?"

"Yes," he firmly answered. "And that means we need to address a few things."

"Such as?"

"Such as no more going out with other men. I told you I can be patient, but I don't share what's mine. So you can tell your mother's friends to take a hike."

"Already taken care of."

He raised a brow. "Are you sure?"

"He's a prick." There was no point in dredging up thoughts of Dawson on such a perfect morning. She refused to waste another thought on that asshole.

"And what did he do that made you reach that conclusion?" His tone was calm, but his eyes were sharp.

"Let's not talk about him."

"Why don't you want to tell me?"

"Why does it matter?"

"Did he do something or say something disrespectful to you?"

His defensive tone sent a small thrill skipping through her. The idea that he wanted to protect her was very appealing. As fun as it would be to see Dawson get his ass handed to him, she didn't need the drama. "Yes and yes. Now let's drop it." She lifted herself out of the water and reached for a towel.

"Why won't you tell me, Kat?"

"I said drop it, Ty."

He became quiet as she twisted the towel around her. "What's that smirk?"

"I like when you call me Ty."

"You're a dork." She laughed and left the bathroom.

"I'm still gonna kick that prick's ass!" he shouted.

She loved him. The juvenile giddiness that accompanied the thought was utterly ridiculous, but no one needed to know what was going on in her head. Thank God for that because it was a parade of mental hearts, stars, and curly little love doodles.

Kat and Tyson.

Tyson heart Kat.

Mrs. Tyson Adams.

Okay, that was going a little too far.

...Katherine Adams.

Stop it.

Shutting the swoony thoughts away, she focused on getting dressed. Her breath quickened as he entered the room with a damp towel slung low around his hips. *I want to bite that hip.* "I guess you don't have a blow dryer?"

"Actually, I do. I have one in the truck for drying Spackle. Do you want it?"

"Nah, I'll pull my hair up when I get home." She slipped her feet into her shoes and quickly made the bed.

"You don't have to do that."

"It's okay." She fluffed the pillows and put them back along the headboard—this time on an angle. "It would bother me all day if I left it. It's easier to just ignore me and my compulsions. You're lucky I didn't sneak away in the middle of the night to do the dishes still sitting in the sink.

I'm trying to convince myself you have a house-keeper that takes care of things, but I know they're really down there, coagulating and getting all crusty and gross."

He froze, one arm in his shirt and the other out.

"What?"

"Coagulating?"

"Yes, coagulating, congealing into thick goop." His eyes rolled as if she was crazy, and she scoffed. "You know I can see you? It's a word! I'm not crazy."

"Maybe a little," he teased under his breath as he continued to get dressed.

"I heard that!"

At the door, he lightly kissed her on the lips and asked, "Can we grocery shop together? I have some things I need to get."

The thought of spending the day doing mundane chores with him made her all warm and squishy inside. "Okay. Why don't you come by around ten, and we'll go?"

"Ah, I still don't get to meet your mom."

Why would anyone want to? "Trust me. I'm doing you a favor. Vivian D'Angelo could make a drill sergeant piss himself."

"Nice."

"That's my mom," she laughed.

He kissed her one last time, leaving her with a sense of being lifted away on clouds. She really needed to grow up. Her feet shifted in an attempt to alleviate the ache that had returned. She considered staying a bit longer, but Vivian could be there any minute.

"Later," he promised, brushing a thumb along her jaw.

She played dumb. "Later what?"

A half-smirk drew out the dimple. His lashes lowered with cool desire. His fingertips trailed over the soft skin of her neck and sucked in a sharp breath, his other hand shifted between her legs. "I know what that look in your eye means." He added a bit of pressure.

She hummed and leaned against him, driving her body against his touch.

"You know, kitten," he said in a slow, gravelly draw. "If I wanted to, I could make you come right here in the hall. I wouldn't even need to take off your clothes."

Lips parted, panties drenched, she panted. He was right. He could make her come.

"Do you want to come, kitten?"

Holy hell.

No one—*no one*—had ever talked to her in such a tone, using such dirty words. The door pressed into her shoulders as her limbs became heavy. Hypnotized, her head lolled back as he gently caressed the base of her throat. "Tell me to make you come, kitten."

She couldn't say it. Her vocabulary was incredibly stunted when it came to actually saying sexual things out loud. His fingers pressed deeper, applying the perfect amount of pressure as her desire spread like wildfire. Thigh to thigh, shoulder to shoulder, her gaze locked on his. "Please, Ty..."

"Please, what?"

His palm continued to rub and press as her knees trembled. She whimpered, her gaze pleading.

The fingers of his other hand covered hers and brought it to the bulge of his jeans. "Feel what you do to me, Kat. I'm just as on edge as you. You do this. Just one breath of your sweet-smelling hair, or one look from those innocent eyes, and I'm hard as a pike."

Her fingers curved around the bulge, and he groaned, pressing himself into her palm. Heady, intoxicating desire flooded her veins. His breath beat at the exposed curve of her shoulder. "Fuck, Kat. You make me feel like a teenager with no control."

Well, it was good she wasn't the only one. Her hand stroked, adding pressure, and his mouth latched onto the flesh of her shoulder. Her knees quaked as he sucked on her skin, and her body tightened and pulsed under his palm. He rocked his hips with hers, riding her touch.

Her lips parted as she moaned. Her orgasm was jarring. Unexpected. Just what she needed to take the edge off. His mouth pulled at her skin as he thrust harder into her palm, pulsing under her touch.

Exhilaration rushed through her as he groaned. Their breathing was the only sound in the quiet house. Less than five minutes ago, she had been ready to walk out the door, and that quickly, he had taken her from start to finish.

"Fuck," he rasped, softly kissing her neck. "I can't believe I just did that. You're a dangerous little woman."

Chapter 17

"MOMMA!" Mia squealed as she jumped down from Jade's backseat.

"Hey, babe! Did you have fun?" Kat asked as she kissed Mia's head.

"Kiki let me sleep in her bed. We went to the bideo store and got popcorn and *Shrek* one, two, and three!"

"Wow! Are you ready to go to Grandma's? She's going to be here in a few minutes."

"Can I watch cartoons 'til she gets here?" Mia asked, bouncing in place as if riding on an invisible pogo stick, obviously all sugared up from Jade's breakfast.

"Sure." Mia raced into the house, and she looked at Jade. "Doughnuts?"

Jade handed her a coffee. "You know I don't cook." They settled in the rocking chairs. "Sooo... Any news?"

Kat rolled her eyes. "None that I can think of."

Jade smacked her palms on her thighs. "Oh, come on!"

She laughed. " Fine. Last night, while you were watching *Shrek,* I was on a private jet to Vegas. I am now Mrs. Tyson Adams. I expect you, as my best friend, to throw me a post-wedding shower and buy me a bread maker. The ceremony was Elvis theme, and I wore a sequenced jumpsuit."

"Come on," Jade impatiently pleaded. "What happened? Did you do it? Was it big?"

"Jade!"

"Well, was it?"

She took a deep breath then a long sip of her coffee. "This coffee is delicious."

"I. Will. Kill. You," Jade growled. *"Come on! Give me details!"*

"Fine." She laughed. "He picked me up at seven and brought me a dozen lavender roses."

"Nice, nice. Then what?"

"Then we left for dinner, but we didn't go to a restaurant."

"Couldn't restrain yourselves?" Jade's mouth pulled to the side and she nodded knowingly.

"No, pervert! I swear, for a girl who has sex as much as you do, you act like you haven't seen any action in years. He made dinner at his house, and it was *amazing*. The food...well, the man can cook! We drank two bottles of champagne, danced, and... he asked me to stay."

"And did you?"

She nodded.

"Oh. My. God. How was it?"

"It was incredible," she sighed. "He isn't like anyone else I've ever known."

"Well, considering your experience stops at Jeremy and Dawson the Dickhead, that isn't surprising."

"No, Jade, this is more than that. I... I think I'm in love with him."

Jade's eyes went wide, and a smile spread across her face. "Well, holy shit."

"I know," she whispered. "What do I do?"

"What do you do? Kat, honey, you enjoy it."

"I know, but what if—"

"No! I refuse to let you ruin this with the 'What If' game. You're glowing, Kat. Glow-ing! The only *if* you're allowed to consider is what if this is the best thing that ever happens to you and you screw it up worrying about the worst-case scenario. I get that you like everything to be nice and neat, but love's better than that. It's spontaneous, passionate, and messy. Be grateful you can share it with someone as nice as Tyson. And as hot!"

"He doesn't love me."

"Who says? Did you ask him?"

"No, but—"

Gravel crunched, and she turned, spotting her mother's SUV.

"Shit," Jade muttered, "To be continued."

She called Mia, who came barreling out of the house, still riding a severe sugar high. "Grandma!" They followed her to the curb.

"Hello, Mrs. D'Angelo," Jade greeted with exaggerated charm.

"Jade," Vivian coolly answered. "Katherine, what happened to your hair? You really need to visit a salon."

"Hi, Mom. Nothing happened to it. I didn't do it yet."

"Well, you shouldn't be standing out front with it looking like that. What if your neighbors saw you?"

Jade snorted, and Kat shot her a reproving look.

"I'll keep that in mind, Mom." She kissed Mia goodbye and buckled her in her car seat. "Well, I have a lot of things to do today, so I'll see you later."

Vivian's eyes narrowed, lips pursing as if sucking a lemon, likely holding back a comment, probably due to Jade's presence. God forbid Kat's friends know what kind of a mother Vivian really was.

"Goodbye, Mrs. D'Angelo," Jade sang.

"Goodbye, Jade. Katherine, I'll speak to you later."

The moment the car pulled away, Jade muttered under her breath. "Bitch."

No offense was taken. It was true, and Jade's memory was long. Kat couldn't object to that sort of loyalty. Jade was a good friend.

~

Kat pushed her cart alongside Tyson's at the local market.

"You should get these for Mia," he said, holding up a carton of patriotic sprinkled cupcakes.

"I only buy what's on the list."

He shopped with a completely different mindset than she did, rolling down each aisle, inspecting everything that caught his eye, and throwing things willy-nilly into his cart. He bought only brand names, whereas she shopped from the generic shelves and according to her coupons.

He shrugged and put the cupcakes in his cart. "Do you do something with your family for Fourth of July?"

"Not unless I'm summoned." She searched for the peanut butter that matched her coupon.

"What's the deal with your mom and dad?"

"What do you mean?" They moved on to the freezer section.

"I mean, why do you let them boss you around?" He pulled out half a dozen *Hungry Man* microwavable dinners and dropped them in his cart.

She stilled. They'd been through this, but now he seemed a little less guarded with his words. "I don't let them boss me around," she argued. "I just don't like disappointing them."

"Do you ever stop to consider if *they*'re disappointing you?"

She frowned. They were her parents. It wasn't her place to judge them. Maybe it wasn't their place to judge her either. She didn't want to talk about this. "I don't know. I'm the kid, they're the parents, it's the way things work."

She didn't like thinking about her family more than she had to. It never brought about any good feelings, and she was in a pretty good mood at the moment. No point in ruining it.

"But at what point do they accept that you're also a parent, and an adult for that matter?"

She lowered the cereal box she was holding and met his gaze. He was leading them into an emotional game of devil's advocate she wasn't in the mood to play, especially in a wide-open aisle of the grocery store.

She took a deep breath and shifted to face him fully. "I don't know, Tyson. They've always been hard to please. In their minds, what I did was unforgivable. I'm lucky they even acknowledge Mia. They didn't, for the first two months of her life. I don't have siblings and cousins like you do. They're all I've got. And if I want Mia to have family that extends beyond myself, my best friend, and a babysitter, then I have to accept them the way they are."

He gave her a sad smile that said he didn't agree, but he didn't press the issue. Leaning close, he kissed her nose. "What are we doing after this?"

"I have to stop at the library."

In the car, he sorted through the novels she'd borrowed. "*Relationships We Don't See?*" He flipped the book over and read the back blurb.

Her hands tightened on the wheel. "I got it because of Gorrum."

"Gorrum?"

She swallowed. "Mia's invisible friend. He's been staying with us for a while."

His expression lit up as he grinned. "I used to have an invisible friend."

"You did?"

"Yup. Clarence. He was a space cowboy."

She laughed. "How long did you have him?"

"I'm not sure. He was around for a good part of my childhood. I don't really remember when he left. Maybe when Sophia was born. He sort of just phased out." He put the book back in the bag. "What did the book say?"

"That imaginary friends reveal a child's fears and anxieties."

"Do you think Mia's afraid of something?"

"No."

It didn't bother her that Mia had an invisible friend. She looked at it as an expression of a vivid imagination. What did bother her was the stigma that Gorrum might represent something more, something lacking in her daughter's life. She wanted Mia to have everything she needed. That meant supplementing all the necessary emotional support. Maybe Gorrum was compensating for something Kat couldn't provide.

"One theory claimed they help children acquire social skills faster. Nothing in that book made it seem like having an invisible friend was a bad thing. And I asked Dr. Stevens about it, and he made it seem like it was a natural part of childhood. I feel a little left out that I never had one."

"Yeah, Clarence was awesome."

It wasn't a laughing matter, so she forced the bubble of laughter back down. "Could you see him?"

"No, but I knew what he looked like. He always wore space boots and a long trench coat. I don't remember his face, but that wasn't important."

"Gorrum's a purple, zebra-striped, dinosaur—that meows."

"Maybe Mia's lonely. When's Gorrum usually around?"

"Maybe you're right. He doesn't usually show up until I'm preoccupied. But then he lingers for a while." Mia once told her that Gorrum, like Mrs.

Bradshaw, was 'lergic' to Trixie, so it made sense Tyson hadn't been introduced. Heat crept up her neck. "Sometimes, we set a place for him at the table."

"You're a cool mom. My parents looked at me like I was nuts whenever I mentioned Clarence, so he usually disappeared for family things. Gloria used to purposely try to sit on him."

She did laugh at that. Listening to a successful adult reflect on their own experiences was more comforting than that dumb book had been. She decided not to worry about the Gorrum issue and let Mia's phase follow its natural course.

When they returned home, Tyson carried in her groceries. He went to his place to unload his stuff and let Trixie out. When he returned, she had the table set with peanut butter and jelly sandwiches, one for her and two for him. "Welcome to Café a' la Kat."

After lunch, she agreed to help him paint one of the spare bedrooms in his house. Being neighbors created a familiarity she didn't think most new couples shared. She never had to worry about looking her best because Tyson had already seen her at her worst. Oddly, that no longer bothered her.

"Do you want to cut in or roll?" He asked, holding up a brush and a roller.

"I'll cut in."

They worked quietly as the radio played random songs on a local station. A smile tugged at the corner of her mouth every time he sang along. He had a nice voice.

The soft squishing sound of the roller and the

bristly swipe of the brush were very soothing. She thought more about the art class he'd mentioned the night before and decided she was going to do it. "Ty?"

"Yeah, baby?"

Her heart did a little cartwheel whenever he called her that. "If you're still willing to watch Mia, I think I'm going to take that class at the community center."

The roller stopped, and he smiled at her. "What?"

Placing the roller in the tray, he slowly walked to where she sat cross-legged on the tarp covering the floor. Without taking his gaze from her, he took the paintbrush and crouched in front of her. "I'm happy you decided to do something for yourself." Leaning close, he ran a thumb over her cheek. "You have paint all over yourself."

She looked down. Little spatters of beige coated her legs, and a long smear marked the inside of her arm. "Maybe I need that painting class more than I realized."

"I think," he said as he moved the bucket of paint aside. "You look sexy, all messed up."

Her pulse quickened as he kneeled, the tarp crunching beneath his weight.

"As a matter of fact, I find myself hard-pressed not to take you right here in the middle of this mess." His gaze smoldered as he looked at her with pure, lustful intent.

A second of complete stillness stretched, and then he was on her. Mouth to mouth then he was kneeling between her thighs, bringing her to completion before taking any pleasure for himself. When he finally filled her, his strokes were hard and urgent.

He gripped her bottom, raising her off the ground and pulling her hard on his cock. His eyes darkened, his thrusts frantic, as he threw his head back and called out her name in a stream of words that added up to something in between a curse and a prayer as he came.

They gasped for air. Slowly coming back to herself, she looked to her right. "Uh-oh."

His face was buried against her shoulder as his breath teased her hair. "What's the matter?"

"We spilled the paint."

Rather than get upset, he laughed. The small bucket was on its side, the brush drowning in a river of beige. "Shit." As he withdrew, her body immediately protested. He adjusted his jeans, and paused as his gaze caught hers. "What?"

There really wasn't anything to say. She shook her head. "I've never had anything like this before."

His expression turned serious as he stepped close, his palm cupping her cheek. "Me neither. Not like this."

After a quick shower, they cleaned up the spilled paint, and Tyson set out a fresh tarp. He ordered a pizza, and they ate while they worked. She helped him wash out the brushes and seal up the paint cans.

As she was kissing him goodbye in his kitchen, her mom's car cruised past the window. "Shit," she hissed and grabbed her keys. Luckily, he didn't try to follow as she raced out the door.

When she reached the yard, her mom was frowning. When Mia disappeared into the house, her mother dropped the sweet grandmother routine. "Where were you, Katherine?"

"I was helping my neighbor paint."

"The new neighbor?"

"Yes."

"Do you think that's wise? What would the neighbors think?"

She rolled her eyes. "He *is* the neighbors, Mother."

"Well, I certainly hope you don't let him hang around here. It's not proper, a single mother entertaining such a man."

Drawing back, she crossed her arms over her chest and scoffed. "And would it be proper if Dawson Price was hanging around?"

"That's completely different. Dawson's a friend of the family."

Yeah, some friend. "Well, Tyson's a friend too."

She ached to tell Vivian what her golden boy had done, but she'd never see it from Kat's side, no matter how badly he treated her.

"Think about your choices, Katherine. You don't need more trouble."

Shifting closer to the house and away from her mother, she huffed. "He's not trouble, Mom. I have to go. Mia needs a bath."

She said nothing, but Vivian's eyes told plenty about her disapproval. It wasn't her life, and based on Kat's past, any consequences she created would only be hers to bear.

Chapter 18

TY WATCHED KAT PULL AWAY, a little nervous for his girl's first day of art school but proud she took the initiative to do something solely for herself. He faced Mia. She sat at the table, the picture of sweet innocence, and smiled at him. "So, what do you feel like doing while Mommy's at class, Miss Mia."

"Let's bake a cake for her."

A cake? Okay, he could bake a cake. "All right." That should keep them busy for the two hours. "Where's your mom keep the mix?" Knowing Kat, she likely had a shelf labeled for things like frosting.

Mia shrugged, so he opened cabinets but didn't find any boxed mixes.

"You could just use a cookbook like Momma does."

He glanced at his little sidekick. She only came to above his knee. Her cute, rosy cheeks pulled as she smiled. How could he disappoint such an adorable thing? "Okay."

He found a cookbook and flipped through the table of contents. "What's your mom's favorite cake?"

"Momma likes white chocolate."

Turning pages, he looked for anything with white chocolate in the recipe. He found something called a Swiss White Chocolate cake. The ingredients all seemed pretty basic.

"Does your mom have white chocolate?"

"In here." She pointed to the freezer.

Hidden on the top shelf in the back, he found a bag of white chocolate kisses. Mia told him where the measuring cups and spoons were, and soon they had themselves set up like a private little cooking show.

"We'll need to add the secret 'gredient too," she said as he tucked a dishrag into the collar of her shirt.

"What's the secret ingredient?"

"Love."

This was the coolest kid in the world. "Of course we do. Luckily, I have some right here in my pocket." He tapped the pocket over his heart, and she smiled approvingly.

He measured out flour, baking soda, sugar, and such as Mia clumsily dumped them into the big bowl. White powder sprinkled the counter, but it wasn't anything that wouldn't wipe up with a little water.

When it was time to crack the egg, Mia assured him she knew how. Tyson winced as her fingers took a bath in the yolk, and half the shell fell into the bowl. Plucking out the pieces, he tossed them in the disposal as he held Mia over the sink so she could wash her hands. His forearms were dusted with white powder, and egg goop clung to his knuckles.

Rather than use a mixer, he handed Mia a whisk. She stood on a kitchen chair and stirred the ingredients into a thick batter while he found a saucepan to heat the chocolate. Turning the dial to medium, he measured out some water and dumped it into the pot. Mia was making a mess at the counter, but having a good time, so he let her go. The water heated to a boil, and he dropped in the chocolate. The white kisses began to melt. He stirred the mixture with a spatula as he consulted the recipe. "Where's your mom keep the cake pans?"

The bowl teetered on the end of the counter. He jumped and caught it as a good bit of batter landed on his arm.

"Oops. Sorry, Tyson."

"That's okay. Why is this so chunky?"

She shrugged.

Something wasn't right. A hiss sounded as the pot of chocolate bubbled like white lava. Dashing to the stove, he stirred the mix, lifting it from the heat. It was smooth but hard on the bottom, sort of lumpy in spots. He frowned and sniffed. The smell of burnt chocolate wasn't too strong. Lowering the temperature, he put the mix back on the stove.

After locating two round cake pans, he frowned. The white sludge was now solidified on the surface of Kat's stove. He looked at Mia, and his eyes went wide. She was elbow-deep in the sack flour. "Mia!"

She jumped, and the bag jerked, falling to the

floor. The heavy sack landed with a thump, sending a mushroom cloud of dust into the air. Particles slowly settled on every surface of the kitchen. Mia laughed.

"Dear God," he muttered.

Mia's strawberry blonde hair was white, her eyes bright and wide against her flour-caked skin.

He breathed. "Okay, don't move. Let me get this frosting started, and then I'll clean you up." Of course, the frosting took more minutes than a three-year-old could stay still. "Snow!" She giggled, scooping handfuls of powder and tossing it into the air.

"Mia, don't do that, sweetie."

She smiled at him, legs twisting in the mess, feet waving left to right. A trail of tiny footprints swirled all around her. He sighed. At least that would occupy her for a few minutes so he could figure out what the hell was going on at the stove.

Quickly scanning the recipe, he realized five things. One, he forgot to preheat the oven. That was a quick fix. Two, he should have removed the first chocolate mix to cool a while ago. Three, the mix was supposed to be added before the batter. Four, he should have constantly been stirring what was now a chocolate boulder glued to the end of the spatula. And five, he was never baking with a three-year-old again.

As the oven preheated, he quickly righted as many wrongs as possible. Pouring the batter into a new bowl, he mixed in the chocolate sauce. There wasn't time to let it cool, and he didn't see the point when it was going into the oven.

Mia ran into the living room, and he tossed the bowl on the counter to chase after her. "Mia, where are you going?"

She giggled as he scooped her off her feet before she could leave a floured Mia print on the sofa. Holding her under his arm like a football, he pulled all the dishes from the sink with his free hand. When the basin was empty, he stuffed a rag in the drain and sat Mia there. "Stay put."

"Why am I in the sink?" she laughed.

"So that I can get this cake in the oven." The burnt smell was getting worse. "Mia, did you put more flour than I measured out?"

Little Miss Innocent shrugged.

The oven beeped. Setting the timer, he slipped the pans in the oven and shut the door. With a sigh, he turned to face the disaster that was Kat's kitchen.

"Shit."

"Quarter!" Mia called from the sink.

One, two, three, four, five, six... He counted until his nerves calmed. Everything—*everything*—was coated in white. Including Mia. He had no idea where to start.

Unsure if giving Mia a bath was a no-no, he reached for a wet rag and started wiping the counters, which was a pain because the minute water touched flour, it formed dough. *Great.*

"Tyson, I wanna get out."

"Okay, sweetie, just give me a second."

He tossed the rag aside and went to the sink. Not good. "Don't move." Running to Mia's room and found a fresh pair of PJs. "Okay, we're going to clean you up before Mommy gets home."

"In my clothes?"

Even the kid knows you don't know what you're doing. "Yup. Head back."

He adjusted the water and used a cup to rinse the flour from Mia's hair and skin. Her clothes clung to her, and she found the entire process hysterical. Him—not so much.

He dried her with a dishtowel and peeled off her clothes, switching them out with clean pajamas. Once somewhat clean, he plopped her on the couch. "Now, you sit here while I tidy up the kitchen, okay?"

She snuggled into the couch with a sippy cup and a wet, messy head. He sighed and looked at the clock. Forty minutes until Kat was home.

For the next thirty minutes, he scrubbed the counters, wiped down the cabinets, swept and mopped the floor, and frosted the most lopsided cake he had ever made. Mia was sound asleep on the couch. When the cake was finally done, he sighed.

"Saddest fuckin' cake I've ever seen in my life," he mumbled, pushing it back on the counter.

The headlights of Kat's car rolled over the front windows. He did a quick scan of the remaining damage. The sink was full of dishes, but the kitchen was—for the most part—clean.

The knob turned, and he straightened, trying to appear relaxed. Her happy expression faltered the moment she saw him. "What happened to you?"

Crap. "Uh, what do you mean?"

"Um..." Her lips pressed tight as her shoulders shook with laughter. "You're all white."

He glanced at his arms and deflated. "I don't

know how you do it, Kat. Mia's an angel, but boy is she a lot of work."

Her smile broadened. "Told you." She shut the door and put down her supplies. "What happened?"

"We made a cake for you."

She stilled, eyes wide with gratitude that would no doubt vanish the moment she saw their culinary nightmare. "You did?"

He nodded. "A white chocolate Swiss cake. I have no idea how it's going to taste, though."

"Aw, Tyson! I want to hug you, but you're filthy."

Eyes narrowing with mischief, he slowly stalked her into a corner, corralling her with his body, until she giggled at his mercy. He pressed a kiss to her neck. "Get messy with me, Kat."

"Where's Mia?"

"Sleeping on the couch." He licked a trail from her collarbone to her ear and pulled the tiny little lobe between his teeth. Everything had the dry taste of flour.

She moaned. "There's a sink full of dishes."

"I'll do them later. After I do you."

She laughed, weakly pushing him away. "Tyson, we can't."

She was right, of course. He couldn't take her with Mia right in the other room. But he wanted to. He pressed his hips against her front, searching for some kind of relief, and kissed her.

Slowly, he stepped back. "Why don't you take Mia to bed while I handle these dishes? I'd carry her for you, but I'm a mess, and she's all clean."

By the time the last dish was scrubbed clean, his hard on had settled. Even in high school, it hadn't been like that with other girls. She wrapped him in such. There was so much he wanted to do with her. As his mind ran through a detailed list of all those things, his body began to harden again.

Down, boy.

He cleared his throat and returned the bowls to the cabinets as Kat returned in a pair of lounge pants that took her ass from adorable to fascinating. "So, how was class?"

"So fun. The teacher's a local artist. She said I had a good understanding of light and told me to practice on landscapes during different times of the day."

"Are you going to?" Painting obviously was something she enjoyed, and she should nurture that talent.

"If there's time."

He closed the cabinet. "Make time, Kat. If you like painting, make room for it in your life."

She shrugged. "I don't know. It's hard when you start caring too much about things. Then life happens, and it's harder to make sacrifices."

"Hey," he tipped up her chin. "Don't be cynical."

"I stopped being optimistic a long time ago." She was joking, but it wasn't funny. True sadness rested behind her words.

"Things will get easier, Kat. Everything takes time." He'd make sure her life got easier. He could afford to help her out here and there. Lightening the mood, he said, "Well, next week we won't be baking."

"You'll sit with Mia again?"

He was a little offended that she assumed he wouldn't. "Of course I will. I told you I would."

"I know, but..."

"Kat, I'm not a quitter. Tonight was an education. Now, when I have my own kids, I'll know three-year-olds are way too young for the culinary arts."

"You want kids?" her words were whispered as if his answer meant a lot.

"With the right woman? Of course." He rested his arms on her shoulders and pulled her close. "I want a big family. How about you?"

Her expression shuttered. "I think Mia's all I'll ever have."

"Why's that?"

She shrugged. "Guys who are interested in a family of their own don't usually start with girls like me."

"That's an awful lot of generalizing, kitten. I'm a guy who wants a family of his own, and I think Mia's an amazing kid. The last thing I see her as is a deterrent. And as far as girls like you...there aren't any."

"Such a sweet talker." She seemed to be laughing with him, not at him.

"Hey, it's my style."

She kissed his chin. "Well, I like your sweet-talking style."

SUMMER HAD OFFICIALLY ARRIVED, and the temperature was at an all-time high, as was her mood, which was probably the result of being sexually satisfied for the first time in her life. It was difficult to keep things platonic around Mia, but Tyson's busy work schedule didn't give them much time together during the week. She got in the habit of calling him at night after Mia fell asleep.

"I bet you're all cozy under those covers right now, aren't you?" he teased. "Are you wearing one of those cute, frilly, little negligee things?"

She looked down at her oversized maternity shirt and snorted. "Sure."

He laughed at her unconvincing lie. "Mmm, is it silky?"

She smirked. "Sure."

"Oh, baby, it's so sexy when you lie to me," he teased. "It's that *Got Milk* shirt, isn't it? Or is it the one that says Parkside High? That one does it for me in a bad way."

"Oh, no," she purred. "This one's a very sexy old maternity shirt that says *Under Construction* with little bedazzled rhinestones. Some of the stones are even missing from going through the wash so many times."

He made a guttural sound of absolute arousal. It was torture talking to him, knowing he was only two doors away, lying in his own bed. "I'm gonna break into your house tonight and peel that shirt right off you."

"Don't lie."

He sighed. "I miss you. I'm seriously considering sneaking into your bed. Mia's a sound sleeper, right?"

"No," she laughed.

"What's on the legs?"

Her mouth pulled into a smirk. "Nothing."

"Panties or no panties?"

"Panties."

"What color? Describe them to me."

"They're black. Cotton. Kind of old lady cut. Try to contain yourself."

He chuckled. "We're going to have to take you shopping. You're way too young for granny panties."

"I didn't say they were granny panties. They're more...middle-aged maiden."

"Hot." His breath echoed against the phone. "Do me a favor."

"Mm-hm."

"Slide those middle-aged maiden panties off that sexy ass of yours."

She stilled, wondering if she could actually have a *serious* and *sexy* conversation with him on the phone. When they were joking around, it was different.

"Did you do it?"

"Um..." Should she lie? He'd never know.

As if he could read her mind, he said, "I'll know if you're lying, kitten, so be honest."

Sighing, she shifted and slid the cotton underwear over her thighs and kicked them under the covers. "They're off." She heard movement on the other end. "Where are you?"

"On my couch, but I'm imagining myself right next to you."

"Ty?"

"Mm-hm."

"What—what are we doing?"

He cleared his throat and sounded like he was lying back. "We're going to play a game."

"A game?"

"Yup. It's called Getting a Pussy Cat to Come. You ready, kitten?"

Her mind froze. She could touch herself, but she couldn't bring herself to orgasm. "Um, I think you're going to lose."

"Is that a challenge?"

"No, I'm just saying...I can't...It's different for me when you're not here with me."

"You never touch yourself?"

"Of course, I touch myself. I just don't *touch myself.*"

"Are you opposed to touching yourself?"

"No, but I don't think you're going to get the results you're looking for."

"I'll be the judge of that. Shut off the lights."

She leaned over and switched off the lamp, submerging the room in darkness. "Okay."

"Good. I want you to imagine me there with you. I'm right beside you, under the covers, very close. Are you imagining it?"

"Yes." This was weird.

"Think of my lips softly kissing your lips,, and trailing down your jaw to your ear. Can you feel me kissing you? You have a very sexy neck. I love how sensitive you are right where your pulse beats. Imagine me licking you there, nice and slow. Do you feel me?"

Her legs shifted under the blanket as her fingers trailed over her throat. Pressure built as she shut her eyes and imagined everything he described. An ache spread from her lower body to her breasts.

"I'm going to nibble a trail down to your shoulder and spend some time where I left that little mark there. You still have my love bite?"

She smiled. It was her first hickey. "Yes. I had to change my shirt this morning so no one would see it at work."

"You afraid other guys might know you're taken? Because I'm kind of liking the idea."

"There are no other guys. I covered it because I didn't want my boss to see it."

"Ah, the infamous Dr. Stevens—my competition."

She laughed, recalling how he'd originally thought she lived with her landlord and boss.

"Okay, back to business," he said. "So I'm nibbling, nice, and slow down your neck and over your shoulder."

"Mm-hm."

"My arm slides under your back, and I pull you close, pull myself on top of you. Make sure your thighs are parted, so I have a place to kneel."

She slowly slid her knees apart, pretending the weight of the covers was actually his hard body.

"Take your hand and pretend it's mine. I slowly lift your shirt up over your breasts—*ohh,* that free *under construction* shirt turns me on. I trail my fingers between your breasts, slow and teasing. Your nipples tighten, but I don't touch them. I just keep teasing the swell of your breasts and the valley in between. Are you touching yourself?"

She sighed. "Mm-hm."

"Does it feel good?"

"Yes," she drowsily answered.

"Don't touch those nipples, kitten. Not yet. I slide my hand down your soft belly. Over and over, I touch you, drawing pictures on your skin, building your desire. Do you feel my breath on your skin?"

Her spine stretched. It was becoming harder to answer as her fingers trailed over her stomach and back to her breasts. Her bottom dug into the bedding. She needed more.

"Take your little pinkie and touch the tip of your right nipple. That's my tongue teasing you."

She moaned.

"Aw, see, you make sounds like that, and my restraint goes right out the window. Pinch your titties, kitten. Feel my mouth sucking, biting, and licking over the tips?"

Small noises formed in her throat. She wedged the phone between her shoulder and her ear so she could use both hands. Pinching and pulling, she played with various levels of tightness.

He groaned. "Now my hand's sliding between your legs. I tease the soft curls over your pussy, and your legs open a little wider. Do you feel me teasing you?"

"Yes."

"Do you want me to keep going?"

"Yes," she breathed as her fingers gently brushed over her dewy curls.

"God, you get me so hard, Kat." Over his breathing, she thought she heard the sound of his zipper coming down. He exhaled a long, slow sigh. "If I were there right now, you know what I'd be doing, kitten?"

"Hmm?"

"I'd be licking up all that sweet, sweet cream. Do you feel my tongue tracing over your wet slit? I'd tease you nice and slow at first, get you shaking and begging. I'd come real close to your pretty pink clit, just like I did with those pretty pink nipples, but I wouldn't touch."

"Tyson..."

"I'm here, baby. My tongue is teasing you with soft little licks as I finally run it over your clit."

She brushed the tight little bud and nearly shot off the bed.

"Don't stop. I'm relentless. Licking and sucking, flicking that little pearl with my tongue. Then, I slide a finger in deep, pumping it into your tight little pussy while my mouth works your clit."

She moved both hands between her legs. Her finger curled and slipped into her sex. Hot, wet arousal coated her to the knuckle. She couldn't reach deep, but her touch still brought relief as her fingers rubbed her clit.

"Fuck. I'm so hard I gotta have you. You feel my big cock pressing at your opening? Stretching you? I can imagine your pussy gripping me."

She finally understood the draw of adult toys, wishing she had one. Her fingers pumped, and she moaned.

"That's it, kitten. So close. I'm fucking you, rubbing your clit, and you're squeezing my dick so tight. Feel me swelling inside you. I'm so close to coming, but I'm waiting for you. Are you close, baby?"

Her body drew tight as a bow, leg muscles locking. Her stomach tightened, and her neck extended. *"Ohmygod…"*

He moaned and breathed into the phone as it slipped away from her ear. Tiny sparks of pleasure lit along her spine as she came undone under her own hand. Minutes passed as she stared into the darkness, trembling, as she slowly came back to herself. She found the phone under her pillow. "Ty?"

"Open the door."

"What?" Her eyes widened as she quickly sat up.

"Open the door, Kat."

Body still trembling, she fumbled through the dark and tiptoed to the front door. The deadbolt clicked, and he was on her before she even saw him.

His mouth crashed over hers, as he backed her up against a wall.

"So fucking hot," he whispered as he ravaged her mouth.

Her hands held on to his head, needing him in that moment apparently as much as he needed her.

"Show me the fingers you used."

She raised the fingers of her right hand and blushed. Nostrils flaring, he sucked them into his mouth, and her sex pulsed.

"Fuck, Kat. You make me crazy. I got a situation in my pants I haven't had since I was a teenager. And yet, I still want to fuck you right here against your fridge."

She wanted the same, but they couldn't. Not with Mia in the house. "This is so hard," she whined. "Maybe I can get Jade to take Mia tomorrow night."

His shoulders sagged. "That's not going to work for me. I have to stay out of town tomorrow night for a job. How about Saturday?"

"Jade has a date."

"So Sunday when your mom takes Mia?"

"I'll go crazy by then." She groaned. "What've you done to me?"

"Me? How about you? I'm the one who needs to go home and shower."

She laughed.

"I want you," he whispered.

Her forehead pressed to his chest as she sighed, the sexual tension an unresolved torture she'd have to tolerate for some time. "I want you too."

~

Tyson looked at Kat with dark, searing eyes as Mia detailed her aspirations to be a princess. According to her daughter, she was quite qualified. Kat glanced at the clock.

Distracted, Mia wandered into the living room, and Tyson's fingers brushed hers. "How long until she's asleep."

"Two hours."

He released a slow breath. "How about I come back then?"

She nodded. Having him there and not being able to touch him was brutal.

His lips briefly brushed her temple as he stood. "Two hours."

One hour and fifty-nine minutes later, Tyson returned bearing two Long Island iced teas. They sat on the front porch while Mia safely slept in her bed. Fireflies hovered low over the lawn like fallen stars as they talked.

The simplest touch had her tensing with need. She never experienced this degree of wanting. She wanted to rub her cheek on him, sniff his neck, and press her body against his for the simple pleasure of it. She wanted him naked and on her in every sense of the word, wanted to feel him everywhere, pushing, pulling, taking, and not stopping until they were both sated.

The hour passed at a slug's pace. Every few minutes, she released a deep breath, needing to let out some of the building pressure. Maybe she should just invite him in. That wouldn't work. Not only did she have to worry about Mia, her mother would be there bright and early the following morning.

His thoughts seemed to be running over the same issues. "What time's your mom come tomorrow?"

"Nine."

He groaned, finished his drink in one long gulp. Her glass had been empty for a while. "I miss you," he said, staring into her eyes and running the backs of his knuckles over her fingers.

"I miss you too."

With a resigned smile, he stood and collected their glasses. "I'll be here at nine oh one."

His mouth brushed hers, fueling the fire smoldering inside of her. She needed something more.

His lips slanted over hers, and she stood, lacing her arms around his neck. The heat from his body burned through the thin layer of clothing separating them. She gripped his shoulders and practically climbed up his front.

He chuckled. "Easy, kitten. Tomorrow."

"I want you now," she pouted.

"I can stay."

She sighed. "No. We're better off waiting."

"Mmm. It does make the heart go fonder."

"Fonder-shmonder. My panties are going to burst into flames."

He quirked a brow and shifted the glasses into one arm, his hand sliding to the damp crotch of her pants. "These panties?"

Shutting her eyes, she groaned.

"You're wet. I can feel it."

Lips parted, she glared at him. "I've never felt

like this before. I'm turning into some sort of deviant."

His hand pulled away as he chuckled. "I'll take care of you tomorrow, baby. I promise. Try to get some sleep."

She sighed. "Yeah, right."

He smirked. "Good night, kitten."

"I hate you," she called as he crossed the yard.

"Do not!" he called back.

She pursed her lips. He was right, of course.

The following morning, as soon as Vivian left with Mia, Kat went inside to do the dishes from breakfast. As she rinsed the last cereal bowl, Tyson knocked on the front door and let himself in. A bolt of anticipation knifed through her, sharp and heated.

Creeping behind her at the sink, he slid his hands under her shirt and over her bra. Warm breath tickled her neck as he placed a teasing kiss at her nape. "Finally," he whispered.

Her nipples hardened as he gently pinched the pebbled tips, her body heating like a brushfire in a drought. He turned her in his arms, and their lips found each other's in a rush as she wrapped her damp hands around his neck.

Squeezing her ass, he lifted as her legs wrapped around his hips. A giggle of excitement raced through her as he moved them toward the bedroom. "This has been the longest damn week of my life." He kicked the door closed and tossed her on the bed. "Clothes. Off. Now."

Stripping away her clothing with frantic pulls and tugs, she squirmed as his body fell over hers, his mouth chasing every exposed inch of flesh with starved intent. Her hands yanked his shirt away as he shucked his jeans. Tangled limbs twisted as laughter interrupted their frenzied kisses.

"This is insane." She rolled with him, arching as he stretched and licked up her side.

"This is what you do to me." The soft tear of foil sounded, her only warning before her thighs were nudged apart to accommodate his broad hips. She was so wet he slid in without resistance and cursed. "Fuck, kitten, you're soaked."

Lifting her hips, she met his thrusts as they quickly gave in to their rushed need. "I barely slept last night. This is all I've been able to think about."

Hips snapping forward, he drilled into her. "God, me too. It's gonna be quick."

Quick was fine. She was desperate for relief. Her body stretched as the sense of fullness stretched her. Reflexively, her fingers dug into his muscled back as he buried her in the bedding with each hard thrust. Her body quaked as he shuttered, and sweet relief came in a fast wave, dulling the edge of need so potent it was nearly frightening.

Their bodies collapsed together, tension giving way to ecstasy. He rolled them to their sides, his heart thundering under her ear as her legs slipped from his, and they panted. "Seeing you only one day a week is not nearly enough," he gasped.

"I have a half-day on Thursday for the Fourth of July. Maybe I could ask Mrs. Bradshaw to keep Mia until the normal time, and I can come see your construction site."

His hand glided over her shoulder, softly petting and holding her close. "That'd be nice. I wanted to talk to you about the Fourth. I'm having a picnic. Nothing big, just family, but I wanted you and Mia to come. You can invite Jade too if you'd like."

Leaning up on an elbow, her trance was broken as she weighed the sincerity in his eyes. "You want me to meet your family?"

"Of course, I want you to meet my family. I told you, you're my girl."

A tight smile teased her lips. "I never met a boyfriend's family before." Giddiness quickly transcended into concern. "What should I wear?"

"A turban," he joked.

Gently shoving his face into the pillow with her palm, she laughed. "I'm serious. I want to make a good impression."

"Wear your normal clothes, Kat. It's a picnic, nothing fancy."

"Should I make something? Oh my gosh, this is so exciting! Will there be music and little checkered tablecloths?"

"If you want to bring something, you can, but you don't have to." His head twisted as he studied her. "Haven't you ever been to a backyard barbecue before?"

"My parents aren't really the grilling type. When I was a kid, I went with Jade's family to a pool party. Other than burgers and stuff, what do people normally eat at picnics? I want to make something really, really great."

"Huh, well, my sister will probably make fried chicken, and my mom will probably bring baked macaroni and cheese. So whatever you feel like bringing, go ahead, but babe, you don't need to impress anyone. They'll love you no matter what. Trust me. Don't stress yourself out."

Finger tapping on her chin, she considered her cookbooks. "Maybe a dessert. Can we go to the library before we hit the market today? I want to go online and look up some recipes."

"Just use my phone."

"Where is it?" She really should save up for a smartphone since she couldn't afford a computer.

He kissed her and pulled her back down on his chest. "Later. I'm not done with you yet."

Sighing, she snuggled into his side. They had all day. Still, she was distracted. "I'm going to make something delicious."

His fingers slowly traced over her breasts as he let out a contented sigh. "I'm sure you are."

~

How had she never experienced something as basic as a backyard barbecue? He and Kat really did come from different backgrounds. Her excitement touched him. He'd throw barbecues every week if they made her this happy.

Their age difference didn't bother him anymore. On the contrary, it made him feel younger. He'd been so convinced thirty-six was the beginning of the end, but since meeting her, he felt like his life had been given a fresh start.

As they lay in a twisted knot of covers and limbs, he considered how happy he'd been this past week. Sure, it was agony, waiting to get his hands on her, but it was more than that. It was moments like this, simply resting beside her, knowing he had the freedom to hold and touch her, breathe her in.

He couldn't remember ever laughing so much with a woman. At the end of the day, his face was sometimes sore from smiling. He liked catching glimpses of her in the morning and after work. Loved talking to her before he went to sleep each night.

Running his fingers through her downy hair, he smiled. He could tell her mind was working over-time, considering what dish to prepare for the little get-together. She was such a contradiction, wild one minute and a conservative picture of domesticity the next. He liked that other people didn't easily see that frisky side of her. He wasn't sure where their relationship was heading, but he knew, without a doubt, he didn't want to let her go. Speaking of which—he rolled her to her back. "Okay, that's enough time spent thinking about desserts. I want mine." She laughed, and he kissed his way straight to ambrosia.

Chapter 20

KAT PULLED into a gated sand lot where several cars and Adams Construction trucks were parked. In the distance, a cement truck poured the foundation for a new project Tyson contracted. She smiled as she saw his broad shoulders standing nearly half a foot above the rest of the men as he held out a blueprint.

He shaded his eyes and smiled as she approached. Handing off the blueprint, he excused himself. A film of grain dusted against her dewy skin as a truck rolled by. Her heart pounded as he stepped within arm's reach.

Smiling, he bent to brush his lips over hers. "Hello, beautiful." Her breath caught as he stepped away.

The surrounding construction had her speaking in a low shout. "This is amazing. You're building a house from scratch?"

"Yeah," he shouted back and took her hand.

"Come on. Let's go into my trailer where we can talk."

He walked her toward an aluminum trailer that reminded her of the mobile classrooms used during high school. Pulling a set of keys from his pocket, he unlocked the door. The chilled air-conditioning blanketed her as she entered the space.

The trailer was bigger than it appeared from the outside. Xerox machines, a large conference table lined with metal folding chairs, a coffee pot, and a desk in the corner were the basic furnishings.

"This is nice," she said as the door closed behind her, muting the sounds of the construction. She bumped into his chest.

His eyes dilated as he caught her shoulders. His mouth pressed to hers with an unmistakable sense of urgency. She moaned into his mouth, lips curving in a smile. Backing her toward the table, he corralled her through the tight space. The back of her legs touched the table as his hands went to the buttons of her blouse, quickly plucking them from their holes.

"I waited all week for this," he whispered as his lips moved down her throat.

"Ty, we're in a trailer."

"We're in my office," he corrected. Unlatching the clasp of her bra, he lifted her rear onto the table and slid her skirt up her legs. "I love it when you wear skirts."

His mouth found her breasts. "I locked the door. No one will bother us," he said, pulling the tight bud between his teeth.

All apprehensions disappeared at the click of his

belt buckle. His mouth was a welcome distraction. His hips made a space between her knees as he dug in his pocket. Lifting his head, he tore the condom open with his teeth. She watched, mesmerized, as he slid it over his long cock. His slow gaze met hers. "Put me inside of you."

Shifting, she wedged her panties aside and gripped him, guiding her to her sex. He groaned with pleasure as he slid deep. Breath mingled as her body awakened under the familiar sense of his possession.

Her feet dangling from the edge of the table, he cupped her bottom as he settled himself deep in her sex. "Ease back. I got you."

Blouse undone, her back lowered to the cool table.

"Raise your arms," he instructed, tugging her blouse open so he could see her breasts. She obeyed and gasped as he gathered her shirt and twisted the material at her wrists, cinching her hands together. "Don't let go."

She lay before him, arms bound above her head, eyes glazing with lust, completely at his command. Withdrawing slowly, his cock rested at her opening as he leaned down and kissed each of her breasts. His hand slid under her right knee, slightly raising her leg, and he slammed back into her core. A sharp cry left her throat as pleasure knifed through her.

"God, you're gorgeous." He thrust again, rocking the table. "So fucking hot, Kat. Here in my office, completely exposed. I wanna lose myself in you."

Arousal trickled from her sex at the erotic imagery, her being taken right there on a table others used for proper business purposes. Fifty plus construction workers continued about their day only a few feet away. It was completely reckless, yet she trusted she was safe with him. She was always safe with him.

She trusted him with everything. With her body. With her heart. With Mia. In that moment, her worries floated away as something inside of her broke free. She abandoned any remaining sense of modesty, too far gone to mourn its departure, and pressed into him. "More," she whimpered.

"More what? Tell me what you want, kitten."

"I want..." He ground his hips into her, filling her completely, yet she greedily wanted more. "Touch me."

"Where?" Leaning over her, one palm planted on the table beside her head, bracing his weight, he stared into her eyes. His thrusts slowed, taunting her, as he ground his cock deeper into her core.

Her eyes widened as he brushed some hidden path of nerves. "There!"

"Here?" The hand gripping her knee let go. She tightened her thighs on his hips. The table rocked as he pinched her nipple. She moaned in pleasure, but it still wasn't what she wanted most.

"Say it, Kat. Tell me what you want and I'll give it to you. I'll make you come so hard you'll still feel me inside your body when you go to sleep tonight."

He increased his pace, and a stack of papers tumbled off the table, scattering across the floor. Her body coiled tighter, peaking, cresting the wave as an intense orgasm threatened to break inside of her. So close.

"Say it," he growled through clenched teeth.

Need overwhelmed modesty. "My clit! Touch my clit, Ty, please—"

His fingers were on her before the last word left her mouth, rapidly rubbing, and she immediately shattered as his body continued to pound into hers.

Her channel tightened, and he groaned. She cried out, arching, her fingers tightening into fists as each wave of pleasure pulsed through her veins. Her mind let go as ecstasy carried her away.

"We aren't done yet."

Her eyes shot open as he raised her legs, securing her ankles over his broad shoulders, his thumbs rooted firmly in the soft underside of her knees. Her ass lifted off the table as he thrust hard, holding her in a way that wrapped her body tight around his cock.

Breath sawed out of his lungs as she cried out in pleasure. Faster and faster, he pumped. His back arched as his release came with a guttural shout. With each pulse of his cock, the echo of her heartbeat filled her ears.

His palms landed with a thump beside her head as he braced his weight over her chest and trembled. Intimacy slammed into her as his heavy-lidded gaze found hers. How could so much emotion stem from such a raw moment of lust? Her feeling went beyond lust, and she had to fight to keep the words locked inside.

He opened his mouth as if to say something and seemed to think better of it, instead kissing her tenderly. Gradually, he pulled back, and she tried to find her bearings.

Flushed and shaky, her hands trembled as she focused on fixing her bra and fastening the buttons of her wrinkled shirt. He gently brushed her hands away and fastened the last few buttons for her.

"How long do you have until you need to get Mia?" he softly asked.

She looked at her watch. "I should probably leave in about twenty minutes. Do you have a mirror? My hair's a mess."

"Sorry," he apologized and stepped closer. "Here, let me see if I can fix it." Fingers gently raked through her hair as he placed a couple of strands behind her ear. "That looks good. You're always beautiful."

"You're biased."

"True." He smirked and kissed her nose, helping her stand. "Come on, I'll give you a tour of the site before I walk you to your car."

She was relieved no one seemed to be lingering near the trailer. After a short tour, he walked her back to her car. "I'm going to be here late tonight since it's a three-day weekend. But I'll see you tomorrow, right?"

It didn't seem right for such a confident man to need her reassurance. Not many people cared what she thought, but Tyson did. Her opinion and presence mattered to him.

"Of course. Twelve o'clock. Mia hasn't stopped talking about it. Jade has another party to go to first, but she'll probably stop by later if that's still okay."

"Sure. And how's your surprise dessert coming along? Can I know what it is yet?"

"No, and it's coming along wonderfully. You'll have to wait and see."

"Fine." He kissed her goodbye and opened her car door. She reluctantly climbed inside the sweltering vehicle and rolled down the windows to let out some of the heat as she waited for the AC to blast.

He leaned in the window, his arm braced above the door. "Well, I gotta get back to work. Drive safe, and I'll call you tonight if it's not too late. Love ya," he said as he kissed her cheek.

Every muscle in her face went numb as her smile faltered, and she gaped at his retreating form.

Did he just say 'Love ya'?

Chapter 21

"COME ON, MOMMA!" Mia called from the door as she bounced with glee.

"Okay, let me get my keys. Am I forgetting anything?" Kat mumbled as she picked up her dessert and followed Mia out the door.

She'd made something called Orange Dessert, a type of ambrosia from Jell-O mix, Cool Whip, cottage cheese, and canned peaches. She had never made it before, but it tasted spectacular when she'd licked the spatula.

It was already twelve-thirty. They were running behind because she'd changed her outfit three times. As they approached Tyson's yard, she could hear music and voices, and her palms began to sweat. Mia raced toward the back gate as Kat fought a tingle of apprehension.

Her steps faltered as she approached the gate. How silly to think her outfit might help her blend.

She swallowed. Sometimes people were weird about mixed-race couples. Funny, that was the first time she actually thought to classify their relationship under such a label.

Once she'd caught an older couple staring at them in the grocery store, but Tyson didn't seem to notice, or if he had noticed, he hadn't acknowledged it. She'd experienced plenty of judgment in her life, but never for something as superficial as racism.

And right at that moment, she finally understood the true definition of privilege.

What if his family didn't want him to date a woman of a different race?

Her hands tightened on the dessert, and her knees grew stiff. There was no hiding that she was different. Shrinking back, she scanned the crowd for Tyson. He was at the grill with his back toward them.

"Come on, Momma!" Mia called, pulling on Kat's skirt and directing them toward the checkered tablecloths covered with food.

So many strangers, ranging from babies to senior citizens, mingled about. Trixie lay in the shade of her doghouse while kids played tag in the back of the yard. Mia tugged Kat forward, dauntless with unchecked courage. She didn't see the difference between them and the others, and had no idea the amount of inadequacy Kat battled on the regular. To her, people were just people.

Maybe you're making a big deal out of nothing.

Mia unhooked the gate and ran to Tyson. When he heard her call his name, he scooped her up in his arms. He whispered something in Mia's ear, and she pointed to Kat, where she still stood on the other side of the opened gate. He met her eyes and walked toward her, Mia perched on his hip.

When he was about four feet away, he said, "Well, come on now. Don't be shy. I've been waiting all week to taste that dessert."

He held out his hand and took another step. She swallowed and reached for his fingers.

"You said a small picnic. You said just family," she whispered, shuffling closer.

His brow creased with confusion. "Kat, this *is* my family." He eased Mia to the ground and took the dessert from her hands. "Come on, baby. Don't be scared. I'll introduce you."

He led her to the closest table, where four women sat chatting. "Everyone, I'd like you to meet Kat. Kat, this is Gramma Tessa."

He pointed to a small woman. Kat nodded and mumbled a shy hello.

"This is my mother, Celia." She looked to be around sixty. Her eyes were the same almond shape as Tyson's.

"Nice to meet you, Mrs. Adams," Kat nervously said.

He pointed to another woman, who Kat immediately recalled by her long, thick dreadlocks. This was his sister, Gloria. "You probably recognize my sister, Gloria," Tyson said, laughter crinkling his eyes.

She nodded a hello.

"This is my cousin, Stasia. And that little guy is Malcolm." She was a teenager and held a newborn baby in her arms.

He threw out their names in one solid breath as

she quickly tried to commit each face to memory. When he finished, they fell silent for a beat, appraising her, and then everyone started talking at once.

"Well, we finally get to meet the girl Ty's talked so much about."

"Ooh, child, aren't you adorable!"

"I can see what he sees in you."

"Come on, now, and have a seat."

"And who's this little angel?"

Overwhelmed, Kat took a seat and simply said thank you. Tyson picked up Mia and said, "This little angel is Mia, Kat's daughter."

All the women fawned over Mia at once. She giggled and announced, "I'm three!"

Tyson's sister Gloria chimed in, "Oh, that's the same age as my Davis. You see that boy over there petting Trixie?" She pointed with a long nail. "That's him. Why don't you go on and say hi?"

Tyson put Mia down, and she ran over to the other little boy. "Okay, I got to go check the grill. Will you be all right here for a few minutes?"

She nodded—a total lie—and he kissed her forehead. Turning to the women, he sternly said, "No embarrassing stories."

The women laughed and as he walked away. His sister yelled, "No promises, Ty! I still owe you from when I brought Darrel home." She grinned at Kat. "Darrel's my husband, and when I first brought him around, Ty told him I sleep with my mouth open and snore."

"Oh, please," her mother scoffed, "There was no surprise there. Darrel already knew how you slept!"

Stasia giggled.

"You shush it." Gloria poked her mother and laughed. She turned back to Kat with a conspirator's smile. "Now tell us, Kat, have you seen the pictures of Ty when he was a six-foot bean pole?"

She laughed, feeling a bit of her tension ease.

The women welcomed her into the fold, telling animated stories of Tyson as a boy that had her laughing to the point of tears. Gloria was hysterical, and from what she could tell, she got a good part of her humor from her mother. Gramma Tessa didn't say much, but when she did, it was obvious she was sharp as a tack and didn't miss a beat.

She shared an immediate camaraderie with Stasia, who also got pregnant in high school and had Malcolm a week before graduation. She was raising the baby on her own because, according to Gramma Tessa, Malcolm's father was a 'no good fool'. It seemed the only difference between Stasia's situation and hers was that Stasia had the love and support of her family.

When Tyson announced that it was time to eat, Kat found Mia and made her a plate. Fried chicken, potato salad, macaroni salad, deviled eggs, fruit salad, collard greens, baked macaroni and cheese, burgers, hot dogs, and a ton of desserts—the selection was overwhelming. She'd never seen so much mouth-watering food.

Her Orange Dessert was a big hit. Tyson loved it and went back for several helpings. She was beyond flattered when several women asked her for the recipe.

After they ate, Tyson introduced her to the rest

of his family. His father was even funnier than his mother. The entire family seemed to love to laugh.

Jade finally showed up around six and showed no hesitation when it came to making new friends. Sitting back, Kat smiled at her best friend's gift for telling anecdotes.

"I can top that! I can top that!" Jade called as Gloria finished an embarrassing story about accidentally getting into the wrong car at the mall last Christmas.

"You go on, girl. Let's hear what you got. Because I gotta tell ya, I don't think nothin' will ever be as embarrassing as me yelling at that poor old man to start the car, thinkin' he was Darrel."

Breathing through cramping laughter, Kat pressed at a stitch in her side. Gloria was hilarious.

"Okay." Jade took a sip of her wine. "So I'm a nurse, right? Well, at work, when a patient comes in, an orderly usually wheels them back to me. When they drop off the patient, the orderly says the name, like Adams or Jones or Smith."

"Sure," Gloria agreed, nodding along with the story.

"Well, a few years ago, when the pope passed away, I don't get the news back at my station, so I had no idea. My orderly wheels back this sweet old man and says, 'Pope's dead'. Well, don't I go through the entire hour calling him Mr. Popestead! *Sit on the table, Mr. Popestead.' 'I'm going to take your blood pressure now, Mr. Popestead.'* He must have thought I was insane!"

Everyone burst into peals of laughter. Kat was

so glad Jade had come. Her presence and support were invaluable.

"I never lived that one down," Jade giggled, never afraid to laugh at life's little faux pas.

When it started getting dark, Kat helped Tyson wrap up the leftovers. As they stood in the kitchen, she sighed, thinking it was a good thing she came.

"Having fun?"

She grinned as she poured the remaining potato salad into some Tupperware. "Yes. Your family's amazing."

"Thank you. I like to think so. They all seem to like you. I knew they would."

She walked around the island in the center of the kitchen and placed the leftovers on the lower shelf in the fridge. When she stood up, Tyson was behind her. He wrapped his arms around her waist and pressed his face into the back of her neck.

"*I* like you," he said as they swayed in place.

"I like you, too," she said, remembering his words from the other day.

"I'm glad you came today." He placed a kiss on top of her head.

"Me too."

"Do you think if we went to bed, anyone would notice?"

"Mr. Adams!" she said in mock outrage. "A host does not rest until the last guest has gone."

"Who said we'd be resting?"

She laughed and playfully smacked him in the arm.

As the guests thinned and said their goodbyes, she continued to tidy up the mess of the party. They were surprised by local fireworks, and all the kids gathered on the grass, watching as the grown ups collected their dishes and said their goodbyes.

Jade spoke to Tyson while Kat folded up the tablecloths. She couldn't hear what Jade was saying, but her stance was severe, as she poked Tyson in the chest a couple of times. Alarmed, Kat took a step closer but paused as Tyson nodded and Jade gave him an affectionate hug.

When the last guest left, it was close to midnight. Mia was asleep on Tyson's couch. Kat covered her with an afghan and removed the glow bracelet twisted around her wrist.

The backdoor squeaked as she slipped outside and waited for Tyson on one of the lawn chairs. Settling under a sky full of stars, she sighed. The door squeaked again, and he appeared, holding a sweatshirt and two Coronas.

"I figured it might get chilly." He handed her the shirt, and she slipped it over her head.

"Ooh, this is soft." She inhaled his scent, which clung to the sweatshirt. "Yeah, you're not getting this back."

He handed her a beer, and they clanked them together. "Happy Fourth of July, baby."

It *was* a happy Fourth of July. Probably the happiest she'd ever had. "Happy Fourth of July, Ty," she said in a hoarse whisper as she took a sip.

They talked until she could no longer keep her eyes open. When it was time to head home, Ty wrapped Mia in the blanket from his couch and carried her to the cottage. Placing her in her bed, he kissed her forehead, slipped off her Crocs, and tucked her little body under the covers.

Kat's heart fluttered at the sight of such paternal sweetness. She forced herself to take a deep, shaky breath.

Don't look at him like that. He isn't her father.

She was entering some really dangerous, emotional territory.

He walked Kat to her room, helped her undress, and watched as she slipped into pajamas. Pulling the covers back, he tucked her into bed and kissed her forehead, much like he'd kissed Mia's. "Goodnight, Kat."

The tender way he cared for her took her breath away. It seemed impossible for someone to be so gentle and strong at the same time. "Goodnight, Ty."

His fingers brushed softly over her cheek as he sat on the edge of the bed. "I love you."

Pressure built in her chest as her throat tightened. He'd been an unexpected part of her life she now believed she couldn't live without. Hopefully, those words carried as much weight for him as they did for her because she rarely heard them, and hearing them from him dismantled the last of her protective barriers. "I love you, too," she croaked.

His soft grin showed immense relief. Leaning in, he brushed his lips over hers. "I'll lock up behind me. Sweet dreams."

Chapter 22

THE FOLLOWING WEEKS WERE
BLISS. Tyson often came over after dinner and
watched movies with them. He was learning the difference between Cinderella and the rest of the
Disney princesses. A few times, Kat even caught him
humming songs.

Mia seemed happy to have him around. On the
nights that he worked late and couldn't visit, she
asked for him. Rather than change their routine, he
seemed to adapt to it, fitting in easily.

Jade welcomed his presence, now bringing three
cups of coffee on her Saturday morning visits rather
than two. The night of the picnic, Kat saw them
talking, but Tyson wouldn't say what her exact
words had been. He did, however, call her an angry
dwarf.

When she asked Jade what was said, she un-
apologetically admitted to threatening his balls with

a dull blade if he ever hurt Kat. But the longer they dated, the less Kat feared getting hurt.

He often took Mia for walks with Trixie and offered a hand around the house, always there to help with simple chores like folding the laundry on the line. They were, in a sense, behaving like a family. They picnicked at the park, visited movie theaters, and went miniature golfing. Sundays were their special days. Tyson came over the minute her mother pulled away and carried Kat right back to bed, where they made love for hours. It was, without a doubt, the best summer of her life.

When temperatures climbed to a record-breaking high, too hot to even sit in the shade of the house, she and Mia often visited the mall for some window-shopping. Returning home after the sun set one evening, she found a large box on their front porch with a bow. "A present!" Mia cheered.

Unwrapping the box, she found an air conditioner. With mixed emotions, she read the tag attached to the bow.

To my hot little kitten,
*   I'll install it tonight.*
*   Love,*
*   Your Handy Man*

When he arrived, tools in hand, she thanked him but regretfully declined the thoughtful gift. "I appreciate it. I truly do, but we can't accept this."

He frowned. "Why not?"

"Because air conditioners cost a lot of money."

"So?"

"So I don't want you spending that kind of money on us."

He rolled his eyes. "Kat, it's a heatwave. You need AC. It's a window unit, for Christ's sake. It's not like I'm redoing your ductwork and installing central air."

"It's still too much."

Dropping his tools, he sliced open the box. "You're being stubborn."

"Don't open it!" she snapped, afraid if the box was opened, he wouldn't be able to get a refund.

"Kat, will you get ahold of yourself. It's fine."

Her gratitude turned to frustration as he persisted in ignoring her decision. "I don't want it."

Frustrated, he threw up his hands. "It's sweltering in here. You're driving all the way to the mall just to cool off. Do you hear how ridiculous that sounds?"

Insulted, she snapped, "You have no right to buy us something so extravagant!"

He scowled. "I can buy you whatever I want!"

Of course, he could because he had money. She'd never be able to repay him for such a gift. It was their first argument, and she didn't want to fight, but he also needed to respect her boundaries. "It's my home, and if I want an air conditioner, I'll buy one myself. I don't need your charity."

"It isn't charity!" he roared. "It's necessary. I don't know how you even sleep in this heat."

"It's not your concern. I want you to take it back."

"It *is* my concern, and it's *not* going back."

Her vision blurred as he refused to budge. "Tyson. Take. It. Back. I can't pay you for it. I want it gone."

Shaking his head, he scoffed. "I don't want you to pay me for it. Fuck, Kat. Why do you always have to make everything about money? I got it because I knew you needed one. Who cares what the price is? It's a gift, damn it."

Her chest tightened. So many times, she had to justify her choices, watched people she loved turn their backs when they couldn't accept her decisions. She was tired of people telling her what to do when the consequences were hers to live with.

"It's easy not to care about price tags when you own your own company, Tyson. I can't afford it! Who's going to pay my electric bill once it's installed? You? Then what? Are you going to start paying my rent too? It's my home and my responsibility. I might live with sacrifices you can't abide, but they're *my* sacrifices, not yours."

Jaw tight, he sent her a hard stare and hauled the box out of her house without another word. Confused and upset, she stomped into her room and paced.

Unsure what to do, she went to the kitchen for a glass of water and came up short when she saw him sitting on her front porch. Scared, she slowly walked to the door. Glad the gift was gone, she worried he might also leave—for good.

Stepping outside, she lowered her head and whispered, "I don't want to fight."

He sighed. "I didn't buy it to insult your pride,

Kat. I know you can take care of yourself and Mia. You do a great job. I just wanted to help."

She sniffled. "You do help, but—"

"I get it," he interrupted, holding out his hand. She slid her fingers into his. "I wasn't thinking that it would make your bills go up. I was only thinking about your comfort."

She smiled sadly. "It was really a thoughtful gift. I appreciate the thought, but our budget's stretched as tight as it can go. If you want, we can hang out at your place more—"

"Don't be ridiculous. A little heat won't keep me away."

She squeezed his hand. "Are we okay?"

He nodded. "We're okay."

"No more expensive gifts," she added.

He pulled her onto his lap and hugged her. "You're a pain in my ass. I never met a girl so impossible to spoil."

"But you love me anyway?"

He sighed and rocked back in the chair. "I love you."

~

Mid-August, an invitation in the mail, and Kat groaned as she read the fancy engraved print.

The honor of your presence is requested at the fiftieth birthday celebration for Mrs. Vivian D'Angelo... Black tie... The D'Angelo Estate...

. . .

It should be a milestone affair, but her mother celebrated her birthday ostentatiously every year, each party more obscenely pretentious than the last. Vivian's fiftieth was sure to be a self-important show with a price tag that could feed a third-world country. And Kat would be expected to play the doting daughter.

When Tyson saw the invitation, he read it carefully. "Are you going?"

"I have to go. My mother would disown me if I missed it."

Eyeing her carefully, he placed the invitation on the table. "Are you bringing a date?"

She smiled shyly. "Are you asking if *you*'re going to be my date?"

"I guess I am."

She sighed. Her parents could find fault in the perfect man. "Ty, it won't be fun. It'll be a bunch of egotistical yuppies and political brats bragging about themselves."

"So? I can grin and bear it if you can."

"You'd have to dress up."

"Also, not an issue. I do own more than work boots and jeans, Kat. If you don't want me to go, just say so."

She groaned and pressed her face in her hands. "I want you to go, but my parents can be cruel. I don't want them to hurt you."

He smirked. "Aw, kitten, you're worried about my fragile sensibilities?" He snatched her hand and kissed her knuckles. "I'm a big boy, kitten. I highly doubt your parents can hurt me."

"But what if they don't like you? They don't like anyone they don't handpick."

"Well, no offense, but I really don't give a furry rat's ass if they like me or not. The only opinion I care about is yours. So long as you like me when this is all over, I'm good."

The idea of attending another one of her mother's parties did seem more appealing with the idea of having Tyson by her side. She turned her fingers in his and squeezed. "Thank you."

"Who knows? Maybe we'll end up having fun."

She highly doubted that.

The night of the party, Jade did her hair and loaned her a pair of diamond earrings and matching satin heels. Kat had found a simple, black gown for fewer than forty dollars. It was asymmetrical and fitted around the bodice.

Mia watched her in awe as she got ready. "Momma, you look like a princess."

"Thank you, baby. I sort of feel like one."

"When I'm bigger, can I have that dress?"

She grinned. "Sure."

There was a knock on the door, and Mia bolted into the kitchen. "Tyson's here! Momma, come on!"

A rush of nerves shot through her, and she faced Jade. "I'm so nervous." This must be what most girls felt before prom. She never went to prom. She'd been home with a two-month-old trying to figure out where her next meal would come from that night.

"You look great. Don't be nervous." Jade adjusted her necklace and smiled. "Let's not keep your date waiting."

The moment she saw him, her heart slammed into overdrive. His broad shoulders filled out the jacket of his tuxedo to perfection. He smiled as she stepped into the room.

Holding a small box with a delicate orchid, he kissed her. "You're stunning," he said in a husky whisper. "This is for you." Opening the box, he slid the flower around her wrist.

"Are you two getting married?" Mia asked as she watched them.

Kat paused and giggled at Tyson. "Um, no, sweetie. We're just going to a party."

"Is it a ball?"

"Sort of."

"Well, then you can dance with Tyson, and then he'll kiss you, and you'll be married," she decided, quite the expert on such things.

Kat looked at Jade, who was unsuccessfully trying to hide a grin. She faced Tyson, and he wasn't trying at all. He wore a huge, dimpled grin. "Well, I suppose we better get to that ball then, so I can dance with your momma."

Mia beamed. "Then I'll have a daddy!"

Kat froze. The comment doused the lighter mood, replacing it with a level of seriousness she hadn't anticipated. Mia had never mentioned her lack of father before.

Thankfully, Jade broke the spell. "Okay, munchkin, let's go. Your momma doesn't want to be late for the ball." She ushered Mia out of the house and said, "I'll have her back tomorrow morning. Have fun!"

Finding it difficult to face Tyson, she searched for her clutch. "Well, we better go if we don't want to be late."

"Hey." He caught her arm and waited as she slowly met his gaze. "You really do look lovely. Let's try to have a good time tonight."

With a shaky breath, she nodded. He shut out the lights, and she locked up the house. When she turned, she gasped. "Is that for us?" A sleek black limo waited at the curb.

"Yup." He smiled, taking her arm. "And I don't want to hear a single word about it. It's my treat. I couldn't have you arriving at your mother's party in that gown and in a work truck."

Giddy with excitement, she grinned at the novel vehicle. "I've never ridden in a limo before!"

Her parents' home had been transformed to resemble an elite country club. The large pillars were decked in twinkling lights that could be spotted from the edge of the sprawling lawn. Limos lined the drive, a battalion of chauffeurs guarding the fleet. Valet attendants shuttled cars to the east side of the property as doormen greeted guests.

A doorman took her bag, and he handed Tyson a small ticket. Floors were polished to a high sheen, and every bit of furniture was draped with pristine linens. Silver vases and beautiful flower arrangements bathed the air in a sweet fragrance.

They followed the other guests to the French doors at the back of the house where the main party was taking place. Across the lawn was a huge, white tent bedazzled with millions of twinkling lights. Tables were dressed in shimmering ivory linens and topped with three-foot centerpieces of cascading flowers and candles.

A well-dressed ensemble was arranged with everything from violins to a baby grand piano. Guests mingled, and their voices carried into the night over the echo of smooth music.

The soft wash of cool summer wind teased her shoulders. It seemed Vivian had even controlled the weather gods in her demand for perfection.

Descending the back steps, Tyson took her arm to escort her across the grass toward the tent. A carpeted pathway was laid out for guests. A woman waiting at the edge of the carpet asked their names.

"Katherine D'Angelo and Guest."

The woman checked her clipboard and informed her they were sitting at *Table 6*. Tyson took the place card and led her into the tent. She recognized several familiar facesbut didn't see her parents. When they located their table, it was half full.

She'd been placed, not with her parents, but with the offspring of close associates. No family table for the D'Angelo's.

She introduced Tyson, and the men at the table queried about Adams Construction. Being an entrepreneur, he fit in well. Hardhat or tailored tux, he was confident and at ease, in any situation, it seemed.

After a few minutes of small talk, he excused himself to get something from the bar. The band started a new set, and the newly wed couples sharing their table excused themselves to the dance floor.

Absorbing the beauty of the evening, she sighed. Despite her tedious nature, Vivian had outdone herself. A small envelope sat at each place setting. She opened the gold filigree favor and read the embossed print. A donation had been made in their name to a breast cancer foundation. She slid the note back in the envelope and reminded herself to show it to Tyson later. He'd appreciate that, since breast cancer was what took his sister.

"Well, aren't you a vision."

Kat tensed and slowly turned. Nathan Lithe stood to her right, holding a place card. "Nathan," she greeted through clenched teeth, forcing a grin.

"And I figured we'd be sitting with a bunch of old biddies and stuffed shirts. This is much better." He took the seat next to her, and she scooted her chair closer to Tyson's empty one.

"So tell me, kitty cat, what have you been up to? I want to hear all about the naughty trouble you've been getting into before Dawson returns from the bar and hogs your attention."

The moment the words left his mouth, her skin grew clammy, and Dawson approached. "Katherine," he tightly greeted, taking his seat on the other side of Nathan.

"Hello, Dawson. How have you been?" The last thing she wanted was a scene at her mother's event. She hoped he'd be cordial.

"Very well, and yourself?"

God, I could vomit. "Busy."

His gaze shifted over her shoulder. She turned to find Tyson at her back, holding two glasses of champagne. "Price," he said by way of greeting.

"Adams," Dawson replied equally as cold.

Neither extended their hand. Nathan's eyes took in the scene and sparkled with mischief. "Nathan Lithe," he introduced proudly, forcing himself into the exchange with the subtlety of a cannonball.

"Tyson Adams," Tyson said, placing their drinks on the ivory table and shaking Nathan's hand.

"Any relation to Senator Adams?"

"No."

Dawson shot Nathan a quelling look, and Nathan laughed at his joke. "Oh, well, I guess not." Senator Mathew Adams was an Irish republican.

"Tyson's the CEO of Adams Construction," Kat informed Nathan.

The master of ceremonies took to the microphone requesting everyone's attention, and the small talk, thankfully, was put on hold. The MC welcomed the guests and, with much fanfare, announced the guest of honor. Vivian appeared in an elegant, white ball gown and stepped to the microphone.

She blushed demurely—an interesting trick under so much makeup. "Touched does not begin to describe how I feel. It's a gift in itself to be surrounded by so many wonderful friends."

On cue, Kat's father took her mother's outstretched hand, perfectly playing his supporting role as doting husband. Vivian delicately dabbed her cheeks. "Edward, you always go above and beyond for me. How did I ever get so lucky? Thank you— thank you, everyone. I hope you enjoy the evening as much as I intend to."

Kat nearly threw up in her mouth. As if Vivian didn't plan the entire evening down to the napkins. Greedily sipping her champagne, her focus was on the dance floor as her mother, and her father danced. When they finished, everyone stood and applauded.

Dinner was served while her parents visited each table, greeting guests. When they arrived at their table, Kat stood and kissed her mother's cheek, wishing her a happy birthday. She hugged her father. "You did a wonderful job with the party, Dad." He had nothing to do with the planning, but her mother appreciated the illusion in front of the others.

Vivian laced her arm with his. "Your father insisted we make this one special. He's too good to me."

At least that was partly true. Kat cleared her throat. "Mother, Daddy, I'd like you to meet Tyson Adams."

Her father, always the politician, shook Tyson's hand. Vivian made no attempt at physical contact. "Mr. Adams," she coolly greeted without even pretending to smile.

Tyson maintained a serene expression as Kat clenched her teeth. After years of playing the polite child for her parents' friends, the least they could do was be kind to *her* friends.

"Well, I hope you all enjoy your evening. Come, dear, we have more guests to greet." Her father smiled before escorting them away. Kat tried not to shake with anger at her mother's obvious slight.

They took their seats, and she clenched her fists in her lap.

"Hey. Relax. Everything's fine. Would you like some more champagne?" Tyson whispered as he soothed her tense muscles.

She nodded. Kissing her temple, he stood to refresh their drinks. Kat's gaze followed his progress as Nathan trailed him.

Dawson slid into Nathan's seat. "So, I see you've thawed after all. He's a little...*tall* for you, isn't he Katherine?"

"Shut up, Dawson." She knew what he was implying and kept her gaze averted, finding the mere sight of him repugnant.

Her fists clenched as her spine vibrated with pent-up rage. By the time Tyson returned, she was strongly considering calling it a night.

Seeing his barb left a mark, Dawson smirked. "Enjoy your date. I'm sure everyone will be talking about you tomorrow—and not because they remember what you wore." He stood. "Nathan, what do you say we enjoy those cigars you brought?"

Prick.

"Are you okay?" Tyson asked once they were alone.

She gave a tight nod. He didn't say anything more, but his stare moved in the direction of the men smoking outside the tent.

"I have to use the restroom," she whispered, trembling and on the verge of tears, infuriated that her family kept such acquaintances but also infuriated because there was truth to Dawson's words. People would talk about them. It didn't matter how successful or kind Tyson was, nor did it matter that he treated her wonderful and was great with Mia. All they would see was his race.

Tyson stood and took her arm. He walked her toward the house. She kept her head down as they passed Dawson and Nathan, enjoying their cigars. Tyson waited just outside the French doors as she entered the house.

In the powder room, she locked the door and winced at her pale reflection. Taking a few deep breaths, she splashed some cool water on the inside of her wrists. Why did people have to be such assholes?

When Kat returned to the French doors, Tyson wasn't there. She looked around and gritted her teeth when she saw him by Dawson and Nathan beneath a cloud of gray smoke.

Descending the steps, she walked as fast as her heels could manage. Tyson said something, and Dawson's features twisted into a sneer. Nathan took a step back as Tyson crowded Dawson, backing him into a pillar.

"Shit," she hissed, dashing off the carpet and cutting through the grass to get to them faster.

Dawson's voice was the first thing she heard, every decibel tightening her insides to the point of physical discomfort. She hated him. "Don't try pulling your shit here, Adams. This isn't Downtown."

Then Dawson whispered something under his breath, and Tyson gripped him by the collar, his eyes hard and cold.

Her steps faltered. This startling threat was not the gentle man she loved. Painfully aware of other guests nearby, she called his name in a desperate plea, "Tyson."

He didn't hear her, his attention solely on the man he hated. "You listen to me, you little prick. You mutter one more disrespectful word to Kat, or so much as look at her wrong, I *will* kill you. Do you understand me?" he growled.

"Take your hands off me, you animal," Dawson snapped, and her eyes widened.

Tyson reinforced his hold with a jerk of his arm, snapping Dawson's head into the pillar. "Do. You. Understand. Me?" His jaw ticked, and his shoulders bunched with tension. He was seething.

"*Katherine!*" Her mother's voice cut through her like an ice pick to the heart. Vivian stood, arms stiff at her sides, gloved hands fisted. "I think it's time for you and your *guest* to leave. *Now.*"

Breath coming quick, she faced Tyson. "What are you doing?" This wasn't what she'd envisioned, no matter how low her expectations of the evening were.

Dawson scoffed, deliberately brushing wrinkles from his tux. "Fine company you keep." He turned to her mother. "Perhaps you should be a bit more selective with your guest list in the future, Vivian."

Her mother's eyes widened, and Kat had heard enough. "Why are you even here, Dawson?"

He laughed derisively. "Take a look around, Kat. Who do you think fits in? Me? Or you?"

"You son of a bitch," Tyson growled, lunging for him.

"Tyson!"

"*That's enough!*" her mother snapped, mouth

tight with disapproval. "Get off my property before I call the police. Who do you think you are, coming here and assaulting our guests?"

"Mother, you don't understand."

Vivian's cold eyes snapped at her. "I understand plenty, young lady. It's you who will never comprehend how civilized adults are meant to behave."

Dawson snidely chuckled, and Kat's breath escaped in a rush as mortification punched through her. But her mother wasn't finished.

"I should have known you would do something like this. Parading in here, making a spectacle—is it never enough to simply be included? Must you always make yourself the center of attention? Will you not be satisfied until you completely humiliate me in front of all of my friends? You think of no one but yourself! I want you to leave!"

Her body shook with such ferocity she feared she'd collapse. She was a teenager all over again, a shameful presence in her parents' otherwise perfect lives. A tear rolled down her cheek, and she stood, paralyzed, and her mother stormed away.

Dawson snickered. "Let's return to the party, Nathan." They walked away, and she stared, unblinking, at the now empty yard.

"Kat," Tyson's soft-spoken voice held concern.

Brushing a hand down her arm, she snapped. *"How could you?"*

He drew back. "I didn't mean—"

"You knew how they were! Did you even stop to think what starting a fight with him would mean to me?"

He scowled and hissed, "I never stop thinking about what my actions mean to you."

"Really? Didn't seem that way two minutes ago."

"You were upset! I know he said something to hurt you. I'm not going to just stand there while some asshole insults you. Fuck that, Kat!"

"No, Tyson. Fuck you because you just fucked me."

She spun away, and he grabbed her arm. "This is exactly what they want. I don't want to fight with you."

Flinging his arm off of her, she choked on the sobs fighting to escape. "It doesn't matter what they want. The only thing that's certain is they don't want me." The soft tinkling of music and festivities hung in the quiet air, totally at odds with the conflict raging inside of her.

"Kat," he pleaded in a soft voice. "I didn't do this to make trouble for you. You have to believe that wasn't my intention. I'm sure we can talk to your mom in the morning and—"

She laughed without humor. "You really don't get it. My family isn't like yours. We don't laugh, and we don't have some warm and fuzzy past full of sweet anecdotes. Since Mia, I've been holding on by a thread, trying to maintain some sort of relationship with my parents for my daughter's sake. This isn't going to just go away, and Mia won't understand why her grandparents disappeared."

"Why would they take it out on Mia?"

"To punish *me!*"

He shook his head, expression wrought with confusion. "I don't understand why you continue to fight to be close to people that treat you like shit. What good is a relationship if it's a dysfunctional one?"

"It's the only kind of relationship I have!" The words left her mouth before she could pull them back.

His hands dropped, and his expression blanked. "I see."

Soft laughter broke the silence as a couple emerged from the tent. "I want to go home." Without waiting for a reply, she fled to the limo.

Chapter 23

AFTER A SILENT DRIVE HOME—KAT refusing to even hear him out—he entered his house and slammed the door. "Fuck!" Stalking to the fridge, he grabbed a beer.

He expected Kat's family to be difficult. He was prepared to swallow his pride to ensure everything went smoothly. What he wasn't prepared for was Dawson fucking Price. When Kat disappeared into the house, he could tell she was upset. He'd been gone for only a few minutes, and the only person that could have upset her was the douchebag sitting next to her in his absence. Figuring he'd get some answers, he'd moseyed on over to where Price and his little toady hung.

"Senator Adams! Someone chase your Kat up a tree?" Lithe had joked.

"Something like that," Tyson drawled, his hands deep in his pockets as he eyed Price.

"Women," Price commented, streams of rank smoke circling his head. "I'll tell you, if they're not on their backs or their knees, they're more trouble than they're worth."

"Is that so?" Tyson asked.

Lithe laughed a little too hard as Price's lips curled around the end of the cigar. "What's the deal with you, Adams? Why's a successful guy like yourself wasting time with some other man's cast-offs?"

His shoulders stiffened. "Excuse me?"

"Kat. Why bother with damaged goods when you could probably have your run at half the untethered women here. You're quite a novelty, I'm sure. And if what they say is true, I imagine—"

Before he could utter another word, Tyson lunged at him. "Nobody gives a fuck what you think, except maybe your little lap dog over there," he growled. "If I ever hear you speak of Kat in such a disrespectful manner again—"

"Oh, please! She's not worth defending, and you know it. You think you're the first man she's spread for? She was knocked up at seventeen, for Christ's sake! You're pissed because I had her before you."

He wanted to fucking disembowel the bastard but knew if he laid one hand on him, he wouldn't stop until the man was nothing more than a bloodied bag of bones.

Chuckling, Price drew a long drag from his cigar and blew it in his face. "She said I was the best she ever had."

Breathing harshly, he tried to reel in his temper. Leaning close, he sneered, "You lie. I know for a fact you're lying. You may be able to fool these idiots into believing you're some prize, but you didn't fool her, and you don't fool me. She didn't want *you*, not the other way around. I know it, you know it, and I bet you even Scrappy Doo over there knows how full of shit you are."

Dawson let out a cocky laugh. "Don't fool yourself into thinking she's better than she is. She may come from money, Adams, but she's trash."

Control snapped, he jerked Price's collar in his fists, making the bastard's teeth clatter. "You think you're such a big man. Let me clear things up for you. She has more class in her little finger than you'll ever have in your entire life. Whatever you think of her, she's still too good for you."

The man had crossed a line, and Ty refused to forgive him. It wasn't long before he'd totally lost control of the situation, and the night went to shit. His stomach plummeted the moment he recognized the humiliation in Kat's eyes, humiliation he'd played a part in putting there. Then he saw her mother, and there was no excusing his behavior.

She looked at him like a stain, a smear of tarnish on a finely polished pearl. She'd judged him before they were even introduced, and he was furious with himself for giving her the slightest impression that she'd judged right.

The woman was vicious. Her words to Kat left him speechless. He understood now, after witnessing how cruelly she spoke to her own daughter, that she'd care little about the fact that he'd been defending her honor.

This hold they had on her, made no sense. Kat seemed to think it was okay to take that kind of belittling crap from people so long as they *pretended* to love her. Then she'd gone and lumped every relationship she had—including theirs—in the same dysfunctional category. He was speechless.

How could she compare what they shared to what she suffered with her parents? Beyond hurt, his mind played over all the times he'd gone out of his way for her, built her up when she was feeling down. The fact that she could even compare their relationship to the one she had with her parents made him sick. And if they honestly could give up their granddaughter to spite Kat, then they didn't deserve to have a kid like Mia in their life. His brain couldn't even wrap around such a gross display of manipulation.

He'd tried to reason with her, but there would be no way of explaining what had actually driven him to put his hands on the man. He could never tell Kat the demeaning things Price said. He dreaded what she might have heard before he realized she was there. His phone buzzed, and he reached in his pocket, but it wasn't there.

Rushing off the couch to find his tux jacket, he hurtled over the ottoman with the grace of a drunken antelope and fumbled with the jacket until his phone clattered to the floor. "Don't hang up, don't hang up, don't hang up!" His thumb slid across the screen. "Kat?"

The feminine voice that purred on the other end did not belong to his kitten. "Hello, Ty."

He frowned at the screen, disappointment flooding him. "Imani?"

~

"I've got coffee!" Jade cheered, entering the house. "I can't wait to hear about your magical night!"

Kat couldn't muster a smile. "I can't. I need to take a shower."

Concern immediately overtook her friend's expression. "What happened?"

Her eyes blurred, but she fought back her outburst, knowing Mia was in the next room. She shook her head and, in a hoarse voice, said, "I can't talk about it. Not right now. I'm sorry. I just want to be alone."

Jade nodded. "Okay, honey. Whatever you want, but you call me if there's anything I can do. I'm here for you."

Kat thanked her for the coffee, and Jade kissed Mia goodbye. Her best friend had seen what Kat's parents were capable of doing to her firsthand, so, mercifully, Jade didn't press her for explanations.

Setting Mia up with a movie, she took a long shower and had herself what she promised was the last cry of the day. Realizing around eleven o'clock that her mother was going to stand Mia up for their outing, she promised a trip to the park.

Bagging some snacks and drinks, she grabbed a picnic blanket and loaded Mia in the car. They drove for several minutes, listening to a CD of *Barney's Greatest Hits* without saying a word. Mia brought Gorrum to the playground, and, for once, Kat was grateful for the invisible meowing dinosaur's presence.

When they got to the park, she spread out the blanket in the shade of a tree, and Mia ran off to play while Kat positioned herself so she could see her daughter. She pulled out a library book and attempted to read. It wasn't happening. After reading the same paragraph a dozen times without comprehending a single word, she gave up.

Her mind went to Tyson. What he did, well, no one had ever defended her like that. However, her aversion to unwanted attention overshadowed his noble intentions. In his attempt to protect her honor, he unintentionally disgraced her in front of her mother—a disappointment Vivian might not forgive this time.

She couldn't hold her mother's shortsightedness against Tyson. As much as he'd contributed to the premature ending of the night, she didn't want what happened to interfere with her future. She was angry and said some things without thinking. It hurt her to know she hurt him when he was only trying to protect her.

When it started getting late, she called Mia, and they headed back to the car. It was time to face the music.

On the way home Kat offered to take Mia to McDonald's, a rare treat. By the time they made it home, it was already dark and past Mia's bedtime. Kat changed her into her pajamas, foregoing her bath, and tucked her into bed.

After she tidied up the house and changed into her pajamas, she grabbed the phone and went to her room. She had six messages. The first was from Tyson.

"Kat, it's me. Please call me."

"Baby, it's me. I don't know where you are, but

we need to talk. Please call me when you get home. I love you."

The third and fourth were also from him and said pretty much the same thing. The fifth message was from her mother.

"Katherine. Call me. We need to speak."

The sixth message was nothing but dead air. About to delete it, she heard the caller clear their throat.

"Kat..." She frowned, not recognizing the voice as the caller cleared his throat again. "It's Jeremy..." Her hand gripped the dresser as her knees gave out. "Jeremy Larson...from high school. I, uh, got your number from your mom. I didn't know how to find you, so I stopped at your parents' house this morning. She said you lived in New Castle now. How are you? I wanted to see if we could meet...to talk. About Mia."

He paused for a long moment, and she panted, a sense of claustrophobia setting in.

"How is she? I'd like to meet her, Kat. Well, we can talk about that when you call me back. I'm staying at the Best Western in Parkside for a couple of days until I make other arrangements. Please call me back. I...I hope you're well." He read off the number to his room and also left his cell phone number.

She stumbled across to her bed and numbly sat, staring at the shoes neatly lined up along her wall. The automated voice on the phone asked her to press seven for more options. Time passed in immeasurable beats of panic. The call eventually disconnected as the phone beeped obnoxiously in her lap. In a trance, she hit the end button. It was only then that she heard the pounding at the front door.

Confused, she wandered to the kitchen. Tyson stared through the window, a look of concern on his face. She opened the door.

"Were you asleep?" he asked, taking in her appearance.

"No." Her voice was hollow and quiet. It didn't sound like her.

"May I come in?"

She stepped aside, allowing him to enter. He shut the door, and she walked into the living room and sat on the couch, staring at a spot on the floor where Mia's *My Little Pony* lay.

"You're avoiding me."

She shook her head, trying to focus on his words, knowing they were important, but nothing made sense at that moment. Jeremy was back?

"Kat, can you at least look at me?"

Forcing her head to turn, she looked up at him with a blank stare. He had a five o'clock shadow, and his clothes were wrinkled.

"I'm sorry. I should've never acted like that. It's just...you wouldn't tell me what Dawson did, and I could tell he did something to upset you. I didn't mean to make a scene. I'm sorry that things got out of hand."

She nodded without really processing his words.

"Will you at least say something?"

She swallowed, but it did nothing to remove the lump in her throat. Swallowing again, she croaked, "It's fine."

He rubbed the back of his neck and squeezed

his eyes shut. "It's not fine. I can see you're upset. Yell at me or something. I can't stand us being like this."

She was unfit for company. Slowly, she stood. "I need to go to bed."

He grabbed her hand, halting her steps. She looked in his pleading eyes, tight with tension and fear. "Kat, please," he whispered.

"I need to be alone." She stared blindly at the wall behind him.

"I love you, Kat. This isn't over." He quietly released her hand and let himself out.

Chapter 24

KAT CALLED out of work and dropped Mia off at Mrs. Bradshaw's. When she returned to her house, Tyson's truck was already gone.

Jeremy wanted to talk about Mia. He wanted to meet her. *Then what?* Would he want to meet her once and then leave again? Last she heard, he was in Japan. Was he visiting?

Would Mia want to meet him? Of course, she would. Mia got a kick out of meeting the grocery clerk at the market. Meeting her father would be— but what if he met her and then disappeared again?

Needing to know his intentions, she dialed his cell phone.

"Hello?" His voice sounded more confident than it did on the voice mail, more grown-up. But no familiar tug at her heart or any nostalgic affection came to life.

"Jeremy?"

"Yes."

"This is Kat. Kat D'Angelo."

"Kat! How are you?" He sounded relieved.

"I'm... good. I, um, got your message."

"Yeah, I hope it was okay that I stopped at your parents'. I didn't know if they still lived there. I went to your old apartment first, but some lady lives there now. It was the only way I knew to reach you."

"No, it's fine. I thought you were in Japan."

"I was in Japan, but then I went to Iraq, and then to Texas. I'm done now. Honorable Discharge. I didn't really have anywhere to go, and I still own the deed to my dad's property, but there isn't much of a house left. I figured I'd come back home and see if the land was worth salvaging. I'm meeting with his lawyer today."

"Oh," she answered lamely, trying to process everything.

"Are you free today?"

"Yes." And they needed to come to an understanding before any more people got involved—especially little people. "I took off work after I got your message."

"Can we meet? I'd love to see Mia."

"Jeremy, I think we should talk before Mia learns you're here."

"Oh, right," he sounded disappointed. "Okay, well, when do you want to meet? I'm heading back to the hotel now, but if you give me your address, I can put it in my GPS and come to you."

"No." She wasn't ready for him to know where they lived. "Why don't I come to you at the hotel? Is there a place we can talk?"

"Yeah. There's a restaurant off the lobby that's usually empty during the day."

She needed to get this over with because the unknown was making her nauseous. "Okay, how's ten o'clock?"

"Great. I'll see you then. And Kat, thanks for agreeing to meet with me."

"Sure." She hung up and collapsed on her bed, letting out a long groan.

~

She arrived at the hotel ten minutes early, with some recent pictures of Mia in her bag. As she entered the lobby, a woman at the front desk directed her to the restaurant. Service staff seemed to be breaking stations down after a breakfast rush. A man drank a cup of coffee at a table in the back, and a busboy pushed a sweeper. She looked around but didn't see Jeremy, so she took a seat in the corner and waited.

Tense and fidgety, her teeth dug a hole in her as her knee bounced incessantly. Nothing was calming her nerves.

"Can I get you a coffee, Miss?" a waitress offered.

"Oh, no, thank you. I'm waiting for someone."

"I'll come back then."

The man having coffee stood, and she checked her watch. She grew self-conscious and averted her eyes as he slowed by her table. "Kat?"

Her gaze jerked in the man's direction, seeing something familiar in his green eyes, something— *it's him.* Her empty belly swished, and she swallowed hard.

"Jeremy?" She wheezed, shaking her head. "I barely recognized you—I mean—I didn't."

This wasn't the Jeremy she knew in high school. This was Jeremy, the adult. Unlike the thin, baby-faced boy who'd kissed her in the back of his father's Bronco, this man was broad and solid. Creases engraved by life experiences surrounded his eyes. His posture was confident, like that of a military man. His hair was shorn, and his eyes were still as green as fresh cut grass, more vibrant than ever against his tanned skin.

He smiled. "You look great. May I sit down?"

"Please," Kat said, unable to absorb that this was the same boy she'd met in high school. "The waitress just came by, but I'm sure—"

He slid into the chair, derailing her thoughts. She had this man's child, yet he seemed a total stranger—*was* a stranger.

"I'm fine for now. Did you want something?"

Shaking her head, she whispered, "No, thank you." Lowering her gaze so as not to stare, she studied the table as they sat quietly for a few minutes.

"I guess this is a little awkward," Jeremy commented, breaking the silence. "I'm sorry to show up like this. When I was in Japan, I thought about you and Mia all the time. I wanted to look you up when I came home for my dad's funeral, but I only had a couple of days' leave. Then I went to Iraq, and I regretted not contacting you. I should've kept in touch."

How would Mia have responded to that? And what if he'd been injured at war? It didn't matter anyway. There was no changing the past. "You didn't want that," she reminded him.

"I was a child."

His age was never going to be a valid excuse for her. "Yes," she agreed with a touch of accusation. "So was I."

"I've regretted not knowing my daughter more than anything else in my life, Kat."

The way he called her *my daughter* hit so many nerves, it seemed to chafe her skin.

"It was wrong of me to abandon you two, but I had no way to support you. My dad was an alcoholic on disability. I wouldn't have been able to land a decent job without joining the military. I needed that. I needed to become a man. I tried to look you up online once I started making some money. I wanted to send you support, but I didn't know how to reach you, and I didn't know if you were still in contact with your folks."

He took a deep breath. "I know that doesn't fix my being absent, but I wanted you to know that I thought of you often."

It took several minutes to organize her thoughts. She couldn't see past his blurred sense of entitlement. Yes, he'd gone and made a career for himself, likely earned a decent degree too. That put him ahead of her in some way, and she couldn't shake the sense that everything she existed for was suddenly being threatened.

"She is *my* daughter," she whispered fiercely. "I raised her when I had nothing. I didn't have the option of running away to establish myself. She needed a parent the day she was born, and *I* was that parent.

I held her and loved her and fed her when her own father couldn't even bring himself to *touch* her."

Her throat constricted as her vision blurred. Blinking away her tears, having wasted enough on him years past, she gritted her teeth and continued. "I was a child raising a child. I became a mother before I even learned how to be a woman. While you were off learning how to be a man, I was on my own using food stamps and government vouchers, struggling to finish my GED. While you were thinking about Mia, I was watching her, teaching her to walk, how to say Momma, because that was all she would ever know. You chose to walk away, and I'm sorry if it isn't right, but I reserve the right to choose whether you walk back into our lives or not. She is *mine*."

Words spilled from her mouth, unearthing resentments she'd buried long ago. The thought of losing Mia—even by small degrees—was unbearable. Without Mia, what purpose would she have in this life?

"Kat, I'm so sorry. I know it must have been impossibly hard to raise her on your own. I can never thank you enough for keeping her safe. I'm not asking for custody—"

Her gaze snapped to his at the mention of custody. "She's not an object, and I'm not a safety deposit box," she hissed. "I kept her safe because I love her, and she needed me. I loved her when no one else did, and that's why I protected her. Not for you, but for *her*, for me. And as far as custody, she will *never* live outside of my home until she's married and having children. Never."

Hands held out in a sign of surrender, he shook his head. "I didn't mean that I wanted to take her from you." His hand rubbed roughly over his face. "This is coming out all wrong. Let me start over. All I'm asking is to see her. I don't even know what she looks like. She doesn't even have to know I'm her father at first if that makes it easier. All I'm asking of you right now is to let me be a part of her world, even if it's as an outsider looking in. I have money, Kat. I've put away money for you guys for years. I know I can't undo the past, but let me at least make up for it in the ways that I can. I have a check." He reached into his pocket and slid a slip of paper across the table. "If it isn't enough, I can get more."

She stared down at the folded check, afraid to lay a hand on it.

"If I agree to let you see her, even if she doesn't know who you are, everything will be by my rules. *Everything*. You can't speak to her without my permission. I will not have her getting hurt if this is some whim and you suddenly change your mind."

He nodded. "Your rules." He nudged the check forward. "Please take this."

Unsteadily breathing, her hand hesitantly reached forward as she unfolded the check. Her fingers released it as if it burned her skin. It was made out to Katherine and Mia D'Angelo in the sum of *twenty thousand* dollars. That was more than she made in a year. Eyes wide, she gaped at him in shock.

"I know it doesn't fix things—"

"It's..." Her vocal cords locked up, trapping her words. Dropping her gaze to the table, the blue penned scrawl ate up her gaze. Swallowing, she shook her head.

This would mean being able to finally pay Mrs. Bradshaw a decent amount for watching Mia. It would mean not having to wash dishes in cold water or worrying that she was in the shower for more than five minutes. It meant finally being able to afford an air conditioner, or name-brand cereal, or ballet classes for Mia.

A child was the responsibility of the parents, meaning both the mother *and* father. This sort of provision was due to her daughter. It wasn't an extravagant gift. It was everything he should have been paying from the start. There were no words for such unexpected support, support from the one person who should have been offering assistance all along.

She managed the only words she could. "Thank you."

"Please don't cry," he said, moving his seat closer to the table. Reaching to comfort her, he hesitated and dropped his hand before making contact.

Searching her purse, she fumbled around for a tissue. "I'm sorry. I have pictures," she rasped, digging further into her bag. She slipped a few onto the table.

Hand trembling, he slowly lifted the photos. "She's beautiful," he whispered.

Their eyes met, both shot with pink and glazed with tears. She let out a watery laugh. He'd never know how much she'd needed that check because her pride wouldn't allow all her sacrifices to be told. But the fact that he'd made such an offer alleviated a great number of her worries, worries she'd carried for almost four years on her own.

There was a marked improvement in her perception of his character, an undeniable forgiveness wavering inside of her. It was the first fatherly thing she'd ever seen him do. And that made her happy—happy for Mia.

～

Once their emotions were under control, Kat let down her guard. She told Jeremy Mia was learning her letters and obsessed with Cinderella. She explained about Gorrum and warned him never to use pepper when he's around because, according to Mia, Gorrum is 'highly 'lergic'.

Jeremy told her about Japan and his time in Iraq. He didn't go into detail about the war but explained why he was home. He'd spent time at a clinic in Texas that specialized in rehabilitating war veterans with post-traumatic stress disorder. He'd lost a good friend and shattered his kneecap during his last tour but walked away with more than some superficial wounds. Realizing he could have died without ever knowing his only child seemed to change his position on a lot of things.

She wasn't sure how she wanted to proceed with Jeremy, but she was glad he was alive. How they proceeded would be by her rules. However, her rules only could protect Mia for another fifteen years. Once she was an adult, it would be her choice to find her father, and Kat would have no choice but to support her decision.

By the time she left the hotel, she was more than fifty percent sure she was going to let Jeremy see Mia. It was wrong for her to let her own insecurities get in the way of her daughter knowing—and possibly having a relationship with—her father.

He was considering building a home on his father's land in Parkside. That would make him a permanent part of their lives. She had a lot to consider.

On the way home, she stopped at the bank and opened a savings account with Jeremy's check. She never had enough money to need a savings account before. There were no qualms about taking that money. Her ignorance and pride never allowed her to file for the child support she was entitled to, but Mia deserved every penny.

Jeremy mentioned setting up a payment plan for additional support once they established a foundation. It was surreal and too intimidating to depend on just yet.

As she unlocked the door that evening, the phone was ringing. Tossing her stuff on a kitchen chair, she raced inside to grab it.

"Hello?" she answered, out of breath.

"Where were you?"

Jolted by his impatient tone, she frowned. "Tyson?"

"Yeah. How come you weren't at work today?"

"How did you know I wasn't at work?"

"Because I stopped by to bring you flowers on my lunch break. Dr. Stevens said you called out, so I swung by the house. Then I went to Mrs. Bradshaw's, and she said she assumed you were at the office."

"You brought flowers to my work?" Sad she missed such a surprise, she softened.

"Yeah. Kat, where were you?" He sounded frustrated and worried.

She looked down at Mia playing at her feet. "I had to take care of some stuff." She couldn't mention Jeremy in front of her, and this wasn't a conversation to be had over the phone with Tyson.

"What kind of stuff? What's going on, Kat? I thought you were in a ditch somewhere. I *swear to God*, tomorrow I'm getting you a cell phone."

Ooh, cell phone! Definitely picking up one of them!

Regretting that she'd inadvertently made him worry, she tried to explain. "Ty, I can't go into it right now. I had a crazy day. A lot happened. I'm taking Mia out to dinner. Can you come over after eight, and we'll talk?"

"You're taking Mia out to dinner?"

He was probably thinking how absurd that sounded, being that she budgeted out her weeks down to the penny. But the truth was, she still hadn't gone grocery shopping, and she felt like celebrating.

"Yeah, it's a long story."

"Is anyone else going with you?"

"What? No, just us. Hey, what's a nice place?"

"A nice place?" His words were slow, tinged with confusion.

"Never mind, I'll go to that place in New Castle that just opened. Can you come over tonight?"

"Yeah..."

"Okay, I'll see you tonight. Love ya."

"I love you too," he said, almost as if he were phrasing a question.

She understood he was confused and going to be as shocked as she was to hear Jeremy was back, but she'd explain everything tonight. For now, it was time to treat her daughter.

"Who was that, Momma?"

She tossed the phone on the counter. "Don't worry about it." Clasping her hands together, she grinned. "How about we go eat at a big fancy restaurant?"

"Yeah?" Her eyes lit at the novelty of such a treat.

"Yeah! Go wash your hands. Mommy's going to change, then I'll get you dressed, and we'll go."

"Okay!" she trilled as she dashed to the bathroom.

~

Tyson stared at the phone. What the hell was going on? Did she win the lottery? The person he'd just talked to was not his kitten.

He paced his living room. Nothing about the way she was acting was making sense. Kat didn't go out to eat. She bought government cheese and discount bread for Christ's sake.

He went to the fridge, grabbed a bottle of water, and dropped into a chair. Trixie came to his side, dripping drool over his arm as she presented him with a half-deflated ball. He took the slimy thing and hurled it across the room.

The dog took off after it. At least he could please one girl in his life.

Last night when he had gone to Kat's, she was beyond upset. She hadn't returned any of his calls, and he was terrified she might break up with him before giving him a chance to make things right.

The moment she'd opened the door, he'd realized he hadn't given her enough time. Seeing her so distant and distraught made the threat of losing her all the more real. He wanted her to talk to him, yell at him if she needed to.

No matter how secure he was in his life, losing Kat would cut him down. It was absolutely imperative that he fixed things between them, which he had all intentions of doing until she disappeared.

Too much had happened. Events began to blur as he played them back in his mind and obsessed over every detail. Was this about Dawson? Everything was suspicious—the missed calls, the disappearing act, her cryptic explanations, and now dinner.

Something was up, and he needed to know what. Having not slept more than a few hours in the past three days, his nerves were shot. Maybe it was time he stopped being so damn understanding and start demanding she deal with this like an adult and confront whatever the hell she was avoiding— mainly, him.

~

On their way to the restaurant, Kat passed a cellular phone store and purchased her first smartphone. At the restaurant, she let Mia order whatever she wanted. She started with dessert, and so Kat did the same. After dessert Kat ordered the almond crusted tilapia, and Mia had mashed potatoes and ravioli. The waiter thought they were nuts, but all was forgiven when she left him a generous tip.

On the way home, they spontaneously stopped at *Wal-Mart*. Kat bought Mia some new DVDs, some much-needed clothes, and a new doll. She also picked up some staples like milk and toilet paper—the expensive fluffy kind!

When they pulled up at the cottage, Tyson was sitting on her porch, expression blank but definitely not happy. He would be once he understood what was going on.

As Mia climbed out of the car, she crowed, "Tyson! Look at my new doll!"

Kat reached into the backseat and pulled the other bags.

He suspiciously eyed her packages. "Go shopping?"

"Yeah. Sorry, we're late. Let me get Mia to bed, then we can talk. I think there's some red wine left from the other night. Why don't you get us each a glass?" Dumping her items on the counter, she wrangled Mia toward her bedroom.

When she returned to the kitchen, Tyson was standing at the counter holding the box that contained her new cell phone and frowning. There were two glasses of wine on the counter.

"Sorry," she said, picking up her wine and taking a sip. "Ooh, that's good. Do you want to sit outside?"

"You bought a cell phone?" His brow crinkled with disbelief.

"I know, isn't it great? Here—" She picked up her purse and pulled out a receipt. "This is my number. Type it in your phone."

He didn't move.

"Don't you want my number?"

"Kat, what the hell's going on? You take off all day on Sunday, and when I come by to talk to you, you can't even look at me. You call out of work today and won't tell me where you've been. Then you act all secretive and won't tell me anything. You go out to dinner—to a *nice* restaurant—buy a cell phone, and go on a shopping spree? And now you're acting like everything's normal."

"It was hardly a shopping spree," she mumbled.

"It is for you!" he snapped. "You won't even buy cupcakes!"

"Shh, you're going to wake up Mia."

"Tell me what's going on," he demanded, expression hard.

Realizing she should probably take it down a notch, she carried her wine out front. On the rocking chair sat a wilted bouquet of lilies, and her good mood faltered. She was a jerk.

Lifting the flowers, she eyed him apologetically. "Ty, I'm sorry," she whispered.

"How about explaining what you've been doing since yesterday morning."

Sitting down, she took a deep breath and explained everything. She told him that yesterday she didn't want to think about her parents and the fiasco at the party. She admitted to having mixed emotions about his confrontation with Dawson.

She told him how disappointed Mia was when Vivian didn't show up for their outing.

As she spoke, the tension in his expression seemed to ease. "Do you ever just feel too wiped to deal? That's how I felt, Ty. I simply didn't have the energy."

"I'm sorry."

She nodded and took a deep breath. *Time to tell all.* "When I finally got home Sunday, there were several messages on my voicemail. I was so happy to hear yours and had all intentions of calling you back, but there were two others."

"Did your mom call?"

"Yeah, but that's not the one that threw me for a loop. The last message was from Jeremy."

His head shot up. "Mia's father?"

She nodded and swallowed. "I know. He was the last person I ever expected to call. He's back."

He didn't move, and she wasn't even sure he was breathing.

"Are you okay?"

He cleared his throat, gaze focused on the ground. "Keep going. What happened today?"

"I called out of work so I could meet with him."

His body tensed, but he didn't say a word, so she went on.

"He looks totally different—grown up. When we first started talking, I was furious. I hadn't expected to react like that. I was scared. He has a degree and is financially stable and suddenly talking about custody."

"Fuck that. Mia's yours."

She swallowed. "That's what I told him."

"Good."

"He's never done anything that showed me he was truly interested in being an active parent. It's really hard to trust the one person who let me down more than anyone else. As much as my parents abandoned me when I could have used their support, it was Jeremy's responsibility. There's so much resentment I buried over the years, for Mia's sake."

She let out an unsteady breath. "But today, he fixed a bit of that broken trust. He's been putting away money, money for Mia, money to help me support her. He gave me a check."

"That's a start," he commented, not seeming overly impressed.

"Tyson, it was for *twenty thousand dollars*." She still couldn't believe she had that kind of money. "Isn't that unbelievable?"

He continued to stare, a million different emotions racing across his face. "Did you take the check?"

"Of course I took the check! He's Mia's father. I never asked for anything from him as far as financial support. If he is willing to pay for things that we've always gone without, then I'm willing to accept."

"But you wouldn't take an air conditioner from me in the middle of a heatwave?"

She frowned. "That's different. That would've been like charity. Mia is entitled to this money."

"Because he's her father?"

"Yes." Why wasn't he happier for her? "Tyson, you have to understand how hard it's been for us, how many things I've gone without to make sure Mia had everything she needed. You have no idea what it was like when she was a year old and had the flu, and I couldn't afford her antibiotics. This money will change all that."

Easing back, but not looking at her, he said, "I understand that a boy got a girl pregnant, shrugged off all his responsibilities, and left all the weight on her shoulders. I also understand that, because of a five-minute act of stupidity, that boy, who is now a man, is entitled to a piece of Mia that no other man can claim. What I can't seem to stomach is hearing you call him her father." Face tight, he finally faced her. "He was a sperm donor up until today. Being a father is more than some genetic link. It's in deeds, in seeing and being a part of her day-to-day life. He doesn't even know her."

"Why are you so angry?"

"Where the hell has he been all her life, Kat?" he fiercely asked. "Where was he while you were in labor? On her first birthday? When she took her first step?"

Not expecting to have to defend herself for accepting child support from her daughter's father, she scoffed. "I know he wasn't there, and he knows it too. What I don't know is why you are taking all of this so personally. It's not like any of this makes your life more difficult!"

"What's going to happen now, Kat? Are you guys going to be this big, happy family?"

"No! I don't even know him, Tyson. He's a stranger to me. I haven't even decided what I'm going to do yet. Why are you being like this?"

He stood and squatted in front of her. Taking both of her hands in his, he met her gaze, eyes pleading. "Where does this leave me, Kat? I love you, and I love Mia. I can't compete with her father. Not when you're willing to take from him what you won't let me provide for you. You two have this past that I know nothing about. You only talk about your history with him in terms of *him* leaving. Does his presence change things between us? What do you feel for this guy? I love you, but the last thing I want to do is stand in the way of a family being together. I can't do that to Mia. But I don't want to walk away. I'm not even sure I have the strength to. If this is going to be some sort of reconciliation for you three, I deserve to know."

"Tyson..." She wrapped her arms around his neck and leaned her forehead to his. God. Any remaining anger from the other night washed away. He was a mess, and it was all her fault. He really, truly loved her. "I *love* you."

His arms pulled her close and hugged her tight. "I don't want to lose you, Kat."

"I don't want to lose you either. Jeremy might've been there when I lost my virginity, but you were there the first time I made love. You were the first person I ever let into my heart. The first person to ever love me back without conditions. There is absolutely no comparison between the two of you. You have nothing to fear."

∿

The following Saturday, Kat made arrangements to take Mia to the park by their house. Jeremy planned to arrive twenty minutes before them. He gave her his word that he would not approach Mia yet, since she was still figuring out how to broach the subject with their daughter. Tyson wanted to come with them, but she asked him to let them go alone and promised him a full report when they returned.

As soon as they arrived at the playground, Mia ran out of her arms and onto the jungle gym. She spotted Jeremy sitting on a nearby bench, but he didn't spare her a glance. His eyes were rapt on Mia.

As she slid down the slide and squealed with delight, his face lit. She pushed Mia on the swings, played on the seesaw animal, and Jeremy never took his gaze off her. Mia climbed across the wooden bridge and yelled, "Hi, Momma! Look how big I am!"

She moved around between the different equipment faster than a pinball ricochets. As she climbed the ladder to the slide, she lost her footing and fell. Jeremy stood and instinctively took a step forward but stilled when Kat met his gaze.

Children fell a lot. Sometimes falls were bad, and sometimes they were only scary. Kat scooped Mia into her arms as she began to cry. The physical restraint it took for Jeremy to respect her wishes and not approach was evident.

Kat brushed off her legs and walked her to a bench. She could never predict how Mia would react to things like this. Sometimes she would pick herself up and move on as if nothing happened, and other times she would milk it for days. The scrape was red but not bleeding. However, this appeared to be one of those times where Mia needed to be comforted.

As she kissed her knee and rocked her in her lap, Mia clung to her. "I wanna go home," she cried.

Kat nodded to Jeremy, letting him know she was okay, and he slowly sat down. When she stood, still holding Mia, and grabbed her purse, his eyes widened with concern.

She gave him an apologetic look and casually waved goodbye behind Mia's back. The look on his face pinched her heart. It was as if she were taking something magical away from him. And in all reality, she was.

Later that day, she told Tyson about the playground as they sat in his backyard while Mia played with Trixie.

"So what do you think you'll do?" he whispered.

"I don't know. I need to be in control, but at the same time, I feel horrible denying him."

He didn't say anything.

"Ty, if you could have seen how happy he was watching her and how sad he was when I took her away..."

"She's a great kid."

They sat in silence, observing Mia. He held Kat's hand, rubbing his thumb back and forth. It was a subtle show of support and affection. They'd gotten more lax about showing affection in front of Mia.

"I miss you," he said in a low voice.

"I missed you too." She gave his hand a little squeeze.

"Is your mother taking Mia tomorrow?"

"I don't know. I haven't talked to her since the party."

"That's my fault," he said apologetically, then laughed. "I guess I deserve being punished by not getting any alone time with you."

She smirked. She hadn't been avoiding him to punish him. "What would you have done if Dawson hit you?" she asked, a little curious at how far he would've taken the fight to defend her honor. It was a *little* sexy.

"I would've buried him in the cement foundation of the house I'm building."

She laughed, and they settled into a comfortable silence. Kat hadn't spoken to her mother since the party. Mia, from what she could tell, wasn't aware anything was wrong. But that would only last so long. Eventually, her daughter would start asking where Grandmom was. Plus, she missed her Sundays alone with Tyson.

"I guess I should call my mother."

"Don't call her if it's going to upset you. We can find other ways to spend time alone. I never mind Mia being around."

He didn't mind Mia being around. Despite her sexual frustration, they still enjoyed each other's company in her daughter's presence. If she could just make amends with Vivian, they could have their Sundays back.

The longer she thought about Vivian, the more her brain hurt. She decided to change the subject. "How did your meeting go?"

He let the topic change. "Good. I'm glad this job's almost over. I have to work out some final details then I'm going to have to fly to Washington to do the final inspection with the client. Wanna come?"

"You know I can't do that. When do you have to go?"

"Probably later next week."

She sighed. More time apart.

Later that evening, Tyson distracted Mia with *Beauty and the Beast* so Kat could call her mother. She took the phone into her room and shut the door.

Vivian jumped right into her role as the wounded martyr. "I don't understand how a guest in our home could behave in such a way. I was *mortified*. He showed absolutely no concern for the sensibilities of our company. Honestly, Katherine, what would possess you to invite such a man? It was barbaric—although I can't say I am surprised."

And there was the root of it.

"A man who loses control like that is someone to worry about. Who's to say where his brutality ends? I hope you're not exposing Mia to his lack of morals."

Her head began to pound. "I'm not calling to discuss Tyson, Mother. But I will say this. Tyson's a wonderful man. He's kind and caring and wonderful with Mia."

Vivian scoffed. "I shouldn't be surprised you—"

"He's a good friend," she interrupted, not wanting to give her mother the chance to say anything more unforgivable than she already had. "I care about him very much—"

"Oh, I do not have to listen to this—"

"No, you don't, but I need to say it. Dawson

Price is an arrogant jerk who's bitter because I wouldn't allow him into my bed. He disrespected me—and while you may not take offense when I'm mistreated—Tyson does. He was defending *me*. I'll apologize for him offending your guests' 'delicate sensibilities, but I won't apologize for my feelings for him—"

"*Feelings?*" Her mother nearly barked. "Dear God, Katherine! Tell me you are not romantically involved with this man."

"I'm in love with him." The line grew so quiet she thought her mother hung up until she vaguely heard Vivian ask under her breath what she ever did to deserve a daughter like her. "I'm an adult, and for the first time in my life I'm happy."

"You may be an adult in age, but I have yet to see you make one responsible decision in your adult life, young lady," she argued.

"How can you say that?" Kat shouted, too offended to pretend indifference.

"Don't you shout at me, young lady!"

"Or what?" she snapped, no longer carefully choosing her words. "Add it to the list of ways I disappoint you! Go ahead! I can't stand it anymore! No matter what I do, it's never enough! I can't believe I even care anymore. Nothing I do will ever be good enough for you!"

"You have no idea what it's been like for us, constantly having to cover up your mistakes—"

Gasping, as emotion choked her, she stilled. Tyson stood in the doorway, his eyes sympathetic and resigned. She looked at him and, in a broken voice, whispered, "I'll never be enough."

He walked toward her and pulled her into his arms as she started to cry. He removed the phone from her numb fingers and ended the call. "Shh..." he whispered, pressing his lips into her hair. "I've got you."

Chapter 25

IT WAS no surprise Vivian didn't show. Tyson was a great distraction, replacing Mia's disappointment with exciting adventures. They visited the petting zoo and a nearby orchard, and by the time they were driving home, Mia passed out holding a half-eaten candied apple.

"She's out cold," Ty said, returning from Mia's room.

"I think that hayride did her in—" Catching the glint in his eye, she stilled. "I know that look."

His gaze smoldered as he slowly stalked her into the kitchen. She giggled as he slid her sweater off her shoulders and let it drop to the floor.

"So this morning was all a ploy to tire Mia out so you could have your wicked way with me," she teased.

He gave her a bashful, dimpled smile, his lips grazing her collarbone. "I told you I would find ways." Entwining his fingers with hers, he backed

379

his way down the hall, tugging her silently toward the bedroom.

"We'll have to be quiet," she warned.

"I'm sure we can manage."

The door shut, and she was yanked into his arms. Chest to chest, she stared at him. Pure lust had her breath coming fast. Pivoting, he firmly pressed her spine against the door, his arms caging her in against the wood. "Has your pill kicked in yet?"

"Last week. " She'd gone to the gynecologist a month ago to see about getting on birth control.

A deep, satisfied growl left his throat as he kissed her. His fingers dropped to the snap of her jeans as hers frantically unlatched his belt buckle. Tilting her head, his mouth bit at her throat, placing open-mouthed kisses across her skin. Hands skimmed under her shirt, over her ribs, and up to her bra, pinching her nipple through the lace, and she moaned. Shucking her pants and panties, she kicked them away with her shoes.

Reaching into his open pants, she pulled his cock free as he gave a guttural moan against the soft flesh of her throat.

"This needs to come off," he said, giving her shirt a tug.

Lifting her arms, he removed the shirt in one quick pull, and she dropped to her knees. Her hand wrapped around his thick cock as she kissed the tip.

Letting out a strangled moan, he braced his arms against the door. "Jesus, Kat, let a man know…"

His feet stepped farther apart as her lips stretched around him. He hissed and went up on his toes, his strong fingers tunneling through her hair. "That's it, kitten. Suck my cock."

Hoping she was doing it right, she measured her strokes by the intense sound of his breathing and half-spoken words of praise. A pearl of fluid seeped from the slit. The scent she associated with intimacy and Tyson was stronger here. He was as hard as steel and soft as satin at the same time. Her fingers wrapped around the base of his thickness as her mouth slid down.

"You look so good down there. Let me see you take me in your mouth again."

Slowly opening her mouth, she took him deep. His face relaxed in ecstasy. "Mmm, that's it, kitten. Just like that." The hand in her hair gently guided her rhythm. "Do you have any idea how fucking sexy you are?"

Easing forward, her palms curved around his muscular thighs, and she gave him control.

"It feels incredible when you do that." His fist tightened in her hair. The pinch along her scalp only added to the delicious mix of sensations. Thrusting his hips, he fucked her mouth, taking quick, shallow dips over her tongue. His thighs quivered under her palms as he grunted and released her hair.

His cock slid from her mouth as his hands gripped under her arms and lifted her off her knees. The cool door pressed into her back. "Put your legs around me," he ordered.

Warm and wet, he pressed against her sex and sank into her core. Her arms caught his neck as his hands slid to support her ass. The sensation of skin to skin made everything better, though a tickle of fear remained.

"Hey," he whispered, nudging her chin with his nose. "It's okay."

Rather than run through the mood-killing statistics of birth control, she nodded and let out a deep breath. He kissed her nose and smiled. "Ready?"

Needing the pleasure to override her paranoia, she extended her spine and slammed her mouth to his. Tongues dueling in a passionate collision of need, he thrust into her. The kiss broke as she let out a cry of pleasure.

"Shh..." he laughed. Lifting her, he walked them to her dresser. Releasing his neck, she braced her arms on the surface.

The dresser rocked, and a picture frame fell to the floor as he thrust into her. His mouth latched onto her breast, his fingers slid down her belly, and sought out that magical spot. As soon as she moaned, he silenced her with a kiss, rubbing harder, faster, as an orgasm crept up on her.

Her channel clenched around him, and he groaned into her mouth. His hips bucked as his spine stiffened. Crying out her release, she tightened again, and the heat of his release filled her as he trembled.

Leaning his forehead against hers, he panted, his gaze meeting hers in an intense stare. "I fucking love you, Katherine D'Angelo. I love you."

How was it nothing they'd just done had been gentle, yet it somehow constituted making love? This intensity, raw affection, and passion she shared with him was ever-growing and changing her in ways she never expected to change. "I love you too."

They slid apart by small degrees, and her skin heated every time she caught him watching her. Straightening her dresser, her eyes widened as she felt another difference between using condoms and not. Heat slowly trickled down her thigh, and she stilled. "I need a shower."

Fleeing the room with only her robe, she raced to the bathroom. As she mechanically washed away all remnants of sex, her body luxuriated in the tender ache that lingered in her muscles. Suds trailed over her belly as— *"Jesus, you scared me!"*

He laughed, climbing into the small tub as steam swirled around them. "Now that's a sight. Mind if I join you?"

He was way too big for her shower. Reaching over her head, he tilted the showerhead and sprayed his chest with water. Rolling his head over his shoulders, he stretched. She stared, mouth open, eyes unblinking. He was so damn good looking—manly—mouthwatering—godly, like Adonis or whoever the hottest god was.

The water turned back on her, and she sputtered. Totally not sexy.

"You're staring, kitten."

"Well, now I'm blind," she gasped, wiping her eyes.

He nudged her shoulder, and she faced the wall. The cap of the shampoo snapped open as strong hands lifted chunks of hair off her shoulders and massaged her scalp.

She leaned into his touch, moaning as he

worked a thick lather into her hair. "I don't think I've ever washed hair so soft," he whispered.

Once clean, he pulled her back against his chest and wrapped an arm over her shoulders, hugging her from behind. They swayed as warm water sloshed over their skin. His lips curved against her cheek. "I love touching you."

She shut her eyes and rested her other cheek on the hand holding her shoulder. He wasn't kissing her, just holding her, breathing her in, pressing his lips to her as if he couldn't bear to let her go. It was likely the most intimate moment of her entire life.

She breathed in, swallowing his scent. *Never forget that smell. No matter what, always remember how great he smelled.*

Soon after their shower, Mia awoke from her nap. Tyson ran home to get Trixie, and Kat's heart tightened as the three of them played in the back-yard. No matter how much the day had strayed from her routine, nothing seemed to break the sense that it somehow found its way to being a perfect Sunday after all.

Leaving Mia in a game of fetch, he smirked and slowly met her at the door. "Do you need to go to the market?"

She didn't want to leave, but if she didn't do her Sunday chores, her week would be a bit harder. "Yeah."

"Why don't you go, and I'll keep Mia? We can have dinner at my place tonight."

This was big. Though her daughter was ad-justing to Tyson's increasing presence in their life, the more time they spent together, the more Mia would assume he was there to stay. She was beginning to wonder why that was such a bad thing. "Are you sure?"

"Of course. Take a break and go get your errands done. Mia can help me cook."

She laughed. "You're a glutton for punishment."

"Nah, I'm just determined to be more successful than I was during our last culinary disaster."

She laughed. "This time, it's in your kitchen. Good luck. I'm still finding flour in crevices."

~

Kat was putting cereal in her cart when someone called her name. She turned around and found Jeremy pushing a cart of food. His long-sleeved, charcoal gray thermal clung to his muscles, showing off his trim physique. "Jeremy," she greeted, thinking it was a pleasant surprise. "What are you doing here?"

"I rented an apartment, so I figured I better stock up on supplies."

She looked at his cart. It was overflowing with everything from paper towels to mustard. "You rented a place in Upper New Castle? What about your dad's house?"

"Well, the house is worse than I thought. It has to be demolished and rebuilt, which is probably for the best. I don't have the best memories from living there. So I figured I'd make other arrangements until I hire a contractor and whatnot. I got a month-to-month lease at The New Castle Crest Apartments."

A shy smile teased his lips. "I wanted to be close to you and Mia."

"Oh." The idea of him being nearby didn't seem to frighten her so much anymore. "I was going to call you this week."

Nervousness replaced his smile.

"I was thinking about arranging a time and place for you and Mia to meet."

His face split with a large authentic grin. "Really? That's great! Thank you, Kat. Thank you so much." She gasped as he hugged her. She tensed, and he quickly drew back and apologized. "Sorry."

"That's okay."

An awkward silence stretched between them.

"Where's Mia?"

"Oh, she's with my neighbor."

"Oh. Can I walk with you then?"

"Sure." She continued pushing her cart down the aisle. He pushed his alongside.

His hug had triggered memories Kat didn't know she had inside. His skin carried the same scent as it did in high school, subtle and kind of woodsy. So much of her memories were overshadowed by consequence, it was strange to think they'd shared an intimate past.

Jeremy had been no different than her parents when it came to support. While Vivian was making appointments at a clinic outside of town for Kat to have an abortion, he was suggesting that might be the best option. As Kat stood her ground, the men in her life lost the strength to look her in the eye, both her father and Jeremy seeing the problem as gone the moment they stopped seeing her and her ever-growing belly.

"Does Mia like to color?" Jeremy asked, bringing her back to the present as he pulled a coloring book off a random rack.

"Sure."

"If I buy this for her, maybe you can give it to her when you tell her about me. That way, she'll know I'm a nice guy."

She nodded. It didn't seem right for this big, strong veteran to need her reassurance about a *Hello Kitty* coloring book, but she liked that he wanted her approval.

After they each checked out, he handed her the coloring book. "Thanks for this, Kat. You have no idea what it means to me."

She took the book and slipped it into her bag. "I'll call you this week."

"Okay." He wheeled his cart through the lot, and she loaded her bags in the trunk of her car.

A male voice called her name. Thinking it was Jeremy, she smiled, but it wasn't him. It was Nathan Lithe. There went her smile.

"I thought that was you, Kitty Kat." He leered from the driver's seat of his Mercedes.

Her expression went blank. "Hi, Nathan." She looked for Jeremy but didn't see him.

"What are you up to?" he asked as if they were buddies.

"Shopping." She folded her arms across her chest to block his wandering gaze.

"Who's your friend?" he asked, tipping up his chin.

She jumped, finding Jeremy right behind her. Scowling. Strangely, his presence brought a level of relief. "Uh, this is Jeremy. Jeremy, Nathan Lithe, a friend of my parents." The two nodded at one another but offered no words of greeting.

"Where's Tyson?"

"He's home. With Mia." At the mention of Mia, Jeremy broke eye contact with Nathan and gave her a curious look, but tucked away his questions for later. "Speaking of which, I'd better get back—"

"Yes, you wouldn't want Tyson getting upset."

At that, Jeremy jerked his gaze back to Nathan and scowled.

"Quite a temper, that one. Anyway, it was nice seeing you, Kitty Kat. Be a good girl now." He slowly eased off the brake. "Jeremy."

It was odd seeing her parents' friends in her neighborhood. As his red Mercedes turned the corner, she tried to put her finger on what it was about him that made her so uneasy.

"Kat, who's Tyson?" Jeremy asked.

She shook off the slimy sensation that always came whenever Nathan was around. "Um..." Something shifted in Jeremy's features. At that moment, he looked like he could kill a man in a split second without even breaking a sweat. Again, she was reminded that this was not the boy she dated in high school.

"Are you okay? Who was that guy?" His shirt tugged across his well-muscled body, and his green eyes were alert and intense. "Kat, who was he? How does he know Mia, and who's Tyson?"

"Tyson's my neighbor. He's also my boyfriend, but Mia doesn't know we're involved. She already adores him, and for her own protection, I didn't want her to get any ideas about him being a permanent part of our lives."

"Is he good to you? To you and Mia?"

"Yes."

"Then why did that guy mention his temper?"

"Tyson had a...a confrontation at my mother's party last month."

"A confrontation?"

"Yes," she continued. "A guy my parents thought to fix me up with made some inappropriate comments about Tyson. I got upset, he didn't like that, so when I was in the house, he called him out on it."

"He beat him up?"

"No, my mother threw us out before he got the chance."

"Kat, if this Tyson's violent—"

"No," she interrupted. "He'd never hurt Mia —or me."

"Can I meet him?"

If Jeremy were dating a woman who was going to be around their daughter, Kat would insist on meeting her right away. She took a deep breath. "He's already insisted on meeting you. When the time is right, I'm sure it'll happen, but for now, I have to get going. Thanks for coming back when Nathan showed up."

"You never told me who he is exactly."

"He's just a friend of my parents, but I won't lie, he gives me the creeps."

Chapter 26

TAKING SEVERAL DEEP BREATHS, Kat sat facing Mia and waited for the right words to come. "I want to talk to you, babe, about something important."

"Do you want to talk about rabbits? I saw a bunny today!" Mia offered.

"Did you?"

"Yeah, under Mrs. Bradshaw's shed. I'm gonna catch one and train it. Mrs. Bradshaw doesn't want them 'cause they been eatin' her flowers. Can I watch cartoons now?"

"Not yet. I need to tell you something. Um, I have a present for you." She knew what to say—she just didn't know how to say it.

"What is it?"

"Well, I have two presents actually." She took a deep breath. "What would you do if your daddy didn't live in Japan?"

"Would he live here with us?"

"No." She had no idea where she was going with

this. "But what if you could talk to him? Would you want to?"

"Does he like rabbits?"

Kat figured she might as well go with it. "Yes, he likes rabbits. He likes a lot of the same things that you like. He was gone for a while, but he may be back now. Would you want to meet him?"

"Today?"

"No, not today, but maybe this weekend." Mia wasn't grasping the enormity of what she was telling her, but maybe that was for the best.

"We can read a story with him. He'll like that." Mia nodded with certainty.

"I'm sure he'd love that. Mia, do you understand what I'm saying to you? You would have a mommy *and* a daddy." She wanted her to understand what she was agreeing to. "Like Mommy has Grandma and Grandpa."

"Would I still live here with you?"

"Of course, baby. You'll always live with me, but maybe when you and your daddy become friends, you can play at his house sometimes, like you play at Kiki's."

"Okay." She rolled on her side and over the edge of the couch, hanging her head upside down, obviously at the end of her attention span.

"I love you, sweetie," Kat said to the upside-down contortionist who was her world.

"I love you too. Wanna spin in circles?"

"Why don't you spin, and I'll call your daddy to see if he can come play on Saturday." She blew raspberries on her belly and stood. Mia squealed and spun away.

Children were so resilient. She just changed Mia's world, and her daughter didn't even realize it. Watching her out of the corner of her eye as she twirled and sang the *Wonder Pets* theme song, she dialed Jeremy.

"Kat?" he said by way of answering.

"Hi, Jeremy."

"Is everything okay?"

"Everything's fine. I talked to Mia. She said she wants to see you, so I was thinking maybe Saturday at our place."

"Saturday would be perfect," he said in a voice filled with gratitude.

"Okay then." She gave him her address, and then, before she hung up, she said, "Oh, and Jeremy, in case she asks you, you like rabbits."

"Rabbits?"

"Yeah. She asked if you liked them, and I said yes. That seemed to be some kind of rating system for her."

"You tell my daughter that I *love* rabbits." He laughed.

"I will. Okay, I'll see you Saturday."

After she hung up the phone, she gave Mia her coloring book from Jeremy and told her that he said he loved rabbits. Mia smiled and said, "That's 'cause he's my daddy."

~

On Thursday night, Tyson dropped off Trixie. He was leaving for Washington, and they were dog sitting. Mia was thrilled. He kissed Mia and Kat goodbye and promised to bring them each back a souvenir.

"Are you going to be all right?" he asked again, a bit anxious he wouldn't be there the day Mia met her father.

"Tyson, relax. Everything will be fine."

"Hey, you can't judge me for wanting to give this guy a once over if he's going to be hanging around my girls."

"I promise, there's absolutely nothing to worry about. Jeremy's a good person who just made a poor choice as a boy. I truly believe he intends to right that wrong, now that he's a man."

On Saturday morning Kat dressed Mia in a new pair of overalls and a pink cardigan. It was getting cooler now that September had arrived. She did her hair in pigtails with little bows. She was very excited to meet her daddy.

"Make sure my bows are just right, Momma." Her daughter sighed as though the weight of the world rested on her shoulders. "Gorrum wants to come today, but I told him he can't."

It had been a while since Gorrum had been mentioned. "Oh no? Why's that?"

She shrugged. "I told him if he wants to see what my daddy looks like, he can hide, but he's not allowed to meet him."

Kat finished her hair and placed her hands on her shoulders. "Mia, does Gorrum have a daddy?"

She shook her head.

"Does that make Gorrum sad?"

"Sometimes," Mia admitted. "But Gorrum has lots of friends, and sometimes grown-up friends are like extra daddies and mommies. Sort of like Kiki and Tyson."

She smiled. "You're very right. I'm glad Gorrum has other friends."

"Me too."

At eleven o'clock, Jeremy arrived. Mia excitedly ran to the door, but when Kat let the strange man inside, her daughter clung to her leg and hid behind her butt. Kat wondered if she thought, because he was her daddy, that she'd recognize him.

He crouched down to Mia's level. "Hi, Mia," he said, voice soft and heavy with emotion.

Mia hid her face behind Kat's legs. Maybe it was a natural instinct for kids to automatically return to the womb when scared.

"I sure am glad to meet you." Jeremy coaxed. "Boy, I'm really nervous. I never had a daughter before, and I'm not really sure what a daddy does. What do you do when you're scared?"

Holding onto the hem of Kat's sweater, Mia peeked around her legs. She evaluated him for a long moment. "When I'm scared," she said with all the authority of a three-year-old, "Momma gives me a magic brave'ry cape."

Jeremy nodded. "Oh, I wish I had one of those."

Mia tilted her head to one side and dramatically tapped her chin. "I know! You can borrow mine." Reaching to her shoulders, she removed her invisible cape and held out her short little arms as she stepped toward him. Her hands touched his shoulders. "Just don't b'ruin it."

"I promise, I'll take extra good care of it." Standing up, he placed his fists on his hips and puffed out his chest like Superman. "I feel braver already."

Mia laughed. Kat was impressed at how easily he pulled her out of her shell.

"Wanna see my room?" Mia eagerly asked.

He looked at Kat to see if that would be okay. She nodded, and he said, "I would *love* to see your room, Mia."

Slipping her small fingers into his large hand, she dragged him off. Kat's heart pinched at the sight.

She tried to give Jeremy and Mia their privacy, puttering around the house, putting clothes away, and organizing closets. Every now and then, she paused to listen, and she'd hear Jeremy telling Mia a story or vice versa. When they laughed together, Kat's hand went to her heart as if she could somehow calm the flutters.

She was in the kitchen reading when Mia came out. "Momma, I'm hungry."

Jeremy stood behind her, watching her closely. He seemed to be absorbing her every word and action. Only parents realized how much children were actually unique little human beings with feelings and opinions and tastes of their own.

"What would you like for lunch?"

"Peanut butter and jelly! Can Daddy eat too?"

"Sure. Is peanut butter and jelly okay for you?"

"That sounds perfect," he said, a sweet grin curving his lips.

"How about we pack a picnic and go to the park?"

"Yeah!" Mia cheered.

They stood at the counter, Mia on her step stool and Jeremy to her left as they made a PB&J assembly line. Once they packed a canvas bag with juice boxes, food, and a blanket, she called Trixie and hooked her to her leash.

Jeremy placed his hand over hers, smiled, and relieved her of the bag. They walked together, as a family. Kat held Trixie's leash in one hand and Mia's hand in the other. Jeremy's held their daughter's other hand and carried the picnic bag. As they walked, Mia sang and pulled herself off the ground, swinging from their arms.

It was amazing how natural the three of them adapted. There was nothing traditional about how their family started, but in that moment, they looked as normal as a Hallmark card. Something about the way he looked at Mia—with such fascination and pride—made her believe Jeremy was there to stay.

At the park, they set up their blanket and ate. Jeremy never tired of all Mia's questions and requests, which was no easy feat.

"Mia, stop feeding Trixie," Kat repeated for the tenth time.

"She's hungry."

Kat sighed, and Jeremy laughed.

Shoving a large bite of bread in her mouth and leaving a smear of jelly on her cheek, Mia turned to Jeremy and asked, "Are you and Momma married?"

"Uh..." He nervously looked at Kat, unsure how to answer.

She smiled. She'd been answering difficult questions since Mia could talk. Let him tackle this one.

"No. Your mother was my girlfriend a long time ago."

"Did you kiss her?"

Jeremy blushed, and she silently laughed as she sipped from her juice box. He sent her a look of panic that playfully promised retribution. "Yes," he finally answered, and his blush crested over his defined jaw.

"Then you used to be married?"

"Um, no..." The pleading look he sent Kat was absolutely pathetic.

She laughed and rolled her eyes. Taking a long, dramatic breath, she announced, "Look, Mia, Geese!"

Mia quickly bolted off the blanket, chasing the squawking birds toward the field.

Jeremy turned. "Thanks for *that*."

"Hey, you wanted to see what it's like having a three-year-old."

Mia chased the geese. After several minutes he said, "She really is incredible. You did a wonderful job with her, Kat. Thank you."

Not many people complimented her parenting, so his praise was nice to hear.

When they returned home, they played Hungry Hippos. For dinner, they ordered a pizza and watched *Cinderella*. Mia asked if Jeremy could sleep over, but he thankfully told her he couldn't.

He helped Kat tuck her in, and then he offered to read her a bedtime story. Mia chose *Goldilocks and the Three Bears.*

"We're like the three bears, Daddy."

Jeremy paused and smiled at her, brushing a

hand affectionately over her strawberry curls. "Yeah," he answered, voice cracking. "I guess we are."

After the story, Kat kissed her goodnight.

"I want a kiss from Daddy too."

Leaning in gradually, he pressed his lips to Mia's forehead and shut his eyes. Her arms wrapped around his neck and squeezed as he slowly embraced her little body.

Standing by the door, Kat's heart pounded, emotion tightening her throat as he held their daughter in his arms for the first time. As her vision blurred, she left the room, busying herself with clearing the table.

Scooping up the marbles from the game, Jeremy came over to help. His hand brushed hers as they chased the marbles with their fingers, and they stilled. A moment of awkwardness passed, perhaps charged with a long-forgotten familiarity or the gratitude of an unforgettable day. Drawing back her hand, she looked away.

"I can't tell you how much today meant to me, Kat."

She smiled at him and folded a dishcloth. "I'm glad."

"Can I see her again?"

"I think Mia would be upset if you didn't see her again. I guess we should set up some kind of schedule."

"What if I wanted to take her somewhere? Would that be okay?"

Don't freak out. "Sure, as long as you had a car seat and I could check in with her."

"Of course," he agreed. "How about next Friday? I could even keep her overnight to give you a break?"

Way too soon! "Can I think about it?" She was still adjusting.

"Of course. Well, I better go. Thank you for what was probably the best day of my life."

"You're welcome. I know Mia had a great time." She walked him to the door.

He placed his hand on the knob. "You're a wonderful mom, Kat. What you have with Mia, it's really special. I...there isn't a lot that impresses me about people these days, but you... you impress me." He kissed her cheek, pulling away before she had time to react to the unexpected gesture.

Letting out an unsteady breath, a smile wobbled on her lips. "I'll call you about next Friday." Kat released a long exhale as he pulled away. As far as expectations went, he'd exceeded them.

~

Tyson walked out of the hotel bathroom in a towel and a cloud of steam. Seeing he had a missed call, he pressed the button on his cell for voicemail.

"Hey, babe. It's me. I guess you're busy with work and meetings. I miss you. Today...today was good. I have a lot to tell you when you get back. I'm going to bed in a little bit, but if you get this before it's too late, give me a call. I love you."

She sounded good, and that made him happy, despite his lingering anxiety that another man was encroaching on his territory. No matter what, he wanted what was best for both Mia and Kat.

Checking the time, he stilled, as there was a knock at the door. He frowned, unsure who it could be at this hour. Opening the door, he mentally groaned. Imani draped against the doorjamb in a low-cut red dress, two glasses and a bottle of champagne dangling from her hands.

"Well, looks like I picked the right time to drop by. I figured we could celebrate a job well done." She pushed past him and sauntered into the room.

Tyson left the door open.

She popped the cork on the bottle of *Dom* and sweet-scented mist filled the air. She grinned triumphantly. "I love that sound."

"Imani, what are you doing here?"

"I told you. I thought we could celebrate." Bending, she filled the glasses.

"It's inappropriate for you to be in my hotel room."

She rolled her eyes. "Since when?"

"You have to go," he said firmly, still standing at the open door.

Ignoring his request, she pressed a glass into his bare chest and let go. His hand quickly caught the flute before it dropped. Reaching past his side, she pushed the door closed.

"Imani—"

"Oh, Tyson, lighten up. When did you get so boring? We're adults. Have a drink and relax."

"I don't need a drink."

"That's your opinion."

"I need you to go."

She emptied her glass and placed it on the table with a frosty clink. "Tyson, Tyson, Tyson. Don't you understand when someone offers you something, you say thank you and accept it gracefully?"

"I'm in a relationship, Imani."

"Since when?"

He owed her nothing. "Thanks for the champagne, but you need to go." He opened the door.

Her red dress slid off her shoulders and fluttered to the ground. Long limbs stretched as she curved her shoulders, drawing his attention to her breasts.

Irate, he quickly blocked the door with his body. "What the hell are you doing?"

"Come on, Tyson. You know we're good together." When he didn't budge, she cocked her head. "Really? What can she give you that I can't?"

He looked her directly in the eye. "Love."

Imani was a lot of things, but first and foremost, she was a realist. For her to claim she would ever love anything more than her career would be a boldfaced lie.

She laughed without humor. "*You* love her?"

"Yes."

"Well... she must be something special."

"She is. And you have to go." He faced the hall and fabric whispered as she dressed. She collected the champagne. "It's a shame, Tyson. We could've been quite the power couple."

"Goodnight, Imani."

With a tilt of her eyes, she sashayed out the door. He sighed as soon as he was alone again then went to find his phone.

~

"Unbelievable!" Jade said, sipping her coffee. "I can't believe Jeremy's back. What does Tyson think of all this?"

Kat gave her a satirical look. "Tyson hasn't met him yet."

"Well, that should be interesting. Two men, one tall, dark, and handsome, the other blonde, green eyes, and..." She paused. "Hey, what does Jeremy look like now?"

She snorted. "Not like he did in high school, that's for sure."

"Really? Is he cuter?" Jade asked, scooting forward in her chair.

"He's, um, older."

"We're all older, Kat."

"I know, but he's—I don't know. Different. He's bigger. He's a man now."

"I bet he's ripped from being in the military. He is, isn't he?"

"He definitely isn't scrawny."

"How not scrawny? Like Tyson?"

"I would actually say he's bigger than Tyson."

"Well, it looks like we need a little high school reunion once you get things settled with Mia. I was always pissed I ended up with Nick when you got Jeremy."

"Oh, come on, Jade! You never liked Jeremy. Nick was just a tool. Besides, if you dated Jeremy, you might have a three-year-old now. Then what would you do with yourself?" she laughed.

"Honey, I never would've gotten pregnant. I

may not always play hard-to-get, but I'm always prepared. I learned that from the Boy Scouts."

"How many Boy Scouts?"

Jade smirked. "Enough."

The door opened. "Momma, I put my crayons back in the box. Can I come out now?"

"Sure, baby."

"Hey you, come over here and give me a hug," Jade said, and Mia skipped into her arms. "Oh, you're getting so big! When are you coming to stay at my house again?"

"How 'bout today?" Mia asked.

"Well, I'm busy today, but soon. Okay?"

"Okeydokey!"

Kat stood and took Jade's coffee cup.

"Well, I better get going. I have a full day ahead of me."

"Thanks for the caffeine fix."

"Anytime." Jade grabbed her purse. "Keep me posted on the ex-lover meets new saga."

"Don't call him my ex-lover. You know we were never that serious."

"True. Huh, isn't it weird you suddenly have more men in your life than I do?"

Kat snorted, following her out to her car. "Doubtful."

"Yeah, maybe not."

SUGAR RUSH IN FULL EFFECT, Mia ran to the window and yelled, "Tyson!"

Kat opened the door, and he scooped Mia into his arms and kissed her. Moving her to his hip, he drew her into a hug. "Ah, there're my girls." He kissed Kat's head. "I missed you guys!"

Trixie came barreling out of the back room. Placing Mia on her feet, he bent and did some *not-so-manly* talking to the dog. "There's Daddy's beautiful lady. Who was a good girl?"

After doting over Trixie long enough to be forgiven for leaving, he smiled. "I'm starved. What do you say I take you two lovely ladies out to lunch?"

Mia cheered and then added, "Tyson, I have a daddy!"

"I heard." He sent Kat a sidelong glance and winked.

She smiled, grateful he was taking Jeremy's arrival in stride. "If we're going out, I need to do my hair." She left the two of them to catch up.

Kat was finishing up her makeup when Mia yelled, "Grandpa!"

Surely, she'd misheard. Her father never came to her home. Walking into the kitchen, she stilled. Sure enough, her father was hugging Mia. Standing, he shook Ty's hand. "It's nice to see you again, Tyson." His gaze found hers, and he smiled sadly.

"Daddy, what are you doing here?"

"I have a daddy too, Grandpa!" Mia proudly added.

"Can't a grandfather come visit his granddaughter?" A bit more forlornly, he said, "And his daughter."

She stared at him, at a complete loss.

Tyson cleared his throat. "Come on, Mia. What do you say you help me take Trixie home? I'm sure she misses her doghouse. Plus, I have presents for you and your mom from Washington."

"Presents!" She followed Tyson and Trixie out of the house, and Kat was left standing in the kitchen with her father.

"If this is about Mom..." she began, thinking that must be his reason for coming there.

"This has nothing to do with your mother," he calmly said. "I missed Mia. She hasn't been over in a few weeks, and that's far too long to go without seeing her. I missed you too, Katherine."

What?

"I heard about what happened at your mother's birthday. That Price kid's a shit. I don't know why your mother insisted on pushing him on you. Kid's got more money than sense."

Who was this man? She stood, speechless. After a long moment of awkward silence, she cleared her throat. "I thought you wanted the match."

"I want you to be happy, Katherine." He grumbled something under his breath she didn't quite catch. "Anyway... Next week's your birthday. Why don't you join us for dinner? I can have the cook prepare that white chocolate mousse stuff you like."

"What about mom?" Vivian wouldn't tolerate being usurped.

"Your mother's had her way long enough. You leave her to me. And bring that Adams fellow. I'd like to see what kind of man's spending so much time with my daughter and granddaughter."

She blinked. Had there been some sort of alien invasion she was unaware of? Because this man was not her father. "Are you sure?"

"Positive." He studied her for a long moment, her shoulders lowering under the weight of his regard. "You look...different. Happy."

"I am happy."

"It's hard knowing, as a father, that I can't take any credit for that." For the first time ever, he appeared unsure. "Is he good to you?"

"Who? Tyson?"

He nodded.

"He's nicer to me than any man has ever been."

Her father noticeably winced. Sometimes the truth hurt. "I deserve that, I suppose." He took a deep breath. "And you deserve to be happy, Katherine."

"Thank you, Daddy."

A long moment passed where neither of them

seemed to know how to move past the emotionally charged exchange. He shifted, pressing his hands in his pockets, and appeared relieved to find his keys. "Right. Well, I'll let you enjoy your day. I'll see you next Sunday?"

"Sure. And you know you're welcome here anytime."

"I might take you up on that invitation." He nodded, hesitated, and left.

Would things ever be normal between them? No matter how much she told herself she didn't need them, she'd always crave that parent-child bond she'd been denied. But there was a huge difference between wanting something and needing it.

Chapter 28

JEREMY CALLED to speak to Mia every night before bed, and with much deliberating, Kat decided it was time for a trial arrangement. Mia would be sleeping at his house that Friday.

Sharing her daughter was an adjustment and not an easy one. As she packed Mia's overnight bag, she continuously reminded herself that this was Mia's father, and he had a legal right to see his daughter. It was better to handle the process amicably and on her terms, but that meant she had to be flexible and figure out how to co-parent, something she'd never considered being an issue in her life.

Tyson came over so he could meet Mia's father. When Jeremy arrived, Mia ran into his arms, and he scooped her off the ground in a show of affection that was undeniably innocent and paternal. He held her as if she were the most fragile gift in the world and as valuable as sunshine. Kat understood that sort of sentiment. Mia was one of a kind.

Anxious, she rambled off several precautions. "I packed her pajamas and an undershirt because it gets colder at night. And there's a list of her allergies and a copy of her insurance card in the pocket. Her pediatrician's name is on the back of the card, but you should call me first if anything's wrong. Unless it's an emergency, then call 911. She typically goes to bed at eight. Make sure she uses the potty before bed. She's usually okay with that, but sometimes she needs help wiping when she poops. Her toothbrush's in the front pocket of her bag. You'll have to put the toothpaste on the brush for her. She can turn knobs, so make sure you use a deadbolt or a chain on the door. She's unfamiliar with your place and may wander around if she wakes up in the middle of the night. It would be best to leave a hall light on for her. And I usually—"

"Kat," Tyson gently interrupted, placing his hand on her arm.

She looked at him and turned back to Jeremy. Realizing he was already nervous and she was only making it worse by scaring the shit out of him, she buttoned her lips and stifled the rest of her warnings —there were a lot.

"How about I call your cellphone if I have any problems or questions?"

Taking a shaky breath, she nodded. "Okay." It was a struggle not to give him a few more valid instructions, like make sure Mia washes her hands before she eats and don't give her sugar before bed. *You're being a control freak.* Her chin trembled as she held back. "Come give me a hug, Mia."

Her arms went around Mia in a tight squeeze. "Momma," Mia wheezed. "You're squishing me."

"Sorry, baby." She relaxed her hold and brushed a curl away from her brow. "I'm gonna miss you."

She walked her to Jeremy's car to check that he had correctly installed the car seat. After buckling her safely, she kissed her again.

"I promise I'll take good care of her," Jeremy said as he started the car.

She shut her eyes and took a calming breath. "Call me if you need anything—*anything* at all."

"I will." He glanced in the rearview mirror. "Ready, Betty?"

"Ready, Freddy!" Mia cheered, anxious for her first father-daughter adventure.

When they drove away, Kat's chest literally hurt. Tyson slowly dragged her back into the house. "She'll be fine, Kat."

"I know." Her eyes glazed with tears. "It's just... this is a super big deal. Eventually, I'll get used to it —maybe when she's sixteen."

He hugged her. "Just think, you had three years with her all to yourself. No one can take that from you."

"I know."

If everything went smoothly, this would be a regular thing. Jeremy would take Mia every other Friday and pick her up from Mrs. Bradshaw's on Wednesdays so they could have dinner together. On the weeks he didn't sleep over, they'd spend Sundays together.

Tyson nibbled her ear. "I know a great way to distract you from worrying."

"Good luck. I think they implanted some kind of worry chip in me when they did my epidural."

He laughed. "And where do you suppose they placed that chip? Here?" He slid his finger under her sweater and up her spine. Shivering, she snuggled closer, needing his strength. "Come on. Let's relax."

He led her to the sofa, drew the blinds, and locked the door. "I should have sent an extra pair of PJs. Sometimes Mia has accidents at night."

Returning to the couch, he slipped off her shoes. "I'm sure Jeremy has a spare t-shirt lying around if that happens." He peeled off her socks and traced a finger down the arch of her foot.

The cottage was cool, but her blood quickly warmed as he massaged her feet. Lowering himself to his knees, he focused on her arches as she rested her eyes and tried to relax.

She caught her breath when he pressed a kiss to the curve of her ancle, a place no one had ever kissed on her. His gaze locked with hers as his pink tongue flicked over her skin and he playfully bit her toe. She squirmed and laughed when his finger traced a sensitive spot that was especially ticklish.

"Ah, I've found your weakness I think."

For the briefest moment, her stress fell away and she fell into his stare, consumed by the safe and protected way he made her feel. She had no one else like that in her life and it was both scary and comforting at the same time.

Big words threatened to burst out, but before she could find the courage, he grinned and whispered, "I love you, Kat."

Her heart fluttered in her chest and warmth spread through her limbs. "Take me to bed, Ty."

Rising, he lifted her off the couch and carried her to her room, not letting her go until the following morning.

~

"Well, lookie here," Jade crowed, parading through the door without bothering to knock. "Please, sir, cover yourself. Oh, my virgin eyes!"

In only a loose pair of jeans, Tyson sipped his coffee, looking prouder than a peacock and more satisfied than any man should be. "Yeah, you're about as virginal as Madonna," he teased. "And I'm not talking about the holy one."

Jade shrugged and grabbed a chair. "Hey, a girl's gotta eat…"

Shaking his head, he placed a kiss on Kat's temple. "I gotta go check on Trixie."

Kat sighed as he left. Jade studied her, ginning. "Aren't you two just *adorable!*"

"Let me put on some pants and brush my teeth." She slipped into the bedroom, and when she returned, Tyson was at the stove making eggs and French toast.

"I really need to get me one of these," Jade said observantly. "Ty, you have any brothers?"

"Nope, just sisters, but I got friends."

Kat sipped her coffee. "What about that doctor that asked you out?"

"Meh, dating work people can get icky. Brian's nice enough and cute, but I don't wanna go down that road in case it doesn't work out. Men have a hard time getting over me."

Ty chuckled and placed a plate in front of Jade. "What're you looking for in a guy?"

"I don't know. Someone nice, caring, but also manly. I like a lot of testosterone with my coffee. Someone fun, who doesn't mind traveling. Romantic, can afford nice things, not a workaholic, but also not a bum. Good looking, I guess."

"Is that all?" He laughed.

"Well, ten inches wouldn't hurt, but it's not like I can be choosy."

Kat choked on her coffee. "Jade! *Ten* inches?"

Tyson placed a plate in front of her. "Ten inches can hurt, Jade. Ask Kat. She knows."

She smacked him in the stomach, and he chuckled.

The sound of a car slowing had Kat turning her head. She jumped from her seat the moment she recognized Jeremy's car.

"Hi, Momma!"

"Hi, baby! Did you have fun?" Unlatching her seat, she pulled Mia into her arms and breathed her in. Jeremy stepped out, holding her dainty overnight bag.

"We had so much fun! Daddy got coloring books, and markers, and Play-Dough, and even a Cinderella doll with a dollhouse. And know what else?" She drew in a deep breath. "Daddy's house has an ele'bator!"

"So you had a good time," she confirmed, relieved to have her back.

"I had a *great* time, Momma! Maybe you can come with us next time."

She smiled and hummed a non-committal response, then looked at Jeremy. "And how did you do?"

"Pretty good, I think. I learned why three-year-olds shouldn't color with markers, but don't worry, they washed off."

"Kiki!" Mia squealed as they entered the cottage, shimmying down her body and into Jade's lap.

Jeremy turned to the table and reached his hand out to Tyson. "How you doing, Tyson?"

It was nice that they got along. "Good. Glad to hear you survived your first night. Want some breakfast?"

"No thanks. We ate before we came." He did a double-take. "Jade Schultz?"

Jade stood. Clearly, Jeremy was not immune. "Well, well. Jeremy Larson." Kat shook her head at the syrupy tone Jade used. "You sure grew up. How have you been?"

Jade's vitality and boldness could make men four times her size stutter. Jeremy didn't stand a chance. Her friend might be tiny, but so was an atom, and once you cracked one of them open, you had a whole explosive mess of crap to deal with.

Jeremy cleared his throat and looked a little red under the collar. "I've been good. And you?"

"Oh, things have improved. Kat says you're thinking of moving back to Parkside, building on your dad's land."

"Yeah, it looks that way. I just gotta clear the lot and find the right contractor."

"Oh, well, *you know,* Tyson here is a contractor."

He turned to Tyson, who was holding Mia as she colored. "You should come see the place, give me an estimate."

"Sure thing, man. I can get out there sometime this week."

Jeremy looked back to Jade and cleared his throat again. "Well, I better get going."

"I'll walk out with you!" Jade shoved her plate away and chucked her coffee in the trash.

"Look, Momma, I drew you a picture! It's a family. Hang it on the 'frigerator."

Kat picked up the picture, complimenting her daughter's work with biased appraisal. "This is wonderful, Mia." The picture was of four figures. One small and child-sized. The other three taller and adult-sized. Two had hair, and one didn't.

"Show Daddy!" She passed him the picture. "It's you, me, Momma, and Tyson."

Ty tenderly ran a hand over the top of Mia's head as she rested her cheek on his shoulder. The byplay was subtle, but it left anyone watching with a clear understanding of where Ty stood in the mix, where he stood in Mia's heart.

Jeremy noticeably observed the way Tyson handled Mia, and a slow grin curved his lips. Kat smiled, taking his expression as approval. She sighed. *This,* she could live with because *this* was extraordinary.

Chapter 29

THE MORNING of Kat's birthday started spectacularly. Mia and Tyson made her breakfast in bed. Tyson had taken her daughter out shopping the day before, and Mia bought her a necklace with both their birthstones.

After a long lecture about receiving gifts gracefully on her birthday, he told her the only thing she was allowed to say was thank you and handed her a gorgeous bouquet of flowers. "This is just the first of many." He grinned, kissing her nose.

After breakfast, she was instructed to shower and dress in comfortable, loose-fitting clothes. From there, she was blindfolded and whisked away to a mystery location.

"No peeking!" Mia warned as they shuffled her into the car.

After a disorienting drive, she was shuffled back out of the car, and the blindfold was removed. Blinking into the sunlight, she focused on her surroundings.

They stood on a cobblestone walk at one of the swankier sections of New Castle in front of a discreet establishment called *Trinidad's*. It looked like a salon.

"Come on," Ty instructed, taking her hand.

The front was set up like a boutique. A cosmetics counter sat to the left and a receptionist desk to the right. In the back, through an archway, customers were getting their hair styled.

By the way the clientele was dressed and the appearance of the employees, she gleaned it was an upscale place. Frowning, she glanced down at her outfit, wondered why Tyson told her to dress in sweats.

Before she had a chance to ask him, he went to the desk and said, "Appointment for Katherine D'Angelo."

"Oh, Miss D'Angelo," the girl at the reception area welcomed. "Happy Birthday! Are you ready for your *Journey*?"

"My journey?"

"Yes, it's our platinum package. We start you off with a paraffin dip, a pedicure, and manicure. Then you head downstairs to the spa for a one-hour facial and massage. You'll take a break in our Zen room, where we bring you champagne, tea sandwiches, and fresh fruit. After that, you shower and return upstairs for a cut and style. We finish your journey off with a professional makeup consultation."

Her eyes widened. She usually got her hair trimmed at The Cut and Curl in New Castle for ten dollars. This place definitely cost way more than that. They didn't even have a board that listed prices. *You know that means it's expensive as hell.*

She bit her lip and kept her promise about accepting Tyson's gifts gracefully, but it wasn't easy. "How long does all that take?"

"Usually four hours."

She turned to Ty and Mia. "And what are you going to do?"

"We're going to the pun'kin patch!" Mia said.

"Don't worry about us," Tyson said as he kissed her cheek. "It's your day. Relax and enjoy. I've got our day covered. We'll be back to pick you up in a few hours."

"Okay, but this had better be it for the presents."

He smiled and waved. "We'll see. Happy birthday, kitten." He left with his little accomplice.

Four hours later, Kat was convinced she'd been drugged. It wasn't natural to feel that good. Her face was baby smooth, her muscles Jell-O, her cuticles gone, and there were no calluses on her feet. Her hair was completely frizz-free, and she had finally learned how to apply makeup properly. It was magnificent. However, relaxing was hard work. After all that pampering, she needed a nap.

But there was no time for napping, and she doubted she'd be able to sleep knowing they had dinner at her parents' in a little over an hour. When they returned home, she went to her room to change and found a blouse, a pale yellow cardigan, and an A-line skirt hanging from her closet door. On the floor sat a pair of brown-heeled boots. A note hung from the hanger.

• • •

Although I find you prettiest in nothing at all,
I thought you would look stunning in this.
Love you,
Ty.

"Aren't you just the sweetest?" she whispered, admiring the clothes.

"Who's the sweetest, Momma? Me?"

She grinned at her daughter, thinking this was shaping up to be the most incredible birthday she'd ever celebrated. "Yes. You're one of the sweetest."

"Tyson picked that out," Mia informed. "He said you look pretty in skirts."

Sighing and unable to erase the smile from her face, she shut her eyes and simply savored the moment, knowing she'd never forget it.

Once she was dressed in her new outfit and had Mia cleaned up from the pumpkin patch, Tyson returned. Her relaxed state ebbed the closer they drew to her childhood home. Tyson must have noticed her tension because he took her hand and whispered, "Everything will be fine."

When they arrived, her father greeted them. "Well, here's the birthday girl!" He kissed her on the cheek, hugged Mia, and shook Tyson's hand.

When they entered the parlor, she braced herself. Vivian sat on the settee holding a cocktail, her back ramrod straight. "Hi, Mom."

"Katherine." Her tightlipped greeting made her feel anything but welcomed.

"Hi, Grandma," Mia called, and Vivian's posture relaxed ever so slightly.

"Mia, darling. I've missed you."

Tyson approached. "It's nice to see you again, Mrs. D'Angelo."

She sniffed and turned away. "Mr. Adams."

"How about some drinks?" Her father announced. "I know one little girl who probably wants a Shirley Temple."

When the cook announced dinner was served, they moved to the dining room. Vivian's lips were pursed so tightly she looked like she was holding her teeth in place. Kat wondered if her father had slipped something into her mother's drink.

Her father was very friendly to Tyson. He treated him as a welcomed guest and talked to him about business, politics, family, and the economy. Tyson's voice filled with affection whenever he mentioned Mia and Kat, and her father's eyes gentled.

As they finished the main course and waited for the ultimate white chocolate mousse to be delivered, Vivian delicately cleared her throat. "Tell me, Mr. Adams, do you find it amusing to play the affluent role, or do you prefer more urban settings?"

Kat's attention jerked to the foot of the table, knowing her mother's silence couldn't last forever and dreading the cutting comments that might come erupting out of her now that she'd finished her cocktail.

Tyson tipped his head. "I interact with some very wealthy clients, but I also enjoy being involved in the construction aspects of each project, so I guess you could say I enjoy wearing many hats, Mrs. D'Angelo."

"Tyson's recently finished a big project in Washington for one of the women who donated to your Independent Women's Foundation, Mother." Kat helpfully added, pushing for normalcy. "Jones, I think her name was."

Vivian ignored her comment. "And no doubt, your parents are impressed by your success. What do they do for a living?"

"My father works for a company that manufactures kitchen appliances, and my mother hasn't worked for the past four years. When she did work, it was as a waitress."

"And why has your mother given up working? She isn't one of those people milking the government with false claims of incompetence, I hope."

"Mother," Kat hissed, but Tyson gave her a quelling look.

"Not at all," he calmly said. "My mother worked since she was nine years old. Four years ago, when I built them a new home free and clear, she expressed her wishes to remain home and give her days to her grandchildren. She often babysits for my sister Gloria's boys, and I believe she's also watching my newest cousin, Malcolm."

"No doubt your family believes in...less conservative family planning."

Kat's shoulders tensed.

"I'm not sure I follow," Tyson slowly replied.

"Well, people of our status believe in limiting a family's offspring to no more than two children in order to keep the economy balanced, but I imagine your culture supports overindulgence rather than proven studies. I believe it's referred to as zero population growth. I'm sure you learned about it in school."

Tyson briefly glanced at her, clearly aware that he had been dealt an insult. "Yes, I am aware of the theory. However, I believe *my culture,* as you put it, believes in having as many children as one can love and support, while also placing a strong value in family history and heritage."

She sniffed, unimpressed. "And do you have any offspring, Mr. Adams?"

"Vivian," her father whispered her mother's name in warning.

"I do not," Tyson said. "But I do wish to marry one day and, hopefully, have a large family." He glanced affectionately at Kat and, despite the cooling climate of the room, her face heated.

"Well, surely you'd prefer to marry within your own. No one wants to burden an innocent child with unnecessary challenges in life."

"Vivian, that's enough," her father said through clenched teeth.

Drawing back, Ty blinked.

Collecting himself, he said, "Every child faces challenges in this day and age. I hope to be a good enough father that my children always know they can come to me, and I'll support them through any difficult time. I plan to love my children uncondi-tionally and without classification. Nothing would *ever* lessen my affection for them."

"But surely you would prefer to father children who look like you, children who fit into your cul-ture," Vivian continued.

Kat gaped at her. "Are you drunk?"

"I'm only asking what others silently assume."

"Vivian, I said that's enough," her father ordered.

Her mother looked at him as if he was without consequence and returned her attention to Tyson. "Sometimes, Mr. Adams, the people we love most in this world disappoint us more than anyone else. And their selfishness is unforgivable. I would proceed with caution if I were you. I mean, if you truly cared about someone, you wouldn't sentence them to a life of ostracism and cruelty. Believe me, I know what that's like."

"Vivian, that is *enough*!" her father stormed, his palm coming down on the table hard enough that the ice rattled in the crystal glasses. He turned to Mia and said in a softer voice, "Sweetheart, there's some candy on my desk in the study. Why don't you go see if you can find it?" Mia left the room, and he turned to her mother. "You will apologize to our guest."

"I will not! This is my home, and I'm free to express my opinions here."

"This is *our* home!" he thundered. "And Mr. Adams is our guest and a friend of Katherine's. I will not have you insulting him or behaving like a self-important bigot. But most of all, I will not sit here and watch you hurt our daughter! My God, Vivian, she's our child. Will you ever be satisfied? I've stood idly by for years and watched you drive a wedge in this family with your relentless cruelty. If you continue, we'll lose Mia as well. And for what? The only person concerned with such petty differences is you. Can't you see that this man makes our daughter happy? Does that mean nothing to you?" He shook his head in stunned disbelief. "Take them away from me, and I guarantee this house of glass you stand in will shatter. *Now apologize!*" he barked in a tone Kat had never heard him use before. Never in her life had she heard him speak with such vehemence.

Vivian sat, scowling venomously. Finally, she tossed her linen napkin on her table and stood, storming out of the room.

Her father cleared his throat. "My apologies to both of you. Vivian seems to have been spoiled by having her way for too long, and I've neglected to remind her of her place." He smiled sadly at her. "I'm sorry, sweetheart. I should've never allowed her such authority. Please, let's forget about her for now and enjoy the rest of the evening."

Tyson nodded, and the dessert was served. However, the rich, feathery mousse had lost its flavor and now tasted like sand in her mouth.

They didn't see her mother for the remainder of the night. Once Mia started to get tired, they gathered their belongings. At the door, her father kissed Kat and held her back as Tyson carried Mia to the car.

"Katherine," he said with a pained look in his eyes. "I owe you an apology. I let your mother decide what was right for this family for too long. I want you to know..." He paused as if searching for the right words. "I want you to know how *proud* I am of you. You're a wonderful mother and a good daughter. I love you."

Her entire body shivered as his words struck

deep. For so long, she'd waited to hear such praise, know she'd earned his approval. No matter how many times she told herself it wasn't necessary, her soul seemed to recognize the arrival of such desired praise. She blinked back tears and rasped, "I love you too, Daddy."

He hugged her, and when he pulled away, he placed his hands on her shoulders. "This Tyson fellow seems like a good guy. So long as he continues to make you happy, he's all right by me."

Smiling, a tear slipped from her lashes. "Thank you."

Something intangible had shifted in her life. It was impossible to place, but it came as if it had always been. The need to continuously justify her choices drifted away and, for the first time in her adult life, Kat was surrounded by a sense of validation. This was her life, and she was doing just fine. The fact that she'd questioned herself for so long seemed absurd now that this newfound confidence surrounded her.

Taking what she wanted felt good, not because it was her due, but because there was no legitimate reason for her to deny herself. As if the walls that contained her for so many years had finally come down, her future was filled with endless possibilities. Though there were plenty of people obstructing her journey toward a happy life, she would no longer be one of them.

The first indulgence, she decided, would be welcoming her relationship with Tyson into her home without veils. The night of her birthday, she invited him to stay. Waking up beside the man she loved was a pleasure she cherished, not because it gave them time alone, but because it gave her a reason to smile before she even opened her eyes.

His scent blanketed her pillows. His warmth heated her skin. It was a comfort she longed for and found it impossible to live without.

After her father had confessed how he felt, a sense of closure came, and she could finally understand that her mother's issues were not his, nor were they hers to bear, and she finally put down that cross.

Tyson was a fundamental part of her life, and Jeremy was becoming a fundamental part of Mia's. The joy Kat took from watching them together was immeasurable. Everything seemed to be fitting together as if it were destined to be this way.

Jeremy had his father's house demolished and contracted Tyson to develop plans for his new home. The two were quickly becoming friends. Sometimes, he even stopped by Tyson's for manly business, such as game watching, beer drinking, and ball scratching. It worked out perfectly because even on the days Mia wasn't scheduled to be with her father, she still was able to see him.

Kat's father started coming to dinner on Mondays, and sometimes they ate at Tyson's. Jeremy took Mia on Wednesdays, which became date night —something she never imagined in her schedule. And on Sundays, like today, Mia was anxious to see one of the men who had quickly become a prominent part of her life.

"Do my hair pretty, Momma." She always insisted on looking the best for her daddy.

Jade made a point to pop in on the days Jeremy visited. The girl was on a mission. Jeremy was resisting her not-so-subtle invitations that they should hang out, and according to Ty, it was costing him dearly. It didn't take a specialist to see the signs. Sometimes he'd blush at the most innocent words, like "underwear", when purred from Jade's mouth.

As Kat brushed Mia's hair, Jade applied a fresh layer of gloss. "Do you like this color?" she asked, rubbing a finger over her teeth.

"I want some!" Mia yelled, and Jade smudged a dab across her lips.

"I think it's fine," Kat commented, pulling Mia back to her lap to add a bow to her ponytail.

Tyson chuckled at the stove. "You don't give up easily, do you, Jade."

Jade tossed the gloss back in her purse and scooped up her coffee. "Until you look me in the eye and tell me he's not interested, I see no reason to back down." She arched a brow at Ty, and he shook his head. "See? You can't say it, so that leads me to believe I'm hot on his trail."

"What are you, a detective?" Kat joked.

"Yes, and I spy a hot guy..."

Kat shook her head.

"Order up," Ty said, sliding a plate of bunny pancakes in front of Mia.

Kat slid her off her lap and stood just as a knock sounded from the door. Jade straightened her posture and smiled. Kat rolled her eyes. "You're relentless." Turning, she opened the door and stilled. "Mom."

The kitchen silenced.

"Katherine." Vivian clutched her purse to her chest. "I came to see my granddaughter."

"Grandma!" Mia broke the silence.

Shifting so her daughter could come to the door, Kat stepped back as Vivian entered. When she caught sight of Tyson in his pajama pants and no shirt, she froze.

"She's going to her father's today."

Her mother stiffly nodded. "I see." Her gaze returned to Tyson.

"Good morning, Mrs. D'Angelo."

"Look, Grandma! Tyson made bunny pancakes."

Apparent disapproval reflected in her mother's eyes. "I've missed you, Mia," she muttered, as though wishing her audience would disappear.

The door opened, and Jeremy stepped in. "Daddy!" Mia sprung into his arms, completely forgetting her grandmother's presence.

Jeremy hugged her. "Hey, princess. You ready for an adventure today?"

"Yeah! Where are we going?"

He grinned and kissed her pudgy cheek. "It just so happens I have two tickets to the aquarium."

Mia cheered. Vivian intensely observed the byplay.

"I'll get Mia's coat," Kat announced, escaping to the hall closet to catch her breath. Not until that moment did she realize how little she missed the chronic tension her mother's judgment triggered.

Ty appeared at the closet door. "You okay?" he whispered, his fingers softly massaging her shoulder.

"Yeah. Maybe once we get Mia on her way, she'll leave."

They returned to the kitchen, and Kat helped Mia with her coat. Vivian requested a hug and Mia then followed suit without further prompting—hugging Kat, Jade, and lastly, Tyson.

Ty kissed her hair as his arms wrapped around her little body. "I love you, Mia. Have a good day."

"I love you too," she said and kissed him on the lips.

Vivian paled.

"Ready?" Jeremy asked with a grin.

Jade followed the two out of the house, and Tyson stood to clear the plates. Kat awkwardly shifted, wondering how long her mother would linger. He disappeared for a minute then returned, wearing a sweatshirt and shoes. "I'm going to let Trixie out. I'll see you later, Mrs. D'Angelo."

As he opened the door, her mother said, "Mr. Adams, wait."

He paused with his hand on the knob.

"I seem to owe you an apology," Vivian said, staring in his general direction but not making eye contact. "My behavior the other night was uncouth and undeserved. I was hoping that we could, perhaps, start again."

"I think that would be a good idea, Mrs. D'Angelo."

"Being that you seem to be important to Mia

and my daughter, I would like it if we could remove any animosity between us."

He shifted but took a moment to consider the truce. "I love your daughter and Mia very much, Vivian. I'd never do anything to hurt them, but I also won't allow them to be hurt by others."

Comprehending the warning, she nodded jaggedly.

Kat held her breath as he leaned close, kissed her ear, and whispered, "I'll be back in five. Don't take any shit."

The door closed, and her mother exhaled. "It seems my advice means nothing these days."

Kat carried the last of the dishes to the sink.

"Mia seems to be adjusting well to Jeremy's return. How does he feel about Tyson spending so much time with you?"

She braced her weight on the counter. "How's he supposed to feel, Mom?"

"Well, I'm just saying, you two have a history."

"What we have is a child together. Don't pretend our relationship was more meaningful than it was. I'm not one of your friends. I know the reality of my situation, and I don't need it sugarcoated."

"But it would be nice for Mia—"

"Mia's perfectly happy with the way things are. We all are."

She pursed her lips. "Why do you always argue with me, Katherine? If I say up, you say down."

"You need to stop trying to make me into a woman I'm never going to be." She held out her hands, encompassing her home. "This is me. I'm not rich. I'm not fancy. I don't care about impressing people who will *never* approve of the life I lead. I'm done apologizing for being exactly who I am. And you need to either accept that this is the life I chose or..." *Butt out.* "You need to accept it."

"I'm trying."

"Try harder. If not for me, then for Mia."

Glancing down, she gripped her purse.

Kat looked at the time. Ty would be back any minute. "Listen, if you'd like to start seeing Mia again, that's fine. I know she'd enjoy that. But Jeremy has a schedule with her, and that comes first. Maybe you can have the Sundays he doesn't take her."

"You would have to let me know which dates," she said as if that minor complication was the end of the world.

"That's fine." Taking a deep breath, she offered an olive branch. "Also, I'm planning a surprise party for Tyson at the end of the month. I mentioned it to Daddy, and he said he'd see if he could make it. Ty's parents will be there, and I thought it would be nice for them to meet you. You're welcome to come too, but Mom, these people are important to me."

"God forbid I make a scene at *his* birthday."

"See," she tsked. "That, right there. That's the crap I'm not going to tolerate."

"Katherine, he accosted your father's associate at a formal affair!"

"Daddy doesn't even like Dawson!"

"That's not the point," she argued, and Kat's blood boiled.

"What is the point, Mom? How would you feel if I told you Dawson practically forced himself on me, thinking because I have a child, I'm some sort of a whore?"

"He wouldn't do that—"

"He did! Right there on my front porch! I had a bruise on my leg because he grabbed me so hard, but you don't want to hear that. You're probably thinking of some excuse, something *I did* in order to provoke him. You might not like Tyson, but I can promise you he'd *never* disrespect me the way that man did."

She sniffed. "It's irrelevant now."

Laughing without humor, Kat said, "You're right, but your feelings on the subject aren't. It matters to me that my mother will defend some asshole before her own daughter. If anyone *ever* spoke to Mia that way or scared her like that, I'd kill them."

"What would you have me do, Katherine?"

"Just be on my side! For once!"

"I am on your side. For years, I've done nothing but try to make your life better. I thought having a husband would—"

"I didn't need a husband! I needed my parents." Lowering her head, she said. "I was a kid. You took me to that apartment, put two thousand dollars in my bank account, and abandoned me when I was eight months pregnant. Do you have any idea how terrified I was? I didn't want your money. I just wanted to know I could go to you when I was scared or confused, and I could talk to you without being judged or made to feel like an idiot."

Vivian met her gaze, her lips tensing, as words seemed to crowd the tip of her tongue. "You're a good mother, Katherine. Sometimes I see the way

Mia looks at you and depends on you, and I... I feel like a failure. All I ever wanted was to be close to my daughter."

Startled by the compliment to her parenting skills, her anger ebbed. "Then you need to get to know who your daughter is. I'm not a debutante. I'm not graduating from some Ivy League school like some of your friends' kids. And I'm not sorry."

She sighed. "I'm tired of fighting, Mom. So what if you can't brag about my car or if you're not brimming with pride over the fact that I rent a home? You have Mia. Be grateful for all the incredible things she brings to our lives, but I'm telling you now, I will *never* let you control the woman she becomes. I want her to be happy, and that isn't a state you get to define for her. It's whatever she wants it to be."

Vivian nodded. "I'm not used to this new side of you, Katherine." She stood. "I will try my best to be better."

"Thank you."

"I'll let you know about next Sunday. I assume Jeremy won't be taking Mia."

She nodded. "Let me know."

Without a show of affection, she opened the door and left.

Kat's shoulders sagged as she roughly exhaled. Ten o'clock in the morning, and she was ready for a drink.

～

Tyson awoke the morning of his birthday and grinned, pulling Kat's soft body close to his so he could nibble her ear.

She stretched and purred, "Good morning, birthday boy." Turning, she nuzzled his neck as her warm hand slid beneath the covers finding him already aroused.

Easing to his back, he grinned as she slowly stroked. "Do I get special birthday privileges today?"

"What would you like, old man?"

"You."

"I believe I can provide that." Slithering under the covers, she crawled between his legs and kissed his chest.

He pulled her closer, so her legs were straddling his. "Put me inside of you, kitten." He groaned as her warmth engulfed him. *Birthdays are good.*

She slowly moved languidly, milking her pleasure. Leaning forward, he took one puckered, pink nipple into his mouth as she slowly rocked back and forth. Making love to Kat in the mornings was his favorite way to start the day. It gave him something to wish for in the future—his future with her.

Falling back on the pillow, he raised his hips and pressed deep into her core. She hissed out a breath in sudden pleasure. With unhurried movements, the tension in her brow eased as he made love to her. "You feel that, kitten? That's me, coming home."

Rotating her hips, sinking fully down onto his length, she pressed so close it seemed they'd never break apart—he could only hope. Leaning forward, her fingers dug into his flesh. It was an exquisitely unguarded moment he committed to memory. She was a vision.

With shallow breaths, they pulled each other close as they worked their pleasure. Her sex fluttered and contracted as she moaned deep and long. His release pulled from the base of his spine as he thrust deeper.

Glancing at her soft belly, the way it folded with each rock of her hips, he envisioned the future and longed for the day his child might be there, their souls entwined in a future that could not be undone. Kat was the one. He'd never been more certain of anything in his life.

A year ago, he thought he'd understood what his family had been pushing him to find. He understood the general process of life. People got married, and people had kids. But not until he had fallen in love with Kat did he truly understand the magnitude of finding such happiness. Now he understood what being in love fully meant, and his definition of happiness had met a new standard. Life was good.

~

Tyson finally left to meet the foreman for Jeremy's project. As soon as he walked out the door, Kat grabbed the phone and dialed Jeremy's number.

"Good morning," he answered, and she smiled, liking this new level of friendship they developed over the passing weeks.

"Morning! Okay, you have to keep him occupied until four o'clock. Just like we talked about. If he tries to come home, you get him drunk. Understand?"

"I accept my mission. And try to breathe, Kat. It's going to work out great."

"God, I hope so."

She hung up and located a bag of paper plates, cups, napkins, streamers, and other party decorations. Mrs. Adams and Gloria arrived as soon as she was dressed, followed by Gloria's husband Darrel, who was delivering the tables and chairs. Darrel also brought little Davis to keep Mia occupied, which definitely helped. There was a ton of work to do.

Mrs. Adams took over in the kitchen, prepping the food for the party as soon as she smothered Mia and Davis with kisses. Kat and Gloria followed Darrel out back and opened tablecloths to dress the tables. The kids played under a nearby tree as they set up for the party.

At eleven, Darrel left to go pick up the cake, and Gloria and Kat made the punch. Mr. Adams arrived at one with the balloons and then took the kids for a walk to the park. The house smelled delicious, and she loved learning all the different ways Tyson's mom cooked.

Darrel constructed a crooked standing grate that he insisted was a fire pit. They were all a little concerned about the soundness of the lopsided structure but didn't want to hurt his feelings. At two o'clock, she jumped in the shower and got dressed for the party.

Guests started to arrive at three. Kat greeted them and took their presents to a table out back. Tyson's mother had set up a buffet, and kids could pilfer the bucket of toys and yard games. Gramma Tessa and Mrs. Bradshaw were in charge of supervising the children as they roasted marshmallows over the sad fire pit Darrel constructed.

By three-thirty, most of Tyson's family had arrived as well as many of his employees and friends. Jade showed up in an adorable dress. "What do you need me to do?"

Kat filled her arms with party hats and noisemakers. "Take these out and try to get people to wear them."

"On it!"

Brushing a strand of hair out of her eyes, she turned back to the cookie tray.

"Katherine?"

Her eyes lit. "Daddy." Abandoning the deserts, she gave him a kiss and hug. "Let me introduce you to Ty's parents."

Tyson's mother was the first to see them as she escorted her father out back. "Mrs. Adams, this is my dad, Edward."

"Well, aren't you a handsome thing." She gripped him in an affectionate hug, and her father actually laughed. It was interesting watching Ty's mom tease her father. The man actually blushed.

Mrs. Adams took over the introductions, pulling her father from one guest to another and handing him a large cup of punch. Taking a deep breath, Kat smiled as the unimaginable seemed to take place and her father easily mingled.

There was no Vivian, but Kat couldn't pretend she was surprised. After their conversation the other day, her mother had a choice to make. The important thing was that Kat made it clear it was her mother's choice, and she'd be the one to live with it.

Not wanting her mother's antics to spoil her good mood, she grabbed a cup of punch and lingered by the gate. Tyson's car pulled up to the house just after four. "He's here!" she called, hushing the guests as they gathered by the back gate.

Tyson entered the house. "Kat?" Opening the back door, he grinned.

"Surprise!" they yelled, and Mia squealed with excitement.

He smiled as he walked over to Kat and gave her an affectionate kiss. "Sneaky kitten," he whispered. Glancing around, he laughed. "You all got me."

As he mingled and greeted his guests, she finally was able to relax. All her hard work paid off. Tyson seemed thrilled and in phenomenal spirits. Laughter mixed with music as guests enjoyed the food. They sang happy birthday, and Jade and Jeremy helped pass out pieces of cake.

When it was time for gifts, everyone gathered around as Tyson opened his presents. Mia sat on his knee and helped him tear the paper, sticking the leftover bows on Tyson's bald head. Kat gave him her gift last—a homemade blanket and two tickets to see Nora Jones in concert.

As he thanked her with a borderline inappropriate kiss, she smirked and whispered, "Did you get everything you wanted?"

"Almost," he said, and she frowned.

"What did we forget?"

"Nothing that can't be fixed. Stasia," he called

his young cousin. "I saw another gift inside on the kitchen counter. Will you go get it for me?"

Stasia passed Malcolm to Gramma Tessa and went into the house. She returned a minute later carrying a small, black gift box with a silver bow on top. She handed it to Tyson.

He took a deep breath and exhaled, shaking his head. "This is what I wanted."

Smiling, she wondered whom it was from. Her face went numb as he dropped to his knee and took her hand. The guests gasped in excitement, and she froze.

"Kat, in the past six months, you've given me more happiness than I have ever imagined possible. You're an amazing woman, an incredible mother, and I think I fell in love with you the minute I saw you gawking at me on my roof with my shirt off."

Her face burned as everyone laughed.

"You let me into your life and made yourself a home in my heart. I couldn't imagine a day without seeing your smile or hearing Mia giggle. I want to grow old with you, watch *Cinderella* until my head's ready to explode, and always keep you cool during heatwaves. But most of all, I want to love you for the rest of my life. Let me love you, Kat. I've never wanted anything more. Katherine Rose D'Angelo, will you do me the honor of being my wife?"

Blinking through glassy eyes, everyone else disappeared as she stared into the face of the man she loved. He opened the box, and there sat the most perfect solitaire diamond engagement ring. Her vision blurred as tears spilled past her lashes.

Swallowing back the lump of emotion clogging

her throat, she sniffled and laughed. "You aren't supposed to buy other people presents on your birthday."

"You're all I want," he softly whispered. "Now, I'm an old man, stop giving me a hard time and say yes."

She sobbed and gave a tearful laugh, then blurted, "Yes, I'll marry you!"

An explosion of cheers rent the air, and as if on cue, Al Green began to play.

Tyson stood and pulled her into his arms, passionately kissing her as the guests went nuts, hooting and hollering. He pulled the ring from the box and placed it on her finger. It was a perfect fit, just like him.

"I love you, kitten."

"I love you too."

Pulling her into a hug, he kissed her ear and whispered, "First comes love, then comes marriage. Soon enough, we'll have ourselves another baby in a baby carriage."

And, once again, she started to cry. Only this time, they were tears of absolute joy.

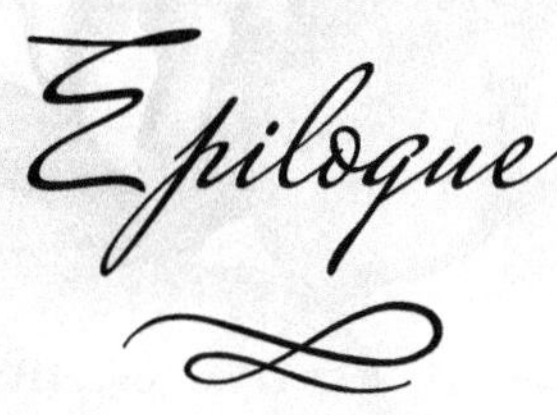# Epilogue

TWO YEARS *Later*

"We're home!" yelled the little witch at her door.

"Did you have fun at your party today?" Kat asked, grinning at Mia's chocolate-stained face. "Did everyone like your cupcakes?"

"My teacher said it was the best frosting she ever tasted, and I told her I made them!"

"Did everyone like your costume?"

"There were three witches, but I told them I was a good witch because I used to be a princess. Tabby was a cat, and Jacob was a Zombie!" She dumped her goodie bag on the table, and Kat quickly moved it out of reach.

"Dinner first. I think you've had enough candy, telling by your face."

Mia sighed. "Is Aunt Gloria coming over to go trick or treating?"

Sliding four-month-old Tyson Jr. into his little pumpkin costume, she blew raspberries on his pudgy dimpled cheek. "Yes, and Grandma Celia, Daddy, and Kiki."

Tyson lifted T.J. from her arms. "How was he today?"

"Perfect."

Holding T.J. up, he nestled his little pumpkin belly as their son giggled and kicked his legs like a happy little grasshopper. "And how's Daddy's big man? Were you good for Mommy today?"

"Is T.J. going trick or treating with us, Daddy?"

Ty grinned, sliding TJ to his hip. "Of course. The whole family's going."

"I'm gonna go get my trick or treat bag!"

As Mia left the room, Tyson asked in a hushed voice, "Jade's coming?"

Kat gave him a warning look. "Yes, Jeremy's bringing her."

"Have you talked to her today?"

The past two years had been a roller coaster for her best friend, filled with joy, tragedy, and acceptance. It was impossible to predict how Jade would act in any situation. She was no longer the same feisty girl she once was, but somehow, she was stronger.

"This morning. She had a session with Dr. Wolfe today, so I don't know how she'll be tonight."

"Do you think it's wise she does all the walking? Maybe she should stay back and hand out candy."

"Ty, she said she wants to go with everyone else. You want to try telling her no?"

"No, ma'am," he quickly answered.

"That's what I thought. Besides, Jeremy will be there."

Gloria arrived with several boxes of pizza. They filled their bellies then loaded T.J. into his stroller as the kids used the bathroom one last time. When they opened the door, Jeremy was helping Jade from his car.

It was funny how life changed. Kat no longer felt the need to bend over backward for those who didn't appreciate her. Her father had become someone she could depend on and laugh with. Vivian was still Vivian, but Kat no longer allowed her to interfere with her own happiness. Seeing Jeremy take such good care of Jade after everything she'd been through was another unexpected gift. It seemed no matter how many hardships they faced, life had a way of always working out for the best.

"Hey, you alright, kitten?" Tyson asked, sneaking up behind her.

"Yes, just thinking." Her hand rested on her belly.

"About what?"

"I was thinking if this one's a girl, we should name her Sophia after your sister."

"If this one—" He paused. "*This one?* As in— you're pregnant?"

A smile broke across his face like dawn breaks across the night, slow and unsure at first, then bold and brighter than ever.

"I am." Sighing at the fulfillment that came with saying the words aloud, she wreathed her arms around his neck. "And Ty, the cravings have already started, so you better do some serious trick or treating tonight and get me some good candy."

"Anything for you, kitten. Anything for you."

The End

WANT MORE FROM LYDIA MICHAELS?

READ *If I Fall (New Castle Book Two)* Now!

Get your next book FREE when you subscribe to Lydia's newsletter!
Click here to sign up for Lydia Michaels' Newsletter.

Follow Lydia Michaels on TikTok, Instagram, and Facebook!
TikTok @LydiaMichaels
Instagram @lydia_michaels_books
Facebook @LydiaMichaels

Sacrifice of the Pawn (Surrender Games #1)
Queen of the Knight (Surrender Games #2)
Breaking Perfect (Menage Stand Alone)
Hurt (Dark Romantic Thriller)
Sugar (Enemies to Lovers)
Forfeit (Degrees of Separation #1)
Lost Together (Degrees of Separation #2)
Atonement (Degrees of Separation #3)
First Comes Love (Single Mom)
If I Fall (Suspense + Secret Stalker)
Something Borrowed (Wife On the Run + Domestic Abuse)
*This list includes Amazon Associate links

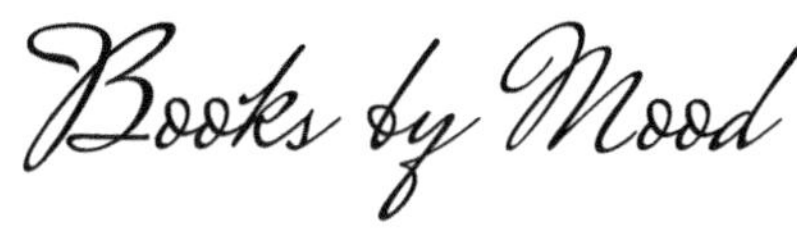

Billionaire Romance

Falling In | Sacrifice of the Pawn | Calamity Rayne | Blind

Small Town Romance

Wake My Heart | The Best Man | Love Me Nots | Pining For You | Almost Priest | My Funny Valentine | Side Squeeze | Beautiful Distraction | Irish Rogue | British Professor | Broken Man (LGBTQ) | Controlled Chaos | Hard Fix | Intentional Risk

Emotional Favorites

La Vie en Rose | Simple Man | Wake My Heart | Sacrifice of the Pawn | Forfeit

Romantic Comedy

Calamity Rayne

Erotic Romance

Breaking Perfect | Protégé | Falling In | Sugar

First Books in Binge Worthy Trilogies and Series

Almost Priest | Falling In | Wake My Heart | Forfeit | Original Sin

Paranormal Vampire Romance

About the Author

Lydia Michaels is the award winning and bestselling author of more than forty titles, a certified life coach, and transformational speaker. She is the consecutive winner of the 2018 & 2019 *Author of the Year Award* from *Happenings Media,* as well as the recipient of the 2014 *Best Author Award* from the *Courier Times.* She has been featured in *USA Today, Romantic Times Magazine, Love & Lace,* and more. As the host and founder of the *East Coast Author Convention,* the *Behind the Keys Author Retreat* and podcast, she continues to celebrate her growing love for readers and the writing community throughout the world!

In 2021, Michaels released the groundbreaking, non-fiction series, **Write 10K in a Day,** to commemorate her career in the publishing industry. She looks forward to many more years of exploring both fiction and non-fiction writing, teaching about the craft, and learning from the ever-changing book industry.

Lydia is happily married to her childhood sweetheart. Some of her favorite things include connecting with readers, helping others, listening to her husband play piano, escaping to her coastal home at the Jersey Shore, cheap wine, *Game of Thrones*, espresso martinis, and kilts. She hopes to meet you soon at one of her many upcoming events.

Follow Lydia Michaels on TikTok, Instagram, and Facebook!
TikTok @LydiaMichaels
Instagram @lydia_michaels_books
Facebook @LydiaMichaels
Subscribe to her newsletter
https://lydiamichaelsbooks.com/newsletter/

Other Titles by Lydia Michaels

WAKE MY HEART

The Best Man

Love Me Nots

Pining For You

My Funny Valentine

Side Squeeze

Falling In: Surrender Trilogy 1

Breaking Out: Surrender Trilogy 2

Coming Home: Surrender Trilogy 3

Sacrifice of the Pawn: Billionaire Romance

Queen of the Knight: Billionaire Romance

Original Sin

Dark Exodus

Prodigal Son

Calamity Rayne: Gets a Life

Calamity Rayne: Back Again

La Vie en Rose

Breaking Perfect

Blind

Untied

Almost Priest

Beautiful Distraction

Irish Rogue

British Professor

Broken Man

Controlled Chaos

Hard Fix

Intentional Risk

Hurt

Sugar

Simple Man

Protégé

Forfeit

Lost Together

Atonement

First Comes Love

If I Fall

Something Borrowed

Write 10K in a Day